Golden Fire

BOOKS BY JONATHAN FAST

The Secrets of Synchronicity
Mortal Gods
The Inner Circle
The Beast
Golden Fire

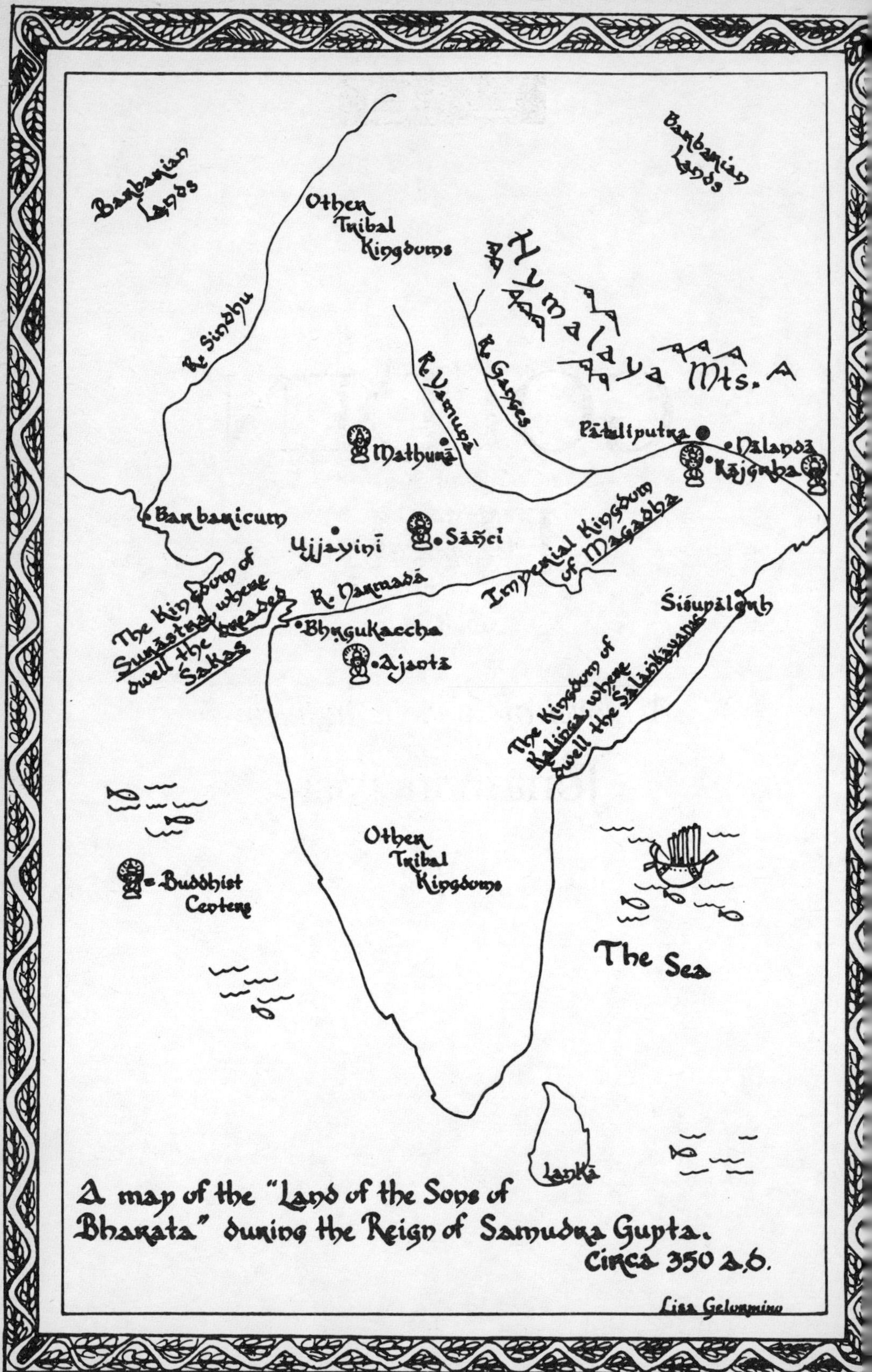

A map of the "Land of the Sons of Bharata" during the Reign of Samudra Gupta. Circa 350 A.D.

GOLDEN FIRE

A Novel of Ancient India by

Jonathan Fast

METHUEN

First published in Great Britain in 1986
by Methuen London Ltd
11 New Fetter Lane, London EC4P 4EE

Printed and bound in Great Britain
by Richard Clay (The Chaucer Press) Ltd
Bungay, Suffolk

British Library Cataloguing in Publication Data

Fast, Jonathan, *1948–*
Golden fire: a novel of ancient India.
I. Title
813'.54[F]   PS3556.A779

ISBN 0-413-41490-6

Grateful acknowledgement is made to the following
for permission to quote from the works listed:

The Kama Sutra of Vatsyayana, translated by Sir Richard F. Burton.
Copyright © 1962 by E. P. Dutton.
Reprinted by permission of the publisher,
E. P. Dutton, a division of New American Library.

The Wonder That Was India, by A. L. Basham.
Copyright © 1959 by Grove Press.
Reprinted by permission of the publisher.

For my wife,
Barbara

Contents

A Guide to Pronouncing Sanskrit Words

The brāmanas believed the gods would not respond to the prayers collected in those holy books called Vedas unless the words themselves were properly pronounced. Thus they developed the first science of phonetics. Although their rules of pronunciation required years to master, the simplified guide shown below takes only a few minutes and may help the reader capture the flavor of the ancient language.

A is pronounced like *u* in but, *ā* like *a* in father.

I like *i* in pit, *ī* like *ee* in feet.

U like *u* in put, *ū* like *oo* in moon.

E like *ei* in reins, *o* like *oa* in moan, *ai* like *ie* in lie.

Ś and *ṣ* are like *sh* in ship, *c,* like *ch* in chip. Otherwise, the *h* indicates aspiration, like the *ph* in upheaval, or the *th* in pothole.

The *ṛ* is pronounced *ri* as in rich. *Ṭ, ḍ,* and *ṇ* are retroflexes (that is to say, they are formed by curling the tongue farther back than in English), but this distinction can be ignored without causing the gods undue anger.

G is always hard.

Śrī Gaṇeśāya nāmaḥ

Reverence to Lord Gaṇeśa,
Patron of literature,
Remover of obstacles

Part I

THE GOOD VAIDYA

1

The jingle of jewelry woke the Vaidya. He lay on his bed motionless, listening to a woman's voice ordering Dūṣaka, his servant, to wake him. The night was hot and noisy with the buzzing of mosquitoes, the croaking of the bullfrogs that lived in the tank behind the house. On the street below, a bullock cart rumbled over the cobblestones, and, from somewhere far away, he could hear gamblers calling in a frenzy for Śiva to bless their dice.

The comet, the Vaidya thought, was to blame. Since it first appeared in the eastern sky seven nights ago, life had been in a state of agitation, and his sleep had been disturbed by every imaginable emergency. A burn that required ointment, an aching tooth, a snakebite. Why couldn't he have pursued a science that let a man sleep? Astrologers and poets could lounge in bed till noon. Why was there always some emergency in the middle of the night that demanded his attention?

He listened to the woman's voice, urgent yet as smooth as the tiger's purring, saying that Samudra Gupta himself, the Great King of Kings, the Supreme Lord of the Land of the Sons of Bharata, had dispatched her, and Dūṣaka had best make haste if he didn't relish the thought of his head atop a pike.

She was evidently a woman of the court, for the Sanskrit was easy on her tongue, and the king's difficult compound title fell like music from her lips. But what sort of woman would be sent as a messenger at this late hour? A gaṇikā, most likely. Perhaps one of the king's own concubines. It occurred to the Vaidya that a great deal must be at stake. A minister might be ill, or a member of the harem—or even the king himself! If he was successful in curing him, unimaginable wealth and honor might be his. And if he did not succeed, he might well be impaled, or mutilated, or left to rot in the palace dungeons, for Samudra Gupta had a fierce temper with those who disappointed him.

The prospect of riches enticed the Vaidya as little as that of suffering in a dungeon disturbed him. Whatever his karma had destined for him, it had been earned over the course of a thousand incarnations. He had an unshakable faith in the accuracy of the cosmic balance that weighed out his fortune, both good and bad, and he tried to accept it with grace.

Reluctantly he rose from his bed, a simple bamboo frame crisscrossed with hemp, which supported a mat and pillows for his head and feet (despite the success of his practice, his possessions remained few and modest, as the Buddha prescribed) and stumbled about the cozy chamber searching, by the light of the ghee lamp, for the box that contained his betel quid. The tile floor was cool under his bare feet, the rugs so finely woven that his toes could not detect the stitching.

A tapestry showing the Buddha taming the mad elephant Malagri, and bordered with an intricate design of lotus blossoms and palms, hung from a pole overhead, dividing the third floor into two parts. It replaced one belonging to the previous tenant, a brāhmana moneylender, depicting the Trimūrti: Brahmā, Śiva, and Viṣṇu. They were the old gods that the people of his land had worshiped since the beginning of time, but they were bad gods for a vaidya, with their prohibitions against contact with the sick, against dissection, against cutting the body with a knife. The all-forgiving Buddha was, as he was fond of telling his students, a better god for vaidyas.

He pushed the tapestry aside and entered the adjoining area, a small sitting room with low stools of an hour-glass shape, formed of woven rattan, and a table of similar design. The ghee lamp provided just enough light to locate his little ivory box of betel quid.

From down below he heard the wooden stairs creaking under the step of his servant, Dūṣaka. He popped a quid into his mouth and returned to the bedchamber in time for the breathless boy to accost him.

"Sir . . . a splendid woman from the palace . . . you must wake up . . ."

He was a brown-skinned śūdra of eighteen autumns, with large, guileless eyes. A sloping chin gave the impression of weak character, and indeed in the brief time he had been employed by the Vaidya, he had distinguished himself as clever only in matters of avoiding work, as cunning only at those times when a few extra kākinī were in the offing. He came from a provincial village to the south, and at first even the everyday sights of the capital had left him wide-eyed. Recently, however, he had adopted the airs of a dandy, growing his nails long, carrying a parasol, complaining about his gambling debts (although he earned only one paṇa a week). Despite this pose, the visit of a woman of the court had left him breathless with excitement.

"Do I appear to be asleep?" the Vaidya replied. The quid was tangy with clove and camphor, and made his mouth burn.

"She says that one of the harem is giving birth . . . a difficult labor . . . the baby will not come . . ."

"Calm down, Dūṣaka."

"Shall I prepare a lather?"

"No time. Get me a clean vasana. Then wake Virata and Kaṅka"—these were his two finest students, who slept on the floor below—"and tell them to prepare to assist me."

"Virata is already awake. He is talking to the splendid woman from the palace."

The Vaidya shook his head; Virata might someday be a fine surgeon, but his weakness for long eyes and a pretty smile threatened to sabotage his studies.

After Dūṣaka left, the Vaidya kneeled before a niche in the wall, where a bronze Buddha sat upon a pedestal, and whispered, "Beloved Buddha, savior of the universe, please grant me success in delivering the baby this night. I am too young to die, and I have too many students yet to teach." He hesitated for a moment, and added, "And if it is my karma to fail in my task tonight, and be executed, please make it quick and without pain. Don't let him impale me."

He took a little rice flavored with saffron and ghee from a brass saucer and pressed it to the Buddha's lips, and licked off a few grains that stuck to his thumb, relishing the sweet taste.

Dūṣaka returned with a clean vasana and the Vaidya wrapped it about his groin, fastening it with a belt of braided silk, and slipped his feet into sandals with soles of buffalo skin. He put an uttarīya around his shoulders, decided it was too hot, and discarded it. A simple pearl necklace and two small gold earrings sufficed for jewelry. He had discovered long ago that more elaborate jewelry with loose stones and dangling strands of gems interfered with surgery; he neither wore them nor allowed them on his students. And when his students complained that people would believe them to be foreigners, or impoverished, or merely poorly dressed (for those of the Land of the Sons of Bharata were dismayed by the sight of a bare neck, a forearm without a bangle, a finger without a ring), the Vaidya said they could wear what jewelry they wished—as long as they abandoned their studies with him forever.

Dūṣaka looked at him with open disapproval. "At least you will make up your eyes."

"No time." The quid was taking effect, and the Vaidya could feel his heart start to pound, a warmth flow through his limbs, as though his blood had been heated by fire. He was ready for whatever the night might ask of him.

"But, sir, you are going to the *palace*. You must consider your appearance."

"I am going to the palace," the Vaidya said softly, "to deliver a baby, not to dally with the courtiers."

The Vaidya was sensitive about his looks, and with good reason. He was thirty-seven autumns, short, and round-shouldered. An early case of pox had left his nose as dimpled as a fig.

"At least your head, sir!" the servant pleaded. "Let me wrap your turban."

But if the Vaidya was sensitive on the subject of appearance, he was even more so regarding his baldness—what little hair he had grew in a fringe about his ears, like a garland—and for an instant he lost his temper.

"Remember your place, Dūṣaka! It is not for a śūdra to instruct one of the upper classes in how to dress. Now away with you, this instant. Pack my bags . . . herbs and ointments . . . surgical instruments . . . dressings. Oh, and a box of ants. Put a piece of sugarcane at the bottom to keep them happy."

"Yes, sir," the servant said forlornly, and started for the staircase.

"And when you are done with that," the Vaidya said, regretting having spoken so sharply, "then you may wrap my turban."

"Yes, sir!" said Dūṣaka, pleased that he had not fallen from the Vaidya's grace after all, and hurried down the stairs.

The Vaidya's house was a narrow wooden structure of three stories, each floor divided by tapestries that hung from poles into chambers as small and cozy as the niches squirrels make for themselves in tree trunks. The attic, with its low barrel-vaulted roof, was used to store provisions; the third floor was the Vaidya's; the students slept on the second floor; and the ground floor was dedicated to their daily work. Around the central lecture hall, which also served as a dining room, were grouped surgeries and consultation rooms, and a library of texts fastidiously lettered on palm-leaf paper and bound in wooden covers. Dūṣaka slept on the library floor so that he would be instantly awakened by any late visitor.

Patients waited in the reception room at the front of the house, and for that reason it was the most beautifully furnished, with a divan—a slab of teak supported by fat columnar legs—for them to sit upon, paintings on the walls to inspire them with holy thoughts, two parakeets in a golden cage whose singing might distract them from their miseries, and a brass bowl of fresh-cut blossoms to sweeten the air.

By this hour the blossoms were brown and wilted, and the parakeets were hanging upside down from their feet, asleep.

The Vaidya's guest was kneeling on the divan, kneading her fingers anxiously. Dūṣaka had lighted some ghee lamps so she would not have to wait in the dark and set out a dish of cardamom candy, which remained untouched.

"May victory be yours," she said, prostrating herself on the floor, and allowing her forehead to brush against his toes.

"No, no," he protested, appalled by an act of obeisance that he considered totally inappropriate, "you musn't. I am only a vaidya." He had prepared to address her in Sanskrit (he had studied it as a boy), but every word left him, like birds fleeing an open cage, the instant he felt the touch of her lips on his feet. Although he tried not to show it, he was so flustered that he could barely express himself in the Māgadhī Prakrit that was his everyday tongue.

She rose to her knees and smiled at him. "You are the Great Vaidya, the Master of Healing. You alone knew how to pull the kidney stone from the stomach of Aṅgada the jeweler. Everyone talks of your skill."

"Well . . ." He shrugged and looked away. "It was a simple operation. Nothing to boast of." His eye fell on his student Virata, who was squatting beside the divan. Grateful for a means of changing the subject, he scolded the young man for his laziness and ordered him out of the room. In fact, Virata was studious and dedicated, but the Vaidya found that he enjoyed showing off his authority in front of the beautiful visitor. He was suddenly envious of his student's ease with women, a quality he had only disparaged in the past.

"I am Sutanukā," the woman said, "a plaything of my lord and master Samudra Gupta."

He had guessed at her high station, for she was so beautiful that she might have been one of the heavenly beings known as apsarases, parading as a mortal for her own amusement.

She was small and exceedingly delicate, narrow-waisted, and broad of hip. She had abandoned her cloak because of the heat, as was the custom among younger women, and her bare, dark-nippled breasts hung like ripe fruit. Her hair was as black as a mynah bird, shaped in an ingenious spiral at the back of her neck and encircled with a chain of pearls. Another string of pearls ran along the parting of her hair, the large emerald at the end of the strand arranged to cover the spot on the forehead known as the tilaka. Somehow, rather than detracting from them, the jewel drew attention to her eyes, which were wonderfully long and liquid and outlined with kohl. It was a time before he could draw himself away from those eyes.

Her earrings were hollow golden orbs, as large and fragile as peacock eggs. Her necklace consisted of five strands of pearls arranged so that while one lay close around her throat, the rest hung between her breasts, emphasizing their perfect roundness and high position. Her girdle, six strands of braided silk gathered at intervals with clumps of precious jewels, circled her hips and joined in front with two golden buckles. Her vasana, a crimson silk of extraordinary delicacy, was draped so that the center fold of it hung between the buckles and the rest fell to her ankles. Gold bangles pinched the soft flesh of her forearms, and her delicate hands were a confusion of rings and bracelets. Her nails were the length of her fingers once again. Red lac, painted on the soles of her feet, had left a trail of pale footprints, impossibly small, across the tiled floor. He found himself wishing those footprints might remain forever.

A score of little bells on her anklets produced the lovely tinkling sound that had first woken the Vaidya.

"The Vaidya will forgive me interrupting his time for sleep?" she asked.

"A vaidya has no time for sleep," he replied ruefully.

"One of the harem is in labor and the baby will not be born. I myself was attending the birth, for I have attended many births and know much of midwifery, but I could not help her. I worry for she is a favorite of my lord."

"You attend a birth dressed thus?" the Vaidya asked, puzzled.

She shook her head. "I donned these ornaments for you. I wished to appear my loveliest, that it might sway you to my plea."

The Vaidya smiled very slightly. Such efforts were unnecessary but flattering.

"The sack of water in which the baby swims," he said with concern, "has it broken?"

"At sunset," she replied.

"Then we have little time to lose. I hope we are not already too late."

"Then you will attend the birth?" A radiant smile spread across her face.

"I am a vaidya," he said, as though that explained all, and busied himself in preparation.

Two splendid gold palanquins waited like crouched lions in the dark cobbled street in front of the house. Eight muscular runners stood in rank beside them, their heads bowed, their palms pressed together in front of their faces in namaste. Up and down the way, those neighbors who were light sleepers, that is to say those who could be awakened by the sounds of bare feet running, peeked from the balconies and windows of their homes to see what wealthy patient had come to wake the Vaidya at this time of night.

Sutanukā pushed aside the curtain of the first vehicle and knelt on the cushion within. The Vaidya, who had never ridden in a palanquin before, climbed into the second, imitating her movements with far less grace. An instant later he felt the surprising, nauseating sensation of being lifted into the air and lurching forward. The runners had shouldered the pole from which the carriage hung and were carrying it at a quick, smooth jog down the broad street that led to the palace. Kaṅka, Virata, and Dūṣaka would be running along behind, keeping pace.

For a time he was rigid, clutching the leather handles for fear that if he let go he would tumble onto the street. But then, as one grows used to the horse's gallop, he grew accustomed to the even rhythm of the runners' feet and dared to lean over and peek out of the curtain. The streets of the city rushed by him, the merchant's stalls and residences all barred and shuttered for the night.

What a delightful sensation, seeing so much so quickly! Life seemed like a drama played for his entertainment alone: three men, booted out of a tavern for being too drunk, or too poor to pay for their toddy; a woman, whose sleep had been disturbed, hurling mangos at the cats who screamed to one another from atop a temple wall; gamblers in an alleyway urging Śiva to bless their dice.

Passing an avenue, he caught sight of the towers and great timber walls that enclosed the city, and beyond them, in the farthest distance, the black hills of Barābar, where miners worked the rich veins of iron and copper that were the strength of the Gupta kings.

They turned down the Royal Way, so broad that ten elephants could march down it abreast. By extending his head beyond the curtain as far as he dared, he could see the many buildings that were the palace, set high on earthwork terraces so that they overlooked the city, and all ablaze with torchlight. His heart, he noticed, was beating very fast.

As they passed some beggars sleeping in the street—they might have been a pile of rags—one of them woke, registered the passing of the palanquin with the cunning of a mongoose who spies a peahen, and set out after it. He was stark naked, black-skinned, with a matted tangle of hair, beard, and a shriveled arm that looked more like the fin of a fish. His gait was an uneven lope, and his long penis swung in a lopsided rhythm. In a moment he was running alongside the palanquin, stretching his good hand toward the curtain. The Vaidya was all ready to call back to Dūṣaka and instruct him to give the beggar a few kākinī, but before he could do so, the rearmost runner, without breaking stride, struck out savagely with his elbow, and the beggar rolled backward from the blow, seeming to collapse into himself like a punctured bladder. The Vaidya started to object, then thought better of it and, sitting back on the cushion, a sour taste in his mouth, let the curtain fall closed.

A stairway, broad and gently sloped, and so long that it seemed the runners would never reach the top, led to the summit of the earthwork terraces. The Vaidya, feeling the palanquin come to a stop and longing, as after a sea voyage, for the feel of solid earth beneath his feet, began to climb out. But then he saw the palace guard everywhere, with their two-handed swords and their long bows and the bloodlust in their eyes, and contented himself with a look past the curtain. It took him a moment to realize that this vast chamber in which they had paused, with its brick walls and stone columns, and roof so high that it seemed like the vault of heaven itself, was merely the gatehouse.

Even at this hour, the floor was crowded with messengers, tradesmen, holy men, guild agents, artists, pilgrims from other lands, and the like, each with one desire foremost in his heart, namely to gain permission to pass through the monumental doors at the rear of the chamber to the wealth and power and privilege that waited beyond it. The air was stifling from the smell of so many of them crowded together for so many hours. The Vaidya squinted at the torchlit dusk overhead, seeking the top of the great doors, and grew dizzy from the effort. They pivoted on massive timber set into stone sockets, and the sheets of bronze with which they had been faced were engraved with the symbols of Gupta royalty—the Garuḍa seal, the lute called the vīṇā, the parasol and sandals, the yaktail flywhisk. On either side of the doors, a great stone lion stood guard, and above the lions, an inscription had been engraved on stone tablets, the same eleven lines in three languages: in Sanskrit, in the tongue of the Yavanas, and in the tongue of the Parthians.

While Sutanukā told the guards of the identity of her party and their purpose, the Vaidya read the inscription:

I AM SAMUDRA GUPTA, BELOVED OF LORD VIṢṆU.

BY THE COUNCIL OF MY FATHER, WHO TOLD ME TO RULE THE WHOLE WORLD, I BECAME THE WARRIOR KING. I CONQUERED THE NINE KINGS OF THE NORTH, HUMBLED THE ELEVEN KINGS OF THE SOUTH, AND MADE THE FIVE FRON-

TIER KINGDOMS MY FEUDATORIES.

NOW I WEARY OF KILLING AND DECLARE MYSELF THE POET-KING, WHO DEVOTES HIMSELF TO MAKING THINGS BEAUTIFUL, TO COMPOSING POETRY, PAINTING, AND PLAYING THE VĪṆĀ. MAY MY SUBJECTS DO LIKEWISE SO AS TO ENJOY EVER GREATER DHARMA, ARTHA AND KĀMA.

OṂ ŚĀNTI.

The Poet-King, the Vaidya thought to himself, and smiled bitterly. From all he had heard, the king was still more warrior than poet.

Apparently those great doors opened only for kings, for when the guards finally agreed to let them pass, a pair of smaller doors, their outline so cleverly worked into the patterns of the larger doors that until then the Vaidya had been unaware of them, swung back instead and the procession continued, under the envious eyes of those forced to remain behind.

Now ten guards, swords clattering at their waists, ran alongside the palanquins as they crossed the royal gardens, past splendid flowerbeds, and grand pavilions, and artificial lakes clotted with lotuses, beneath whose surface the straw-colored moon seemed imprisoned like an infant in the womb.

There, among the other buildings, was the decaying palace of Candragupta Maurya, the king who, some six hundred years before, had made an empire of the Land of the Sons of Bharata. Not only had the present dynasty taken his name, but also the plan and pattern of his palace, scaling it up in size to reflect their own greater glory.

The newer palace was seven stories high. A great columned veranda surrounded the first floor. Each succeeding floor was slightly smaller than the previous and ringed with balconies. The barrel-vaulted roofs were topped with golden finials, from which flew brilliant silk banners. The walls were framed with mighty timbers, filled with burnt brick, and faced with great sheets of gold engraved with heroic images of Samudra Gupta on his throne, with Viṣṇu watching over him and endless rows of servants and soldiers in attendance. The wooden railings around the balconies and fretwork screens across the windows were carved and painted in brilliant colors, as were the lintels, jambs, sills, and joists. It seemed almost a paradox that a structure so enormous could boast detail so delicate and exquisite. From a distance, it resembled nothing so much as a great enameled candy box.

The harem, a smaller structure alongside it, had walls faced in silver, engraved with rows of voluptuous women involved in all the womanly diversions of the upper class: braiding flower garlands, bathing beneath a waterfall, combing their hair, playing the vīṇā.

Here the palanquins were finally set down. The Vaidya emerged, staggering like a drunkard. Kaṅka and Virata, though amused, dared not smile or show any other disrespect for their beloved teacher.

The small, olive-skinned women guarding the harem allowed Sutanukā to pass, but crossed their pikes in front of the Vaidya and his assistants, barring the way and giving them a fright. Being Roman Yavanas captured on one of the king's campaigns and pressed into service, they wore the Roman costume—tunics and helmets of metal—and carried pikes and swords.

Aware that every passing moment brought their venture closer to ruin, Sutanukā cursed and threatened them, but to no avail. Men were not permitted within the harem, and that was that. Subtleties were wasted upon them, for they spoke no Prakrit beyond, "Halt or you shall be killed," and understood even less. Exasperated, she insisted they wake Triṇaka, the keeper of the harem, the only authority who could countermand them.

While they waited, the Vaidya demanded an account of the labor thus far.

"It lasted for six hours," she said, "and still the opening of the inner yoni was no more than a finger's breadth, and the mother was in such pain that she cried to her god, and the sweat from her body soaked the bedding three times."

"Did you feel the contours of the stomach to determine the baby's position?"

"I could tell nothing. Sir, I beg your indulgence. While I am skilled in the sixty-four arts and many tricks of midwifery, I understand little of those juices and winds that are called doṣas and keep the fire of life aflame within us."

"I assume the Purohita has been busy." The Vaidya was referring to the royal priest.

"He has been in the temple all night, singing hymns and making sacrifices to Viṣṇu."

"Then the gods will certainly favor us," the Vaidya said, "for I have heard it said that he is the most holy of brāhmaṇas. What about the astrologer? Are the stars fortuitous?"

"That is curious," Sutanukā replied. "For a week he has sequestered himself in his observatory and has not appeared once, not even for meals."

"Is he often given to such asceticism?"

"No. Never before, to my knowledge, has he behaved thus."

"The comet!" the Vaidya said, suddenly recalling that frightening manifestation of the heavens. He looked to the sky, and there on the eastern horizon was the white curl, the shape of a tiger's claw, that had first appeared seven nights ago.

"Yes, the comet," she whispered, smiling at the excitement in his eyes.

May the Buddha protect me, the Vaidya thought to himself, for he knew, as well as any who dwelt within the Land of the Sons of Bharata, that the comet heralded the birth of an avatāra, a bodhisattva, a cakravartin, one who would somehow change the history of the world. Since its appearance, the people of Pāṭaliputra had spoken of little else; each mendicant and ascetic had his own interpretation, and the fortunetellers and palmists who cluttered the bazaar were filling their pockets with paṇas, telling every pregnant woman in the kingdom that her baby was to be another Buddha. But now the Vaidya knew that the comet was intended for the prince who was soon to be born, and the fact that he was to participate in that greatness, in however small a way, filled him with awe. At the same time, all fear left him, for he understood that he was simply the tool of the gods, expediting their will, doing their handiwork. Perhaps his whole life, his years of training in surgery and healing, his experiments in concocting herbs and ointments, and with the forbidden art of dissection, were nothing but preparation for this night, and that once this night was over, his work on earth would be completed. He could feel the great wheel of the dharma turning beneath his feet, grinding out his destiny.

In time the harem keeper, a doddering old brāhmaṇa with a cane, arrived.

"What man thinks he can sneak into the royal harem when Triṇaka is on watch?" he declared in a creaking voice. He was evidently half deaf and half blind, for he did not recognize Sutanukā, who was a frequent visitor there. "Guards, seize them!"

But the guards only smiled at one another.

Sutanukā put her hand on his arm and said gently, "Triṇaka, it is I, Sutanukā, I have come with the Vaidya. He will deliver Sāvitrīdevī's baby. These other men are his assistants. We would enter the harem if you permit it."

The brāhmaṇa looked back and forth between them, understanding dawning in his eyes. He went on quickly, trying to cover over his own ineptness, "Of course you may enter! How else can you help the queen? Move quickly now, if you are to serve her." And he muttered to himself, "These women dawdle so. It is a wonder they ever accomplish anything."

The bedchamber they entered was small and dark, and oppressive with the smell of flowers. Golden bowls set on wooden tripods had been filled to overflowing with garlands. A collection of dolls made from wood and ivory and clay, dressed in real silks and ornamented with real jewels, was a curiously touching reminder that the queen was barely past puberty.

A sturdy wooden couch occupied the far end of the chamber, and Sāvitrīdevī lay upon it, a pillow for her head and a pillow for her feet, and nothing over her but a sheet of sheer white silk. She was groaning in pain, twisting and turning and calling for help in a language that sounded like babble.

The Vaidya came closer and gasped with amazement, for her coloring was unlike anything he had ever known. Her skin was as white as rice flower, her hair like burnished gold and her eyes—this was strangest of all—blue as the sky!

The tapestry that separated her chamber from the corridor was being constantly pulled aside so that a procession of women might come and go as they pleased, so many of them that the tiles were red with their lac footprints, and the atmosphere was more like that of the place on the riverbank where the women meet to draw water, do their wash, and exchange gossip than a sickroom. They swarmed about the anguished queen like so many honeybees, wiping her forehead, cooing reassurances in her ear, massaging her great belly with honey and ghee. The Vaidya had never heard such a jangle of golden jewelry or smelled such a confusion of perfumes, or seen so many swaying bosoms and narrow waists. Everywhere he looked his eye met with sensuous smiles and sly sidelong glances, completely inappropriate for married women. Evidently any break from the tedium of harem life was looked upon as an occasion for merriment.

Only Sutanukā seemed to realize the gravity of the situation. Or perhaps she alone cared that tomorrow might mean one less queen in the harem, one less favorite to compete for the love of the king.

One of the queens prostrated herself before him and offered him rice and a bath, as was customary, to put him at ease before he started his work. He growled at her something to the effect that his stomach could wait while that of Sāvitrīdevī could not.

He called to Virata to help him prepare the soma drug, but his assistant did not respond. He was staring at the throng of women as though they were so many flowers arranged for the picking.

"Virata!" the Vaidya whispered furiously. "Remember the punishment of Indra."

He was referring to a popular folk tale about the great god Indra, and how, in punishment for enjoying kāma with the wife of the sage Gautama, his body was covered with a million yonis.

Virata recovered his senses and immediately set about preparing the drug that eased all pain. He took some dried mushrooms from one of the bags, rehydrated them in water, then pressed a golden liquid from their stems using a pestle. This he mixed with barley water and honey and ghee until it was a thick syrup.

Once this soma had been a sacrament for the brāhmaṇas, but they had turned away from it centuries ago, and now only the vaidyas recalled the secret of its preparation and its use was solely medicinal. Once a year the Vaidya would make an arduous pilgrimage to the foothills of the Himalayas in order to collect the wonderful white-flecked, scarlet-capped mushrooms from beneath rocks and pines. In addition to relieving pain, it gave the body marvelous strength to aid in recovery and the mind visions of glory and godliness to overcome depression.

"Drink this," he said, sitting at the edge of the bed after the contraction had passed. "It will ease the pain. I am the Vaidya and I will help you have your baby."

But before she could take the cup, another contraction racked her frail body. Sutanukā restrained her lest she tumble to the floor, while the Vaidya tried to make sense of her mutterings. Something about "filius" and "Christus." Alas, it meant nothing to him. When the pain had passed, he repeated what he had said before.

She stared at him blankly.

"She doesn't understand you," Sutanukā explained. "She is a Goth princess, from the Land of Ice far to the north. She has lived here a year, but her ear for the royal tongue is poor."

"Then she speaks neither Sanskrit nor any of the Prakrits?"

Sutanukā shook her head. "Her father was a general in the great army of the Roman Yavanas, and thus she learned the Roman tongue. But now that the Romans are no longer our friends, those who might have understood her words have departed."

The Vaidya looked around in despair. How could you diagnose a patient without learning of her dreams and delusions? His heart went out to the girl, so helpless and alone in a strange land. His glance strayed to the doll collection, and he noticed that several of them had blue eyes and blond hair. He mimed for her to drink from the cup, then closed his eyes as if to sleep. Hesitantly, she took the cup and raised it to her lips.

"Yes, yes," he said softly, "that's a good girl, that's a brave girl."

She had to endure many more contractions before the draft took effect. The precise moment of the soma's dominancy became obvious, for she smiled, and her eyes glazed over. She sank back onto the couch and in a minute her breathing was slow and even.

The Vaidya lost no time. He felt the blood in her wrist and found it quick, but not exceptionally so. He examined her complexion and breathing, in the way described by Suśruta in his famous textbook on medicine. But the color of her skin was so odd, he could not tell if it was pale or dark. Next, he raised her legs and examined the opening of the inner yoni. Indeed, though nearly a day had passed since the onset of labor, it was still no more than a finger's breadth.

Could an exceptionally long labor be peculiar to the people known as Goths? He doubted it. From his own experience he had come to believe that race, despite what the brāhmaṇas said, involved no more than skin, hair, and bone structure. Clearly the baby was improperly positioned in the womb. He pushed and prodded the enormity of her belly, the skin stretched so taut that it had grown shiny and translucent and patterned with a tracery of fine blue veins, and tried to determine whether hip or shoulder was foremost.

Suddenly a tiny arm, covered with a clear fluid and thin as a sapling, slipped from the yoni, its miniature hand grasping and opening as though trying to grab hold of something, as a man does when trying to save himself from quicksand.

One of the queens screamed and fainted, and had to be attended to by a dozen other queens, thereby doubling the confusion.

The Vaidya turned to Sutanukā and said, raising his voice to be heard above the hubbub, "Most likely, one must die, either mother or child. Can you make this decision?"

"Only the king can make such a decision," she said.

"Then we must speak to him."

There, in the ghee-lamp lit twilight of the king's bedchamber, four men were gathered around the gaming board, squatting on cushions, tossing the oblong dice, cheering their luck or cursing their defeats. They were engrossed in the game of Caturaṅga—Four Armies—and seemed oblivious of the musicians serenading them and the servant women who fanned them and shooed away the flies with yak-tail whisks.

To the east of the board was Samudra Gupta, the Great King of Kings, the Supreme Lord of the Land, tall and broad of chest, with muscles that bulged like braided serpents beneath his red warrior skin. He had a jutting chin, a straight nose with flaring nostrils, and eyes that seemed perpetually to squint, as if measuring a man's truth or trying to see better some vague form that was always just beyond sight. Two men dwelled within him in an uneasy truce, the warrior and the poet, each suffering the other, their violence and sensitivity eternally at odds. Though only forty-five autumns, his hair, bound by the uṣṇīṣa, which was the symbol of his power, had turned white as a toll of the conflict.

He wore a necklace of emeralds and sapphires in a setting of gold, earrings shaped like great golden wheels, and a dozen jeweled bracelets on each wrist. Because he was a kṣatriya, the sacred thread that crossed his chest was of braided hemp. Just below his right breast, it intersected a savage red scar inflicted years before by a Śaka warrior.

To his south sat the Purohita, tall and gaunt, stiff with brāhmaṇa dignity. Although he was sixty autumns, he seemed ageless, as though he had been as he was now since the beginning of time. The high dome of his head was shaven but for the topknot that hung to the left. His nose was hooked like the beak of a hawk, and his stare was hawklike, too. It was said that gods could be distinguished from men on three counts: that they neither blinked, nor perspired, nor cast a shadow. If the Purohita had not cast a shadow, his humanity might have been in question.

To his west sat the king's vidūṣaka, a thick-fingered dwarf named Vāmana, after the fifth incarnation of Viṣṇu. He was not well proportioned as dwarfs go, his head being too large, and squarish, his neck too small, his gait awkward because of the way his feet turned in. The king of the Śālaṅkāyanas supposedly had a much better-proportioned dwarf, like a grown man perfectly shrunk, and an expert singer to boot. But Samudra Gupta would not have traded, even with a thousand head of cattle to sweeten the exchange, for Vāmana was known to be the cleverest vidūṣaka of any size or shape.

And to the king's east sat a small, wizened man named Dakṣa, chief of the silk guild and a citizen of enormous wealth. Dissolute living, wine, and womanizing had ravaged him, leaving his skin the pale yellow of parchment, his face haggard and lined. His frame was gaunt from bouts with the fever, his spine bent like a shepherd's crook by that disease that makes stiff a man's joints. His teeth were mostly ivory. His eyes had a shrewd, cynical glint to them, tempered with just enough humor to save him from ugliness.

Each player had an army of eight pieces—king, elephants, horse, chariot, and four footmen—and each army was wrought from a different substance to distinguish it from the other. Thus, the king's pieces were gold; the Purohita's, ivory; the vidūṣaka's, iron (a present from the king, a jest); and Dakṣa's, crystal.

The king's three weary companions remained awake by virtue of the betel quid they had been chewing all night, and would stay up till morn, were it asked of them, to distract their lord from the age-old drama taking place in the harem. Through years of loyal service and unquestioning obedience, even during the king's least rational moments, they had distinguished themselves as the most loyal members of his innermost circle (though whether that loyalty was without opportunism or guile was a question better not asked) and as such were privileged to see him, on rare occasion, without the mask of strength required by office. Tonight, for example, he was neither the Chosen of the Gods, nor the Great King of Kings, nor any other of his other glorious titles, but rather another expectant father, experiencing the fears that had beset that occupation since the dawn of time.

They did their best to distract him. The dwarf was particularly good at this, it being his profession. Now that his turn in the game had come, he put the dice in the cup and shook them, mocking all the mannerisms he had seen other gamblers effect—the prayers to the gods, the lucky hand gestures known as mudras, the squeezing of the lips and grunting, as though will alone might make them fall proper surface up—and doing so with such cleverness that even the dour Purohita smiled. If he rolled an eight, his elephant could trample his opponent's king; other combinations might result in his forfeiting the piece or losing his turn. And yet, despite the dwarf's entertaining gyrations and the fact that this move might decide the game, the king's attention wandered as it had all evening.

"My king," the dwarf said, in the most elegant Sanskrit, "who conquered the nine kings of the north is in risk of losing his kingdom to a dwarf, but cares not a whit."

"My thoughts are with Sāvitrīdevī," the king admitted. "Even a first birth should not take so long. Dattadevī delivered Prince Rāma in less than a night."

"Some women take longer, Your Excellency," Dakṣa remarked, "and some take less. My third child was two days and three nights in coming. The longer the labor, the more the likelihood of a boy."

"Is this true?" the king asked the Purohita hopefully. The Purohita had been his teacher since childhood, and the king turned to him out of habit whenever he was in doubt.

"Some say so," the priest replied offhandedly. "It is not written in the Vedas."

"Is the playing of Caturaṅga described in the Vedas?" the dwarf asked innocently.

"He tries to provoke me," the Purohita commented dryly.

"He is the only one who dares," the king said, smiling.

"I simply wonder," the dwarf went on, "why a thing must be written in the Vedas to be believed."

"Aha," said Dakṣa, "a Buddhist."

The dwarf shook his head.

"A materialist?" Dakṣa pressed.

He shook his head again.

"Certainly not a Jain," Dakṣa said.

"I believe," the dwarf began, in a deep voice, as though he were an ascetic expounding a new doctrine, "in keeping things short."

"Bravo," said Dakṣa. "I shall be your first disciple."

"And what about this comet that has my kingdom in such an uproar?" the king went on, oblivious of the conversation around him. "My astrologer promised to tell me what it portended three days ago, but still he does not emerge from his tower."

"I have never seen him take so long," the dwarf agreed. "Perhaps he has fallen asleep."

"Sometimes the complexity of the cosmos," the Purohita remarked, "is more than a man can calculate in an afternoon."

"Isn't the meaning of a comet," Dakṣa suggested, "obvious when it coincides with the birth of a prince?"

No one responded, and the merchant, realizing the sensitivity of the subject he had stumbled upon, withdrew and grew suddenly absorbed in his next move.

For all gathered there knew he was correct, but none cared to admit it. If a comet portended the birth of a great leader—and all agreed it did—then what of the king's first son, Rāma Gupta, the crown prince? The competition of two sons for the kingship was a thought no one wished to dwell upon.

Mercifully, the dwarf broke the silence. "I still think that lazy astrologer has fallen asleep. We should send someone to tickle him and thus keep him awake."

"Tickle him?" Dakṣa laughed, and said to the king, "My, Your Excellency, but he is a fine dwarf! Had I one such as him, I should never be gloomy."

"I would trade him," the king replied soberly, "for a pound of salt, or two coconuts."

"If I dare disagree with the king," the dwarf said, "I am worth three coconuts at least. Possibly four, if their size is not too—"

The conversation was interrupted by the gong that signaled the arrival of visitors. All eyes turned toward the entrance of the bedchamber, where two figures had appeared in the dusky twilight of the ghee lamps.

The guard who blocked their way with his sword cleared his throat and said, "Sutanukā, the gaṇikā, desires an audience with her lord, Samudra Gupta, the Great King of Kings. She brings with her a vaidya."

"Yes, yes," the king said impatiently, "let them come to my feet."

Meanwhile, the Purohita had turned away and moved to the farthest corner of the chambers. Since the Vaidya was in constant contact with the sick, he was ritually impure. Even to overcome this brief exposure to him, the Purohita would have to perform rites of purification that might last for hours.

To the Vaidya, the march to the king's cushion seemed an endless journey.

While in the harem he had been too busy to admire—or grow intimidated by—the wealth and splendor everywhere displayed, here the Vaidya could no longer ignore it. The chamber itself was so large that four stone pillars were required to support the timber roof beams. The walls were covered with gold leaf, in which scenes of the king engaging in cultural pursuits had been engraved and highlighted with embedded gems and pearls. The windows, shaped like upturned scallop shells, were glazed with single sheets of crystal. There was the king's canopied bed, all of filigreed ivory, as delicate as ice crystals hanging from a window ledge. Hundreds of ghee lamps set in sconces and on low tables of brass with wooden legs bathed the room in eternal twilight. Everywhere the eye rested it was dazzled by the profusion of artwork from all over the civilized world, cloisonné barouches and dagger handles from the savage Hunas to the north, jade statues and yellow glazed vases from China, rugs and tapestries from the Parthians, ivory carvings and glass goblets from the Yavanas.

The king's own guards stood in the shadows, ready to draw

their swords and strike the Vaidya dead in an instant if he so much as spoke a wrong word—or so the little man felt certain as he traversed the long distance to the king's cushion.

Now they approached the splendid gaming table, and the four men turned to stare at him. He felt undressed, exposed. His heart slid into his throat.

Why hadn't Sutanukā chosen another vaidya for this "honor"? Why couldn't she have left him home in bed? He was more than content with his humble practice, healing the poor and the unimportant.

Now his mind grew blank with fear. Not knowing what to do, he simply copied Sutanukā's every move, kneeling before the king, pressing his forehead to the king's feet, repeating the complicated honorifics in a trembling voice. He heard in his head, over and over, words a patient had once spoken to him: "Better to have nothing to do with courtiers—look at them the wrong way and the next thing you know, you've lost your nose."

"What news have you of Sāvitrīdevī?" the king demanded before they had even risen.

"This unworthy woman," she began, "comes to tell the most excellent King of Kings and Lord of the Land that because the baby was so long in coming, and because I feared for the health of both mother and child, I sought the help of he who is known to be the finest vaidya in the land. He came gladly even though I woke him from the soundest sleep. He examined the queen and . . ." She hesitated. "Perhaps he himself is best suited to tell you the rest."

The Vaidya was so frightened by now that when he attempted to speak, all that came out was a croak.

"I am but flesh," the king said, trying to put him at ease. "I do not breath fire or eat men alive."

The others at the gaming table laughed.

"Y-y-yes," the Vaidya stammered, "but when I tell you the truth you will have me impaled."

"I have punished men for lying," the king said, "but never for telling the truth. Do you practice according to the oath of Caraka? Can you recite the oath for me now and swear to it before the Purohita, the holiest of the brāhmaṇas?"

The Vaidya faced the Purohita, who remained in the corner with his back turned, and began in a faltering voice to recite the verses he had learned as a young man, had lived by all his adult life, and had taught to his students in turn: "I shall dedicate myself entirely to helping the sick, even though this be at the cost of my own life.

"I shall never harm the sick, not even in thought.

"I shall always endeavor to perfect my knowledge.

"I shall observe all rules of good conduct.

"When I am with a patient, I shall concern myself with nothing but the welfare of that patient.

"I shall not speak outside the house of anything I see or hear within the house.

"I shall not speak to a patient of his death if by doing so I harm the patient or anyone else.

"In the sight of the gods I pledge myself to this. So be it."

By the time he had finished, his voice was firm and strong and self-assured. The pledge of his profession had filled him with strength.

The Purohita nodded, but remained turned away. "The impure one speaks the truth."

And the king said, "Say what you have to say."

"The baby is turned about," the Vaidya replied in Sanskrit, which now fell easily from his lips, "and cannot leave the yoni. By surgery I can save mother or child. The decision is left to the king."

"You are the greatest vaidya in the kingdom," the king said skeptically, "and yet you cannot save both?"

"There is a chance I can," the Vaidya replied, "but it is no more certain than the role of those dice that you hold in your hand."

"Give me odds," said the king.

"I have performed the operation"—the Vaidya thought for a moment—"forty-two times. Twenty-nine times—no, twenty-eight—the child survived. Four times both mother and child survived. If there were someone who spoke the language of the golden-haired queen, that would make it easier. As it is, I cannot learn the details of her pains or the nature of any dreams or visions that might possess her."

"There is no one," the king replied. "She is of the people called Goth, who live to the north and speak a barbarous tongue. Her father was a general in the Yavana army—the Roman Yavanas—which today numbers many Goths, for they are wonderfully savage and strong. She was captured by the Parthians and given to me in homage. If our Roman ambassador were still at court, he could interpret, but he was recalled a year ago because of our refusal to limit our exports."

"The Romans love their luxury," Dakṣa said with a smile. "If they must spend their money, it is better they buy our silk than that poor cloth the Chinese manufacture."

"There is one phrase she cries over and over," the Vaidya said. He tried to recall the strange syllables as she had spoken them. " 'Christus filius Dei. Adiuva me in derelictione mea.' If only I knew what those words meant."

" 'Christus' is the name of a Yavana god," the Purohita said coolly. "He died some three and a half centuries ago, but only now does his cult grow popular in their land. Those who worship him drink his blood."

"Then they are cannibals?" the Vaidya asked, puzzled.

"Sāvitrīdevī is no cannibal," the king said, a flash of fire in his eye. "She practices ahiṃsa and eats no flesh."

"I only meant . . ." the Vaidya began, fearing that he had made precisely the fatal slip he had been trying to avoid.

"If she practices ahiṃsa, it is because of the king's civilizing influence," the Purohita explained, still without looking at the Vaidya. "There are many barbaric people living beyond the borders of the Land of the Sons of Bharata. Someday our great king will bring civilization to them all."

"Tell me then, Vaidya," the King said, fastening him with his stare, "can you guarantee the success of the operation?"

"No," the Vaidya replied. "But if I do not perform it, I guarantee you that the baby will die, and possibly the mother too."

The king closed his eyes and for several moments sat completely still. The rest of them, having grown so sensitive to his every mood, were careful even with the sound of their breathing. The Vaidya had the unsettling impression of a cobra about to strike. Suddenly the king's eyes flicked open and he said, "I have made my decision. If the child is a girl, kill it that the queen may survive. If it is a boy, let the queen die."

"I am sorry," the Vaidya said, "but I cannot determine before birth if the child is girl or boy."

"Vaidya, you vex me! Even an old hag of a midwife who

cannot write her name knows whether the child in the womb be boy or girl."

"Sometimes they know," the Vaidya replied, "and sometimes they do not. More often, they do not."

"Then save the child," the king cried in frustration, "and pray for the sake of your life that it is a boy."

The Vaidya bowed very deeply and backed out of the room.

"Clear the room of these women," the Vaidya ordered when he returned to the queen's chamber.

"I should like to stay," Sutanukā said boldly. "With my experience, I may be of assistance."

The Vaidya considered her dubiously. Her beauty, her makeup, her jewelry. Her fingernails, which were as long as daggers. Had the woman ever used them for anything beyond stroking a man's liṅgam?

In response to his thoughts, which she devined from his gaze, she began to peel away her fingernails one by one, for they were not real, but contrivances of polished horn stuck to her fingertips with a glue made of tree sap.

"To look like a goddess and work like a man," she explained, "those of my trade must sometimes resort to artifice."

Satisfied—to the extent of her ingenuity at least—the Vaidya permitted her to stay.

Dūṣaka cleared one of the tables of unguents and cosmetics, and dragged it over to the couch. He spread a sheet of clean white silk across the top and arranged upon it, as he had a hundred times in the past, the knives, pincers, trocars, and cauteries his master might require.

The Vaidya instructed Kaṅka to wash the queen's belly thoroughly, for the honey and ghee with which she had been anointed had attracted hundreds of flies. While the Vaidya did not understand precisely why it happened as it did, he had noticed that the cleaner the surroundings, the less frequently fever followed surgery, fever that nearly always meant death. If only he could find a way to fight the fever, how many patients he might save!

Dūṣaka and Sutanukā were put to work snapping fly whisks, while Virata lit incense of camphor, sandalwood, and musk with the hope of driving the insects out of the room. But while the Vaidya himself grew nauseous from the billowing smoke, the flies only settled more thickly.

Now the Vaidya took the skin of Sāvitrīdevī's arm and pinched it between thumb and forefinger, so hard that it turned green and gray. The girl did not respond. Satisfied that she was in the deepest state of soma sleep, a total disassociation of consciousness from the body, he sliced the skin from the navel to the top of the yoni. It slid easily apart making an opening the shape of an eye. The Vaidya's two students closed in on either side, pressing sponges to the open edges of the incision, to the smooth flesh with its underlayer of severed veins and oily yellow globules, in order to slow the bleeding and absorb the liquid. Kaṅka, who was the best of the Vaidya's students and had assisted in many operations of this type, went about his work with speed and precision. But Virata, who was less experienced, seemed uneasy. To be cutting the stomach of so lovely a young girl affected him in a manner that numerous operations on older and uglier patients had not.

Sutanukā, too, appeared shaken by the color of the blood, and its quantity.

"So, you cannot shed your fear as easily as your fingernails," he muttered.

"Fear?" She stared him in the eye. "Sir, I have been on the battlefield. I have seen men cut to pieces."

"But have you seen them put back together?" He smiled for the first time that night. "That is the trick."

Now as he went about his work, he lectured her as though she were a student: "The body has three hundred bones, five hundred muscles, two hundred and ten joints, and seventy canals through which flow the four doṣas: wind, gall, mucus, and blood. Of the winds, there are five, and they control the bodily functions. Udana comes from the throat and produces speech; prana, from the heart, allows us to breath and swallow food; samana fans the fires in the stomach so they may cook the food and separate that which a man can digest from the rest; apana in the abdomen drives the waste from the bowels and the semen from the liṅgam; and vyana is responsible for the motion of the blood throughout the body.

"Thus the food digested by the fire in the stomach becomes chyle, which flows to the heart—the seat of all intelligence—and from there to the liver, where it is converted into blood. Part of the blood becomes flesh, part bone, part marrow, and part semen, a process that takes some thirty days in its entirety. If the semen is retained, it produces energy, which is returned to the heart, and from there spread throughout the body. Hence the importance"—he paused and glanced significantly at Virata—"of retaining the semen.

"Since all the canals begin at the navel, we are now cutting very close to the source of the blood and must be extremely cautious. Those wonderful devices my assistants use to control the bleeding are called sponges. They come from Macedonia, from deep in the ocean. They must be very clean. I have washed these a dozen times myself."

The Vaidya looked down at the queen's stomach, the creeping stain of blood, near-black against the chalk whiteness of her skin. Flies swarmed about the opening and clung to the sponges as though they were hunks of fresh meat. The little monkey-hand that reached from the yoni opened and closed more slowly, like the plea of a drowning man.

Again he assessed his assistants. While Kaṅka and Sutanukā had gotten past their squeamishness, Virata seemed worse than before. His brow was beaded with sweat, and his eyes shifted restlessly, like the eyes of a thief.

"The next layer of skin," he continued, indicating the transparent membrane now revealed, "is the sack-that-holds-the-bowels. While thin and simple to cut, its manipulation is fraught with hazard. If not properly severed, the fires of the stomach may go out of control and consume the body with heat."

He moved the blade of the scalpel along the membrane, and it curled aside like the peel of a grape, revealing an enormous mass of throbbing purple muscle, slick and striated.

"This is the egg-in-which-the-baby-waits. Prepare yourselves, for the blood here is richest of anywhere in the body. Kaṅka! Virata! Hold your sponges very tight! Do you understand? If the gods are willing, perhaps we can save two lives this night."

They nodded. Kaṅka's hands shook. Virata's curly black hair stuck to his forehead with sweat.

The Vaidya plunged his knife into the purple mass and made one long cut. The sack opened like the mouth of some living creature gasping for air, and a river of blood poured from the lips. It poured over Sāvitrīdevī's pale white stomach and down the sides of the couch and onto the floor. The Vaidya could feel it, hot and wet, trickling on his feet.

The flies swarmed, sensing the richness of the food laid before them. Somewhere in the open cavity of her stomach something squirmed and shifted, something indistinct and shrouded in milky fluid. Sāvitrīdevī groaned and twisted upon the table.

Kaṅka was doing his part, but Virata had frozen. His mouth hung open, and his grip on the sponge was slack.

"Virata!" the Vaidya barked. "Wake up! Come to your senses!"

But Virata paid no attention. He took a step backward, then another. Then his eyes rolled upward and he crumpled to the floor as though struck by an arrow.

"Take his place," the Vaidya shouted to Sutanukā, "quickly! Another second may mean life or death."

The gaṇikā, kneeling beside Virata's body, pulled the sponge from his hand and looked at it with dismay.

"It is dirty," she said. "It has touched the floor."

"There is nothing to be done now," the Vaidya replied. "Wipe it off and press it to the side of the cut as Kaṅka is doing."

As he spoke he pulled a small object out of the pit of the queen's stomach. The tiny arm protruding from the yoni slipped away as from a bangle and reappeared joined to the shoulder of a squirming, struggling little monkey, strung by a cord to its mother. The Vaidya held the creature by its feet so it dangled upside down and, with the thumb of the other hand, removed the clot of blood clogging its mouth. The baby screamed.

Sutanukā smiled and whispered, "Long life to the prince."

Reluctantly she put aside the sponge, one of the few threads that tied Sāvitrīdevī to this life, and ran to get the Purohita, who was waiting in an adjacent chamber. He would perform the jātakarma ceremony, the ceremony that welcomed a soul to three score and ten autumns of joy and suffering on this earth. By the law of the brāhmaṇas, the jātakarma had to be performed before the umbilical cord could be cut.

The holiest of brāhmaṇas would not even enter until the "impure" one—the Vaidya, that is—and his assistants had been dispatched to the farthest corner of the room.

Then the Purohita hurried to the infant and, taking him up in his arms, began whispering mantras in his ear. He placed a drop of honey and ghee and powdered gold on his tongue and gave him the holy name that his parents would keep secret until the day of his initiation, eleven years hence.

Meanwhile the Vaidya, filled with a sense of hopeless frustration, watched the blood streaming from Sāvitrīdevī's stomach, knowing that to administer to her during this auspicious moment would be unpardonable.

After the cord had been cut, the wet nurse arrived, a plump and agreeable śūdra woman with breasts like melons. Laughing with joy—as much for the miracle of birth as for her own good fortune in attaining this enviable employment—she took the baby to the chamber that would be his nursery, where she would bathe and feed him and swaddle him in clean silks. She treated the bleeding body of the queen as though it were already the husk of one who had gone to the next life. Once she and the baby were gone, and the Purohita had performed his slow shuffling step to the door, the Vaidya rushed to the queen's side.

"Now let us try to save *this* child," he whispered.

He set about clearing the cavity of her stomach, but the flies had doubled in number. No sooner had he brushed away one swarm than another would alight, their feet sticking in the blood as though it were honey. Finally, an instant came when the cavity seemed empty; quickly he pulled together the sides of the purple "egg" and then the layers of flesh that covered it. With the bulk of the baby gone, the skin was loose and willing to be formed.

"The ants," he called to Dūṣaka. "Now!"

The servant brought him a carved box, inside which black ants the size of betel nuts, from the province of Samatata, swarmed over a section of sugarcane, their tough sickle-shaped mandibles opening and closing with remarkable force. The Vaidya caught one between his fingers and, carefully positioning its head over the juncture of the flesh, allowed it to bite down. The next instant he pinched off its body so that only the head remained, the mandibles holding the flesh closed as a thred would bind cloth. He took another ant and repeated the operation, then another and another, until the entire length of the incision had been sutured closed.

"You will not allow the flies," Sutanukā said with interest, "but you yourself provide ants." The comment was inappropriate, but she could not contain her curiosity.

"The ants are clean and industrious. Their mandibles stop the bleeding, and the foul-smelling juice that drips from their body seems to retard the deadly fire. They are truly the friends of the vaidya. They do their job quietly and efficiently, and never criticize their master."

He glanced at Dūṣaka, who looked down with shame. Kaṅka squatted beside his friend Virata, trying to revive him with a jar of camphor.

The Vaidya placed a silk sheet over the incision and laid a small iron bar gently on top of that.

"The weight of it," he explained, "will help stop the bleeding."

Indeed, the torrent that still flowed from the yoni, saturating the sponges and silk sheets that the Vaidya had placed between her thighs, began to subside almost at once. For the first time since his arrival, the Vaidya relaxed somewhat. Squatting beside the queen's bed, he felt her pulse, examined her complexion, and listened to her breath.

"She will live?" Sutanukā asked.

"If her karma wills it," he replied. "For the moment she survives."

He looked down at the figure that seemed to sleep so peacefully, golden hair in disarray, mouth half open, one slim arm dangling over the side of the couch. Through the sheer white silk one could see the sole remnant of his surgery, a jagged purple line studded with severed mandibles, that began at her navel and vanished into the diamond of pale curls between her legs. The Vaidya wiped a string of saliva from the young queen's mouth with a lover's touch.

"There is nothing more you or I can do," he continued, "but wait and pray to the Buddha, or Viṣṇu, or whoever remains awake at this time of night."

Birds were chirping. He looked to the window, and outside, the black of night was turning gray. The stars were gone, and he could make out the shape of the king's palace, its ornate finials outlined against the ever-lightening sky. Then he heard it: the blowing of the conch shell, echoing from the balconies of the palace to the ramparts of the great timber walls that surrounded the city. And from far away it came to him bit by bit, the sounds of crowds surging forward, of bullock carts clattering down the stone-paved streets, of marching musicians, drumming and blowing horns.

He looked at her, puzzled. "Is today some sort of festival?" Since he had become a Buddhist he had found it more and more difficult to keep track of those festival days observed by the brāmaṇas.

She smiled sympathetically at him, a poor exhausted little man with a nose like a fig and hands covered to the elbows with blood.

"It is the birthday of the prince."

"Oh, I'm a fool," the Vaidya said, shaking his head.

"No, no, you are a wonderful vaidya, kind and compassionate and wise. Come, let me feed you and wash the blood off your hands."

2

In the chamber set aside as a nursery, the wet nurse was already busy bathing the new prince in a basin of chased gold—a gift from the guild of metalsmiths—in order to make him presentable to the king, who would be visiting within the hour. As she washed him, she sang with joy and he screamed with indignation, lusty howls that penetrated to the most remote chambers of the harem, yet brought no complaints.

She considered herself the luckiest woman in the land to have such enjoyment, for just last week her husband had lost his position as servant to Jubala the cart maker, and a few days later, following a silly quarrel between her husband and her uncle about which was the greater god, Śiva or Viṣṇu, her uncle had banished them from the mud hut on the outskirts of the city that had always been her home. As a final blow—why did bad things all happen at once?—a thief had stolen their jewels and bangles, all that remained of their small wealth (unless, as her uncle suggested, her husband had sold them without telling her, to support his drinking, gambling, and womanizing, an idea she simply could not accept).

And so she had found herself without a home, or anyone to turn to, or any means of supporting herself and her children, the youngest of whom was only a month. In her darkest moments of despair, she spoke of becoming a beggar or a prostitute, though she was not sufficiently repellent for the former profession or enticing enough for the latter.

But then a neighbor whose brother was a messenger at the palace learned that one of the queens was expecting and a wet nurse would be required. Interviews were arranged. Having no jewels, the wet nurse had to borrow bangles of iron and glass from the neighbors. Unable to find an ornamental girdle big enough to circle her wide hips, she went to a jeweler and, by weeping and threatening to drown herself in the Ganges, convinced him to make her one on credit. She even went so far as to lac her nipples, to emphasize the hugeness of her breasts, and their inexhaustible milk.

And here she was, installed in the palace's luxurious servants' quarters with husband and children, being paid what seemed to her a fortune to nurse and care for an infant—a prince no less!—something she enjoyed so much she would, speaking frankly, have done it for nothing.

She leaned over the golden basin, supporting the baby's head in her left hand, and scrubbed his belly with her right, being careful of the stump of the umbilical cord as the Vaidya had instructed her, lest it tear and cause a wound. She lathered his arms and legs with phenaka, his tiny blossom of a penis. As she worked she wondered that a creature so mindless, so red and wrinkly and bawling, could turn, in time, into a man like the men she had known, capable of surprising tenderness at one instant, horrifying cruelty the next.

Lulled by the warm sun streaming through windows shaped like upturned scallop shells, she began to daydream about inviting her uncle to the palace, showing him how well they were living, and doing everything else within her power to make him realize how badly he had behaved. When he begged forgiveness, she would forgive him, thereby demonstrating how much finer her nature was than his. What a pleasing daydream it was!

She removed the scabs that caked the prince's hair as though she were peeling some big soft fruit, admiring the beautiful swirling designs they made as they fell into the water. At first she attributed the odd color of his scalp to accumulations of the doṣas that pulsed through the womb. But as she scrubbed she grew ever more amazed, for she saw that the color was not the fault of anything but the hair itself.

It was the shade of honey.

She had never seen such a thing. Honey-colored hair! Was this a deformity? Everybody knew that a prince born with a deformity could never take the throne. Rāma Gupta, the crown prince, had a harelip, and much of the gossip at the time of his birth centered around whether it would make him unfit to be king. But even a harelip was less bizarre than these honey-colored locks.

Suppose the Purohita construed them as an evil omen. Then might the king have the infant put to death? A shiver passed through her and a cry escaped her lips at the thought of it. This innocent infant, this lovely wrinkly pink thing, put to death!

And what of herself? She would no longer have work, would be out in the indifferent world with husband and child and no way to support them. How would they live? Her thoughts turned again to the profession of begging. She had heard that the competition among beggars was so fierce that they occasionally cut off their children's arms and legs to make them more effective instruments of pity.

She couldn't go on. She collapsed on a cane stool, which groaned under her weight, clutched the royal infant to her breast, and wept. In a few seconds she had passed, in her mind's eye, from glory to destitution. She wept for herself, for her own children, now without prospects, and for her husband.

She heard the gong that signaled a visitor's approach and rose, wiping her eyes, trying to compose herself.

One of the guards who was standing just outside the doorway said, "The Great King of Kings Samudra Gupta would see his newborn son."

Her heart began to pound. "Oh, yes," she called back, "but he must wait a moment—the baby's not ready yet. He wouldn't mind waiting a moment, would he?" And she added, "Please?" realizing that this was not the proper way to address the king.

Indeed, another servant would have been slaughtered for such familiarity, but the mixture of earnestness, naïveté, and goodhearted confusion in the wet nurse's tremulous voice reminded the ruler, who was listening from beyond the tapestry that closed off the nursery, of his own wet nurse, who cared for him until the time of his initiation, and he simply smiled indulgently, stationed himself in the hallway, and sent a return message that he would wait a few minutes, but (and this ironic) that he, too, had other duties to perform that day. His good mood was in part due to the news, just imparted to him by Sutanukā, that the infant was a boy and that Sāvitrīdevī had survived the operation.

The wet nurse looked around the chamber in desperation for something with which she might hide or disguise the baby. A few of the presents had already arrived: the golden basin she had bathed him in; a golden cradle encrusted with precious gems from a Pallava king; a toy palace cunningly carved out of elephant tusks from the royal mahout; a fabulous chest from the silk merchant's guild, overflowing with fine silks in every color, particularly saffron, which was auspicious. Perhaps she could tear a strip from one of the silk sheets and wrap it like a turban around the infant's head. But no, he would ask to have it removed. He would want to examine every inch of the baby, as new fathers do.

Then her eye fell on an ivory jar of kohl—a paste of ground antimony used to outline the eyes, that they might appear all the longer and more beautiful—probably left behind by one of the queens. She dipped her finger in it and applied it to the prince's hair. It adhered to the fine strands, she saw with relief, blackening them and making them lie smoothly across the scalp, as if oiled with ghee, something she had intended to do in any case.

"The king grows impatient," the guard called to her in a warning tone.

"Just another instant," she replied. She put more and more of the kohl on his hair, until it was a rick uniform black, then wrapped his tiny body in a silk of brilliant blue and hung a string of pearls around his neck. Only then would she let the king enter.

"So at last I am allowed to see my son," he said in his booming voice. He took the infant and held it at arm's length, high in the air.

The baby's big head lolled to the side. It rolled its eyes, and stuck out its tongue, and waved its arms and legs without purpose.

"You must support the head," the wet nurse scolded him.

"I know. Because I am a warrior does not mean I am ignorant of babies." The king made a comical face, stretching his lips like a monkey and making clicking sounds with his tongue. "Why does he refuse to smile?"

"They cannot smile yet. Not for ninety days."

"So long? No, I can't believe that. I think he does not smile because he is hungry. Have you fed him? Is your milk rich enough for his appetite? He is like his father, I wager. Always hungry." He held the baby close to his face and gazed into its huge round eyes.

"If you're quite done," the wet nurse said, "it is time for his nap."

"Wet nurse, look! Here on his back, a birthmark in the shape of a cobra. Is it thus, or do I imagine it?"

The wet nurse squinted at the brown mark on the baby's back and nodded. "It does seem to have the shape of a cobra."

The king roared with pleasure. "No birthmark could be more auspicious. My son is destined for greatness. He is the chosen of the gods, perfect in every respect. Well, is he not?"

"He's a beautiful baby," the nurse replied, hiding her anxiety.

The king raised an eyebrow. "You hesitate. Is there some defect you would hide from me? A shortage of fingers or toes?"

"See for yourself."

"You have your nerve, wet nurse, talking to me thus."

"See for yourself, O Great King of Kings, if you please."

The king laughed. "That's better." He examined the baby's hands and feet. "Yes, the child is perfect. And of a fine temper. He hardly cries at all."

"Hardly at all," she agreed and, remembering, added quickly, "O Lord of the Land."

The king gazed at his new son, as though he were gazing into the future, and in time his boisterous good humor gave way to a kind of melancholy.

"Perhaps, my son," he whispered, "you are too perfect for your own well-being."

The wet nurse did not understand, but knew enough not to question him.

Tens of thousands of subjects crowded that part of the gardens that was open to the public, waiting for the king to appear on his balcony with news of the new prince. The hot sun and bright banners flying from the palace finials added to the festive air. Some of the men raised their children on their shoulders so they could see above the heads of those in front of them, while others, weary from standing and waiting so long, squatted down on the grass and saw nothing but a forest of legs. Vendors took advantage of the idle crowd and hawked their sweets and cakes, while acrobats and magicians performed in the hope of gathering a few kākinī.

Suddenly the crowd began to cheer. Those who were squatting stood, and those who were standing rose onto their tiptoes and strained their necks. The great Samudra Gupta, weighted with jewelry, stepped onto the balcony, followed by his favorite porter, carrying the white parasol and sandals that were the symbols of his authority.

Samudra Gupta could actually feel the floor tremble and wondered, for a fraction of a second, if the vibrations might split those wooden joists that held the balcony aloft and send him tumbling to his death. But he felt no fear, for death, in the face of such adoration, was meaningless. He was, for the moment at least, eternal as a god.

He gazed upon his subjects, a sea of gleaming brown skin, glittering jewels and flower garlands, and smiled with pleasure. Pressing his palms together in front of his chest, he saluted them in namaste. It was a gesture of humility, but somehow, he felt, insufficient. The moment called for the grand, the unusual. He had an inspiration; he fell to his knees on the space in front of the throne, lowered his chest and then his forehead to the wood. Never in his knowledge had a king done such a thing, prostrated himself in public, to his public. It was a way of saying, "I am your servant, I exist only to serve you," to all those gathered before him.

A cheer welled up, a thunderous roar of appreciation. He had never heard such a riotous outpouring of approval. He rose and looked back into the dark portal behind him for the reactions of his two principal counselors, the Purohita and the mahāmantrin, as well as that of the crown prince, who was standing beside them.

The mahāmantrin, a plump, cunning Buddhist by the name of Vasubandhu and a respected philosopher in his own right, brought up his right hand and made the chin mudra, the symbol of wisdom, by forming a ring of the thumb and the index finger and allowing the other three fingers to point straight out.

The Purohita's approval was more reserved, but the king had expected that.

Young Prince Rāma was least pleased of all. But that, too, was to be expected, the king thought sadly, for the birth of a second prince could only bring trouble to the firstborn, particularly when that firstborn had a handicap, a harelip, jeopardizing his claim to the throne.

The crowd grew quiet as the king prepared to speak. While the distances and acoustics were such that even those standing near him would have difficulty understanding, hundreds of men who had already memorized the details of the address had been placed throughout the crowd so that they might pretend to listen, and then relay, clarify, and rectify the king's words to those around them.

"A prince has been born!" the king shouted. He waited for the inevitable cheers to subside before he continued, a pause he repeated at the end of each statement.

"He is big and strong and perfect of features.

"He is called Candra Gupta the Second, after my own father, the greatest lord to ever rule the Land of the Sons of Bharata.

"He is blessed by Viṣṇu and by all the gods.

"In honor of his birth, today shall be a festival day. No man shall work at his trade. Those of all classes—brāhmaṇa, kṣatriya, vaiśya, and śūdra—shall for this day only forget their class distinctions, and dance and sing and drink as though they were all of one class.

"Musicians and actors shall perform works of a joyful nature. Poets will receive a prize for the finest new ode. Those who beg shall come to the royal almshouse for a double share."

He performed the salute of namaste again, turned, and left the balcony.

As was his habit following appearances such as this, he went directly to the small meeting hall to meet with his advisers and learn their opinion of what he had said and how the public had reacted to it.

"Victory to you, my lord," Vasubandhu said, hurrying up to him. "An excellent speech! A daring gesture! Another king might fear a loss of dignity. But not this king. One who has conquered the nine kings of the north can afford to bow."

As the Purohita advised the king in spiritual matters, the mahāmantrin counseled him regarding questions of state.

The king nodded. He was still elated by the crowd, the size of it, the intensity of their adoration. He took to the balcony infrequently, for it was a heady drug of the sort that interfered with a king's real work.

"And you, my teacher," the king inquired of the Purohita, "what did you think?"

"My lord knows how I feel about abolishing class distinctions, even for a day."

"It is a traditional way of celebrating the birth of a prince."

"What was permitted in previous ages is prohibited in this evil Age of Kali."

"Dear teacher, you are too hard on your student," the king said, laughing at his sternness.

He turned next to his oldest son, the crown prince. Oddly, it was his approval he wanted most. "And you, young Rāma, what did you think?"

"It was an excellent speech, Father."

The boy didn't look at him when he spoke, but directed his attention to the monkey he carried in his arms, a brown, short-haired, long-limbed creature with protruding ears, a flat black face, and pointed teeth. It wore a diamond-studded collar and leash that Rāma had ordered, at his father's insistence, after several of the courtiers had complained of being bitten.

"Then why do you frown?"

"You misread my face, Father. It is not a frown, but the fault of my divided lip."

It was indeed difficult to read Rāma's expressions, for the sides of his palate had remained unjoined at birth, and his upper lip was split all the way to the base of his nose, making his lower face resemble nothing so much as a camel's snout, to which vicious and haughty animal his detractors were fond of comparing him. When he spoke, his voice escaped through the fleshy fissure in a thin, high whine.

He was thirteen years old, tall for his age but pudgy, round-faced, with thick black hair that began low on his forehead. His cheeks were marble-smooth, without so much as a trace of fuzz; this, along with large, sensual eyes and a thickness of the body, gave him a womanly appearance. And like a woman, he was far more comfortable with the intrigues of the court than with his instructions in warfare. Knowing that his deformity might one day prevent him from gaining the throne, he had begun, at an early age, to curry the favor of the more influential courtiers and ministers. Many of them, realizing how dangerous life might be were the crown prince a foe, allowed themselves to fall under his sway.

"In fact," Rāma continued to his father, "I smile for you.

And for my new little brother. When may I set eyes on him?"

"Soon. I shall call an assembly so that all the members of the court may see him. Ah, my son, I am pleased that you greet your little brother with love. I cannot tell you the nights I stayed awake, worrying that envy and suspicion would be a barrier between you."

"The behavior of children is not a fit matter to occupy the mind of a king, Father."

"Of course, you are right. I am proud to have a son of such wisdom."

While the king smiled at the boy, and spoke words of praise, and touched him affectionately as he spoke, a subtle discomfort was always evident. Those who understood the king very well knew that he blamed himself for his son's disfigurement, and suffered the guilt of it, if not every day, at least during those hours in the dead of the night when no diversions stand between a man and his conscience.

One evening, late in the pregnancy of Rāma's mother, whose name was Dattadeví, the king had disguised himself as a common soldier and, leaving by one of the many secret subterranean passages that honeycombed the earth beneath the palace, wandered the city unnoticed, a practice he was fond of and indulged in at least once a month. During these outings he had two principal aims: to overhear as many conversations as possible and thus learn how the common man felt about how the land was being ruled, and to lose a few thousand paṇas at the cockfights. This latter diversion was among the great pleasures in his life.

Later, while returning through a poor part of town, he saw, down a dark twisting alley, a man forcing a woman to the ground and struggling to mount her. She cried for help. The king came running. The rapist fled, the king pursued him. Cornering him in a courtyard, the king drew his two-handed sword and made a stroke so swift and clean that for moments afterward the man remained standing, unaware that his neck had been severed. Then, with a look of surprise upon its face, the head rolled from the neck and thudded to the ground. The body, gushing blood from the opening, dropped like a felled tree. The king carried the head by its oily black hair, trailing blood along the paving stones, back to the woman, so she might do as she liked with it. The rapist, she told the king, had been one of a gang hired by a feuding family. Just before the king's arrival, they had murdered her husband and brother-in-law, and had he not come to her rescue so promptly, they would have murdered her as well. The king, deeply moved by her distress, gave her the money he had won at the cockfights—he had been lucky that night—to hire mourners and prepare a pyre so that she might burn by her dead husband's side. Her gratitude was such that she had virtually forced him to worship Kāma with her. They did so in four different positions: the splitting of the bamboo, the fixing of the nail, the lotuslike position, and the crab position.

No sooner had the pressure in his liṅgam been relieved than the scarlet veils of bloodlust and passion were torn from his gaze and he saw that he was in the house of a butcher, a slaughterer of livestock and a member of the loathesome caṇḍāla, the class beneath all others. He dressed and left without another word. Returning to the palace, he went directly to the Purohita and confessed his act. The Purohita spent days making sacrifices over the holy flame and chanting the most sacred mantras. But even with all his magic, he warned the king, there were bound to be repercussions for such a serious violation of the dharma.

And then Rāma had been born with a harelip and cleft palate. The Purohita never said a word, but the king understood that his dalliance with the caṇḍāla woman was responsible for his son's disfigurement. Such was his guilt that he never scolded or punished the baby Rāma, even when he tore precious silks, or shattered crystal, or nearly burned down the palace by overturning a flaming ghee lamp. Since everything his father did took the form of an apology, the son, ignorant of the transgression, came to think of his father as a weak man and a fool. Without a model to respect and imitate, Rāma became cynical and amoral. Without discipline, his character grew misshapen, like a tree that no man bothers to prune.

Later that same day, Prince Rāma climbed the steep stairs that led to the highest parapet of the palace. From the slot-shaped windows along the way, he could see the palace complex spread out beneath him, the golden finials and silk banners dazzling in the sun; and the city, its grid of orderly streets and avenues lined with stately whitewashed houses and verdant gardens, deteriorating toward the outskirts into cramped tortuous alleyways clumped with mud hovels. He was so high now that he could even see, beyond the great timber walls and towers that girdled the city, the river Son flowing into the great muddy Ganges, crowded with rafts and barges plying the commerce of the empire. This godlike perspective, combined with a sense of violating the forbidden, made him dizzy with excitement. He whispered to the monkey, which was clutching his shoulder, to be calm. The air smelled musty and old, and the dust on the treads showed how few feet had passed this way before him.

Reaching the doorway, he boldly pulled aside the beaded curtains and entered a tiny chamber. Everywhere around him were rattan footstools piled with fibrous paper pressed from palm leaves, upon which had been scratched all manner of mathematical calculations and planetary symbols. Hanging from hooks on the walls were intricate devices of brass and teak, studded with wheels and levers, inscribed with finely calibrated rules. Try as he might, Rāma could not deduce their purpose. In the center of the room, a great brass sphere rested on a bamboo tripod, its surface engraved with all the stars in their constellations.

From overhead he heard a slow shuffling step, and as he watched, a figure began to descend from what must have been an observation turret up above, first sandaled feet, then the bottom of a long vasana, then the astrologer himself, old Vahara Mihira, with his flowing gray beard and hair, his forehead ever wrinkled in concentration, his eyes like glowing coals beneath thick gray brows. He was muttering to himself, so absorbed in thought that he seemed unaware of the intruder, as he was unaware of the twig of a hibiscus tree that had lodged in his hair the last time he walked in the garden, perhaps weeks ago, and had been there ever since. He wandered over to one of the stools, picked up a blank piece of palm-leaf paper, and began to scratch calculations with his stylus.

Rāma cleared his throat self-consciously.

The astrologer squinted from beneath the hedge of his brow. "Who's that?"

"I, Prince Rāma."

"Did I send for you?"

"No, old man."

"Then go away."

"I would learn about the stars, old man, and how to tell the future. Treat my entreaty with respect or I shall have my father cut off your nose."

The astrologer ceased his scribbling and eyed his visitor

suspiciously. "Why, Rāma, I never knew you to have an interest in the sciences."

"Oh, yes. I am a man of many interests, like my father."

"Not quite like your father."

"By the tone of your voice, I presume you think me less."

"A boy is always less than a man."

"It is because of my harelip, is it not?"

"I once knew a sage who was blind and had lost both legs, but he knew one hundred of his previous incarnations."

"Then why do you say that?"

"That you are not like your father? Because you are not. A prince is not a king. A peacock is not a crow. Nor is lead identical with gold."

"Old man, you speak nonsense. I think you spend too much time staring at the stars and not enough looking at the politics of the court. That is the real world. That is where your attention should lie."

"The glitter of the court is too brilliant for my poor old eyes. I must be satisfied with the stars."

The monkey swung down from Rāma's shoulder, grabbed a palm leaf that was covered with notation, and began to chew on it.

"Give me that," the astrologer cried.

When the old man reached for it, the monkey drew back his lips, baring his sharp white teeth, and screamed "Chee-chee-chee!" Then he leaped to Rāma's head.

"I would like my calculations," the astrologer said, unamused. "They have taken me weeks."

"They are probably worth more as monkey food," Rāma said, laughing as he struggled with his pet.

By the time he secured the leaf, it was ripped down the middle and a bite had been taken from the side. The astrologer regarded it with irritation, then placed it carefully on a stool.

Rāma found himself losing patience. "Get on with it, astrologer. Teach me about the stars. I would have our lessons start this instant."

"I would teach you manners first."

"Old man . . ." he threatened, making a scissors of his fingers as if to cut off his nose.

"The problem is, I cannot think where to begin, and there is so much to it." The old man stroked his beard and spoke in a manner so carefully calculated that Rāma could not decide if he was mocking or sincere. "And everywhere the practice is different. In the Land of the Sons of Bharata, we say that each day of the month the moon visits a different part of the sky, and these parts are called his mansions, or nakṣatras. But in the land of the Yavanas—and they are very wise astrologers—they divide the sky according to where the sun dwells each month, and those are called the solar mansions. As for the Chinese, they love the number five and so divide their heavens into five parts—four that correspond to the seasons, the fifth in the region of the Pole Star, which corresponds to their emperor. Now they, too, have the division of twelve, but instead of dividing the transit of the sun or the moon, that is to say the solar or lunar ecliptic, they divide the equator—"

"Enough talk of Chinese!" Rāma interrupted, stamping his foot. "I wish to learn the future, right here in this city of Pāṭaliputra."

"To learn, we first need patience." The astrologer stared at him a long moment before continuing. "Since a man's fate is determined by his karma, so is the moment of his birth. As he has been brave in previous lives, and paid homage to the gods, and refrained from eating meat, then will he be born at an auspicious moment. As he has been evil, and deceived men, and neglected the rituals of the brāhmaṇas, then will his birth come at an inauspicious time. This moment of birth is all-important. Which mansion was just over the eastern horizon at the time? And the planets, the sun, and the moon—where did they lie? The Yavanas say that the placement of the sun—the sun sign—is most important in determining a man's fate, but we in the Land of the Sons of Bharata pay more attention to the moon."

"I am still confused, old man. Let us talk less in the abstract. Give me an example from real life. What about—" he thought for a moment—"the prince who was born this morning? What do the stars say of his moment of birth?"

The astrologer picked up a palm leaf and frowned at his calculations. "The Lagna of Karkaṭa—that sign the Yavanas call Cancer—had begun its ascent. Thus the moon was leaving the mansion of Pūrṇavarṣu and entering that known as Puṣya. But most interesting of all is the influence of the comet. It dwells, along with the planets Mercury and Mars, in Aśvinī, creating a—"

"You speak another language, old man," Rāma shouted in frustration. "Tell me in the royal tongue, what does it mean? Will he be king?" Realizing that he had said too much, Rāma stopped suddenly and held his fingertips over his mouth.

"He will be," the astrologer said slowly, "the greatest king to ever rule our land."

Rāma kept his expression neutral, though his insides were churning with misery.

"But you could be mistaken, could you not?"

"That is why I have spent the week secreted here, eating nothing but a fig now and then while I did each of my calculations one hundred times over."

"But you *could* be mistaken. Admit it. Even the gods make mistakes. Rāma, my namesake, mistook Mārīca for a golden deer."

"I am not mistaken."

Rama tried another tack. "Have I not heard you ask a certain boon of the king, that he allot ten million paṇas for the building of a vast stone platform, a sort of man-made mountain, higher than the Himalayas, from the top of which you could observe the stars with ease?"

"An observatory," the astrologer said sadly, "like those of the Babylonians. We have discussed such a project. But without slaves to perform the labor, the cost is impossibly vast. The king thinks such funds could be better used to stock the granaries and care for the beggars."

"I disagree with him," Rāma said thoughtfully. "I believe that studying the stars should have precedence. Beggars are born beggars by dint of their acts in previous lives. Let them work off their own karma. Why should we suffer as a result? Yes, if I were to be a king—and I am thirteen years old, the time of my coronation may be much closer than any man imagines—I would make the building of such an observatory my foremost priority."

The astrologer stared at him stonily.

"What I am trying to say," Rāma continued, "is that if you have made a mistake, if indeed my little brother is not destined to be king, if instead my auspicious planets occupy the proper lunar mansions, indicating my own indisputable royal destiny, then you will certainly get funding for your observatory, and very soon."

"If we are not faithful to the truth," the astrologer said, as though in grave pain, "then the greatest observatory in the world is of no more use than a footstool."

"I do not understand," Rāma said.

But the astrologer had turned his back on the young prince and returned to his calculations.

While outside the people of Pāṭaliputra celebrated, the Vaidya remained in Sāvitrīdevī's close, airless chamber, moistening her lips with ghee, readjusting the weight on her stomach, feeling her temperature, and listening to her breath. Occasionally Sutanukā brought him betel quid, or a cup of spiced milk, or some fruit. He chewed the quid, but barely tasted the food, and then only out of politeness to her.

As the crystal windows reflected the setting sun in their uneven surface, Sāvitrīdevī stirred, indicating that the soma had begun to wear off. She opened her eyes and smiled to see the Vaidya. Then she struggled to her elbows and looked around with a troubled expression. He reassured her, in pantomime, that the baby was well, while Sutanukā ran to get the king, who had ordered that he be summoned the instant the queen regained consciousness.

While waiting for their return, the Vaidya raised the queen's head on pillows. By making all kinds of threats, he managed to separate the wet nurse from the infant and place it in its mother's arms. It sucked at her breast for a few moments, then drifted off to sleep, saliva bubbling from the corner of its mouth. The queen stroked it with her free hand, occasionally bending forward to kiss it gently on the top of its head, then leaning back on the pillow and smiling shyly at those assembled around her. Now and then she would murmur words of endearment in a language nobody understood.

The king arrived while the servants were lighting the ghee lamps. Sāvitrīdevī's face became radiant, and she tried to rise so that she might prostrate herself on the floor before him. The Vaidya pressed her gently back on the bed.

"Not yet my dear. In a week when you are stronger. The

king will forgive you for not rising, won't he?"

The king didn't bother to answer. Kneeling beside the bed, he bent over to kiss her and let his fingers drift along the curtain of golden hair that spread across her pillow.

"She lives!" he whispered to the healer. "By the eyes of Viṣṇu, you are the greatest of the vaidyas in my land, or anywhere on earth. From now on you will be vaidya to my court, and your title shall be mahāvaidya."

At just that instant Sāvitrīdevī shivered, even though the evening was so warm that no one had bothered to cover her.

A grave expression crossed the Vaidya's face, a look of tragedy. "No," the Vaidya said. "She dies."

"What?" the king said. "Vaidya, you talk nonsense. Look at her! She is awake, she smiles and embraces her son."

"She dies," the Vaidya said. "The fires burn out of control."

"But surely there is a way to stop it? With all your knowledge of herbs and ointments—"

"With all my knowledge I know there is no way to stop it."

"But I feel her face. It does not feel hot."

"It is hot, and it shall grow hotter."

"Vaidya, there must be a way!" the king said, gripping the little man by the shoulder so tightly that he cried with pain, and actually lifting him off his feet. Then he let go and shouted, "Get the Purohita!"

One of the guards who had accompanied him turned and ran like a wild deer. Sometime later he returned with the high-domed, dour priest who was the holiest of the brāhmaṇas.

"He says she will die," the king told the Purohita, as a child pleads with a parent to fix a favorite toy. "He says the fires will consume her. Do something. Save her."

"The fires from the stomach rage out of control," the Vaidya explained. "They will consume her before dawn."

"Although he is impure," the Purohita said, "he is a wise vaidya. Heed his words."

"No," the king said, shaking his head emphatically. "He knows much, but you know more."

"Remember a tale I taught you when you were a boy?" the Purohita said, with surprising gentleness. "About how all the eldest gods once gathered on Mount Meru for a horse sacrifice, an asvamedha. And the Lord Śiva, discovering that he had not been invited, grew so enraged that a single drop of sweat fell from his forehead. And when it touched the earth, a great conflagration appeared, which turned into a monster named Fever, a gruesome troll with bloody eyes, a tawny beard, and hair that stood on end. He had a gaping mouth and teeth like daggers and was dressed in blood-red robes. And as he stalked the earth, everything he passed—man and beast, tree and flower—was incinerated by his unbearable heat. Then the Grandfather, the one called Brahmā, took pity on the human race, and went to Śiva and pleaded for him to destroy this creature called Fever before it turned the entire earth to a cinder. Now, Śiva could not destroy what he had created, but, moved by the Grandfather's plea, and also by receiving a piece of the sacrifice, he divided Fever into a million parts. So the world was spared, but in return, Fever takes his victims. My lord must try to grasp the essence of my story. Do not deny the gods what is theirs. Though our sacrifices be indescribably painful, they keep the wheel of the dharma in motion."

"No!" the king shouted, "I will not let her go!" And he threw himself across her, as though protecting her from the onslaught of warriors. "Get you to the temple, Purohita! Make offerings to Viṣṇu and Brahmā and Śiva, chant the most holy mantras you know, and have your assistants read the Vedas from beginning to end—" He broke off, his voice choking with grief.

"I am the king's servant, and shall do as the king wishes. But all the ritual in the land cannot undo the karma of one evil deed."

"Evil deed? Can this child have ever even thought evil? Look at her face! It is the face of an apsaras."

"In this life. Perhaps she was born thus so that she could learn the meaning of righteousness and atone for past evil. Do not make me try to explain the ways of karma, for few things are so subtle and complex, and beyond the grasp of man."

"If this lowly woman might speak?" Sutanukā said, rising. The king nodded and she continued, "I have heard of a magical way to combat the fever."

"Go on," said the king.

"One heats the head of an ax until the metal is red, then plunges it into a bucket of cold water. Thus the fire travels from the sick person into the ax, and then into the water to be dissipated."

"I know this trick," the Vaidya said. "I learned it as a student. For a time I performed it whenever the stomach fires went out of control. Not once did it work."

"Did you chant mantras as you performed it?" the king pressed. "Did you do it in the presence of a brāhmaṇa?"

"Those of our profession are by and large Buddhists," the Vaidya replied.

"Buddhists." The king shook his head. "You are so impure, Vaidya, how do you expect any sort of magic to work? Get me axes," he shouted to his guards, "a hundred of them, and a cauldron of the coldest water. Then build a fire in the courtyard, that we may heat them."

The Vaidya was exiled from Sāvitrīdevī's chamber. He squatted in the hallway, watching sadly—nothing saddened him like a man denying the truth—as through the night the guards came running up the steps with axheads heated red as kiṃsuka blossoms. A hundred times he heard the hiss of hot metal plunged into water, a hundred times he saw the guards reemerge with axheads turned dull gray. Throughout it all, the king's noble servant the Purohita, defying exhaustion, chanted mantras with an obstinacy that might have driven a weaker man insane.

A long while later, the king emerged. He was broken, defeated. All that was kingly in his bearing had for that moment abandoned him. He ordered the Vaidya back to the queen's bed chamber.

Sāvitrīdevī's body was covered with sweat, and her face was so hot the Vaidya pulled his hand away, as though from a pot straight off the hearth. The beat of the blood in her wrist was very fast but very faint. Her eyes rolled in her head, and she babbled as if in a dream, and struggled against the women guards who had been enlisted to hold her down. The baby had been taken away from her.

"What say you, Vaidya?" the king asked.

"She will die before sunrise. O King of Kings," he went on, trying to approximate the humble tones others used when about to tell him something he would certainly not care to hear, "if I may make a suggestion? Why don't you send away the priests and this band of wood choppers"—he indicated the guards running back and forth with the axes—"and spend the last few hours alone with her?

A queen should be allowed to depart this life with some measure of dignity."

The king considered the Vaidya's words with great sadness. Then he did as the Vaidya suggested, dismissed the priests and the ax carriers, and everyone else for that matter, so that he and the queen were alone. He sat on the couch beside her, clutching her hands in his, and told her stories of future incarnations when they would live together until their hair was no longer black and gold but a common shade of gray, and die together, and throw off the yoke of karma and spend the rest of eternity dwelling with the gods.

Alas, she understood not a word.

Dawn came again and with it the caṇḍālas who would take away Sāvitrīdevī's body. As divine as she had been in life—that her name ended in "devī" implied the stature of a goddess or nearly—she was, like all creatures, impure in death. That such loathesome work as laying out and shrouding her body, and carrying it to the cremation grounds, be performed by those classes that were twice-born, or even by the lowly śūdra, was unthinkable. Only the caṇḍālas, who lived like dogs, were fit servants to Yama, the god of death. What remained of her earthly form after three days in the fires would be thrown in the Ganges.

The Vaidya, assuming that at last his work was through, ordered Dūṣaka to pack up his tools. Already he was thinking forward to the time when he would reach home. He would instruct his servant to turn away all callers, and he would retire to bed for as long as he wished. Ah, bed. He had not slept in two nights and a day.

He looked about for Sutanukā, yearning to say one last word to her, but the guards explained that she was attending the king. Perhaps, he imagined, he would run into her at the bazaar. Or how nice if she came to his home to secure his services for some trivial problem, a splinter or a cinder in the eye. Then he would invite her to walk with him in his garden—he had a very fine garden—and perhaps even sit with him on the swing. Beyond that he dared not allow his imagination to wander, for Sutanukā was the property of the king.

A porter, accompanied by four guardsmen, intercepted the

Vaidya and his party as they were descending the harem stairs and informed them that they had been summoned to an audience with the king. Something about the porter's tone of voice, as well as the way the guards closed in about them, hands on sword hilts, filled him with trepidation. It might be a long time indeed, he thought sadly, before he saw his bed.

The throne hall was crowded with men of all classes and colors, many of whom had been returning day after day for months in the hope of the king hearing their petition. But for the Vaidya and his party there was no delay; no sooner had they arrived than they were led the length of the vast hall, toward a gilded throne on a stone pedestal, where Samudra Gupta sat on high, watching their approach with all the wrath of Kali the Destroyer. Ten rows of ten sandstone columns divided the distance, and the tile floor had been polished until it reflected the undersides of the elephants sculpted on the capitals, holding the roof timbers aloft with their mighty trunks. The Vaidya and the rest prostrated themselves, remaining with their foreheads to the floor until he commanded them to rise.

Sutanukā, standing to the left of the throne, glanced at the Vaidya with a fearful expression, and he felt an awful sinking sensation in the stomach. The wet nurse stood beside her, cuddling the infant prince, whose hair, the Vaidya was puzzled to see, had been covered with a strip of silk. The Purohita and the mahāmantrin were also there, on the other side of the king, stony-faced.

The whispering that had begun at the Vaidya's entrance ceased at the sound of the king's booming voice: "Sāvitrīdevī is dead. Whose fault is it?"

"It is," the Vaidya replied in a small voice, "nobody's fault. Before I performed the operation, I told you that most likely she would die."

"You said there was a chance she might live."

"A small chance."

"The holiest brāhmaṇas chanted the most powerful mantras for most of the night. Ghee and oblations were burned in the sacrificial fires. Isn't that enough to turn a chance into a certainty?"

The Vaidya hesitated before replying, realizing what treacherous ground he now trod. Sutanukā watched him with concern.

Carefully he began, "Even you, O King of Kings, who has conquered the nine kings of the north and made the kings of the western frontier bow in tribute, even you cannot influence a man's—or woman's—karma."

It was as though the king hadn't heard him. Although his voice was level, fire blazed in his eyes. The poet no longer tempered the warrior within him. He was a general who had suffered a terrible defeat and would exact retribution for every one of his losses.

"Sutanukā," the king went on, "told me about the operation. She said that your assistant, the one called Virata, dropped a tool on the floor, and because the tool was sullied, Sāvitrīdevī died. Is this true?"

Behind him, the Vaidya could hear Virata's breathing grow quick and tremulous. The Vaidya looked at Sutanukā, who raised her shoulders and turned up her palms in a gesture of helplessness and apology. She looked so small in the shadow of the king's great throne.

"It is true that cleanliness seems to better the patient's chance of survival," the Vaidya said. "But many times I have been rigorously clean and despite all my precautions—"

"Is it true," the king interrupted, "that the one called Virata dropped a tool and thus dirtied it?"

The Vaidya sighed. "Yes," he said reluctantly, "it is true. But—"

"Then this one called Virata is responsible for her death."

"No," the Vaidya objected, "it is not his fault, and to punish him would be a great mistake."

The Vaidya could not believe how bold he had become! Just yesterday he had been so cowed by the king that he had lost the power of speech altogether. But now he was determined to stand by what he knew to be the truth.

"But, Vaidya, you contradict yourself. In one breath you tell me that Virata dirtied the tool that caused the queen's death, and then you say that to punish him would be a mistake."

"If you would just allow me to explain—"

"I have heard your explanations!" the king bellowed. "Now let us address ourselves," he continued, his voice dropping to a whisper, "to the question of the infant's hair."

"I do not understand," the Vaidya said, looking back and

forth between the faces gathered before him for a clue to the meaning of this curious pronouncement. They all avoided his eyes.

"Sutanukā discovered it while helping the wet nurse care for the infant. Show him," the king instructed the wet nurse.

The big woman pulled aside the silk that covered the baby's head. His hair, where the kohl had been removed, was the color of honey, half of it was black.

"Some man would trick me," the king said, "by coloring my son's hair. You had the opportunity, Vaidya."

"But why would I have done such a thing?" the Vaidya asked.

"Perhaps the honey shade of his hair is the result of some mistake you made during your operation. Perhaps you thought you might conceal your mistake from me until you had time to flee the city."

"He was so caked with blood and mucous when I delivered him," the Vaidya admitted, "that I knew not his hair color. If it is like honey, it is a blend of his father's hair and his mother's—of black and gold—just as a black bull mating with a white cow will sometimes produce offspring who are dappled or gray."

"Do not liken us to bulls," the king whispered.

"I only meant to draw an analogy."

"So you deny you were the one who tried to deceive me by coloring his hair?"

"I have no wish to deceive the king," the Vaidya replied. "I like the honey-colored hair. I find it perfectly appropriate. And I should think the king would appreciate this reminder of his beloved queen who is gone to the arms of Yama."

"Now I remember," the wet nurse said, as though just struck by a revelation. "It was the same man, the one called Virata. He was waiting in the hall when I took the baby to the nursery. I remember he stared at me in a frightening way, and moved his lips as though chanting a mantra to himself, and made a magical mudra with his hands. Yes, that was it. He used sorcery to change the color of the baby's hair. I am certain of it. I would stake my life on the fact."

"If I may speak," the Vaidya asked. "I have known Virata since he was a child. While he has his faults, the practice of sorcery is not among them. He is by and large an honest and hard-working student."

"Of course, you would not know about it," the king said. "Sorcery is a secret art. He would not discuss its practice with you."

"The work of the vaidya is a science and thus antithetical to the practice of sorcery," the Vaidya continued, his voice taking on a note of desperation. He could see where this audience was heading, and he wanted with every ounce of his will to stop it or divert its path.

"Let this Virata speak for himself," the king said. "Do you practice sorcery?"

The Vaidya turned, for the first time since entering the hall, and regarded his student, who was standing behind him. Virata was quaking with fear and for a time could not find his tongue. Finally he said, "No."

"What think you, Purohita? Does he speak the truth? Does he practice sorcery?"

"My lord, to my knowledge he seems a simple young man."

"My Purohita, your eyes cloud. You can no longer see the truth when it stares you in the face. But I shall prove his guilt." He called to one of his guards. "Bring me a hot plowshare."

"No," Virata mumbled, realizing the ordeal in store for him. His bowels failed, to the amusement of the court, soiling his vasana. He fell to his knees, trembling, holding his palms together in namaste. "Please, my lord, my King of Kings, I do no magic, I am a simple student, please spare me. I did not touch the infant's hair. I swear it by the witness of all the gods."

"We shall see," said the king.

While they waited for the plowshare to arrive, the king attended to other petitioners.

Presently the smell of burning logs drifted in through the windows. Virata whispered, "Master, help me. I am afraid for my life."

"In that you have done nothing wrong," the Vaidya replied softly, "you have nothing to fear."

He tried to sound sincere, for he knew that fear dried the mouth, and the drier Virata's mouth became, the worse his odds of surviving the ordeal.

The sound of a gong announced the entrance of a guard carrying the hot plowshare, holding it in wet cloths to protect his hands.

Virata was dragged forward and made to kneel, to open his mouth, and to stick out his tongue.

The Purohita began chanting mantras, but broke off almost immediately to reassert his conviction of Virata's innocence and ask the king to reconsider the ordeal.

The king would not be swayed, even by his own guru, the holiest of the brāhmaṇas. He ordered the guard to touch Virata's tongue with the tip of the plowshare.

The court grew silent. The trilling of songbirds in the courtyard seemed suddenly deafening.

The metal hissed as it touched the delicate skin. Virata screamed and clasped both his hands over his mouth. Curling into a crouching position, he rocked back and forth, moaning, whimpering with pain.

"What say you now, Purohita?" the king asked. "I can see no better evidence of his guilt."

The Purohita was silent.

The king turned to Vasubandhu, who was standing a little way to the right of the throne, and said, "Tell me, what is a fitting punishment for murdering a queen and trying to deceive a king?"

The mahāmantrin gave the question due thought. He saw the wildness in the king's eye, heard the bloodthirst in his voice, and tailored his response accordingly. Even more than the others did he wish to keep the king's favor, for it was his presence in the court that made the Viṣṇuite king tolerate the troublesome religion called Buddhism.

"The king is known throughout the entire world as a ruler of benevolence and humanitarian ideals, who has, following the example of the great cakravartin Aśoka, nearly banished torture and cruel means of administering death. However, living in the Age of Kali as we are, he must not forget his duty to uphold the dharma. He must be firm and set an example for others, lest the land turn to anarchy, to matsyayāna, the way of the fishes. I would say this is particularly so in a crime of this severity. As for a just punishment, the *Arthaśāstra* recommends burning alive for those who would plot against the king. On the other hand, beheading is prescribed for willful murder."

The king nodded thoughtfully. "He shall be burned and beheaded."

"No!" the Vaidya cried. "You must not. He is a good young man; he has done no harm. This is all a tragic mistake."

"Another word," the king said, fixing the Vaidya with his squinting stare, "and you will follow him to the arms of Agni."

The Vaidya was crossing the palace gardens when he heard the jingle of tiny bells behind him. He turned and saw Sutanukā running to catch up with him. Two nights and a day without sleep had taken their toll, a fact made more apparent by the harsh noon sun. But even with her makeup smudged, her chignon in disarray, her features puffy and eyes ringed, she was more beautiful than any woman he had ever seen.

"I had to wait until the king dismissed me," she apologized. "I was afraid you would be gone."

"I am still here," the Vaidya said.

"I can tell you are angry at me. I can hear it in your voice. Please understand. The king bade me describe every detail of the operation. I had no choice." She moved closer to the Vaidya, so that he could smell the musk with which she perfumed her breasts, and lowered her voice to a whisper. "He was so angry that Yama had taken his queen. When he grows thus, there is no reasoning with him. He strikes out like an animal, and whoever is within reach must suffer. Vaidya, listen to me! I shifted the blame to Virata because I had to. He was going to condemn you to the stake instead!"

"I wish he had," the Vaidya replied, quite sincerely and with no intention of provoking guilt in her. "I fear I shall not be able to go on living in a universe where kindness is rewarded with torture."

"Being but a lowly woman, I have never studied the Vedas. But isn't it written somewhere in those holy books that the workings of karma are beyond our understanding? Are we not, kind Vaidya, like the ant who says there is no order to a shrine, because he can see no farther than the crumbling corner of the stone block he climbs?"

"I do not know about karma or stone blocks or ants. All I know is that here in my heart the world has ceased to make sense."

He turned his back and continued to walk. She hesitated, then ran after him, tiny bells jingling.

"Where are you going now?" she said, catching up with him.

He didn't look at her. "I do not know. Home, I suppose. I think I will stand in my garden and see if the flowers still have beauty."

"May I walk with you?"

"You may do as you like."

They passed a grove of kadamba trees and slowed to let a flock of peacocks, dragging the burden of their long feathery fans, cross in front of them.

"It has been very special to me," Sutanukā said shyly, "knowing you."

The Vaidya didn't reply.

"I feel as though perhaps we were friends in another time, another life."

Still the Vaidya was silent.

She went on, "What I mean to say is—"

But now he interrupted her. "Save your words. Whatever affection we may have felt for one another last night exists no longer. When your lord and master burns Virata, he will burn part of me, too. What shall remain will be insufficient to share with another."

"I see," she said. She stopped walking.

He continued and soon, reaching the great gatehouse, passed out of sight. Sutanukā stood there for some time, gazing after him. She nearly forgot where she was until a voice intruded on her thoughts.

"Why are you crying?"

She looked down and there was the dwarf, standing beside her.

"Why does a woman ever cry?" she said, sniffling.

"It is dangerous to trifle with the property of the king. The Vaidya has trouble enough already."

"No cause to worry. He has no interest in this plaything called Sutanukā."

"No man is immune to your charms," the dwarf said.

"The Vaidya is not like the others. He is deep as the Ganges. He is almost like a holy man."

"Believe me. I saw the way he looked at you in court. It was not the look of a holy man." The dwarf laughed.

"Truly? Did it appear thus to you?"

"It did. Right now he probably grieves for his student who would die upon the stake. But once his grieving is past, he would take you for his wife in an instant. Were you not," the dwarf continued with emphasis, "already the property of the king."

"I could buy my freedom," she said, wiping the tears from the corners of her eyes and forcing a smile. "Other gaṇikās have done so. I might do the same."

"You are too useful to him," the dwarf said. "I have heard him say so a hundred times. However, there may be another path to your freedom. Let me think on it."

"Dwarf, answer me one question. And please speak frankly. I have watched you, with the king, for many years now. Clearly he trusts you beyond all others. Why would you jeopardize such a trust to help a poor gaṇikā?"

"I am thirty years old," the dwarf replied. "We dwarfs do not live long. Thanks to the king's pity, I have tasted the pleasures of kāma with many women. I loved none of them, and so it was like drinking from an empty cup. For once before I die, I would like to enjoy kāma with a woman I love."

"And I am this woman?" she asked with a trace of amusement.

The dwarf looked away. He could not meet her eye.

She reached down to smooth his hair, as one would caress a pet. "Get me my freedom, dwarf, and you shall have your wish."

By the time Prince Rāma sauntered into the throne hall, swinging his parasol from one hand, his pet monkey clinging to his shoulder, court had already been in session for some time. He greeted, with a namaste so sophisticated and world-weary that his fingertips barely touched, four friends who had been waiting for him in the shadow of a certain column toward the rear of the hall. Because the prince favored it, this particular column had become a meeting place for his clique, a band of wealthy fops a few years older than he, who carried parasols, advertised their indolence by wearing their fingernails long and thought nothing of betting a thousand paṇas on a single roll of the dice.

Of them, three were particularly favored by the prince: Nandana, because he was terribly strong and would fight anyone; a skinny slip of a teenager named Kubera, because he was clever and could always make Rāma laugh; and Rāma's cousin Karabhaka, because he was handsome, and older, and understood palace politics, as well as the best places to play.

Rāma struck a pose, leaning lazily against the column with just the proper attitude of boredom, disinterest, and amused superiority, while the three friends described an episode he had just missed: how some fellow, an assistant to a vaidya, had been accused of causing Sāvitrīdevī's death during the birth of the new prince. Gleefully they recounted the young man's humiliation, how he had fallen to the floor quaking, how he had loosed his bowels, how he had wept like a girl and pleaded for mercy.

Rāma was pleased by the news of her death, for the king had been lavishing attention on the golden-haired freak ever since her arrival, at the expense of Rāma's mother, Dattadevī, who was after all mahiṣī, first among his wives, and thus most deserving of honor. Still, he troubled to frown and express his regrets as a matter of form. In truth, the matter was of little concern to him one way or the other. He had more important issues on his mind.

His real reason for coming to court that day was to hear the astrologer speak and see what could be done to discredit the old man. He had already instructed his army of spies to spread themselves around the throne room. Following the astrologer's pronouncement, were it favorable to the newborn infant, they would shake their heads and express the opinion that he had grown dim-witted with age. Then they would recall previous predictions of his that had not come true and tell stories of other times when he had behaved foolishly.

Rāma's spies numbered more than twenty, including gaṇikās (though not Sutanukā, whose loyalty to the king was unquestioned) courtiers, servants, and even a few ministers. The ministers were not true spies—they were not in his pay—but rather those who Rāma had noticed were growing disaffected with the king and whose favor he had subsequently cultivated with gifts and kind words. The prince had even located a young astrologer with very fine manners and appearance, and planned, if he could sow sufficient discontent, to press his father into retiring old Vahara Mihira and hiring his candidate instead.

He lingered through several more audiences, the boredom of which he and his retinue survived only by dint of the comic antics of his monkey, which had decided to unwrap the turban of a courtier standing in front of him.

Finally the moment arrived: the gong sounded, and the ancient astrologer shuffled the length of the great hall, stroking his beard and mumbling to himself, weaving a path between the columns and nearly losing his way to the throne in the process. He clutched a bunch of palm leaf pages, the future of the empire, in his right hand.

When he reached the king's throne, he prostrated himself, slowly and laboriously, his bones seeming to creak with the effort. Rāma covered his mouth with one hand and, under the pretext of a yawn, whispered to those around him, "I wager a hundred paṇas he will not reach his feet again, or we shall all die of old age waiting for the event." They laughed until the king silenced them with a look.

Contrary to Rāma's expectations, the astrologer regained his stance.

"You have been a long time in your chamber," the king said, staring down at him critically from the height of his throne.

"The more important a pronouncement, the more one desires to be certain of his calculations."

"The young prince's horoscope is complete?"

The astrologer nodded his shaggy brow. "It is. He was born just as the mansion known as Puṣya ascended above the horizon. This makes his moon sign . . ." The astrologer shuffled the papers in his hand, looking for a specific document.

The king cut him off.

"Do not bother me with lunar mansions and the moon's ascending mode, and cusps and degrees, and what planet has gone visiting his neighbor. I wish to know the future of my son. If he is destined for greatness, tell me that. But do not hesitate to tell me also if karma would make him a rogue fit to die on the stake."

The astrologer paused, waiting for silence. Then he said slowly, "If you truly desire to know these things, than I shall tell you all, for my astrology is a science of extraordinary precision."

The king hesitated. (What man wouldn't when offered the chance to learn the future of his children?) Finally he said, "I do so desire."

"In his eighteenth year, the new prince shall commit an unspeakable crime."

People gasped; the whispering in the throne hall grew as loud as a raging river. The king, astonished and outraged, as much by the prediction as by the noise, bellowed for silence. As soon as quiet had returned, the astrologer continued. "He shall commit an unspeakable crime, yet the gods shall favor him. The people themselves shall make him king. His empire shall reach from sea to sea. He will be"—the astrologer hesitated to catch his breath, which was coming fast with excitement—"the greatest king ever to rule the Land of the Sons of Bharata. He will be cakravartin, the universal emperor!"

Prince Rāma's lips began to tremble, and tears welled in the corners of his eyes. He fled the great hall before his friends noticed.

"May I bother you, Mother?" Prince Rāma asked, drawing aside the tapestry at the entrance to the chamber.

"Sweet son, can it wait?" she said, with a long, sensual sigh, the sound a cat might make were human speech bestowed upon it.

She lay face down, naked on her wooden couch, her black hair coiled behind her head, her heavy breasts bulging from beneath her ribcage. A handmaiden leaned over her, massaging her with an ebony roller, while another fanned her with palm leaves, and a third snapped the fly whisk.

"I wish," she went on, "for nothing to disturb the mood of my massage. I lie on the brink of Nirvāṇa."

"I must talk to you now. Alone."

"But what of my massage?"

"I will massage you."

She sighed and said, "To be a mother is to sacrifice everything for your children," and a trace of humor in her voice showed that she was not oblivious to the irony. She raised herself on her elbows, so that the dark tips of her breasts just brushed the surface of the couch, and ordered everyone out of the room. Rāma saw her face now, the strong bones, the long eyes outlined in kohl, the beauty mark on the left cheekbone, the large mouth, the thin lips. How he loved her, she who had always been so gentle and patient with him, whether he came to her with a scrape on his knee after playing or a wound in his heart from overhearing a courtier making fun of his hare lip.

She smiled at him, the smile that was his alone; to the rest of the world she was cool and distant, and full of scorn. She had not always been so. After all, Samudra Gupta had loved her enough to make her mahiṣī; there was a time when he had showered her with gifts and sought her company before all others. How could she ever forget his delight on learning that she had borne him a son?

Or the look of repulsion that had crossed his face when he saw the child's deformity?

He turned his back on her after that, abandoning her to the luxurious prison of the harem, to watch him wed one young wife after another in the quest for a perfect heir.

Lowering herself against the table, she closed her eyes, and whispered, "The roller, sweet son. On my back."

Rāma wrapped the leash of his pet monkey round the leg of a rattan footstool, offering it a betel nut to keep it quiet. He picked up the ebony instrument and began to work it slowly, dutifully, down his mother's spine.

"I was just in the court, Mother. I heard the astrologer speak of my new little brother."

"And what did he say?"

"Among other things, that he would be cakravartin."

"The old fool. There are no cakravartins. It's a child's tale. A little lower, sweet son, and press harder. Harder. Ah, yes, that's the way. Ah, it's bliss."

Just as the people of the Land of the Sons of Bharata believed in the coming of avatāras, reincarnations of the God Viṣṇu who would bring salvation to mankind, thus did they also believe in cakravartins, great kings who would crush all enemies, unify the land, and make men live in accordance with the dharma.

"What of the emperor Aśoka?" Rāma asked. "He was a cakravartin, they say."

"Aśoka." She laughed deep in her throat. "He stole the throne and murdered his rivals. He slaughtered a million men to conquer Kaliṅga. And then, because he became a Buddhist, and stopped eating meat, everyone said, 'Ah, he is cakravartin!' "

"Whether or not cakravartins exist is beside the point," Rāma said. "Now that the astrologer has said it, people will believe it, for such is the nature of fortune-telling. In time they will make it true." He lowered his voice to a whisper. "You know how weak father is. They will convince him to install little brother on the throne in my place."

For some time his mother made no response. She was considering her son's future. His ambitions to the throne were no secret. If the king decided to leave his crown to the honey-haired prince instead, he would probably take care to dispose of Rāma, too; otherwise, the rivalry would be too fierce, the throne too insecure. They would surely try to exile her son.

Or murder him.

And where would that leave her?

An old woman, no beauty left, no power in the court, no one to champion her.

"Strike against him before he can strike against you," she whispered. "But first find a powerful ally."

"I have allies, Mother. I am not a child."

"You have nothing. A few servants, a few spies. I know all about them. They are useless. Now listen to me. Yājñavalkya, the minister of war and peace, wishes more than anything on this earth to conquer the Śakas. Know you his pearl eye? He lost that eye to the Śakas when Samudra Gupta and he first did battle with them. Yājñavalkya was his general in those days. After that Samudra Gupta was convinced that the Śakas could not be vanquished, so ferocious were they on the battlefield. Hardly a day has passed, since that battle long ago, that Yājñavalkya does not plead with Samudra Gupta for permission to head an expedition against the Śakas. The king refuses, saying that they could never be conquered, that it is enough they pay tribute to him and allow our ships to set sail from Bhṛgukaccha and Barbaricum on their western coast."

"But I have heard the minister of trade complain of the tariff they charge us, that it is an outrage, a humiliation."

"Thus precisely does Yājñavalkya argue."

"So you suggest," Rāma continued thoughtfully, "that I use Yājñavalkya's frustration to my own advantage."

"Men who harbor such obsessions may be manipulated as easily as donkeys. One must not, however, appear overeager."

"Thank you, Mother. You are as wise as you are beautiful." He had been moving the roller farther and farther down her back, until now it reached the cleavage between her buttocks. The motion of the soft mounds of flesh fascinated him. As he manipulated them, he probed the notch in his upper lip with the point of his tongue, a habit he had practiced since infancy, that brought comfort as would the sucking of a thumb.

"Mother," he said presently, "are you very sad?"

"Do I seem so?" she asked softly.

"I know the king never visits you. I know he blames you because you gave birth to me, and I was born like this." Rāma touched the crack in his upper lip.

"What nonsense!" she exclaimed. "The king does not visit me because he has tired of me. After all, he has but to raise his hand, and there is a new bride, a brāhmaṇi maiden with a yoni like a fist, or some exotic, golden-haired thing who babbles in foreign tongues."

"I worry for you when you seem so sad. Why don't you leave this place?"

She uttered a deep throaty laugh, and what he could see of her breasts, rolls of dark flesh squeezing from beneath her chest, shook like puddings. "Where can an old woman go?"

"The Buddhist monasteries take in single women. They seem to have a good life, caring for the poor and the ill, meditating and studying the scriptures."

"You would make a nun out of me? Oh, my little Rāma, how I love you!"

"Mother, I am serious! I think the king might let you go."

"I have no doubt. He would supply me with a palanquin and the fastest runners in the kingdom, so long as I swore never to turn back."

"You are sarcastic. You mock me."

"My little Rāma, do you know the story of the wind antelope, from the *Jātakas?*"

"The *Jātakas* are tales for children. I am a man."

"No, there is great wisdom in the *Jātakas,* even though they were written by humble folk and not by the wise brāhmaṇas that my lord loves so. Here, come and sit by me. Let me pretend that you are a baby again and that I am putting you to sleep, telling you a story."

"If that is your wish, Mother."

Rāma sat on the side of the couch. His mother rested her head so she faced him, and placed a hand on his thigh. She took a moment organizing her thoughts and then she began. "When

Brahmadatta was king of Benares, he had a wise old gardener named Saṃjaya. One day Saṃjaya mentioned to the king that he had seen a wind antelope at the edge of the garden. The king grew very excited, for wind antelopes were among the most timid creatures on earth, and no man had ever succeeded in capturing one alive. He asked the gardener if he thought it possible to have this one for his zoo, and Saṃjaya replied, 'Just give me a crock of honey, my lord, and the antelope shall be yours.'

"Saṃjaya went to where he had seen the wind antelope, and spread honey on the grass. Then he waited behind a tree. When the wind antelope returned, it tasted the honey cautiously and, finding it delicious, ate until there was none left. Every day Saṃjaya spread honey on the grass for the wind antelope, and every day the antelope returned for it. Then, one day, Saṃjaya showed himself. The antelope dashed away in a frenzy. But the next day it returned, and in time it no longer ran from the sight of the gardener.

"Now Saṃjaya came with a gourd of honey and a beltful of grass. As he walked, he dipped the grass in the honey and tossed it on the ground. As you can imagine, the wind antelope followed him, eating the sweet grass, losing all track of time and place. Suddenly it looked up and saw that it was in the palace courtyard. The gates swung shut, and the poor animal was caught."

"And did it never escape?" Rāma asked. Here, at his mother's side, his sophistication slipped away. He became a child again, wholly caught up in the story.

"Well, King Brahmadatta put it in a cage in his palace zoo for twelve moons. But then he felt sorry for having penned in such a graceful wild creature and tried to set it free. Alas, it would not leave, for it had grown to love the honey grass more than its own freedom."

For a time she was silent. Then she said, "Do you understand, my little Rāma? Now go find Yājñavalkya and do as I have told you. Go, little one. My heart is with you."

Yājñavalkya, stripped of jewelry, stood on the sun-baked practice field behind the barracks, training with a machine called the spinning tree. It consisted of a central pole the height of a man, into which several very long, very sharp blades had been anchored at different heights. A servant would turn a crank connected to the pole by a buffalo-skin belt, and when the blades were rotating fast enough, the soldier would step into their range and dodge them by ducking his head or leaping into the air. Those soldiers who were liable to distractions or were not sufficiently nimble would soon lose a foot or be otherwise maimed and, thus dishonored, would spend the rest of their lives as beggars or servants, dreaming of battles unfought and valor lost. But those who survived it swore by it as a means of quickening reflexes, of keeping the mind alert and the body agile.

A number of guards had for the moment abandoned their own practice with sword and bow to observe Yājñavalkya dodging the blades. Over the years he had refined his motions to an elegant, effortless dance in which his limbs moved so rapidly that they blurred like the wings of a hummingbird. First he faced the blades, then, still leaping and ducking, he turned his back to them, then, miraculously, he shut his one good eye and went on as though blind. The members of the guard whispered to one another, as connoisseurs always do when witnessing a supreme show of skill, regarding the fine points of his technique, and agreed that no other soldier, one-eyed or two, had ever been so adept. They would have watched him all afternoon if not for the approach of Prince Rāma. "The Little Camel," they whispered contemptuously and dispersed.

Yājñavalkya leaped out of the circle of jeopardy, as the area within the reach of the blades was known, and, breathing heavily, sank to a squatting position to rest. Noticing Rāma, he smiled and placed his palms together.

"Victory to you, my prince. Do you care to challenge the spinning tree?"

Rāma shook his head. "Thank you, but I was up late drinking, celebrating the birth of my little brother. This morning my thoughts are blurred, my senses sluggish. I dare not."

Though he forced himself to keep smiling, his heart ached, for he knew that Yājñavalkya's offer was a mockery. The whole court whispered about Rāma's incompetence as a warrior. From the age of five, the finest members of the guard had attempted to train him in the use of the two-handed sword, the long bow, the dart, and the cakra. Alas, he proved as clumsy with one weapon as with the next. The first time he ever tried the spinning tree, harmless wooden paddles were substituted for the metal blades. Although they were being turned very slowly, one struck him in the head and knocked him unconscious, leaving him with vertigo for a week. His martial studies were curtailed one day soon afterward when, while drawing back the two-handed sword in preparation for a blow, he miscalculated and made a gash in his own shoulder. The guard who was training him was put to death, supposedly for teaching a poor technique, but actually for laughing at the moment of the accident. From then on it was decided that Rāma's education should emphasize statecraft rather than swordsmanship.

So Rāma's heroics were confined to his fantasies, during which he was a great warrior, was Arjuna himself crossing the battlefield with Kriṣṇa as his charioteer. As that handsome, heroic figure, that favorite of the gods, he would raise his sword against the Śakas and slaughter them by the thousands. Later, when he was alone in bed, relieving the tension that is the plague of all pubescent boys, he imagined the most beautiful Śaka queens visiting his battle pavilion, offering themselves to him. Often in these fantasies, he would pierce their cheeks with a dart as he came, or bite off a piece of their ears and feel their hot blood run down his chin.

Yājñavalkya rose to his feet. He was a small, volatile man of extraordinary strength and agility, with a pleasant, open face and barely enough guile to survive in the court. His left eye, a great pearl inlaid with an ebony pupil, always stared straight ahead, independent of the right, leaving those he spoke to unsure as to whether they were the true object of his attention. He grinned again, bent his knees, and, snapping his legs straight, did a backward somersault in the air. He landed slightly off balance and fell, but was up again in a second, laughing, brushing the dust off his vasana.

"But I know just what you mean! This business of being a minister makes you soft as a woman. If I do not come down to the practice field every afternoon and play with the weapons, my mind goes into a stupor. It's all these banquets, the rich food, the drinking. Last week I had to entertain a trade delegation from China, then a Parthian prince passing through on caravan. Just when I thought it was all over, your little brother was born, and there I was, sitting at the banquet table for four hours, listening to every courtier and his uncle make some long-winded toast. Ah, for the simple, hard life of the warrior!"

"It is a shame," Rāma said, holding the monkey in his arms

and stroking its little head, "that we no longer fight real battles."

Yājñavalkya shrugged. "Your father, having spent many years in battle, now wishes to spend the rest of his years in peace."

He walked over to his jewelry, which he had left piled on a square of silk on the ground, and began to dress himself, fitting the enormous earrings into his pierced earlobes, straightening the links of his golden necklace, sliding the bangles over his hands.

"I know," Rāma said. "I have heard his pronouncements. Personally, I think it a mistake. There will be no real peace until the Guptas rule the entire land. The Śālāṅkāyanas and the Pallavas in the east, the Kadambas and Gaṅgas in the south, the Ārjunayānas and Mālavas in the north. They must all be conquered and subjugated. And of course the Śakas." He mentioned this last as though it were an afterthought.

"The Śakas," Yājñavalkya whispered. His right hand strayed to touch the great pearl that had replaced his lost eye.

"Of course, Father says that we can never win a battle against the Śakas. . . ."

"They are marvelous horsemen. Their cavalry is superb. But we could defeat them. We could build a cavalry of our own. In five years I could have twenty thousand men on horseback, with five thousand elephants to guard them."

"In five years I would be eighteen. Old enough to be king. Old enough to order such an expedition."

Yājñavalkya fixed him with his good eye. "You would do that?"

"Without question," Rāma replied. "And with your permission, I would have you made general of our army so that you might lead it. I can think of no other man who would be so capable."

Yājñavalkya got a faraway look. "To lead an army against the Śakas . . . that would be a great pleasure."

"But this is idle talk. I will never take the throne. You heard the astrologer. My new brother is a cakravartin."

"He is only an infant. You could rule for ten years, then cede the throne to him."

"And go to the forest and live as a hermit, like Viśvamitra," Rāma said, his voice steeped in sarcasm. "No, I am not one for renunciation."

"Now that the astrologer has made his prediction, people will expect the new prince to be king. I see no alternative."

"Unless he meets with an accident."

The minister of war and peace eyed Rāma closely. "What are you suggesting?"

"I suggest nothing. I simply state that were the infant to have an accident, the throne would be mine. And the Śakas would be ours."

"Accidents such as that are rarely accidental."

"If no one knows," Rāma said, "then the difference between accident and assassination becomes a matter for the logicians."

Yājñavalkya's voice grew very soft. "Your father and I have been like brothers. He carried me across the battlefield when another might have left me for dead. He made me his minister and entrusted me with the military strength of his empire." He looked away, as though the very idea was more than he could bear. "How could I then partake in the killing of his son?"

"When he saved your life, he robbed you of a valorous death in battle. When he made you minister of war and peace, he took you away from the discipline you loved most. He wages no more war so that he can sit on his pillows and practice his vīṇā. Meanwhile, his army grows weak, and the Land of the Sons of Bharata is threatened on every border. As for killing his son, *I* am his true son, I am the son of the mahiṣī. This little brother of mine, what was his mother? A mleccha, a blond-haired barbarian Goth! Are we to rid our land of foreign rule, only to put a Goth king on our throne?"

"Ah, but you have a quick mind, young Rāma. You make me question that which I always knew to be true. The world turns topsy-turvy, and what was once solid ground now appears to be the sky overhead."

"As I see it," Rāma went on, pressing his advantage, "it is a choice between your loyalty to the king and the welfare of the kingdom. We both know that war with the Śakas is inevitable. We know that in order to succeed, we must wage this war soon, while you, our greatest general, are still young enough to lead the troops. We know that father, while he is king, will never permit such a war, but I, who am nearly old enough and certainly clever enough to rule the kingdom, will make it my first order of business. It seems to me that you have only one course left."

"How simple to kill an infant. A scorpion in the bedclothes.

It would seem for all the world like an act of nature. And yet, even as we speak, I feel that we rend the dharma, that we draw evil karma to ourselves that will haunt us through a thousand lives."

"What if the astrologer were wrong? After all, he is doddering with age. What if this little brother of mine grew up to be a tyrant who failed to fill the granaries, or feed the beggars, or keep up the roads? Then to kill him might be to accrue the very best karma."

"Mights and what-ifs are not a bulwark on which to base such decisions."

Yājñavalkya folded his arms across his chest and looked toward the palace of the king, the golden finials glittering in the sun, the banners lying still in the heat. Some of the harem had gone swimming in the pond—the gardens were not far beyond the barracks walls—and the two men could hear them splashing, their shrill voices laughing and calling to one another.

"There is a caste that specializes in murder," Yājñavalkya continued, his voice having grown very faint. "For a price they would even murder a prince. They are as expert in their craft as I am in mine, and so cunning that they can make even the foulest crime appear an accident or act of nature. They worship Śiva in the left-handed way, turning all the virtuous forms of pūja upside down. Thus, instead of facing east when they worship, they face west, toward the land of the dead. Instead of circling the altar clockwise, they circle it counterclockwise. Where Śivaites believe that man must never kill, they kill in Śiva's name. Their symbols are Śiva's darkest symbols—the trident and the garland of human skulls. Members of this caste must be approached with the greatest care and subtlety. An intermediary, fully trusted by all, must make an appointment. Such a meeting should take place in the dead of night, and he who would hire them must bring silver paṇas, at least ten thousand. At the slightest suspicion of treachery, the murderers will not appear, nor will they ever again make themselves available."

"Ten thousand paṇas? That is a month's allowance for me."

"It is more than a cowherd makes in a lifetime."

Rāma fingered one of several bangles that adorned his wrist, a golden cobra with sapphire eyes, its fangs stretched open to accommodate a ruby the size of a robin's egg.

"I would like to give this to you as a present," he said, slipping the bangle over his hand, "in appreciation of the years you have spent preparing me for the throne."

"May the gods forgive me," Yājñavalkya whispered, "for the course I enter upon this day."

Virata was led through the streets of Pāṭaliputra naked, his hands tied behind his back, his skull shaven and colored red with brick dust, a garland of bright red blossoms around his neck, the trappings of a condemned man. One of the śūdra class walked before him, banging a drum so that those of the upper classes might avoid laying eyes on one who was so impure, who had killed and deceived the king and betrayed the rules of his caste. Most of the citizens of that great city ran inside when they heard the ominous thud of the drum, the curious contenting themselves with a peek from a balcony or a window obscured by gratings. But a few—and such people exist in all lands, at all times—ran along beside him, throwing stones, yelling taunts, striking at his naked flesh with thorny branches until he bled from a score of wounds. If he had any comfort, it was from the soft crushed garlands that still lay scattered across the cobblestones, remnants of the festival celebrating the prince's birth.

Virata thought of his father, a mender of silks, who had saved for years so that his son could learn the healing arts. How poorly he had treated that good man, condescending to him and mocking his simplicity. Now the chance of making amends was robbed from him forever. If customers continued to visit his father's stall in the bazaar, they would do so as travelers slow their carts when passing a disaster, to gape and thank the gods it was not they who had been struck by such misfortune. He would be dismissed from the guild and prohibited from practicing his trade. If he couldn't find other work, he would join the ranks of the beggars.

And what of the rest of his family—his mothers and brothers and sisters? Particularly his little sister Sarasvatī, who idolized him as only an eight-year-old girl could, showering him with trinkets on his trips home, little clay likenesses she made herself of the elephant-headed god Gaṇeśa or the monkey Hanumān. Despite his parents' attempts to shelter her from the truth, she would, sooner or later, learn of his debasement.

And the Vaidya. The image of the little man with the figlike nose swam before his eyes. His endless patience. The hours he had spent explaining the effects of the different herbs, the meaning of the visions that came with illness, the manner of hearing a man's breath, of feeling his blood by squeezing the wrist. The Vaidya had invested all his knowledge in the pupil, and the pupil had failed him.

How unjust it was! How unbearably unjust. He had committed no crime, besides the crime of a weak stomach. No crime in this life, but in another . . . ?

Yes, without doubt. He was paying now for some horrible violation of the dharma in a past life. If only he could, like the great holy men, recall those other lives, then he would understand it all. But such powers were granted only to those who practiced the most severe austerities for years on end, not for students who had neglected their studies to strum the vīṇā beneath a pretty girl's balcony.

The plaza at the entrance to the city was a confusion of oxcarts and chariots, merchants with sacks of goods and women balancing urns, wealthy pilgrims in litters and saffron-clad monks on foot, mahouts herding elephants and snake charmers carrying cobras in wicker baskets, deformed beggars and old women peddling spiced rice balls and sweets. The monks chanted, the mahouts cursed, the snake charmers bragged, the beggars moaned. The air was sweet with spices, and stinking from the elephants, who left their dung in a line down the middle of the street. The royal guards stood at every corner, and more of them patrolled the plaza on horseback, with an eye out for vandals and thieves.

Carved on the great stone pillar in the middle of the plaza was an edict of Samudra Gupta, the Kāvyarāja, or Poet-King, as he fancied himself, welcoming travelers to the city. Children and adults alike strolled clockwise around the pillar, stroking it with their right hands for luck. The timelessness of this tradition was evident from the shiny groove that had been worn in the stone at shoulder height.

The crowd parted at the approach of Virata, like filings of iron repelled by the wrong pole of a magnet. Eyes were averted. Conversations ceased, and the quiet spread until only the shuffle and trumpeting of the elephants remained. The lips of those of the three upper classes who were the twice-born could be seen moving as they whispered to themselves the death-conquering mantra:

How we adore the sweet-smelling Tryambaka, who blesses life,
May I be liberated through death, as a cucumber from its stalk,
But not from immortality.

Even the most grotesque of the beggars, a man with no face, sidled out of the way of the procession and hurried to touch the pillar for luck.

Now they marched Virata toward the great gates of the city. The gatekeeper, a gross fellow with one tooth, ran out on the bridge and managed to get close enough, before the guards pushed him away, to send a stream of urine across Virata's leg. It burned where it struck his wounds, but he was hardly conscious of the pain.

From the elevation of the far bank, Virata could see the brown waters of the moat flow into the river Son, and, in the valley beyond, the Son join the Ganges, that holiest of rivers, which wound its way from the Himalayas to the ocean like an endless prayer. Its waters were crowded with barges and rafts, and all along its banks women knelt, beating their wash against the rocks, collecting water in urns, bathing their children in its holy water. Monks lifted their robes so they might wade deeper in it and poured handfuls of it over their heads. Lush, irregular paddies of rice, a vibrant green, spread away on either side of the river, giving way to the forests and rolling hills that were the king's hunting grounds. As if in sympathy to the flowing waters in which he had played as a child, Virata's eyes, dry since his verdict was imposed, began to stream tears.

They walked for miles, away from the Ganges and toward the black hills of Barābar. They trudged past villages of round-roofed mud huts, past herds of russet cattle and flocks of geese and chickens, past dwellings were holy men who had renounced the world sat in solitary meditation, until, in time, they reached a place where the land grew arid and cracked, and as hard as stone, and could be neither planted nor grazed, nor put to any other constructive use.

Here were the burning grounds, here where the earth was charred and barren of vegetation and blackened pieces of old pyres rose at crazy angles against a red sky. For centuries the inhabitants of Pāṭaliputra had brought their dead here to be burned or, for the families who could not afford the luxury, merely left for the carrion. The bones that had survived the pyres—and rarely did the flames burn hot enough to consume them all—had been raked into piles by the caṇḍālas who lived on the outskirts of the field. An ivory hand jutted from one pile, its fine web of bones still intact, and there, in another, was part of a pelvis, a bludgeon of a leg bone, a skull sitting at a crazy angle smiling sardonically. As they passed, a snake slithered from an empty eye socket. Startled by the drumbeat, the wild dogs that prowled among the piles of bones fled, and the vultures skipped clumsily into the air, to circle until it was safe to return.

A caṇḍāla woman, dressed all in rags, squatted beside a pile of bones, sifting through the ashes for a ring or bangle that might have been overlooked, anything of value that she might exchange for a handful of rice or a bit of cheese. The guards who led the procession threatened her with their swords and laughed as she fled, bent over, no better than the other carrion, they agreed.

The stake had already been erected, the wood piled high around its base. The guards pushed Virata up the mountain of sticks and branches and dried cow dung, and lashed him to the stake with yards and yards of hemp. He could barely breath from the tightness of the rope around his chest.

"Any last words?" the guards asked him.

He shook his head. He had no voice. And even then, what was there to say?

One of the guards was twirling a fire stick. A second later the ghee-soaked torch burst into flame. Now they were holding it to the twigs. A crackling sound, waves of heat, smoke that burned his nostrils and made his eyes tear. He hadn't imagined it would come so soon. He had assumed they would wait. In his culture, every stage of life—birth, the beginning of formal education, coming of age, marriage—all were marked with ceremony, and every ceremony involved waiting. Waiting for the brāhmaṇa to arrive, waiting while the altar was prepared, waiting for the most auspicious moment of the day. But today, he realized, for the first and last time, there would be no waiting. No brāhmaṇa. No sacred fire or oblations. The lack of ritual disturbed him nearly as much as the fact of his dying.

He felt a sudden awful concern for the ātman, that part of the cosmos that had broken away to form his consciousness at his birth and would now survive his death. What would become of it without brāhmaṇas to drive off the demons, without a cow to sacrifice, without mourners to weep and beat their breasts, without relatives to take down their hair in sorrow?

The heat made the air around him swim, made the landscape

appear as though behind melting glass. His sweat mingled with the brick dust on his shaven skull, and drops of it rolled like blood down his face. The heat was unbearable. He looked down at the red, blue, golden tongues of fire licking at his feet. For an instant he felt nothing, then the pain came to him and he screamed. He screamed again and again. For him the universe narrowed down to the small space of his feet, the knot of excruciating pain. Slowly, slowly, it expanded, it crept up his ankles, it engulfed his calves. A smell came to him, indescribably vile, and a bubbling sound. With horror he realized that it was the smell of his own flesh burning, his own blood coming to a boil.

He had never had much to do with the gods, but now he prayed for Viṣṇu to intercede, prayed from the depths of his being. Let me die, he pleaded, stop the pain. But Viṣṇu remained nothing more than a distant idea, a rock carving on a temple wall, a character in a tale told by the bards. He grew faint and vertiginous, and still the light of his consciousness refused to be extinguished. He called on other gods, on Brahmā and Śiva, on the beloved Kriṣṇa and the ancient Indra, on Durga the destroyer and Yama, the guardian of the underworld. And still the flames inched higher, moving like a million busy knives up his knees, his thighs, his shriveled genitals. His thinking ceased to make sense, became a confusion of voices, of frightening images and dismaying ideas. He was so overwhelmed he could no longer recall his own identity. How desperately he longed for help! And then he heard, through the babble of his thoughts, the bell-clear voice of the Vaidya, repeating one of his favorite sayings: "The old gods are bad for a vaidya. . . . The merciful Buddha is a better god for a vaidya."

For just an instant his mind cleared. He had a vision of the Buddha sitting in blissful Nirvāṇa, eyes half closed, lips curled in the faintest of smiles.

Stillness.

Kindness.

Emptiness.

The sword slashed through the air.

A geyser of blood spurted from the severed neck, and his handsome head rolled through the flames, coming to rest some twenty feet away.

The guard who had wielded the sword, proud of the cut, went

to recover the head, to put it in a sack and bring it to the king, to show that his orders had been properly executed. He lifted it up by the hair and regarded the face with surprise.

"Look at this!" he shouted to the other guard. "He was smiling! Must have gone mad from the pain."

Samudra Gupta felt good enough during his public audiences that morning, but later, in the bathhouse, reclining on a crystal throne while servants filled the golden tank in which he sat with tepid, perfumed water, an uneasiness crept over him.

He achieved a certain peace during his visit to the temple, meditating upon the divine union of the adorer and the adored. But later, while he was being massaged, the uneasiness returned, as persistent and bothersome as a gnat on a hot day.

Following a splendid lunch, which he hardly tasted, he returned to one of his sleeping chambers for a nap. Yet rather than falling straight to sleep as he usually did, he rolled and tossed like a man with a fever, his mind troubled with a hundred unimportant matters in order to avoid the one matter that was the true source of his anxiety.

Finally he gave up in irritation—nothing irked a king more than a subject who would not bow to his rule, even if that subject happened to be himself—and, thinking some music might distract him, took down his vīṇā from the wall. Seating himself cross-legged on the cushions, balancing the polished gourd that was the body of the bulbous lute between his legs, taking a tortoiseshell plectrum in his right hand, and twisting the pegs at the end of the bamboo neck with his left, he sought to bring it into tune. Satisfied, he embarked upon the raga called "Dīpaka," which was meant to be played in the afternoon and to convey the sentiment of love. After the slow, nasal, twanging exposition of the seven-note theme, he began a series of melodic improvisations, each quicker and more complex than the previous, increasing in tempo until the notes poured from beneath his calloused fingers in glittering cascades, conveying feelings of overwhelming intensity, and even a glimpse of that cosmic order that was so often spoken of in the holy books, so rarely perceived.

Barriers fell, and those emotions he had kept repressed all day—elation over the birth of his son, despair and rage over the loss of Sāvitrīdevī—flooded up from the seat of his being. Through the magic of his art, he suffered an illumination. He threw down his instrument and called for a servant to fetch the dwarf.

When the dwarf arrived, the king was pacing the room, his hands clenched together, tears streaming down his face.

"Ah, dwarf," he said, relieved by the presence of his old friend, "we must talk."

"If it will cheer my lord, we will talk day and night."

They sat down together on the mat where he had earlier attempted to nap.

"You were in court today, my dwarf? You saw the man I sentenced to burn at the stake?"

"I did, my lord."

"And you found me just in my pronouncement?"

"My stature is such that I see only the low things. The higher things I leave to you, my lord."

"I was not just, dwarf. Now I see it all clearly. I was an angry child, wishing to avenge the death of my beloved Sāvitrīdevī, and not caring who would suffer so long as I inflicted such pain as I myself had felt. This assistant of the Vaidya—I do not even recall his name—he was guilty of nothing. He died for no cause. His family was dishonored for naught."

"Even the gods make mistakes," the dwarf said.

"Tell me, dwarf, how can I undo this dreadful thing I have done?"

"Such questions are best left for my lord's wiser council."

"You are my wisest, dwarf."

The dwarf thought for some time. Then he gave up and shrugged. "My brain is too small. The problem comes out my ears. How would the king counsel himself?"

The king sighed. "What is left to do? A public pronouncement of his innocence? A gift of a thousand head of cattle to the boy's father?"

"That would seem generous."

"It would not bring him back to life." The king picked up the vīṇā where he had dropped it and turned it over in his hands. "And what of the Vaidya? Never did I so much as thank him or offer him silver, even though he spent two nights and a day without sleep. He saved my son's life and I, in turn, executed his disciple. To a great teacher, a disciple is sometimes dearer than a son." He plucked a string, then tightened its peg and plucked it again. "I might appoint him a member of the court. He is indeed a marvelous vaidya."

"A little thought comes to my little mind," the dwarf said. "What if you gave him someone to replace his student? I have heard that Sutanukā was an able assistant to him during the birth. She is worth a thousand head of cattle. What if you gave him Sutanukā?"

The king frowned. "I could not do that. She is like my right hand. She is a woman with the strength of a warrior. They are more rare than the giant pearl." He played a scale, made a fine adjustment in the tuning, played the scale again. "And yet, I suppose that if I feel no sense of loss, then I have made no sacrifice. What is the loss of a gaṇikā when compared with the loss of a son or a disciple? Yes, I shall give him Sutanukā, though it pains me gravely. Why are you grinning like a monkey, my dwarf?"

"Because of my pleasure in serving such a wise king," the dwarf said, bowing deeply.

When the Vaidya returned to his home, he stood for some time in the garden, gazing at the flowers. He had an herb garden, too, where he grew garlic to treat bleeding stomach, turmeric to purify foods, henbane to calm the nerves, and hemp to induce appetite, but he loved his flower garden better.

Here were hibiscus and jasmine, bold yellow champaka and pale sirisa, white atimukta and scarlet kiṃsuka. He went over to examine a small aśoka tree he had planted a few months ago that refused to bloom. What was the legend about aśoka trees? That in order to blossom they had to be kicked by a beautiful maiden. He thought of Sutanukā. Then he thought of Virata being consumed by flames.

He went back into his house. His seven remaining students were gathered in the common room, practicing their surgical incisions on hollow lotus stalks, bandaging a wooden mannequin with hinged joints, suturing animal skins, or poring over long palm-leaf books with wooden covers.

While they were diligent workers, they had never been known to study with quite such intensity. In fact, they were avoiding the Vaidya's eye, praying he would not speak to them. Word had already reached them of Virata's execution, the disgrace in which they, by association, shared.

The Vaidya called Kaṅka into one of the small consultation chambers. When they had sat down together—there were stools here of woven rattan for the comfort of his patients—he saw that the young man had been crying.

"Kaṅka," he began. He had to clear his throat several times. "Kaṅka, you have been my student for seven years. I have given you my knowledge and you have been a worthy student. You have learned everything I have to teach. Now you must take over my practice, my teaching. Today I make you vaidya."

"Oh, no, master. I could not be vaidya. I know nothing. You are vaidya."

"I am in my thirty-seventh year. My wife is long dead, my children are far away. The time has come for me to enter the final stage of my life. I shall renounce all and become sannyāsin."

Kaṅka let out a cry of grief. "Oh, master, I plead with you, do not! We can not survive without your teaching. We will be like a chariot without a driver. We will certainly be doomed."

The Vaidya smiled. "I have trained you well. You will be victorious."

"Oh, Vaidya," Kaṅka said, falling to his knees and embracing his master's feet. Now he wept like a baby. "It is too much loss for one day. Too much loss for a lifetime. Can't you please stay with us, just for a few weeks more? A few days then!"

"Get up, my new vaidya. I must be on my way, and you must get to work. There is so much to do. You will be overwhelmed at first, but in time you will learn to attend to everyone and everything. Do not forget the pledge of Caraka. And make sure you take good care of my garden."

"I shall, Vaidya. I swear I shall."

The Vaidya returned to the common room with Kaṅka and repeated, more or less, what he had just said. It was unnecessary, the consulting chamber being separated from the common room only by a tapestry, but he did it as a matter of courtesy.

The students were astonished and heartbroken. Some of them wept, some of them pleaded with him to stay. Some of them were in such shock from the events of the day that they simply squatted down and hid their faces in their hands.

He gave them further instructions about running the house, and to each of them a warning regarding areas of their practice in which he had noticed they were lax. He reminded Dūṣaka that Kaṅka's orders were to be obeyed without question. Then he kissed each of them and, carrying nothing more than a clean vasana and a bowl with which he might beg, he walked out the front door and down the street that led to the gates of the city.

3

In the cool of the afternoon, the wet nurse decided to take the infant prince for a stroll around the palace gardens, so he might breath the fresh air that everyone knew was beneficial to the health. She dressed him in fresh silk and nestled him into a bamboo carriage, a gift from Jubala the cart maker, the same rogue who had fired her husband. How the strands of karma drew together disparate corners of life, like some great fisherman's net! Despite her resentment, she had to admire the clever way he had crafted it to resemble a miniature battle chariot, the nurse substituting for the horse (that made her laugh). The device rolled so smoothly that the infant, sated from the last feeding, fell asleep at once.

The wet nurse rearranged his silks and kissed his forehead. Just thinking about suckling him made her breasts swell, and a drop of milk expressed itself on the very tip of her left nipple. Laughing, she wiped it away with her finger.

The gardens were at their loveliest this time of day. A peacock strutted back and forth, exhibiting the dazzling iridescent fan of his feathers, while in the pond swans drifted lazily among the islands of water lilies. Three of the queens sat on the bank, weaving garlands and giggling over some bit of gossip.

But she could not enjoy it, for at times like this, when she was idle, the Vaidya's assistant would appear to her, as real as if he were standing before her, his face melting like tallow behind a curtain of flame, and she would tremble and grow faint.

She had to accuse him, she argued to an invisible inquisitor. She had no choice! Otherwise, she might have been executed herself, and then to whom would her family turn? Better one man suffers than an entire family. The king would have burned him anyway for ruining the surgery. Death is death. If a condemned man is on his way to meet Yama, what difference is the weight of a second crime on his already bent shoulders? Certainly such a sacrifice would earn him high status in his next life.

Another possibility: What if he actually was a sorcerer and really had been responsible for the infant's honey-hair? Perhaps the gods themselves had put the thought into her mind, that the dharma might be served. After all, an idea is something, and something cannot come from nothing. Perhaps the gods arranged the entire incident so that she, the wet nurse, might be the instrument of the young man's punishment. That being the case, she had nothing to feel guilty about; on the contrary, she had enforced the dharma. What greater virtue might a person accrue?

"Victory, madam," said a small dark man standing beside her. "You are the wet nurse of Prince Candra?"

Something about him made her want to draw back: the painful thinness of his body, the eyes, huge as a child's yet forbidding as the entrance to an ancient cave. Yet, because he carried the white parasol of the palace porter and addressed her in the language of the court, she made an effort to be polite, acknowledging her position and adding that, while she knew the royal language, she never spoke it because a missing tooth made proper pronunciation impossible, and she felt that to mispronounce Sanskrit was a sin against the gods. This was her standard response and, although it deceived no one, the courtiers, perceiving her simplicity, usually allowed it to pass unquestioned.

"A gentleman wishes to see you. He waits in the gatehouse."

"What is his name?"

"He would not give it. He wished to surprise you."

She frowned. Who could it be? Her husband was in the servants' quarters, taking care of the children. What other man did she know who would come here to the palace to see her? Then she had a thought. "A man of sixty years? With a mole on the side of his nose, and bags beneath his eyes? And a way of talking . . . very . . . slowly . . . like . . . this?"

"Yes, that's right, precisely as you have said."

She beamed with pleasure. "It is my uncle. He has come to beg my apology. You see, we had a falling out. But I intend to forgive him. Forgiveness is always the virtuous path, don't you agree? Please escort him here."

"I would, but he is afraid of the palace. He will not venture beyond the gatehouse unless he is by your side."

She sighed. "The silly old man. He is śūdra, you know, always boasting about how comfortable he is among the upper classes. And now he is afraid to enter the palace, where śūdras come and go every day!" She shook her head and laughed.

"I know exactly what you mean," the porter said. "My mother-in-law is the same way. She would have us believe that she is as worldly as an ambassador of the court, but just let a brāhmaṇa come around the house, and she grows as stiff as a dried flower."

"It is their generation," the wet nurse agreed. "They are all thus."

"You don't have to tell me. Go get your uncle, and I will watch the infant until your return."

"No, I couldn't. What if someone noticed my absence?"

"All the important members of the court are in temple doing afternoon pūja. As for the harem guards"—he indicated the olive-skinned, helmeted women standing by the buildings—"they are mleccha and only know a few words of our tongue."

"Well . . ." The wet nurse hesitated. She knew she shouldn't, but the thought of her uncle seeing her in these splendid surroundings was simply more than she could resist.

"If you hurry," the porter said, "you won't be more than a few moments. He's sitting directly beneath the inscription. Go now. Don't worry, I'll watch the infant. I've raised four of my own, I know how to handle them."

"And you won't leave him unattended—not for an instant?"

"I won't take my eye off him."

The wet nurse smiled and hurried across the gardens toward the gatehouse, her cheeks hot with anticipation. The guards, recognizing her, opened the small door embedded in the great gate so she might enter. Inside, hundreds of men squatted on the floor waiting for permission to enter the palace complex on one piece of business or another. She searched for her uncle, a smile set to burst at the sight of him, but she caught no glimpse of him—or anybody else she knew. Puzzled and disappointed, she trudged back across the gardens to the place where she had left the porter watching the baby carriage.

There was the carriage, but the porter was nowhere in sight.

Her blood turned to ice water. Her thighs slapped against each other as she ran and she had to hold her hands over her breasts to stop their painful swinging. She was unaccustomed to any sort of physical exertion, and by the time she reached the carriage, her lungs ached and the air burned her throat.

She leaned over the carriage, gasping for breath, her heart threatening to tear from her chest, and laughed with relief. There was the infant precisely as she had left him, gurgling with pleasure. Evidently the porter had been called away, but far from neglecting the child or harming him as she had imagined—she was embarrassed by the violent fantasies she had entertained during those few awful moments—he had left him with a toy, a beautifully carved ivory rattle. The baby was sucking on it as though it were a nipple.

"Oh, yes, my dear, my beloved," the nurse cooed. "You're hungry. It's time for your meal."

Her breasts were heavy with milk, aching for his lips. As she reached down to lift him, she thought she saw something move within the cage of the rattle. She watched with fascination as a scorpion emerged from the slot in the rattle and danced across the baby's cheek. It was small, milky-white, and segmented, as though its body were a string of fine, flat pearls. It scuttled along on eight slender legs, feeling ahead with its pincers. Its stinger, she noticed absently, was poised above its head, tense as a curled spring, ready to loose its deadly energy. Now a second scorpion emerged from the slot in the rattle, and a third. Another stuck its head from the opening, ascertained that the climate was to its liking, and followed the rest. One after another, they crowded across the infant's face. The occasional glimpse of a leg or a curled stinger led her to believe a half dozen more lingered inside the rattle, waiting for their turn.

She acted without thinking, grabbing the rattle, hurling it as far as she could, then gingerly picking the scorpions off the infant's face and crushing them between her fingers, hardly aware of their stings. How dare these wretched creatures threaten her baby!

She didn't reflect upon her own condition until she had rid the carriage of scorpions and satisfied herself that the baby had not been stung even once; then she glanced at her right hand and saw that the fingers were thick as potatoes from the swelling.

Several of the women harem guards were watching curiously from beneath their helmets. She called to them for help, but they did not understand. Some thought it a game to amuse the infant. Dizzy and numb, she took a few steps toward them. They seemed impossibly far away, as though seen through the wrong end of a magnifying glass. She tried to take another step, but her legs failed and she toppled to the ground. There was no pain. With what remained of her consciousness, she realized that she was dying. She saw the face of the Vaidya's assistant consumed by flames and marveled at the precision with which the great wheel of karma had turned full circle. Her last thought, as her ātman departed the fleshy pile of her body, was not of immortality, afterlife, or reincarnation, but that she had died without her uncle witnessing her life at the palace, her moment of butterfly-like splendor.

The regret would last a thousand lives.

They caught the assassin quite by accident. The head of the guard had posted two of his men behind the kitchens to keep watch over a clay crock filled with pickled tongues of hummingbirds, which had just arrived from the south by special order of the mahāmantrin, a notorious gourmand despite his Buddhist vows. A certain amount of food pilfering was common around the palace, and the tiny tongues were worth their weight in gems. Still, the guards felt their assignment demeaning and would have rather joined the others in their search for the rogue who had tried to assassinate the infant prince. Furthermore, the delicate smell of frying vegetables in chick-pea batter wafting from the holes in the kitchen roof was driving them mad with anticipation for lunch. In order to pass the time more quickly, they decided to hold an archery contest. Near them, along with sacks of grains, and trays of legumes that had been set out in the sun to dry, were a pile of gourds and a number of large clay urns of the sort used to store honey and cane syrup. They would stack several urns, they decided, one on top of the other, and shoot gourds off them at five hundred paces.

One of the urns was so heavy it would not move. They turned it over and discovered inside it a small man curled into a posture called Yoga Nidrāsana, wherein the body is bent double, the ankles crossed behind the head, the fingers intertwined behind the back. It was a position that a proficient yogi could maintain for hours or even days. They pulled him out of the urn and, without allowing him to untie the knot he had made of his limbs, carried him straight down one of the dank subterranean tunnels that led to the king's inquisition chamber, pausing only long enough to dispatch a runner for the king and his closest advisers.

These passages, which honeycombed the earth beneath the palace, were used by the king's spies and, occasionally, by the king himself when he wished to leave the palace unnoticed. Some of them led to the homes of loyal citizens, while others, dug so that the king might flee if the city were under siege, extended so far that they emerged outside the walls of the city altogether.

The inquisition chamber was located along the deepest of these tunnels, where a man's screams, no matter how piercing, would be swallowed by layers of stone and earth. Furnishings were limited to a sturdy wooden table with shackles at either end, a rack of ingeniously conceived iron instruments of pain, and a brazier with which to heat them (though it was rarely necessary, for they usually proved effective enough cold). A grating overhead shed dim light on the rough-hewn timber supports and crude earthen walls. Because of the constant leakage from the moat, the floor was covered with an inch or so of stinking polluted water, which even the sweet smell of the ghee torches blazing in brackets on the wall could not conceal.

The guards had just finished securing the assassin to the wooden table when the king arrived. He approached the suspect for a better look, his sandals making a sucking sound, scaring the rats from their hiding places. The man on the table was small, and so thin that the pulsing of the blood could be seen in the large vein that ran alongside his neck. He had a ferret's face and enormous unblinking eyes that returned the king's gaze without so much as a trace of fear. He had been stripped of his turban and vasana, and shackled, spread-eagled, by chains around his wrists and ankles.

"You tried to kill my son," the king said.

The chamber was silent but for the sound of water dripping from the roof beams.

"Yes," the man replied.

"Why?"

"For the same reason you are king. Because it is the work of my caste."

"I have seen those of his caste before," the Purohita said, "and always involved in the darkest deeds. They kill for a fee. It is part of their pūja. They worship Śiva the Destroyer by acting the destroyer themselves."

"What could be more insidious," the king mused, "than one who justifies his own bloodlust as the will of his deity?"

"How many have you murdered," the assassin whispered, "in the name of Viṣṇu?"

"It is quite another thing," the king replied, "to kill in order to build an empire of lasting peace."

"I think not," the assassin said, "for Yama is Yama in all His splendid forms. You and I are alike, but I lack your delusions of righteousness."

"Were he not an assassin," the Purohita remarked dryly, "he might be kept at the court to amuse us with his sophistry."

"Who hired you," the king asked, "to perform this commendable deed of murdering a helpless infant?"

"I cannot say. Would you have me violate the laws of my caste just now, when my death looms so near?"

One of the guards bowed. "O King of Kings, if this lowly guard might speak? We found this inside his turban."

The guard presented the king with an exquisite bangle, a golden cobra or "naga," as they were called, with sapphire eyes and a giant ruby wedged between its fangs.

The king turned it over in his hands. "It resembles," he said cautiously, "a bangle Dattadevī gave to Prince Rāma on the event of his upanayana."

"You are mistaken, Father."

The king turned toward the sound of the voice. Prince Rāma was standing at the entrance to the chamber. Vasubandhu arrived a few steps behind him.

"Good afternoon, my son," the king said, smiling uncomfortably. "Implication of guilt was the farthest thing from my mind. I have seen a thousand such bangles, a million. Those who make jewelry are always eager to sculpt the nāga."

"My father defends himself when no one has attacked. I mean to say, it does not resemble my bangle in that a thing cannot resemble itself. In other words, dear father, it *is* the bangle my mother gave me, without a doubt."

The prince smiled at the anxious expression upon his father's face, and continued. "I left it upon the bank, wrapped in my vasana, when I went swimming in the pool last week. Afterward, when I dressed, it was gone. I should have told the guard there and then, but frankly, Father, I was ashamed. The heir to the throne should not be so irresponsible as to lose his favorite piece of jewelry. After all, it was a gift from the mahiṣī, that queen whom we must both honor and respect above all others."

The king's cheeks burned at this obvious reference to his ill-treatment of Dattadevī.

"I suspect," the prince continued, "that someone, be it guard, courtier, queen, or even minister, stole my bangle from where it lay and used it to hire this assassin. It is even possible, I believe, that he arranged for the assassin to be caught, and the bangle to be discovered, in order to lead the trail of suspicion back to myself. I am an easy suspect. Every second-rate Sanskrit author has tried his hand at a work about brothers who battle for the throne."

"It is a popular theme," Vasubandhu said cautiously. "In other lands, where the rules of royal succession are more rigid, the problem is less common. Perhaps we would do well to follow their example."

"A man cannot change tradition as he changes his ornaments," the Purohita said.

"Let any man say a word against my son, and I would slit his throat in an instant."

"And I would do the same for you, Father," Prince Rāma said, grasping the king's hands in his own and looking deeply into his eyes, "as I would for my little brother."

Rāma turned and approached the assassin who lay chained to the table. "This is the man who would take my brother's life?"

"It is," his father replied.

Rāma addressed the assassin. "Who hired you to do such a dark deed?"

"By the law of my caste," the assassin replied, "I cannot say."

"Perhaps I can persuade you to speak," Rāma said, gently. Having been granted permission by his father to interrogate the prisoner, he instructed the guards to free him and bind him again, face down. He pulled a dagger from his waistband and, standing over the assassin, inserted the point of it into the man's rectum.

The Purohita turned his face to the wall and began to chant

the gayatri to himself, to cleanse himself of the terrible impurity he bore witness to. Vasubandhu, on the other hand, watched with fascination.

"Who bade you murder my little brother?" Prince Rāma inquired.

"By the law of my caste, I cannot say."

"Each time my question goes unanswered, my dagger digs deeper into your bowels. Now tell me, who bade you murder my little brother?"

How gently he pressed the dagger's jeweled handle! The blade cut into the ring of pink muscle and blood oozed from it like excrement. Those watching Rāma perceived in his manner the existence of a most refined sensibility. They waited for the assassin's cries, but all they heard was the water dripping from the timbers that supported the ceiling.

"He is a yogī," Samudra Gupta said. "He knows the secret of pain."

"I am beyond your reach," the assassin whispered, in a voice that did not even waver.

"Who bade you murder my little brother?"

The assassin began to sing to himself, "Oṃ namaḥ Śivāya, Oṃ namaḥ Śivāya . . ."

Prince Rāma pressed the dagger a hair's breadth deeper. Some artery must have been severed, for the blood came in spurts now, wine-dark.

"Who bade you murder my little brother?"

"Oṃ namaḥ Śivāya, Oṃ namaḥ Śivāya!"

His voice grew exultant. Suddenly he stopped singing. His face turned red, then blue, and his eyes bulged from their sockets.

"What's he doing?" Rāma demanded.

"Strangling himself with his tongue." The king was matter of fact. He had known all along that they would learn nothing of the force behind the assassin. Yogīs were beyond human persuasion.

"No," Rāma exclaimed, "stop him! He will not cheat me of my pleasure!"

The guards pried his mouth open and tried to extract his tongue from his throat, but they were too late. The pupils of his eyes rolled out of sight. With a clatter of chains, his body shuddered as the ātman sloughed off its fleshy cage. The assassin lay limp and lifeless.

Enraged, Rāma plunged the dagger down the man's rectum, all the way to the hilt, again and again, until his bowels fell out upon the table.

Then he excused himself and hurried along the subterranean tunnel that led to his wing of the palace. He could not reach his chamber in time, his excitement was so great. Looking around, making certain that he was alone, he took his throbbing red liṅgam out of his vasana. The mere touch of his hand was enough to make him ejaculate. He leaned against the wall, gasping for breath, spurting jet after jet of milky semen against the coarse earthen wall. He closed his eyes and imagined that his penis was the dagger that took the assassin's life and all the world was awash in blood. Afterward, he staggered to his chamber, lay down on his bed, and fell into a deep, dreamless sleep.

When the king returned to his chamber, the Purohita was waiting at the entrance. "I would speak with my lord," he said, lowering his high shaven dome and pressing his palms together in namaste.

"I've little time," the king said briskly. "I've called a meeting of my spies so I may find the brigand who would plot against my sons. I will not rest easy until I see him impaled, with the carrion pecking at his eyes."

"That is the subject I wish to discuss."

With the king's permission, he followed him into the chamber. They sat down on cushions a few feet from each other, and the king offered him sweetened milk, which he declined.

Suddenly the king smiled and, reaching over, patted him on the knee. "I am sorry if I spoke harshly, but I worry for the safety of my child. When we sit together like this, I am reminded of the days when I studied the revealed books with you. Ah, you were a fine teacher! I still do not know how you drummed any knowledge into this hard warrior head of mine. Remember when we read the passage in the Upaniṣads, where Śvetaketu's father tries to show him that brahman permeates the entire universe?"

The Purohita smiled and nodded. He half closed his eyes and

recited from memory, " 'Put this salt in water,' the father said, 'and come to me in the morning.' But when, next morning, the father asked for the salt, the son could not find it, for it had dissolved."

"Yes," the king said, nodding, "and then he instructs the boy to taste the water from the top, and the middle, and the bottom. And the boy replies that each part tastes equally of salt."

"And the father," the Purohita continued, "said, 'You do not perceive the One Reality that exists within you, but nonetheless it is there. Everything which exists partakes of that subtle essence. Such is Reality! Such is the soul! Tat tvam asi, Śvetaketu!"

"Tat tvam asi," the king repeated, reliving the wonder he always felt pronouncing those sacred Sanskrit syllables. "Thou art that!"

"I was such a donkey," he went on, laughing at the memory of himself. "I missed the point completely. For weeks afterward I drank salt water in the belief that in doing so I was partaking of the brahman."

The Purohita shook his head. "You were a devoted, conscientious student. Like a warrior, you wrestled with an idea and did not let go until you had subjugated it completely."

"Ah, to be that child again," the king said wistfully, "so carefree in my ignorance."

"Careful of even your casual wishes. The gods hear the muttering of mice."

"Would that we could sit and reminisce all afternoon! But I must be off to my meeting. Tell me what you came to discuss, my teacher."

"You need not attend the meeting," the Purohita said, his voice suddenly grave. "You know who hired the assassin."

"You are mistaken. I do not."

"The salt is in the water. Its taste is everywhere, yet you deny it."

"If you know who hired the assassin, tell me this instant. Do not game with me."

"His name is Rāma."

The smile vanished. In an instant the king was transformed from the adoring student to a cold, dangerous beast. "You accuse my own flesh? Proceed with care, Purohita. State your case well, for you tread a floor of thin reeds."

"The bangle was Rāma's—"

"Of course it is Rāma's," the king said with irritation. "He said so himself! He left it on the bank when he went swimming and someone stole it, to cast the shadow of guilt upon him."

"Yet he saw it not. He was standing at the entrance to the inquisition chamber when the guard presented it to you. The guard's body blocked his view. How could he have known it was his bangle without laying eyes on it?"

The king started to answer but could find no response. His face twisted in anguish. "There is some other explanation," he murmured to himself. "There must be."

"Is it so unusual? Does not Kauṭilya, that great authority on statecraft, say in his *Arthaśāstra*, 'Beware of princes, for like crabs, they eat their own parents.' "

"I know what Kauṭilya says," the king snapped. He rose and paced the room. Returning to the Purohita, he said, "And if it is so, then what am I to do? Exile my son so that he may form his own army and join the ranks of my enemies! Or put him to death and be known throughout the land as the king who practiced infanticide? The thought of it chills my blood."

The king reflected for several moments. Then he went to the entrance of the chamber, pushed back the tapestry, and ordered the guards and porters and servants, who had been waiting outside, to call together those of his innermost circle—all but Prince Rāma.

In no time the king's closest circle of advisers—Vasubandhu, the Purohita, Sutanukā, Vāmana the dwarf, and Dakṣa—were gathered in his chambers. That the king began to speak without waiting for Rāma to arrive was so unusual that from it alone the others guessed the purpose of the meeting.

He told them all about the assassination attempt (all but Dakṣa had already heard), the inquisition, and the Purohita's observations regarding Prince Rāma and the bangle.

When he had finished, Vasubandhu said, "I noticed it, too, how he claimed the bangle without seeing it. When my lord called for me, I was lost in thought, trying to find a way to tell him of my suspicions. I can only thank the Purohita for sparing me this unpleasant task."

"It is a most delicate and difficult situation," the Purohita agreed, "and one that causes us all pain."

"Let us dispense with such sentimentality," the king said with a sudden, deliberate coldness that shocked the others, even those who knew him longest and imagined they understood him best.

"Granted he has done evil," the Purohita said gently, "he is still your son. No civilized man can disregard his love for a son."

"I am not any man," the king bellowed. "I am the King of Kings! I am the Supreme Lord. I have done what no man has done before—united the many kingdoms of the Land of the Sons of Bharata! The dynasty of the Guptas shall rule until Kalkin comes on his white horse, with his flaming sword, and no prince shall blacken its name with fratricides and battles for the throne!" The king's voice dropped to a whisper. "We have only to decide how best to proceed. What thoughts have you, my beloved friends? My trusted council?"

"A naughty child," the dwarf suggested, simply to fill the lingering silence, "should be punished."

"Were our enemies to perceive a division within the Gupta dynasty," Vasubandhu replied, "they would drive in a wedge and split us asunder. It must not be."

"Yet the baby must be protected," Dakṣa said. "He must grow up to be cakravartin and fulfill the prophecy."

"When the infant Kriṣṇa was in danger," Sutanukā said, having been granted permission to speak, "he and his brother were sent to be raised by the cowherd Nanda and his wife, Yaśodā. Likewise, Prince Candra might be put in the hands of some trustworthy citizen until"—she hesitated, searching for the right expression—"the political climate has changed."

"I would take him into my home and love and cherish him as though he were my own son," Dakṣa said.

"Your offer warms my heart," the king said, "but it would be discovered too easily."

Vasubandhu agreed. "Everyone in the city knows of your friendship with Dakṣa. Living there, the infant would not even have the benefit of the walls and guards of the palace, for what little good they did."

"My thoughts ran along other lines," Sutanukā said. "When the king, in his wisdom and impeccable regard for the dharma, chose to make a formal apology to the family of Virata, he sent this unworthy woman"—she was referring to herself—"as his emissary."

"Of all diplomats," the king said, "Sutanukā is the most subtle and full of tact. Were she a man, I would give her Vasubandhu's job in an instant. But what has this to do with—"

"If I may finish," she said, gracefully raising a forefinger that glittered with rings. "I was taken in by the family of the Vaidya's disciple. They treated me with hospitality. The father—Govinda is his name—though a lowly mender of silks, is a kind and generous man of unusual intelligence. He has a large family, where there appears to be very much love and very little discord. Might there be a certain justice in sending Prince Candra to live with him?"

"He is a mere silk mender," Vasubandhu said disparagingly. "We discuss the destiny of a future king."

"Be not so quick, my minister, to dismiss this idea," the king said. "There is indeed justice to it, and such a symmetry that I wonder if the gods themselves did not have a hand in its arrangement. Much might be learned from a humble man that could not be learned in a palace. And, while today he is a mere mender of silk, I plan to give him restitution in the form of a thousand head of cattle. With such wealth he could practice any number of respected trades."

"I know this Govinda," Dakṣa said. "He has worked in my guild for many years. His mending is faultless and his prices are always fair. As Sutanukā has remarked, he seems an intelligent man, with a knack for business. What if we lent him money, set him up as a silk merchant? He certainly has a knowledge of the trade. We might even see a profit, for there are fortunes to be made by the man who knows when to buy—and when to sell."

"With Dakṣa as your liaison," Vasubandhu said, "you could keep a close eye on the child, and nobody would be the wiser. Indeed, the more I think about it, the more excellent an idea it seems, assuming this Govinda is as fine a man as the gaṇikā would imply."

"He is not a Buddhist, is he?" the king asked. "I would not like my son to be raised as a Buddhist."

Vasubandhu, who was a Buddhist, grunted and looked away.

"To the best of my knowledge," Dakṣa said, "he is a Viṣṇuite, like my lord."

"But what of the infant's honey-hair?" the dwarf said. "He is the only one in the kingdom with such hair. Everyone will recognize him."

"Those who care for him will have to make certain his hair is always dyed black," Vasubandhu said. "They must be sure he never bathes in public or takes a lather where others may see him. Such precautions will be difficult to maintain, but not impossible."

"I would feel better," the king said, "were there someone I could send with him. Yet those few I trust are gathered in this room today, and number one less than I trusted yesterday."

"I would happily spend the rest of my life as a servant in a house of strangers," Sutanukā said, bowing deeply, "if it would let my lord rest easier one single night." It was a safe offer since, her appearance being so singular, he could not possibly send her.

"I, too," the dwarf volunteered, realizing that he could not be sent for precisely the same reason.

"I believe we would all be glad to serve the king in this manner," Vasubandhu said, "but we are all known and would create more risk than we might alleviate. Dakṣa alone will be the king's eyes and ears, since only his visits to the Govinda household will be beyond suspicion."

"And what shall we tell Rāma," the king continued, "if we proceed with this plan?"

"As far as the world beyond this small chamber is concerned," Vasubandhu said, "Prince Candra is dead. We shall say that one of the scorpions succeeded in its deadly work. We will stage an elaborate funeral service, complete with pyre and mourners." He hesitated. "An infant's body must be obtained to burn in his place."

There was a moment of silence. As much as those gathered there wished to show their loyalty to the king, they had a horror of contact with death.

Finally Sutanukā said, "I will do this task for my lord. As a woman—and a śūdra—I am already impure. The presence of death will taint me less than the others."

The king bade Sutanukā remain with him after the rest had left. She knelt beside him on the cushions, her gaze lowered demurely, her hands crossed on her knees, waiting for her lord to speak.

"My mind," he said presently, "is in turmoil. I pretended to have an icy heart for my son Rāma so that my council might divine a plan without worry that they would offend me, but in truth, I love him still. That he has tried to kill his brother makes me love him not one bit less. I have anger, yes. Anger enough to wage a war, to burn and pillage and plunder, but no less love. Do you find this strange, Sutanukā?"

"That a man love his son? No, my lord. That the man happens to be king and lives in a palace, that the son is prince and fights with all means at his disposal for what might be his—these are unusual circumstances, but they alter not the essence of it."

"Ah, Sutanukā, you are so wise, you have the woman's knack of seeing beyond the bangles to the business beneath."

"I live to bring comfort to my lord." Saying this, she bent toward him and, still averting her eyes, rubbed her breasts gently across his chest. This was the rubbing embrace, an invitation to worship Kāma.

The king put his arms around her and drew her to him. She seized his lower lip between her sharp white teeth and tugged at it, while drawing her long nails lightly across his back. They kept on with this and similar sorts of love play for a few minutes more, but then the king shook his head and pulled away. "It is no use. My mind is so fixed on the problem of my sons that it denies the pleasure of your touch."

"Then let us distract the mind," Sutanukā suggested. "For, as a bullock draws a cart, so, too, does the mind precede the body. I could pose you a riddle, or teach you a tongue twister, challenge you in dice or composing kāvya."

"A kāvya contest! Yes, that's a fine idea. We shall battle wits and at the same time solve my dilemma, for when we create kāvya, a fragment of the gods enters us and advises us. What metric pattern shall we use?"

"That known as malini is both pleasing and challenging. That is, four lines of fifteen syllables, accented—"

"I know how malini is accented, insolent girl. Am I not called Kāvyarājah, the Poet-King?"

"Of course, my lord. I shall remember that and try not to best you too badly."

"Oh, insolent thing. I should punish you for speaking so to your lord."

"It is only the truth," she said teasingly.

"We shall see." He thought for a moment more, and added, "The game would have more spirit if we played for stakes."

"My lord is a gambler at heart," Sutanukā said, smiling.

"Show me a man of the Land of the Sons of Bharata who is not. But we must bet something of real value, for only thus does a game take on the kind of excitement that makes the blood race and the fingers tingle, that makes, in effect, the game not a mere game but an event in a man's life. What can we bet that is of value?"

"That is a puzzle indeed," Sutanukā responded, "for I enjoy perfect contentment here, at the palace. I want for nothing that my lord has not already given me, and I doubt if there be anything I would not gladly give to my lord."

"Ah, I know of something, but it will shock you hearing it now, in this manner, for it is the sort of news that so alters a person's life that it is usually imparted with elaborate warning, in special audience. Can you bear the sudden shock, my Sutanukā?"

"I will certainly do my best, my lord."

"Well then. As you know, I am giving Govinda the silk mender a thousand head of cattle in restitution for killing his son. Now, it has occurred to me that the Vaidya deserves something, too, for I also stole from him, in the rashness of my rage, one of his finest disciples. Since you were an able assistant to him . . ." He didn't know quite how to put it.

"Yes?" she said anxiously.

"I would give him—"

"Go on."

"—you."

She gasped and held her hand over heart.

The king nodded with satisfaction. "So, we have found something we both care about. You wish to stay at the palace, while I would give you to the Vaidya. Very well then. If you win, you stay. If I win, you go. That should give our game excitement enough. What say you?"

She lowered her head. A single tear rolled down her cheek, yet her voice was steady: "If my lord would have it."

His heart overflowed with compassion for her. That the prospect of leaving the Gupta court be met with dismay was only to be expected. It was not, after all, unlike an exile from paradise.

"Three rounds," the king said. "We shall toss the dice to see who goes first. You are the odd numbers, and I am the even."

He called for his dice, and shook them, and blew upon them, and finally tossed them down on the mat. They fell four dots up.

"I will start." He was silent for some time. Then he said,

"At the bazaar, the fruit seller slices a mango
and finds,
To his humiliation, the pulpy flesh crawling
with maggots . . ."

He looked toward Sutanukā. After several moments she responded,

"His customers care little for they know that
Brahmā makes the fruit,
And that butterflies have no beauty without
maggots for comparison."

The king smiled and nodded his approval. "You win the first round. Not only does your Sanskrit have beauty, but there is also wisdom to your versifying. Now you choose. Would you make the starting verse or the answering?"

"The answering, I think. Such is the work of a woman."

"Very well," said the king. This time it came to him more quickly:

"The infant scorpions devour their mother that
they may survive,
The mother thinks not of herself but the good
of her children . . ."

Sutanukā said almost immediately,

"The king rules two families, those of his
blood and those of his state.
Can he sacrifice himself for a hungry few when
the welfare of many is at stake?"

"It is a good verse but too many syllables, I think," the king said, frowning. "This round I win. And so it stands, one to one. This next round decides it. I will make the starting verse." He hesitated a long time, determined to come up with something she could not match. After all, he was kāvyarāja, the Poet-King.

"Even a sage, asked to choose between sons,
which one may live,
Finds it easier to count all the numerous
bends of the Ganges . . ."

He had used that line about counting the bends of the Ganges in other kāvya contests with the gaṇikā, and he hoped she would not remember.

In fact, she took no notice of it. She began to recite, then shook her head and said in a trembling voice, "I cannot make an answering verse. Not a single handsome phrase or cunning conceit comes to my mind. You are the winner, my lord." She began to weep. "I fear I must leave the court."

The king shook his head. "I cannot make you do it. You have served me too well for too long. I will send him cattle instead."

"I would not make a liar of my lord."

"It's all right. You do not have to go. Neither the Vaidya nor anyone else knows of my plans. I have discussed it only with the dwarf."

"But we have gambled, and I have lost!" A distraught look entered her eyes, and her voice rose to a wail. "I could not live with the dishonor of an unpaid debt. I would drown myself in the Ganges!" In her misery she pulled her hair from her chignon and began to wail and beat at her breasts.

"Woman, please!" the king said. "If your honor means so much, and if you insist on adding such weight to a simple game and a lightly made promise, then go, serve the Vaidya. I would not have another meaningless death on my conscience."

"Thank you, my lord."

She prostrated herself, and kissed his feet.

"But first you shall procure me an infant's body, as you promised. It is a matter of such delicacy I dare not ask another."

"I shall, my lord."

"And then you will go to serve the Vaidya. That is, if you are still so determined."

"I must not waver from my decision."

"The thought of dismissing you fills me with misery and guilt."

"It may be for my own good. Wise men say that from suffering comes growth."

"If it is too awful, you can come back. You are always welcome."

"Thank you, my lord."

"I shall miss you, Sutanukā."

"And I, you, my lord."

Imagine how surprised Samudra Gupta would have been to see her, only a little while after this tragic farewell, riding the swing in the gardens, pitching joyfully back and forth and chanting, in time to the motion, the verse that had eluded her—or so she claimed—earlier that day:

"Yet a gaṇikā, when asked to choose between
duty and love,
Finds it as easy as losing a contest by playing
the fool."

Sutanukā's skill in improvising kāvya was legendary throughout the state of Magadha. If she had one person to thank for it, one person to credit for everything she had become, it would be Saṃjñā the gaṇikā.

While Saṃjñā was not the most beautiful of women, her skill in the sixty-four arts as well as her wit and learning had attracted to her home, over the years, most of the great poets and artists of Pāṭaliputra. Since, like artists of every era, they were often without a paṇa to their name, she let them enjoy kāma with her in return for the kind of brief immortality artists can bestow. As a result, there existed a number of outstanding odes to her and some beautiful sculpture, including the carving of Lakṣmī that graced the city gates, which resembled her down to the curl of her lip and the shape of her chignon.

Sutanukā's parents, being śūdras and thus destined to serve, were employed as servants in Saṃjñā's home. By the time Sutanukā was four, she had thoroughly impressed the famous gaṇikā with her cleverness and charm. When the child reached puberty, and her bosom and hips swelled to their present excellent proportion, Saṃjñā suggested that she be given to her as a disciple, to train in the sixty-four arts. Sutanukā, who loved to watch the other gaṇikās adorn their bodies with pastes and scents and bangles, was delighted, and her father, too, was pleased (for an unmarried daughter was among a poor man's greatest fears).

Her arduous training began.

By her sixteenth autumn she was at least proficient at singing, playing the vīṇā, dancing, doing all three together in conjunction, writing and drawing, tattooing, adorning an idol with rice and flowers, arranging flowers, coloring the body, making tile pictures on the floor, arranging carpets and cushions for reclining, playing on musical glasses filled with water, storing water in tanks and urns, trimming and decorating pictures of cloth, stringing garlands and wreaths, binding turbans and topknots, acting, making ear ornaments, preparing perfumes, decorating the body with paste and jewelry, performing sorcery and sleight of hand, cooking, making drinks and spirits, sewing, making tufts and tassels and the like from yarn, solving puzzles and riddles, playing memory games, mimicking others, chanting, reciting tongue twisters, dueling with weapons, demonstrating knowledge of logic, carpentry, architecture, precious metals and gems, chemistry and mineralogy, mines and quarries, coloring jewels and gems and beads, gardening, arranging cockfights and quail fights and even ram fights, teaching parrots and starlings to speak, dressing the hair, deciphering codes, speaking in a mangled dialect that only a few could understand, speaking Sanskrit and Prakrits, making flower carriages, drawing mandalas and reciting mantras, versifying in contest and other such mental exercise, composing entire poems, knowing many words and their meanings, creating disguises, knowing how to make materials appear finer than they actually are, knowing many ways of gambling, as well as ways of taking the property of others by means of mantras and spells, playing the sports of children, demonstrating the manners of every class and caste, intelligently discussing warfare and armies, performing gymnastics, knowing how to divine a man's character by his features, scanning verses, solving mathematical games and puzzles, making artificial flowers, and sculpting figures and images in clay.

She was also unequaled as a guide in the pursuit of that god called Kāma, whom all men worship in all lands at all times.

While the other women of the city were confined to the small world of home and children, Sutanukā found herself conversing with the best minds of the day, the most famous artists, politicians, astrologers, and philosophers. Occasionally, even a holy man would explain to her a verse of the Gītā or some parable from the Upaniṣads. She had personal wealth and freedom to go where she liked, when she liked, even in the dead of night if she so chose. She had somehow transcended not only the class into which she had been born, but even the narrow niche to which those of her sex were confined.

Men who came for kāma, discovering her wisdom, returned for counsel regarding matters sometimes as important as life and death. Among their number was a tall, broad-shouldered kṣatriya, whose squinting gaze made her feel as though he were trying to look beneath her skin.

On one visit he told her that he was king, that he dressed as a common warrior so that he might walk the streets, bet on a cockfight, and learn what his subjects thought of him. He invited her to come live at the palace and serve him alone. She assumed that he was insane, for many of the warrior class seemed to suffer from delusions of grandeur. Imagine her surprise when, after finally consenting to his invitation entirely in the spirit of play, a fleet of golden palanquins arrived at Saṃjñā's house to move Sutanukā and her possessions to the palace.

Aside from the king, she had never considered devoting herself exclusively to any one man, though many had asked, even pleaded with her. But the Vaidya was different. From the instant she first saw him, shambling into the reception room in the middle of the night, only half awake, with his fringe of hair in disarray and betel quid fresh on his breath, she had known that their fates were intertwined like the garden creeper and the fig tree.

That he might not feel the same way—that the death of Virata might have cooled his ardor toward her—was a source of the greatest anxiety. Lying in bed the night after the king had granted her freedom, the thought so troubled her that she could not return to sleep. The bed sheets were like ropes of bondage, the pillows as hard as the stone altar upon which sacrifices were made.

In time she devised a simple plan: she would put a cinder in her eye and, on that pretext, visit his house. Diagnosing his emotions would be easy during the examination. If he cupped her face in his hands, and leaned so close that she could feel his warm breath, and lingered there even when the cinder was removed, then she would reach up and embrace him, and draw his mouth to hers, and practice all the methods of kāma she had learned in her short life, until he was so intoxicated by her skills that he could no more live without her than a smoker could without his churrus. But if he was curt and abrupt, and spent only the time required with her and not a second more, well then, she would thank him politely and leave his house, and make sure that she never laid eyes upon him again.

Ah, the pleasant hours she passed trying to decide which sort of kiss a man like the Vaidya would most enjoy, which soft sounds and bites and caresses. She would coax him, and he would resist, fearing the king's retribution were he to learn of their coupling. Knowing that such fears often add an extra dimension of excitement, she would wait until afterward to tell him the truth, that she was his forever, to do with as he liked. A woman, like any fine possession, was always more enticing when a man believed she belonged to another.

Yet as she dreamed of life with him, she could not also help considering life without him, an endless procession of days, each exactly like the one before and those to come, filled with the empty pleasures and meaningless prattle of the palace, leading to nothing but an old age without honor or sense, and death. What if the king predeceased her? What would become of her then? The thought of being passed on to Prince Rāma chilled her blood. Although she was not a queen, she might still be granted the privilege of throwing herself on her lord's funeral pyre. That was her only consolation.

Although the sky was still dark, she heard the deep tolling of the gong that signaled the time for the virtuous Viṣṇuite male to wake and begin pūja. She rose from the bed and began to dress by the light of a single ghee lamp. She would have time, she calculated, to offer a prayer to Gaṇeśa, the elephant-headed god, the remover of obstacles, and to perform her endless toilet and consult with her old friend Vahara Mihira as to whether the stars were auspicious that day for a visit to the Vaidya.

But first she would keep her promise to the dwarf.

The dwarf had his own suite of chambers in the king's palace, his own entrance, even his own little walled garden and bathing pond, all of it constructed at half size. Only the tiniest flowers had been planted there, and the aśoka trees had been bound at the root and carefully pruned so that the dwarf might enjoy them as a normal man enjoyed their full-sized counterpart. Two miniature deer, imported from China, wandered in the garden, and for a time there had been a little horse from Tibet, but he had proved so cranky and unmanageable that he had been set free. The entrance was low enough that a normal man could negotiate it only by crawling on his knees. The bed chamber featured a library, including, in addition to many of the revealed books, two different versions of the *Jātakas*, the dwarf's favorite stories, inscribed on palm-leaf paper in the tiniest nāgarī script, handsomely illustrated, and bound between long wooden covers. The little boxes in which he kept his betel quid and sweets, and the jars for scents and unguents, were all halfsize, and even the brass altarpiece in the pūja chamber, with its figure of Viṣṇu and Lakṣmī astride Garuḍa the eagle, had been cast and hammered in miniature, with remarkable attention to detail, the tracery of the feathers, for example, and the fine shell of Lakṣmī's ear. His visitors, who were mostly young women, always spent some time admiring the ingenuity and craft with which his entire world had been shrunk—for everyone loves things made smaller, the suggestions of childhood, the intimations of manageability—before being escorted to the one full-sized piece of furniture in the entire suite, the bed.

When Sutanukā arrived, the dwarf was standing in the garden, concentrating on a palm leaf in his hands. She had sent a message warning of her arrival, so his being there, and in such a romantic mood, was no coincidence. She prostrated herself before him and kissed his feet. When she rose, he handed her the leaf. He had torn it, with great skill, into a silhouette of a man and a woman in a twining embrace. She complimented him on his handiwork and promised to keep it in her girdle until it withered. She then improvised a kāvya to the effect that a man and a woman were like his leaf carving, fresh and young one moment, withered the next, and that was why opportunities for kāma had to be seized when and wherever they presented themselves.

"I assume by your visit," the dwarf said, "that the king has given you to the Vaidya."

"Thanks to you, my dwarf, my fondest wish has been realized. I should only be happier if I could remain here with you forever, in your tiny, perfect world, and turn my back on all things large and coarse."

"You are a most excellent liar," the dwarf replied, smiling. "Does the king know the purpose of our meeting here today?"

"I told him I had wagered that you were too large to fit within an unguent jar. And you, I said, had produced an unguent jar as large as a water urn and curled yourself neatly within it. For your boon, I said, you had requested kāma with me. Knowing that the kṣatriya often feels himself a stronger warrior denying a permission than granting it, I asked that I be relieved of my duty to fulfill that boon. He denied it. I did not make too much a show of protest."

"Were all men as wise as you, war would disappear and the world would turn as smoothly as a water screw."

Taking her hand, he showed her about the garden, pointing out all the wondrous details, the miniature deer, the trees with bound roots, the golden carp with fins like silk veils that swam in the pool. Of course, she had seen it all before, but in order to create the proper mood for their congress, she expressed her wonder again and again, as though it were all new. They sat together on a marble bench under one of the taller trees, and he quoted a Prakrit kāvya, from the *Seven Hundred Poems of King Hala*.

"This morning, my friend, I heard a man
singing, and his song reminded me of my
lover,
And opened all the wounds that the shafts of
the Love-god had made in my heart."

As he recited this love kāvya and others, he placed his little foot upon her foot and one by one touched each of her toes with his and pressed the ends of her long polished nails. Then, meeting no rebuff, he took her foot in his hands and, caressing it as he would a dove, worked his index finger into the space between the large toe and the second toe.

Sutanukā, imagining she was sitting with the Vaidya, allowed her breathing to grow heavy. Over the years she had grown adept at worshiping kāma with those for whom she felt little affection, or even outright repulsion. It was no coincidence that acting was included among the sixty-four arts indispensable to the gaṇikā. That she truly admired the dwarf for his kindness and humility made it that much easier. When at last she saw the hard little point of his liṅgam pressing up through his vasana, she leaned over, under the pretext of picking a flower, so that her breasts pressed against his thigh. This movement, known as the piercing embrace and traditionally reserved for a man and woman who had caught each other's eye but had not yet even spoken to each other, used in this context, between old friends who knew that they were about to taste kāma together, took on a thrilling coyness. He took hold of her breasts and, with a sigh of pleasure, pulled his fingernails teasingly along their soft round geometry until he reached her nipples, which he pinched and caressed until they grew dark and stiff.

Sutanukā's breath caught in her throat. She made the soft, moaning cry of the green pigeon, appropriate to a person whose lover has caused her pain, thus implying that even his gentlest touch cut her to the soul.

Without a word, he rose and led her to his bedchamber. There, beside the bed, he embraced her. She drew her fingers through his hair, pressing his face into her stomach. His childlike size gave her, who had never been a mother, a strangely maternal sensation, a sudden insight as to why so many women enjoyed kāma with him.

She drew back from him and removed her girdle and vasana. Having tweezed all her body hair just that morning, her nether lips, those surrounding the yoni, were large and dark, textured like a cock's wattle, completely exposed.

Standing there naked except for her jewelry, striking the casual saucy stance of a statue, the three bends of the body at head, hip, and shoulder, she said, "What would you do to me, dwarf?"

"Had I eternity, I would practice every way of kissing you, of biting you and stroking you and leaving the marks of my nails upon your body, until I were an expert at the art of pleasing Sutanukā and could write a learned treatise on the subject, like that of Vatsyayana. But since I have only this afternoon, I would begin with that sort of congress to which all else leads."

"But . . ." Sutanukā hesitated; as well as she knew the dwarf, she felt on shaky ground. "But would that not be precisely the sort of union we wish to avoid? After all, I am, in the depth of my yoni, what men call the mare. And you. . . ."

The dwarf laughed. "Feel no discomfort, dear Sutanukā. I have come to terms with what I am long ago." He unfastened his silk belt and pulled off his vasana. His liṅgam, while stiff and engorged, was no bigger than her smallest finger. "But what man cannot do alone, he achieves through artifice and ingenuity—is this not so? Consider how the architects of Pāṭaliputra, using earthwork ramps and rollers, erected the great stone columns upon which rests the roof of this very palace."

"Oh, dwarf," she said, grateful for all the embarrassment he was sparing her, "you are very droll."

He disappeared into an adjacent chamber and reemerged a moment later wearing a device quite unlike any she had ever seen. It was of the class of objects known as apadravyas, things that are put on or around the liṅgam to supplement its thickness or length, but of such formidable size and realism that it might have been a real one, on loan from a camel. It had been carved, she imagined, from some smooth substance, like wood or horn, painted to resemble the dwarf's own flesh, and secured to his groin with a variety of buffalo hide straps and belts. It was, he informed her, a new version of a time-tested device, prepared especially for their meeting that afternoon, sized according to the information he had been able to gather about her yoni. The engorged bottom of his own small organ extended beneath the bottom of the wooden liṅgam in such a way that it could benefit from friction with the yoni, and thus bring him satisfaction also, though of a limited sort.

"And so," the dwarf said, with a self-mocking smile, "we triumph over our physical shortcomings."

"When you turn," she said, half in jest, "be careful of knocking things over, like a careless monkey with his tail or an elephant with his trunk."

Wary of the device, she abandoned the exotic poses that were second nature to her—the mixture of sesame seed and rice, the mixture of milk and water, the splitting of the bamboo, the fixing of the nail, the lotuslike position, and the crab position—and lay like a virgin on her back, her legs spread apart. The dwarf climbed up beside her, but at the last moment—and wasn't this what men usually did when about to possess that which they had coveted most for years?—at that last moment, miscalculating the size of the new liṅgam, he caught the tip of it beneath Sutanukā's hip and twisted it halfway around.

Groaning with pain, he rolled onto his back and struggled to detach the straps. Finally he ripped away the device and held his hands over his own little liṅgam, which had been badly bent and was turning an ugly purple at the base and beginning to swell. Sutanukā helped apply cold compresses to it. Then she put him to bed and read him some stories from the *Jātakas*. This seemed, for both of them, the most gratifying moment of all. When he fell asleep, she kissed him on the forehead and left without a sound.

4

The Vaidya's plan was, for the moment, to walk along the Ganges, stopping at the shrines and temples that had been erected along its hallowed banks until his karma manifested itself and the design of his future became apparent.

But as he crossed the moat, leaving the walled city of Pāṭaliputra behind him, he was suddenly overcome with a desire to see the place where his disciple had died. So he turned away from the holiest of rivers, the barges that drifted along its muddy currents, and the verdant rice paddies that lined its banks, and turned instead toward the arid land beyond the hills, where a plume of black smoke led like an arrow to the burning grounds.

In time he came to the infernal plain, with its piles of bones and blackened timbers. Distant bonfires filled the sky with smoke, so the sun appeared dull red, as though even Savitar, the sun god, was dismayed by what he saw.

A little girl no more than eight years old, her breasts having yet to bud, wandered from one bone pile to the next like a sleepwalker or one in a trance. Her hands and face were smudged with ashes, and her necklaces were in disarray. At first the Vaidya thought that she was a caṇḍāla child who had strayed from her hut and gotten lost, but when he came closer he saw the quality of her vasana and her bangles, and the light shade of her skin. She had enormous unblinking black eyes and a little curl of a nose. He noted, with professional interest, her bowed legs, something he saw occasionally among children. If caught early on, it could be treated by feeding the child ground bone, but it was too late for this little girl; her legs would be bowed for the rest of her life.

Although she was alone, she showed no fear at his approach.

"What are you doing here?" he said, squatting beside her. "This is no place for little girls."

"I've come to give my brother his last sacrament." Her voice was solemn, her brow furrowed in concentration. "The king burned him like a criminal, but he didn't do anything wrong."

"Are you Sarasvatī?" the Vaidya asked.

"Yes." Her eyes grew wide. "How do you know?"

"Virata was a friend of mine. He always spoke of his little sister, and how he loved her. Once he showed me a clay statue you made for him."

"I know. You are the Vaidya. But why are you carrying a staff and a begging bowl?"

"Because now I am no longer the Vaidya. Do your parents know you are here?"

Of course they didn't. Who would let their child come to such a place alone?

The little girl was slow to answer. "They forbade it. They said if I was caught, I would be beaten. He who is burned alive is not allowed the sacrament."

"I understand," the Vaidya said.

"Will you help me anyway?"

"Yes," the Vaidya said.

"What makes it so difficult is that all the bones look alike. I cannot tell which are those of my brother."

"I think it does not matter. He is not in the bones, any more than Viṣṇu resides within one of his wooden idols. The bones, like the idols, are only a trick to make it easier for us, with our simple minds, to worship that which we cannot see."

"Then is there no point—"

"Of course there is. He is here and he will hear us. Come now."

He took her hand in his, and they crossed the burial ground together, looking for a suitable pile of bones. Scrawny yellow jackals, alerted by the slap of his sandals against the hard ground, turned and bared their teeth, then fled. Ungainly vultures took to the air with a frenzy of flapping wings and circled overhead, waiting for them to pass so they might return to the business of stripping flesh.

They chose a pile of bones that seemed more recent than the rest. The skull was faced down so they would be spared staring into the empty eye sockets, those black pits that speak so eloquently of mortality.

"We have no fire," the little girl said sadly.

"It's all right. The fire has already burned."

"No ghee, or rice, or wood chips."

"The gods will forgive us."

"And I do not know any mantras."

"Just speak the mantra that is in your heart."

She lowered her head for a moment, deep in thought. Then she said, "Good-bye, my brother. I know you are innocent and the gods know it too. I hope I die soon so that we may be brother and sister again at a time when kings are less cruel."

"You mustn't wish that," the Vaidya said. "You are young yet and have many wonderful things to live for."

"That is the thought that is in my heart. I cannot lie at a time like this."

The Vaidya didn't know what to say. He had never met so somber and straightforward a little girl.

Together they circled the pile of bones three times in the inauspicious counterclockwise direction, as was proper during a funeral.

Then the Vaidya whispered,

"Let your eyes go to the sun,
Your life to the wind,
May the virtuous acts of your days lead you to
heaven and rebirth in this world,
Or in the water if you are happy there,
Or in the grass where all things come to rest."

"Thank you," she said, prostrating herself before him and kissing his toes. Then she rose.

"I should take you home," the Vaidya said. "A little girl must not travel alone at night, or during the day for that matter."

"I came here alone, I will go home alone. You are so big and clumsy; if you came too, you'd wake my father and he'd beat me for disobeying him."

"If I were your father," the Vaidya said, "I should be angry at you—but also very proud."

"Good-bye," she said, gazing at him with those great, sad eyes, and suddenly she was running across the burning ground, quick as her crooked little legs could carry her.

"Wait!" he shouted, and started after her, but a stitch in his side bent him double. He was not used to running, or even walking for that matter. He dropped to his knees, trying to catch his breath, waiting for the pain to go away.

As he knelt there, listening to the blood ringing in his ears, the night world spinning around him, his attention gradually focused on the bonfires that blazed in the distance. Straining his eyes, he could see, through the black-particled curtains of smoke, the silhouettes of men dragging bodies from the mud huts at the edge of the plain and piling them upon the fires. He heard, over the crackling of flames, women wailing with grief, a sound that raised the little hairs on his neck.

He clambered to his feet and approached the fires, a dreadful suspicion growing within him. When he was near enough that the soot fell upon his hair and face, and left its gray trails across his vasana, a caṇḍāla lad, black-skinned and ragged, blocked his way with a bamboo cane. One look at his monstrously pockmarked face, and the Vaidya's worst fears were confirmed.

Smallpox.

He had been wondering what he would do, having renounced his profession, when confronted with people who needed his skills. Now he knew, and knew also that there had never been any question, nor would there ever be. If people were sick, he would help them. He could no more renounce that part of him than he could renounce his heart.

He explained to the boy that he was a vaidya, and that Sitella, the goddess of smallpox, had visited him when he was a child, cursing him with scars, blessing him with immunity. Like a fickle mistress, he explained, she visits a man only once in his life. If she chooses that he will live, she never bothers him again.

He entered hut after hut, each one as hot and airless as an oven and filled with the fetid odor that came of breaking pustules. The dung floors were so crowded with victims that he had to step carefully between them. With their black cracked skin they were like logs piled for a fire: children and old men, young men at their prime and women whose worn breasts bore testament to any number of children, all laid low by the same enemy. Those who had just felt Sitella's touch lay sweaty and shaking, thirsty and feverish, their pulses racing, pinpoint pustules rising on their scalps; those whom she had lain with longer were delirious, their faces creviced and cratered like the face of the moon. The pustules had left some blind and others deaf; still others they had slowly suffocated by swelling within their throats. The fortunate few who could still walk had more than they could do to drag away the bodies of those who could not.

The Vaidya remained with them for three days. His first task was to segregate the sick from the others, confining them to "hospital" huts, where holes had been knocked through the mud walls to allow the air to circulate. Those who showed no sign of infection were sent to the opposite corner of the settlement, while the few who had survived the pox were designated as his assistants. Under his tutelage, they moved from patient to patient doing what little they could, making sure, for example, that the light did not harm their eyes, feeding them dal and milk, sponging their flaming skin with wet compresses and then rubbing it with ghee after the pustules had broken and dried in order to soften it and speed the healing.

When he asked the survivors to send their fleetest runner to an herbalist in the city for healing plants, and they complained that they hadn't a paṇa left to pay for them, he offered his staff and begging bowl to trade for turmeric, laudanum, and a decoction of hemp. He was going to give them his sandals, too, but the sight of this small funny-looking monk offering up his last few possessions to help those who were treated by the rest of society as dogs, or worse, moved them to extraordinary acts. One after another, they recalled family treasures hidden over roof beams or buried under doorsteps, wealth in the form of jewelry mostly, that had been passed from generation to generation as a safeguard against just such an emergency. Thus when one man behaves extraordinarily does he bring out the finest nature in others too, sometimes changing the course of human events.

He showed them how to boil the turmeric and use it in a

compress to relieve inflammation, and he showed them the way to alleviate delirium with laudanum and suppress pain with hemp. After three days, having revealed his meager store of secrets, he decided his work was done and prepared to take his leave. Overwhelmed with gratitude, the caṇḍālas tried to press money into his hand, and food, and their poor bangles of iron and glass. He refused all but a few mouthfuls of rice, and those he took more to please them than himself, for he had little appetite.

Sutanukā stood on the doorstep of the Vaidya's house, gathering her courage to knock. The cobbled street was noisy with children playing tag, the rumble of oxcarts, and the occasional clatter of a horse's hooves. The noon sun glittered off golden cages of twittering songbirds hung in the balconies and gables of the homes along the street. She had been standing there some time already and was worried that if she delayed much longer, the sun would wilt the flower garlands she had arranged so carefully in her hair and round her neck to please him.

Meanwhile, she rubbed repeatedly at her eye. It was interesting to note that, while during those times when a woman didn't want a cinder in her eye, it was almost impossible to get rid of it, on the rare occasion when she *did*, the eye steadfastly refused to cooperate. Every time she had tried to insert one of several she had gathered from the hearth of the palace kitchen, the eyelid had closed against her will or a wave of tears had washed it away. Finally, by pinching the eyelid between thumb and index finger—thus immobilizing it—and tilting the head back so that the tears formed a stable lake, she managed to get one to stay. The effect, when she regarded herself in a looking glass of polished metal, was gratifying: the eye was red and watery, and burned from the irritation.

Now she gathered her courage and rapped on the door. In a moment Dūṣaka the servant opened it. He began to bow deeply; then, recognizing her, his jaw dropped in surprise and he simply stood there, as though turned to stone by an enchantment.

"I would see the Vaidya" she said briskly. "I have something caught in my eye."

"Y-y-yes," he stammered, "of course, come this way."

She followed him down the corridor and past a tapestry, into one of the small chambers that was used for consultations.

"If you'll just wait a moment," he said, "the vaidya will see you," and backed out of the room, his mouth still gaping.

She shook her head and laughed to herself at his behavior. The simple fact of being back in the Vaidya's home filled her with pleasure. She knelt on the couch, straightening her girdle, adjusting the drape of her vasana, pinching her nipples so they appeared dark and large. Then she tilted her head in a way that she knew made her most beautiful and lowered her eyes demurely toward the floor. In a moment she heard the creak of buffalo-skin sandals enter the room. She smiled in a way both coy and seductive and raised her head, saying, "Vaidya, I hope you do not mind my coming—" But then she stopped short, for the man who had entered was not the Vaidya, but Kaṅka, his assistant.

"I would see the Vaidya," she snapped. "I have little time and many obligations."

"I am the vaidya," Kaṅka said gently.

"Do you take me for a fool? I was there at the palace when you assisted him. You are one of his disciples, nothing more."

"My lady, please do not excite yourself. True, I was an assistant, but now I am vaidya. My guru bestowed the title upon me before he departed."

"What?"

"He is gone, my lady."

"But, where could he go?" she said helplessly, as though the world beyond the doorstep of the Vaidya's house was beneath contempt.

"He has entered the fourth stage of life. He has become sannyāsin."

"No!" she cried, rising. Her voice grew shrill. "It is not true! It is a lie he had you tell me because he does not wish to see me."

"Were it a lie," Kaṅka said sadly, "I should be the happiest man on earth. I miss him more than an orphan misses father and mother combined."

"If you are lying, boy, I will have you impaled and left for the carrion to peck at your eyes!" She was snarling now, like a tiger.

"I do believe you, my lady," Kaṅka replied in measured tones, "for I have seen the justice of your king. He is skilled at ordering innocent men burned at the stake."

"I will not tolerate such insolence from one of your class!"

"My class? Inspect the holy thread, my lady." He hooked his thumb beneath the thread that crossed his chest, so she might examine it more closely. "As you see, it is braided of cotton. I've chosen to worship Buddha out of deference to my teacher, but I am born a brāhmaṇa. I tell you this only to prove I do not lie, for as you well know, those of my class value truth above all else."

She took a few deep breaths. "Forgive me. Sometimes the truth is difficult to accept. For those of any class."

"I understand."

"So he is sannyāsin." Her voice grew indifferent so suddenly that not even the simplest of fools would have been deceived. "Where did he go? To a thatched hut in the forest? To a cave in the high Himalayas?"

"The last I saw of him," Kaṅka replied, "he was leaving the house with nothing but a begging bowl, a staff, and a book of the sutras."

"I see. And when he reached the street, which way did he turn?"

"My lady, a man becomes sannyāsin because he wishes to leave the world behind and dedicate his thoughts entirely to solving the riddle of his existence on earth. If I may speak frankly, you are a woman of pleasure. Even if you managed to find him, he would have no use for you. You would only slow his progress upon the path he has already chosen."

"If he can renounce being a vaidya, then I can cease being a gaṇikā. Did not Sita accompany Rāma to the forest when he retreated from the world? Does not Parvatī keep eternal company to Śiva during his meditation?"

Kaṅka countered, "When Nanda asked what to do about women, the Buddha replied, 'Do not see them!' And if seeing them could not be avoided, the disciple asked? 'Do not speak to them!' And if one had to speak to them? 'Then keep alert, O Nanda!' Such is the Buddha's opinion regarding women, my lady."

"What did the Buddha know of women?" she muttered to herself, rising from the wooden couch. "I go to the palace. If by chance the Vaidya should change his mind and return here, swear that you will tell him of my visit. Do you swear it?"

"I have known the Vaidya many years. He is not one who would take the vows of sannyāsin and then change his mind."

"Just swear it. Swear it on the eyes of your beloved woman-hating Buddha."

"Yes, yes. I shall tell him. I swear it."

She started for the door.

"My lady, before you go, I should look at your eye."

"My eye?" In her grief she had forgotten it completely.

"It is badly inflamed. You would not want to lose your sight in it?"

"I hardly care," she said and left.

She was halfway down the street when she heard the patter of bare feet on the cobblestones. She turned and saw Dūṣaka running after her, waving his hand. She stopped and waited, striving for a look of studied impatience despite the tears streaming from her swollen eye. Being śūdra herself, she knew how to deal with śūdras.

"I beg your forgiveness, my lady," he said, when he caught up with her, "but I could not help overhearing your conversation with my master. I believe I can help you find the old Vaidya. His whereabouts are not such a mystery as my master would have you believe."

She betrayed no evidence of her excitement. "Well? Speak then, and be quick! I am expected back at the palace."

"The problem, my lady, is that my talents are wasted at my present work. I am a man of wit, ambition, and intelligence. If not for the accident of my lowly birth, who knows what heights I might have gained?"

"Get to it!"

"I only say that my skills would be put to much better use in some function at the palace. I might even be fit for a position as a royal porter."

"Tell me where I can find the Vaidya," she said, her teeth clenched, her patience strained, "and I will see if there is a place for you at the palace."

"What kind of a place? I would not be a lowly servant again."

"Śūdra, you try my patience!" She thought for a moment. "The king did mention he would have a new barber, for the old one lost his hand in a duel and cannot hold the razor."

"Royal barber?" Dūṣaka smiled. "That is a good position. I could do that well. My master was always pleased with the way I shaved him. Though he was so careless about his appearance. I used to say to him—"

"Enough of this prattle, whore's son! Tell me what I wish to know—and tell me now!"

"Of course, my lady," he said, hurrying to appease her anger. "You see, every day I go to the bazaar to buy herbs from Kraṭu the herbalist—what herbs we cannot grow in our own little garden. Well, yesterday I visited his stall, and there was a caṇḍāla, one of the tribe that lives by the burial ground. He had with him a list, scratched on a palm leaf, of medicinal herbs. He had been sent to purchase them by a monk—a vaidya—who was staying in their village, treating a smallpox that was among them."

"Smallpox?" she whispered. Her eyes widened with terror, and she edged away from him without even realizing what she was doing.

"Fear not, my lady. The messenger bore the scars of a survivor. He could not infect me."

"How do you know this vaidya is your old master?"

"Well, the caṇḍāla and Kratu were having trouble deciphering the handwriting. So they gave it to me, knowing my skill with such things. And it was the Vaidya's, without question. All vaidyas write thus, like the marks a peacock leaves when crossing clean tile with muddy feet, but the old Vaidya's was particularly messy, as though the peacock had gone and come back again."

"Impertinent servant! But you are certain it was he?"

"I would stake my reputation on it." And he called after her, as she hurried away, "Don't forget your promise! I am a first-rate barber, a master with the razor . . ."

The bonfires shed a ghastly flickering light across the burning grounds. The piles of bones shone red from the light of it, and the stars and the moon were obscured by black particles.

A caṇḍāla boy squatted before the circle of huts, half attending the fires, half asleep. Although the hissing, crackling sounds of burning corpses masked the intruder's approach, something awoke him, and he grabbed the bamboo staff on the ground and sprang to a defensive stance.

"Who is it?" he cried in a Prakrit so coarse and grating, so ill-accented and awkward in rhythm that it seemed to the intruder almost like a foreign tongue.

"A visitor," she replied, stepping foward.

"Come no closer! Sitella visits us, and until she leaves, no other person may pass."

The fire flared, illuminating the boy's face, a monstrous mask, torn and pitted as though a demon had drawn its talons through the flesh. His eyes, watery from the heat and ashes, were old, tired as those of a warrior who has seen too much death.

She reached into a secret pocket of her vasana and brought forth a handful of gold coins. "I come for the body of a newborn child."

The firelight glittered off the coins, but the boy showed no interest. "Are you some sorceress who would use an infant's blood in her potions?"

"Yes," she said, "that is right."

"I guessed that beauty such as yours must be magic. Have you a potion to protect yourself from the pox, sorcerer woman? Is that why you show no fear?"

"I have fear," she said. "But I have needs and duties too."

She thought of the Vaidya, and her heart filled with worry about what he would think when he saw her bare of jewels, her glossy hair dull with soot, her body covered with ashes, like an ascetic.

Hope glimmered in the young man's eyes. "Have you a potion that will clear my face of these scars? I once loved the daughter of a cowherd. We were to be married, but Sitella visited me first. When I saw my beloved again, she screamed and hid beneath the bed, and would not come out until I swore never to return. Make me a potion to cure my scars and I shall let you pass."

"No potion of mine will change your karma. But I will give you a word of advice, for I know the workings of the human heart better than an archer does his bow. Return to your beloved and spend time with her, under any excuse. Let her come to know you all over again. When a woman knows a man well enough, then she forgets his outer face and sees only what is within. Do you understand?"

Perhaps he did and perhaps not. Still he let her pass. She moved from hut to hut, peering into the darkness, surveying the rows of writhing figures within, searching, or so she told herself, for the newly dead infant she had promised the king. Although she had walked the battlefield in the wake of war, wading between dismembered heads and limbs and leaving her footprints in blood instead of red lac, she had never seen anything as dismaying as this. The stench made her want to retch; the chorus of moans seemed a detail from her worst nightmare. At every instant she fought her need to turn and flee.

In time she came to a hut where a young mother knelt, holding a limp infant in her lap, fastening a necklace of pebbles and glass around his neck.

"Your baby . . . ?" Sutanukā said, bending down so she could enter.

"Dead of the pox," the mother replied. "He caught it while he was in my belly and lived only two days." She looked up and, noticing in the ambient light of the bonfire that her visitor was an outsider, a member of the upper classes, touched at her hair as though to make herself presentable. She was no more than sixteen autumns, and her former comeliness could be deciphered like a code beneath her scars. "You are an upper-class woman, are you not? A kṣatriya or a brāhmaṇa? It is evident from your bearing. Tell me honestly, don't you think he is a beautiful child?"

She held up the infant. "See how well-shaped his head is, and the fineness of his hair? His skin is smooth and light as a brāhmaṇa's. You can barely see the pox. And look at his little hands! How perfect the fingers, the joints, the nails. The soles of his feet are as soft as down. Here, touch them. See how soft they are."

Sutanukā tried to oblige but her hand seemed repelled by an invisible force.

"Have you any children?" the mother asked.

Sutanukā shook her head. "I am a gaṇikā. I must not have children."

When she had first begun to menstruate, Saṃjña had shown her how to fashion a cap from beeswax and fit it over that part, deep inside the yoni, from which a woman's semen drips, thus preventing the mixture of doṣas that creates life.

"The Vaidya said I will never have another child. He said that the pox has ruined my—"

"The Vaidya? A little man with a round nose, and a belly, and a fringe of hair?"

"Yes."

"Where is he? Where will I find him?"

"He said that the pox has ruined my insides. The bag-in-which-the-baby-swims can no longer hold children. I will never bear another—"

"Tell me where he is!" Sutanukā snapped.

"Who?"

"The Vaidya! The Vaidya, the Vaidya, the Vaidya!"

"He left days ago. I know not where he went."

All the life went out of Sutanukā. She seemed to collapse in upon herself, as though she had been struck a blow.

The mother returned to the decorating of her baby.

"You must sell me your child," Sutanukā said, after a few moments.

"What?"

"Sell me your child. It is bad to go on playing with the body, as though it were a doll. Here, I will give you all this gold." She held out a handful of coins.

"What will you do with him?"

"I cannot tell you. But I promise he will be treated with the greatest respect. He will be given the funerary rites of a prince."

"The Vaidya said no one must touch a poxed body after its death."

"I tell you it is all right. No one shall touch it. He will be wrapped in a shroud and burned. The Purohita himself will say a blessing over him."

"I do not understand."

"You do not have to understand. Simply do as I say."

"All right. But one copper paṇa will suffice. After all, we are caṇḍāla. That is all we are worth."

Sutanukā forced the gold on her. Then she took the baby, wrapping it in a silk she had brought for that purpose, and left the hut without daring to look back. She carried the dead baby as far as the edge of the burning grounds, then put it down so that she might retch freely with what little was in her stomach.

* * *

The death of Candra Gupta II, the infant prince, was proclaimed a time of mourning for the entire city. The wild call of the conch shells sounded from the parapets of the timber walls that surrounded the city, and the banging of the drums was like the beat of some monstrous heart buried beneath the cobblestones.

As a cobra moves through the grass, so the procession wound through the streets of Pāṭaliputra: at the head of it, three kings of neighboring states who had allied themselves by marriage, each carrying a firepot; then the four eldest members of the king's family supporting the bier on which the infant's body lay, rubbed shiny with ghee and covered with garlands; then the king's eldest uncle leading ten sacrificial cows by ropes attached to their right forelegs; then all the other members of the Gupta family, marching in order of age, eldest first, youngest last. Following at a distance came a thousand female mourners hired especially for the occasion, sobbing piteously, beating their breasts, and tearing at their disheveled hair, and behind them a crowd of townspeople, perhaps more interested in joining in the spectacle than in the grief.

One hundred brāhmaṇas waited at a site by the Ganges. Under the Purohita's supervision, they had erected a pyre of freshly felled timber as tall as a two-story building, with a roof of foliage to protect the body from the blazing sun.

The dead infant was placed atop the pyre, on an antelope skin surrounded by kusa grass. Around him were arranged his birth presents—the golden cradle, the ivory palace, the chest of silks, the bamboo carriage shaped like a warrior's chariot. Of the three firepots, the first was placed at the northwest corner of the pyre, the second at the southwest corner, the third at the southeast.

Since the days of the Buddhist emperor Aśoka, whose love of animals and disdain for violence changed the face of the country, the ritual slaughter of cows had been outlawed, and the presence at funerals of those venerated animals, whose milk and dung and urine were so valued by the inhabitants of the Land of the Sons of Bharata, had become wholly symbolic. Recently, however, in an attempt to fight off the moral and spiritual decline of the Age of Kali, the Purohita had returned to the brutal form of cow sacrifice described in the Vedas. Using a specially consecrated knife, he slaughtered one cow after another, ten in all, and cut up the carcasses, arranging the kidneys, hearts, livers, and stomachs around the pyre as prescribed in the ancient books.

Having arrived at the auspicious moment, he then seized a torch and moved from one firepot to the next, igniting them. The funeral procession, holding its breath almost as one, waited to see which of the three fires reached the corpse first. If it were the fire in the southeast, then the ātman had been borne off upon the smoke and would experience liberation; if it were the fire in the northwest, then it would dwell in the World of the Fathers with the gods; but if the fire in the southwest reached it first, that was the saddest of all, for then it was destined to be reincarnated as a man.

The fire to the southwest reached it first.

In time the fires combined in a great tongue that leaped into the clear blue sky, consuming the baby and his precious things almost at once.

For hours the procession stood without moving, listening to the Purohita chant mantras, and reflected on the puzzling behavior of the gods, who would send a cakravartin to aid mankind and snatch him away before he had been given an opportunity to act.

At sunset, the king and those closest to him circled the mountain of cold ashes three times in the inauspicious counterclockwise direction. Then they bathed in the Ganges and returned to the city, this time in a procession led by the youngest, never looking back.

When they reached the palace, the king and his party, ritually impure from having participated in the procession, made auspicious mudras with their hands, and recited that most auspicious of prayers, the gayatri, rubbed the smooth little stones called salagramas for luck, and tasted ghee, which was also lucky, being the product of a cow.

For ten days afterward the infant's ātman existed as a miserable ghost, unable to pass on to the next stage of its existence, and in its confusion and anger, liable to harm its surviving relatives. During this dangerous time all work in the palace ceased. The king and his party ate saltless foods, and slept on the ground, and denied themselves kāma. Libations of water were poured for the infant, along with offerings of rice balls and vessels of milk. A golden tub was filled with milk and water, and left in the prettiest part of the garden for the spirit to bathe in.

On the third day, the child's bones were thrown into the Ganges. On the eleventh day the ātman acquired its subtle body and could at last continue on its journey through the afterlife. Those who had participated in the funeral ceased to be impure. Life at the palace returned to its normal course.

Coincidentally, at the same time the comet that had been blamed for so much trouble disappeared from the skies of Pāṭaliputra.

Thus, the funeral rites of the orthodox Viṣṇuite had been followed to the letter, and everybody in the city had been convinced that a second heir to the throne, a cakravartin perhaps, had been born on this earth and a few short weeks later had departed it.

Everybody, that is, except Prince Rāma, who, noticing the absence of tears in his father's eyes, had grown ever so slightly suspicious.

Part II

GOVINDA THE SILK MERCHANT

5

Be there one passion that afflicts all men regardless of class or caste, it is neither the desire to aid one's fellow man, nor the thirsting for power, nor the compulsion to make great art, commendable as that desire may be, but rather the urge to shop for fine and pretty things. Thus, while all roads in Pāṭaliputra led to the palace, all life seemed to flow in the opposite direction, toward the bazaar.

In a great open square, beneath canopies of bright cloth, farmers stood by stands heaped with radishes, potatoes, blood-dark beets, wormwood, mangoes, cucumbers, eggplants as purple as the head of a lover's liṅgam, kushmandas and pumpkins, suranas, garlic cloves whose stems had been braided into ropes, onions with skin like gold leaf. Sacks of rice, barley and sorghum, lentils and chick-peas, rice flower and wheat were piled in bullock carts, and big clay urns of sesame oil and mustard oil, of ghee and whey, sealed with wax and stamped by the tax collector, stood stacked in pyramids. There were rows of barrels filled with toddy from the south and grape wine from the northeast, as well as rice beer and liquor distilled from cane syrup. Sometimes at noon, when the heat grew too great, one of the barrels would explode, and the beggars would knock one another aside, scrambling to scoop some of the warm liquid out of the gutter in their cupped hands and drink of it. And then there were butcher stalls, shunned by all who called themselves twice-born, where men of the lowest class slaughtered cows and goats and pigs, drained off their blood, hung the sides of meat on iron hooks, and slapped them to shake off the flies. Wives and servants moved among the wagons, bargaining down the farmers by finding a rotten spot on a mango or a bruised eggplant. The farmers complained, in turn, about bad weather and vengeful gods, reminisced about how big fruit had been in Vedic times, before this evil Kali Age, and reluctantly lowered their prices.

On the streets leading off the square the artisans had their homes, and in front of their homes, the stalls where they sold their goods. There were perfumers grinding sandalwood for incense, jewelers polishing stones with rice husks, garland makers threading fresh flowers with bells and colored beads, idol makers chiseling images of the gods, potters guiding the clay beneath their wet fingers, and candy makers with children lingering underfoot, waiting to be tossed samples less perfect than the rest.

And on a certain spring day, not long after the rains had passed and the cycle of life was beginning all over again in such an emphatic manner that even the most skeptical materialist believed rebirth a possibility, an unusual party could be seen making its way past the crowded stalls: a little girl with a perpetual pout, affecting the airs of a grown-up though she was no more than ten years old, and dressed in such lavish ornaments that she could only be a princess; accompanied by her grandmother, an imperious woman with a shock of gray hair on one side of her head and with eyes ringed like an owl's; and followed by four handmaidens, their arms loaded with packages. From the wondering way they took in their surroundings and stopped at every stall to sample a pepper fried in batter or admire a jeweled anklet, one assumed they were strangers to the wondrous bazaar of Pāṭaliputra, the largest, most splendid in the land.

A tall man balancing bamboo cages filled with ferretlike creatures on his head wove his way toward them, chanting, "Mongooses for sale! Mongooses for sale! Kill rats and snakes and mice faster than a flash from Śiva's eye! Yet will not harm children, even newborn babes!"

"Oh, Grandmother," the little girl said, "buy me a mongoose! I'll take care of it, I promise."

"What use have we for a mongoose? There are no rats or snakes at the palace."

"But these are so pretty! They're red, almost."

"Victory to you, sir," the grandmother said to the man carrying the mongooses. "Can you guide us to the stall of Govinda the silk trader?"

"Down this street to the end, then a little ways to the right.

But you'd be making a mistake, passing up my mongooses. They're on sale today." He winked at the little girl.

"No, thank you," the grandmother said curtly, and handed him a copper kākinī for his trouble.

The rest of the party started forward, but the little girl folded her arms across her chest and refused to move from her spot. "I want a mongoose," she said resolutely.

"Little one, be reasonable!"

"I want a mongoose and I shall not move until I get one."

"But your handmaidens are so loaded down with packages they can barely walk. And, who knows? Prince Rāma may not like mongooses. You must think of the wants and needs of your husband-to-be."

"I happen to know," the mongoose seller offered, "that Prince Rāma has been talking about buying a mongoose for months. You'd be doing him a favor if you brought one as a gift. Of course, you could always return it."

"Oh, please, Grandmother?"

The grandmother sighed and purchased the mongoose, and they continued on their way.

When they were out of earshot, the mongoose vendor said to himself, "So she is to wed the Little Camel. May the gods help her."

They had gone only halfway up the street when the little girl grabbed her grandmother's hand and gave it a mighty tug. "Grandmother, it's a magician!"

"If we keep stopping like this," the grandmother said, "we will never get there."

"Oh, please, Grandmother! Can't we watch just for a moment?"

The grandmother saw the size of the crowd that had formed around the elderly magician and his young assistant; she recognized the pile of hemp rope, the sword, the wicker basket, all the props of the infamous rope trick. While she had never witnessed it herself—her life had been a sheltered one—she had heard many stories about the screams, the dismembered limbs, the bloody stumps.

"The rope trick is not for little girls. It will give you nightmares."

"Oh, please, Grandmother! I won't be scared, I promise."

"Absolutely not."

"I won't eat ever again. I'll fast to the death. I'll stop breathing. I'll—"

"I no longer have the strength to fight. Watch if you like, but do not run to me in the middle of the night with your bad dreams."

"Oh, thank you, Grandmother, thank you. I won't ask for anything ever again."

They joined the crowd, the little girl pushing her way to the front for a better view.

The magician made a brief benediction to the gods. Then, having inserted the end of a rope through a wooden nut, he hurled it toward the sky. It ascended with such speed that it made a whizzing sound, higher and higher, ever uncoiling, until it vanished into the mist. The crowd gasped to see gravity defeated, the rope hanging before them so steadily that it might have been tied to a celestial tree limb. The magician ordered his assistant to climb it, and the boy obliged, scampering up the rope like a monkey until he, too, disappeared. Moments passed and when he did not return, the magician grew angry. He gripped a sword between his teeth and, uttering oaths, climbed the rope, too. Soon shouting could be heard from overhead, reprimands and excuses. The bloody, severed limbs of the assistant rained down from above, as real as starlings slashed from flight by a hawk. Finally, the magician slid down the rope, holding the boy's severed head by the hair.

The little girl said, "Ick."

Her grandmother gasped.

A young woman used the opportunity to swoon into the arms of her lover, who, touched by woman's frailty, kissed her brow.

Although one of the royal guard was standing in the crowd, he made no motion to interfere, for the rope trick was, after all, only a trick.

The magician threw all the parts of his assistant into the wicker basket, shut the lid, chanted a prayer to Śiva and a number of Oṃ śāntis. Then the lid flew open and the assistant jumped out, whole again, and ran about the circle, collecting praise from the crowd and coins in his turban.

Snake charmers, palm readers, astrologers, letter writers who turned the thoughts of amorous illiterates into neat nāgarī script, magicians and sleight-of-hand artists, potion makers who would influence the minds of one's enemies—they passed them all and stopped before each, so that it was nearly noon before they finally reached the stall of Govinda the silk merchant.

The stall was deeper than it was wide, with a floor of tamped cow dung and wooden shelves along the back, sagging under the weight of the goods. There were bolts of coarse fabric woven from silk "yarn" spun from the loose woolly silk that covers the outside of the cocoon, and bolts of fabric whose surface was as smooth as polished tile, woven from the finest thread, the stuff of the cocoon itself. Smaller pieces of silk, folded into squares, were stacked on other shelves, and silk cords and braided belts hung from hooks. A red and white silk canopy stretched overhead, shielding two boys from the searing noon sun. The red and white stripes slid across them as they moved from the front of the stall to the shelves and back again.

One boy was stocky and just into his teens; the other was a few years younger, slim and graceful. They were everywhere at once, organizing the wares, sweeping the floor, keeping a tally of the day's business on a banana leaf. An ivory cage containing a bright yellow parakeet hung from a crosspiece, and the bird sang his delicate three-note song with equal industry.

"I am looking for Govinda the silk merchant," the grandmother announced in a haughty tone.

"This is his stall," said the stocky boy. "I am his real son, Mitra, and this is his adopted son, Dattaka. We help the customers while Father is away."

"We must speak with Govinda himself," she said. "I am Nāsatyādevī, and this," she continued, indicating the little girl, "is my granddaughter Dhruvādevī, of the state of Kaliṅga on the eastern coast, princess of the great and noble tribe of the Śālaṅkāyanas, brave warriors and traders whose ships have traveled to the edge of the earth."

Dhruvādevī received the tribute with her nose in the air, her eyes averted, as if the boys were beneath her notice.

"She comes to Pāṭaliputra," Nāsatyādevī continued, "to wed Prince Rāma Gupta and must have the most splendid silk for her wedding outfit. We have heard tell of a Chinese silk so fine that it has the appearance of liquid gold and so bright in color it seems to glow of its own accord. I believe it is called Golden Fire. Would you have it in your stall or know where we might find some?"

"I've heard about this Golden Fire," Mitra said knowingly. "No one ever has it, but everybody pretends they can get it. They'll take a payment and tell you to come back in a week. And a week later, they and your payment will be a hundred miles away."

Dattaka nodded. "It's a story, like the urn of ghee that never runs dry or the potion that turns lead to gold."

"As for Chinese silk," Mitra went on, "we have it, but I think you do your granddaughter a disservice, particularly on a joyful occasion such as this."

"Oh?" the little girl said.

"It is crude stuff," Dattaka agreed, "fit only to make blankets for camels."

"We have nothing to gain by selling you our native silk," Mitra said. "We make the same profit selling you the Chinese stuff. But we would hate to take the blame if Prince Rāma was displeased with his bride's attire."

"I think," Nāsatyādevī said, "we had better come back when your father is here. Meanwhile, we shall try to find satisfaction at one of the other silk stalls."

"All right," Mitra said, "but let me show you one piece of silk before you go. So you'll know what really good silk looks like." He leaned across the front of the stall so he could lower his voice and still be heard. "Do you know what most of these other silk sellers do? They buy Chinese material, unravel it, and reweave it into our own patterns. The threads become bruised and lose their sheen. Now, the silks from Govinda's stall are all once-woven."

While the boys were occupied getting the bolt down from a high shelf, Dhruvādevī peeked at them.

She could not help but notice how beautiful Dattaka was, long-limbed and lightly muscled, graceful as a deer. A few weeks shy of his eleventh autumn, he was balanced in that fragile moment when one is neither man nor boy but partakes of both. His black hair was curly; his cheekbones were strong, and his eyes bright. His smile—and he smiled often, for he could find the bright side of the worst situation—was winning, and open, and showed off fine white teeth. Nor did Dhruvādevī fail to notice the reddish cast of skin that marked him as a kṣatriya, one of her own class.

The other boy, Mitra, had the coloring of the vaiśya class. He was three years older than his brother, with rounded shoulders, a barrel chest, short legs, earthy tastes, and a love of laughter. He was trying to grow a mustache, but all that would come were a few fine hairs. Having already celebrated his upanayana, he proudly wore the woolen thread of his class across his chest.

The boys spread a bolt of their third finest fabric, a crimson silk bordered in yellow diamonds, across the counter, so that the sunlight caught like a liquid in its folds. Over the years Govinda had taught them to divine precisely the silk their customer would buy, then start with a bolt of material third best to it and in due time present the remaining two as though they had been forgotten and only recalled as the customer was leaving.

The grandmother looked at it and shrugged. "I have seen better."

"Let us go, Grandmother," the little girl said. "I am growing bored."

Suddenly Dattaka recalled a cloth of exceptional quality. They pulled down the bolt and laid it beside the crimson. It was a green as dark and rich as a pine forest, overlaid with an intricate floral design.

Dhruvādevī tried to look away, but it drew her eye as the kadamba blossom does the honeybee. Her grandmother grudgingly admitted that it was one of the nicer silks she had seen.

"The weave is so tight," Mitra pointed out, "that you could carry water in it."

"Suitable for a brāhmaṇa," Nāsatyādevī allowed, "but not for a princess."

"I'm afraid that's all we have to show you at the moment," Mitra said. "We're expecting new cloth in a week or two. You could come back—"

"There's the purple cloth," Dattaka said.

"No," Mitra replied quickly in a low voice, "we couldn't. What would the queen say? If she found out, we would be impaled."

"What cloth is this?" Nāsatyādevī asked with interest.

"Nothing," Mitra said. "My little brother should not have mentioned it."

"We could tell the queen that the shipment was held up," Dattaka suggested. "Perhaps she would take the green cloth instead."

"Dattaka, are you joking? Father would have our heads!"

"Could we just look at it?" Nāsatyādevī asked.

"There's no point, really," Mitra said.

"Oh, please," Dhruvādevī said.

"What's the harm in letting them look at it?" Dattaka asked.

"It makes me nervous," Mitra replied. He looked up and down the street as though the fictitious queen might arrive at any moment. "Oh, all right."

He went to the back of the stall and returned with a bolt of the deepest, purest purple, with threads of real gold and tiny mirrors of polished tin incorporated into the auspicious svastika design along the border. This was the silk he had known they would buy all along. All the rest was the theatrics that accompanied any sort of shopping at the bazaar.

Nāsatyādevī and her granddaughter both gasped when they saw it, their voices so well synchronized that it was almost comic, and for once there was no argument between them.

"We must have it," the older woman said.

"I'm sorry," Mitra said, "you cannot."

"What if we sold them only a few yards?" Dattaka asked his brother. "Wouldn't that be all right? We could tell the queen that the bolt was short."

"We are guests at the palace," Nāsatyādevī said. "If you told us which queen it was, we might speak to her ourselves. . . ."

Both boys objected at once. There could be no sale if either of them ever mentioned this to any of the queens.

They haggled, first over whether the silk could be sold at all, then regarding the amount that could be spared without enraging the fictitious queen to the point of punishment, then regarding the price, then regarding who would sew the silk into the garments (the princess had her own tailors, but the boys insisted that Govinda's tailor was more adept with fine silk), and finally regarding the style of the wedding garments (Grandmother opted for the traditional long vasana and uttarīya, while the princess wanted them in the "Asian" style, quilted pants and jacket).

Nāsatyādevī took a fat purse from a pocket sewn into her vasana, but before she could open it, a street sweeper who had been working in the vicinity since the princess and her grandmother had arrived, threw down his broom of rushes, grabbed the purse from her hand, and fled into the confusion of the crowd.

Before the others could even react, Dattaka had leapt over the counter that separated the stall from the street and was running after the robber, legs pumping furiously, bare feet slamming the cobbles. He dashed around crowds of shoppers and knocked aside a stately brāhmaṇa. The sweeper looked over his shoulder, saw him coming, and doubled his pace, pausing first to overturn a cart of coconuts to bar the way. The coconut vendor cursed and waved his hands in the air, while his goods bounced down the street with a hollow drumming sound. Dattaka skipped between the coconuts, then clambered across the cart.

The sweeper had disappeared.

Dattaka ran to the corner. Ahead of him, nothing unusual. Likewise, to the right. On the street to the left, a procession of elephants in royal armor, with gilded tusks and headdresses of gold plate. As they lumbered along, their knees struck bells hanging from their breast straps, making a rhythmic clanging. Dattaka looked again and saw the sweeper creeping along in the shelter of the last elephant's rear leg.

Realizing he had been spotted, the sweeper screamed and punched the last elephant in the testicles.

The elephant puffed out his ears and, bellowing in pain, charged, frightening the two animals ahead of him into doing the same. Terrified shoppers ducked into doorways and jumped behind stalls, while those lucky enough to be safe inside buildings, crowded the balconies for a better view. The mahout, thrown to the ground, got back to his feet and ran after them, calling to them by their pet names, trying to calm them. Some quick-witted men managed to roll two bullock carts across the end of the street, blocking the way. The elephants turned back, but by that time the mahout had arranged to block the other end of the street with a flaming torch. With no place to go, the elephants ran back and forth, soon tiring themselves. Seduced by the soft, familiar voice of the mahout, they finally allowed themselves to be taken with as little trouble as if they were cows.

As for the sweeper, he was trapped in the crowd as they pressed against the buildings, as surely as a fly in amber. Dattaka came up behind him, drew the dagger from his own belt and, pressing it to the sweeper's kidneys, suggested they return to the stall together. So imposing was his courage and self-assurance that the thief never questioned the fact that he had been taken by a little boy more than a head shorter than he.

Mitra met his brother halfway and walked back with him, praising his courage, cursing and shoving the sweeper when he walked too slowly.

Reaching the silk stall, Dattaka threw the knave into the dust at Nāsatyādevī's feet. Ordered to turn over the purse by the count of three or suffer a dagger in the heart, the trembling sweeper tore off his turban, within the folds of which he had secreted the bounty, and threw it toward Dattaka. Dattaka handed it to Nāsatyādevī.

Then he turned to Dhruvādevī and prostrated himself at her feet. "How, my lady," he asked, "shall we punish this brigand?"

She blushed at being so honored, but did not look away from him. "Give me his ear," she said in her little voice, "as a keepsake, so I may remember this moment always."

Dattaka grabbed the sweeper by the ear and raised his dagger.

In a trembling voice the sweeper said, "Please, young man, have mercy. I would not have stolen but my children are starving."

"Such is his karma," Nāsatyādevī said self-righteously. "Had he upheld the dharma in previous lives, he would not be in this predicament."

With a single motion so sudden it made the others gasp, Dattaka took a slice with his dagger. But it was only a slice of air. When he raised his hand, rather than the bloody shell of an ear, he held the sweeper's earring, a piece of cheap colored glass in an iron setting.

The sweeper felt the side of his head, ascertained that his ear was still in the location it had occupied that morning, and embraced Dattaka's feet with gratitude.

"Swear to me," Dattaka said, "that you shall never steal again. Swear it on the eyes of Brahmā, and Viṣṇu, and Śiva, and whatever other gods you may hold dear."

"Oh, I do, I do, I do." He was weeping.

"The gods love those who uphold the dharma," Dattaka said. "Take this for your children."

Leaning over the stall, he found a gold paṇa and tossed it to the sweeper.

"What are you doing?" Mitra said in distress. "Father will kill you!"

"Now be off," Dattaka said. "And if I ever hear of you stealing again, I shall have both ears and the nose."

"Thank you, my young friend, thank you." He rose and backed away from Dattaka, bowing again and again. He directed more thank yous to Mitra and to Dhruvādevī and her grandmother. Then he turned and ran.

Dattaka laughed. Falling to his knees, he presented the iron earring to Dhruvādevī, while Mitra watched in horror. "My lady, if you will forgive me, it is not an ear, but only an ear ornament. A better keepsake, I think, since it will not sully your silks, nor summon the flies, nor grow to stink after a day or two."

"You are a very strange boy," Dhruvādevī said, taking the ornament and slipping it into the pocket inside her vasana. "Grandma, I am tired from so much excitement and wish to return to the palace and rest."

"Of course, my dear," Nāsatyādevī said, and without another word, they left, followed by their entourage.

"What about the purple silk?" Mitra called after them.

They appeared not to hear him.

Mitra rested his elbows on the edge of the stall and buried his head in his hands. "Oh, Dattaka," he moaned, "whatever am I to do with you? Here was an opportunity to make a pretty profit. Not only did you spoil it, but you gave away money to boot! I suppose this is what happens when you try to make a merchant out of a warrior."

"I am sorry, dear brother," Dattaka said, putting his arm around Mitra.

"But you're *not* sorry. You're grinning like a monkey who's gotten into a cache of bananas."

"I am thinking of all the excitement! The charging elephants, the flash of the sunlight on my dagger. The color of the princess's eyes when she looked at me."

"Well, you can forget about the princess's eyes. Offering her that cheap piece of jewelry. Of all the rude gestures. Brother! Do you realize that, had you behaved, we might have become silk vendors to the palace? Now we'll never see them again."

No sooner had they reopened the silk stall the following day, than Dhruvādevī appeared with her grandmother and handmaidens in tow. The little princess wore the glass and iron ornament as a pendant from a string of pearls around her neck. The grandmother, her attitude somewhat warmer than the previous day, purchased the purple silk with the gold threads, enough to make two costumes, one in the traditional style and another in the "Asian" style. She purchased a second bolt of silk to make a wedding costume for herself, and five less expensive patterns, one for each of the handmaidens. Never had the stall brought in so much money in one day.

In subsequent days Dhruvādevī and her handmaidens became a common sight, sometimes accompanied by her grandmother, at other times by her aged nursemaid or another of the older courtiers who had accompanied them to the state of Magadha. At first she came to make certain that the wedding outfits were being properly tailored (she had decided to trust the work to Govinda's tailor rather than her own), then in later weeks to order minute alterations in one item or another, sometimes changes as small as the letting out of a single stitch or the taking in of a finger's width of seam. Once, Dattaka, in the midst of writing down some new instructions, glanced up and saw her studying him as closely as one would a verse of the Vedas.

One day the tailor, who happened also to be Dattaka's great-uncle, stopped by the stall for a talk. He had bulging eyes and a frame so skinny that his vasana hung from his hip bones as though they were hooks. He had spent so many years bent over his work that he found it impossible to straighten up.

All the senseless alterations, he explained to Dattaka, were damaging the wedding outfit. Already the weave was growing loose from being sewn and resewn so many times. Dattaka must take the initiative and arrange some secret meetings with the princess before the garment was ruined completely.

Dattaka could not believe she was having all that sewing and resewing done simply as an excuse to see him.

"That is the nature of women," the tailor replied, fixing him with a bulging eye. "They must do everything in a roundabout way. If they want one thing, they pretend they want something else. It's as simple as that."

The tailor considered himself a worldly fellow and an authority on females.

"But she is promised to Prince Rāma," Dattaka said. "If she agrees to meet with me and he learns of it, he will get very angry. He might have me killed."

"Nonsense. You are but children. Can a grown man be jealous of a little boy? Furthermore, Dattaka, if you don't meet with her, the wedding garments will be ruined, and we may *all* be put to death—or at any rate lose the palace business, which means a great deal to your father. I am not asking you to marry her, little one. Simply meet with her. Chat. Play games. Do whatever it is that children your age do in such situations."

"I don't know what children do in 'such situations.' I have never been in 'such situations.' "

"Toss the ball with her. That was my favorite game when I was a child. Or play tag. You will know when you are there. It will come to you. These things do."

"Father would not approve," Dattaka said.

"It's him you're helping. It's his business you're trying to save." The tailor reflected for a moment. "Don't tell him."

Dattaka was unconvinced. Later when he made up his mind, it was not because of the tailor's urgings or concern for the much-altered wedding garments, but rather feelings of his own, powerful feelings he himself did not entirely understand.

When Dhruvādevī appeared that afternoon, he maneuvered her to the back of the stall under the pretext of showing her some new bolt of silk. Fortunately, she had come with her old nursemaid, who was half blind and far less suspicious than her grandmother. Mitra, having voiced his opinion that the scheme would get them burned at the stake as their big brother Virata had been nearly eleven years before, had fled previous to her arrival.

Dattaka and the princess stood together in the cool shade of the red and white canopy, the sun projecting stripes across them and along the cow-dung floor.

"Here is the silk," he said, pointing to one of their worst weaves, a cloth that happened to be close at hand. He was so nervous he could not think.

"It is very beautiful," she said without taking her eyes off him.

"I would like to see you somewhere else." The hardest words he had spoken in his brief years. He wondered that they could be heard above the pounding of his heart.

"They never leave me alone," she said, seeming much more at ease than he.

"Well then . . ." said he, relieved to drop the plan.

The little yellow parakeet in the cage overhead trilled, it seemed, with amusement.

"However," she went on, "Grandmother has been planning to take me bathing in the Ganges, by the abandoned Śiva shrine. We could meet there as though by accident. . . ."

"I cannot bathe in public," Dattaka said. "It is a rule."

"You need not bathe. You could be waiting in the grove behind the temple. I could tell her that I wished to be alone, to reflect on spiritual matters. I will send one of my handmaidens to confirm it once the precise place and time have been arranged."

She glanced toward the street where her handmaidens were waiting in a group. They giggled and covered their mouths, and looked away.

"The silly hens," Dhruvādevī said.

"Then you will require no further alterations of your wedding garments?" Dattaka asked.

Dhruvādevī laughed as though this were the cleverest quip. She stood up on her toes and, switching suddenly to Sanskrit, whispered in his ear, "I love thee."

Then she hurried out to join her handmaidens and her nursemaid. Dattaka watched her go, the sunshine on the cobblestone street painful to his eyes. The blood was pounding in his cheeks. He could not move. His first brush with love had left him feeling godlike and terrified.

"You have chosen a date for the wedding of Prince Rāma and Princess Dhruvādevī?" the king asked.

"It might as well be next week," the old astrologer replied.

"Might as well?" the king said in amazement. *"Might as well?"* He looked over at the Purohita, and that venerable old brāhmaṇa also acknowledged the peculiarity of the statement. The three of them had gathered in the king's bedchamber to discuss plans for Rāma's wedding.

"You, whose lifework has been correlating man's fate with the motion of the planets, now tell me, after thirty years of being my adviser, that one day is as good as another?"

"In some instances, this is the case."

"I do not understand. What of the stars?"

"They remain in the heavens. They have not fallen into the moat."

"And what of the moon? Does it radiate good fortune on this undertaking?"

"It nourishes the water lilies."

"Damn it, astrologer, do not talk riddles like some mountain sage."

"On past occasions," the astrologer said in his gravelly, creaking voice, "when I have brought my lord displeasing predictions, I have been asked to be more circumspect."

"And so you mean to tell me that the subject of Rāma's wedding is so inauspicious that you can only discuss it by discussing that which has nothing to do with it?"

"Precisely, my lord."

The king sighed and rested his chin in his hand. "I should have guessed as much. My right eye has been throbbing for days."

"I suggest," the Purohita said softly, "that we have him tell us all that he knows. He is a splendid astrologer, the likes of which shall not be seen again in this evil Age of Kali. And the truth, no matter how inauspicious, is always the warrior's mightiest weapon."

"Proceed," the king said.

"Sparing you the details of lunar mansions and the like, in which I know my lord has no interest, let it suffice to say that, Prince Rāma's ascending sign being Jyeṣṭha, the constellation that the Greeks refer to as Skorpionis, while Dhruvādevī's sign, she having been born in the same nakṣatra but at a lower latitude—"

"First you say you will spare me the details, and then you launch a fusillade!"

"Forgive me, my lord, but I am like the old warrior who must swing his ax, gaining confidence, before venturing onto the battlefield."

"Well, swing it and get on with it."

"To be brief, there is no auspicious day or hour for this wedding, so in conflict are the astrological elements of the two parties. I have calculated the juxtaposition of the stars ten years hence, and it remains inauspicious even then! Every object in the heavens—moon and planet, comet and star—frowns upon this union. If permitted, it shall set in motion a chain of events that will end in death and disgrace."

"What else can I do?" the king beseeched him. He rose and paced the chamber anxiously. "We must forge this bond with the Śālāṅkāyanas, for they control the eastern coast. They alone know the secret of sailing to China and the islands in the east. We must have those trade routes if our economy is to flourish."

"I am not a minister who would make suggestions regarding the rule of this mighty empire," the astrologer said with exaggerated humility. "I am only the reed that shows which way the wind blows, so my lord can prepare himself for the onslaught of the rains."

"I have heard this 'only the reed' speech before," the king grumbled. He approached the old astrologer and shook a finger at him. "Of course, you have been wrong in the past. You told me Candra Gupta would be a cakravartin. Yet a few days later his tiny bones were scattered to the Ganges."

"Monkey bones they must have been, for my science of prediction shows that Candra Gupta II still lives, and it is only a question of time before—"

"Silence!" the king said. "We shall have no more talk of the dead. Let us concentrate instead on the living. You say Prince Rāma's union will end in death and disgrace. And is there no way to prevent this tragedy?"

"No. But as the moon wanes and waxes bright again, the tragedy shall pass. Led by the Guptas, the Land of the Sons of Bharata shall enter the glorious Age of Kṛta."

The brāhmaṇas believed man's history was divided into four ages, which they named after the four sides of the dice. In the first age, the Age of Kṛta, men were giant in stature and long-lived, loved the gods, and venerated the dharma. But in the later ages, the Age of Tretā and Age of Dvāpara, all these qualities declined, and the final age, the Age of Kali, was marked by a confusion of classes, by disease and malnourishment, by the neglect of the dharma and the rule of cruel foreign kings. At the end of that time, the Age of Kṛta would come once more, the cycle would begin again.

Vahara Mihira, like the rest of the court, believed himself to be living in the evil Kali Age. He looked back, as do men of all times and nations, toward a past that he believed to be better, and forward to a future he assumed would be worse.

"And this Age of Kṛta," the king said mockingly, so as not to reveal the true hope in his breast, "shall this old Samudra Gupta live to see it?"

Vahara Mihira fixed him with the milky-white orbs that had been his eyes (in the years since the infant Prince Candra's death, he had grown completely blind and had to be led about by one of his disciples) so steadily that the king had the unpleasant sensation that he still saw, and shook his head. "No."

"A curse on you," the king cried, "who are so loyal to the truth that you would deny your lord the pleasure of hoping," and ordered him out of the chamber.

"I am sorry that Prince Rāma's wedding should proceed under such an ill omen," the Purohita said.

"In fact, I care not," the king said. "My mind is fixed on another son, another celebration."

"Prince Candra's upanayana ceremony?" the Purohita asked in a low voice.

The king was pleased that he had remembered. "It will be eleven years, come next week, since his birth. Eleven years since I saw my son. When last I held him, he was a pink wrinkled thing, sticking out his tongue and sucking on his fingers. Today he is a young man, a warrior, preparing for the ceremony that will make him one of the twice-born. Oh, what I would not give to lay eyes upon him, even for a moment."

"It is too dangerous," the Purohita said. "We should not even speak of it here in your chamber."

"Tell me, my beloved guru, what harm there would be in walking by his home one morning while he was playing in the garden? Or strolling by the stall where he sells silks in the afternoon? Perhaps I draw as much attention to him by avoiding these two places as I would by visiting them as casually as I visit any place else."

"So it would be if Prince Rāma's spies observed the places you failed to visit as carefully as they observed the places you visit." The Purohita gave one of his rare smiles, the slightest upturning at the corners of the lips. "But since that first category comprises most of the earth, I doubt if they scrutinize it with such care."

The king laughed. "Of course, you are right," he said, and moved on to another topic.

That day the sun was a perfect jewel in the turquoise bangle of the heavens. Young cowherds, the image of lord Kriṣṇa, grazed their cattle across rolling hills, while in the nearby forests, hermits dressed in crude garments of tree bark, practiced meditation for years on end. However, because these were the king's hunting grounds, the peace was frequently interrupted—as it was now—by the clatter of chariot wheels, the drumming of horses' hooves. A speckled deer leaped across a meadow, so lightly that its feet barely touched the ground, and a chariot raced along behind it, drawn by two white horses, their nostrils flared with effort. Two men stood in the chariot: a driver, snapping the reins, and a hunter with a bow and a quiver.

The hunter was Crown Prince Rāma, grown to a young man. He was as tall as his father but still adolescent in appearance, plump and soft-skinned, with breasts that were almost womanly. The hair on his head was unusually thick and black, his hairline low on his forehead, his cheeks plump, his lips thick.

If he now displayed a confidence he had lacked as a child, it was the result of his having learned to use weapons. Yājñavalkya had insisted that he could never lead an army against the Śakas without being at least competent with bow and sword. And so Rāma had walked out on the training field, the scene of his worst childhood humiliation, and taken up the weapons with new determination. Even now, his technique was still so poor that he could have been beaten by the rawest apprentice, but the praise heaped upon him by those who would encourage him in his practice, as well as by those who simply wished to curry favor, misled him into believing that he was the equal of his namesake, the great warrior of the epic *Rāmayāna*, and he had begun to long for battle as a horse longs for an open field to test its legs.

As he had grown more proficient with weapons, he had also come to love the hunt. Quite simply, he enjoyed killing. What pleasure to see a hawk cut from its heavenly flight, or the head of a boar lopped from its body by a single swing of the sword and left lying in a mandala of its own blood! Sometimes (and this was his favorite sport of all) he would hire a caṇḍāla, paying him enough to raise his family from poverty, take him to the hunting grounds, set him loose unarmed and on foot, and then chase him down in a chariot and cut him to pieces. Alas, rumor had reached his father of the practice and the fun had come to an end.

Now the deer he was hunting, cornered in a cul-de-sac of

boulders, ran back and forth anxiously. Rāma drew his bow—a small hunting bow rather than the enormous device used in warfare—lined up a feathered shaft and let it fly. The sharp brass head fell short of the heart and lodged instead in the animal's rear flank. The deer lost its balance, twisting as it fell, hindquarters first. Regaining its legs only with difficulty, it limped away. Rāma drew another shaft but this time missed the target completely. The charioteer suggested they dismount and crush the animal's head with a rock to relieve it of its misery, but Rāma was determined to shoot it with an arrow. Having ordered the charioteer to follow along close behind it, at a pace somewhat slower than a man's walk, he launched shaft after shaft. One of them stuck in the deer's neck, another just below its jaw. Soon the deer's progress was no more than a hobble. Its velvet coat was stained black with blood, and the shafts were a crippling weight. It teetered and fell, then miraculously regained its legs and walked a few steps more. The charioteer had to exercise all his self-control not to go ahead and kill the deer himself, but he knew that in this situation such insubordination might mean two deaths that afternoon—the second being his own.

With the chariot moving so slowly, Rāma could hear the runner approaching from behind. He turned, irritated at the distraction, and saw Dūṣaka, the palace barber, jogging toward him. He was panting for breath, stumbling from exhaustion. The bare soles of his feet were bleeding, leaving red prints on the ground, like the lac-tinted footprints of royal ladies.

"My lord! My lord!" Dūṣaka called as he reached the chariot. "Victory to you, my lord," he said, falling to his knees, and lowering his face to the dirt.

"Rise," Rāma said, "and tell me what was of such importance that you ran all the way from the palace to my hunting camp, and all the way from the hunting camp to this green hillside?"

Dūṣaka tried to speak, but could not catch his breath.

Rāma bade him sit on the rear edge of the chariot, which made a comfortable seat, and, sensing that something confidential was at hand—something conceivably of great importance—sent the charioteer far away. Then he sat down beside Dūṣaka as though they were old friends, smiled at him, slapped him on the thigh, and nodded encouragement while the barber tried to compose himself after such exertion.

Since his arrival at the court, Dūṣaka had done everything within his power to win over Prince Rāma, including offering himself as a spy. (Barbers made excellent spies because customers, while having their hair shaved and tweezed, tended to divulge their most solemn secrets.) Rāma, sensing that this dark-skinned bumpkin of a śūdra wished to become not simply a servant but a friend, a part of his circle of dandies, considered him a fool beyond contempt. Still, he was so useful a spy, so loyal and eager to please, that the prince occasionally smiled at him or slapped him on the shoulder, as one throws scraps to a pitiful jackal.

"And how is the hunting, my lord?" Dūṣaka said finally, as though he had happened to be in the area and stopped to pass the time of day. He tried to address him in Sanskrit, which he had studied on the sly, but hopelessly fouled up the sandhi, the complex system of rules that governs elision of words, making himself sound more the fool than ever.

"Good," Rāma replied, amused by this pretense of manners.

"Your new bow of horn? Does it work to your satisfaction?"

"Indeed. It is light of weight and easy to draw. I had wounded a deer and would have killed him if not for your interruption."

"My lord, forgive me." Dūṣaka looked truly concerned. "I would wait by yonder tree while you finish the task you have begun."

"No, no, my friend. I am only teasing. I would gladly put aside the hunt to spend a few minutes with my friend Dūṣaka. You know, when I was a boy I used to have a pet monkey. He was always getting me into trouble, frightening the horses, biting the courtiers. But something about him pleased me, so I cared for him and protected him. Then my monkey died."

"I'm sorry," Dūṣaka said, assuming a mournful expression.

"It was so sad." Rāma nodded. "But now I am happy because I have a new monkey. A monkey named Dūṣaka. And as long as he pleases me, I shall care for him and protect him."

"Thank you, my lord."

"Now tell me why you have run all this distance. Have you news from the palace? Has something of interest happened during my absence?"

"Oh, yes, my lord. I am not sure what it means, but it is

something most irregular. I thought you would want to know of it immediately."

"Ah, you are a good little monkey. You think always of your lord. In my opinion you are too wise and loyal to be a simple barber. I think your karma has destined you for greater things."

"Like what?" Dūṣaka said eagerly.

"First tell me what you saw."

"Early this morning I am sent for by the king. 'Shave my head,' he tells me. 'And mention it to no one.'

" 'Very well,' I say. So I work industriously for a time, and then I say, casually, 'And why would my king, who has such excellent black hair, without even a trace of brown to it, wish to rid himself of it? I hope he is not planning to renounce the throne and join an order of monks.' "

"If only he would cede his throne so gracefully," Rāma murmured.

"Just as I thought myself. But he shakes his head. 'Many years,' he says, 'do I expect to rule this fair land.' So I say to him, 'So why do you have me shave your hair if you do not intend to renounce the throne and join an order of monks?' "

"And he replies?"

" 'Keep to your work and don't talk so much.' "

Rāma laughed. "Is there more to this fruitful inquisition?"

"One other thing. Once I am done shaving him, and his head is as smooth as a pumpkin gourd, and I am thinking that the shape of his skull is such that he would indeed make a handsome monk, a royal porter arrives with a cloth sack. 'That will be all,' says the king, shooing me out like I am some common servant. But I stand a moment at the door, as though straightening the knot on my vasana, and I see him take from the cloth sack—"

"Yes?"

"—a common begging bowl!"

"Good work, my friend." Rāma grinned at him and massaged his shoulders as though they were fellow warriors. "Good work indeed."

"Do you understand what it all means, the bald head and the begging bowl?"

"Perhaps."

Behind them, the horses whinnied and scratched at the earth

with their hooves, eager to return to the chase.

Dūṣaka waited, hoping that Rāma would share his suspicions. But the prince simply expressed his appreciation and sent the barber back to camp, to eat and bathe before returning to the city.

In time he rose from the edge of the chariot and searched for the deer, hoping it might still have the breath of life in it. But the creature was lying on its side, not far from the boulder where he had trapped it, its tongue lolling from the side of its mouth, its eyes rolled up so that only the white showed. While pulling loose some of the barbed shafts that riddled its coat, that he might have some arrows in case he encountered game on the way back to camp, he noticed a depression in the animal's skull as might be caused by the blow of a heavy object, a rock or club. He called over his chariot driver and demanded an explanation. The driver pretended to know nothing about it. He said that the deer must have hit its head falling.

Prince Rāma was not pleased.

Next week would be Dattaka's eleventh birthday, and Govinda's household was in an uproar preparing for his initiation. At that time he would receive his sacred thread and experience the symbolic rebirth that would make him one of the twice-born. He would enter the stage of life known as brachmācārin, and study Sanskrit and the sacred books, and take a vow of celibacy until he had finished his work. It was an important time in a boy's life, and an important time for his family.

Govinda's two wives, Yāmunī and Anusūyā, and his mother-in-law Mālatī, as well as Sarasvatī, Anusūyā's daughter, had been crowded into the kitchen all day, beginning preparations for the feast that would follow the ceremony. (Even though Govinda kept an entire family of servants, being śūdras, they would, by handling it, spoil the ritual purity of the food.)

The wives could never agree about anything. That they had agreed upon a menu (an appetizer of assorted vegetables deep-fried in a batter of chick-pea flour; yogurt with lots of sugar, cardamom, nutmeg, and ground pistachios for the sweet dish; spicy cauliflower and peas for the dry dish; eggplant and potatoes in a garlic-flavored tomato sauce for the wet dish; various fried breads stuffed with onion and potato; sweet and bitter relishes of mango, coconut, and mint; rice with raisins and nuts; the traditional broth spiced with turmeric, cumin, coriander, and ginger; and finally fresh fruits, and curds and cane syrup to drink) had less to do with diplomacy than the dictates of convention, which allowed little variation regarding the courses at a feast. Obviously the fried foods would have to be prepared at the last moment; the lentil broth, rice, and vegetables would be begun the morning of the feast. The relishes, however, which were a vital part of the feast, might be started well in advance. And now that the time for cooking had come, they could do nothing but quarrel.

Anusūyā, Govinda's first wife, a small, plump, energetic, sixty-year-old woman, whose hair was streaked with gray, was berating Yāmunī, Govinda's second wife, for starting the feast preparations without laying down new cow dung (once dry, a floor of this substance was soft and odorless and, being one of the five by-products of the cow, sacred), washing out the brass pots, bringing several fresh urns of water in from the tank, and all the other acts that in her mind constituted good housekeeping. She had a kindly though officious manner—as was required to run a household of this size—and a quick temper.

Yāmunī responded that Anusūyā was always accusing her of not doing her share. Here she was, trying to make a simple date relish, and all the elder wife could do was criticize, criticize, criticize.

Govinda had married Yāmunī after deciding that Anusūyā would never bear him a child, and in fact Yāmunī had given birth to four children, three of them male. Full of herself to begin with, this accomplishment had left her unbearable. All she would do was lie around the house eating nuts and combing her hair. When Anusūyā gave her an order—and as the senior wife, it was her position to retain authority—Yāmunī responded so slowly and so grudgingly that it was scarcely worth the effort. Although she behaved like a teenager, she was forty-four, a slow sultry woman from the south, with long eyes and a beauty mark on her left cheek.

Mālatī, Yāmunī's mother, who also lived with them, joined the fray on her daughter's side with a familiar refrain. Her daughter had borne Govinda three boys, and that was work enough for a lifetime.

"If you will not clean, you must not cook," Anusūyā said, moving menacingly toward the corner where Yāmunī squatted on the floor, dicing a twisted root of ginger.

As if the anger between them was not discomforting enough, the little room was sweltering from the fire blazing in the hearth and crowded with cookware and provisions. Ghee, honey, sesame oil, rice, and beans and the like were stored in clay urns of diminishing size, stacked one atop the other, so that the lid of one was the base of the next. Other pots, some of brass, hung in nets from the roof beams, along with braids of garlic and onions, and drying spices. The hearth was like a little hut, its mortared stones coated from years of use with a shiny residue of ghee and sesame oil. Several ancient iron pots hanging from a rod above the fire contained the food for that night's dinner.

"It is not *your* kitchen," Yāmunī replied, dark eyes flashing. "You cannot order me around." She raised the knife ever so slightly.

"Heed her words," Mālatī whined. She was seventy and wore a shawl over her head to hide her baldness. Her mouth was a dark hole with only one tooth. "When Govinda dies, her sons will inherit everything, and they will throw you in the gutter."

"Mother," Yāmunī remonstrated her, "don't say such things. My sons will always find a place for Anusūyā. As a sweeper woman, perhaps." One of the things that made her so infuriating was that she never raised her voice, but always spoke in low, evenly modulated tones.

All this was idle talk, for Anusūyā had raised the boys and they had more love for her than their real mother, whom they treated more like an older sister. But Yāmunī was so self-absorbed she did not realize this.

"If you want fresh cow dung put down," Yāmunī said reasonably, "then have Sarasvatī do it."

Sarasvatī was the child Anusūyā had finally borne once relieved of the pressure to supply her husband with an heir. Now a girl of nineteen, she was squatting by the hearth feeding cow chips to the fire. The heat made the sweat bead across her brow and trickle down between her breasts and drip from the end of her braid. Stray tendrils of hair stuck to her temples and neck. While she was not unattractive—she had the same plump pleasantness as her mother—the fact that her legs had grown bowed in childhood had left her despising herself. So it is with women that they will find one small flaw in their appearance and worry it to the proportions of a hideous disfigurement. (However, in fairness to Sarasvatī, it should be pointed out that those of the Land of the Sons of Bharata considered crooked thighs particularly unattractive.) While from time to time men expressed an interest in her, she turned them all away. As far back as she could recall, she had been taught that deformity was a punishment for a previous life misled, and this life would be passed in penance so that the next life might be passed with pleasure.

Sarasvatī looked over her shoulder at the other women, but said nothing. She was always quiet around them, never entering into their disputes for fear of being forced to side with one mother against the other.

"Sarasvatī is busy with the fire," Anusūyā said protectively.

"She has been feeding the fire for an eternity," Yāmunī said with contempt. "It is hot enough to roast a camel. Dinner will be ruined. Look at her! She doesn't know what she's doing. She crouches in the kitchen, but her soul is dreaming of a husband."

Sarasvatī blushed deeply and looked away. It was true.

"Foolish girl," Mālatī chimed in. "You waste your time dreaming of marriage. You are too old. I was married when I was only seven. Better you join a monastery and stop being a burden on our household. You don't even know how to feed a fire properly."

Sarasvatī burst into tears and ran from the room.

"How could you say such a thing?" Anusūyā demanded. "Haven't you a drop of pity?"

"I think mother does her a favor," Yāmunī said, "to remind her of the truth. She is such a daydreamer."

"How could you be so cruel? To take out your anger on a young thing—"

"Nineteen autumns?" Mālatī grunted. "That's not young. I was married when I was seven."

"Oh, shut up!" Anusūyā snapped and turned her back on them.

Sarasvatī ran out into the garden. What a relief to be out in the cool air! The shadows were growing long and the frogs in the tank had begun to croak, signaling the onset of evening. She had hoped to be alone, but Govinda and his eldest son, Viśvāvasu, were arguing with the stonemasons they had contracted to build a steambath, and a little distance away, Mandarikā, Viśvāvasu's wife, was tossing a buffalo-hide ball stuffed with rags with her three children. They laughed and shouted to one another as they raced to catch it. Nipa and Pinaka were twins, a girl and a boy of eight, and their little brother, Nanda, was seven. Usually Sarasvatī enjoyed watching their joyful play, but now their very existence seemed a rebuff to her own unmarried state.

Mandarikā, seeing Sarasvatī so upset, stopped the game of ball, and called to her, "Sister, what is the matter?"

She called her "sister" from affection. In fact, she was her half sister-in-law.

"Nothing," Sarasvatī replied.

How trying to live in a home with thirteen other people, not to mention the five servants! Half the time she felt as though every move she made was under surveillance, and half the time that she was being ignored. When she wanted to use the washbasin for her morning toilet, she had to stand on line like a beggar at the almshouse. When she tried to sleep at night, there was always a child crying with a nightmare, or a row between the wives. She could not help overhearing things she had no desire to know about, such as Yāmunī's difficulty making Govinda's liṅgam erect, and Mandarikā's worries regarding her husband's fidelity. Sometimes she wished that she could rid herself of them, slough them off as a cobra does its skin! Yet she was also wise enough to know that they were part of her, part of what she was, and never to be discarded, not even in death.

While she loved them all in varying degrees, even shrill old Mālatī, who never had a kind word for her, there was only one whom she always longed to see, who always had time for her, and understood her, and managed to ease her suffering even when her own mother could not. That was Nanā, the mysterious woman who had appeared on their doorstep, along with the infant Dattaka, eleven years ago.

"Have you seen Nanā?" she called to Mandarikā, trying to restrain her tears and keep her voice level.

"I think she is on one of her walks," Mandarikā replied, withholding the ball while her children squealed for it. "Dattaka will know. He and Mitra are upstairs in Father's room, studying the Vedas. His initiation is next week, you know. How hard he works!"

Indeed, Dattaka and Mitra were both in their father's room, poring over one of the long, narrow, wooden-covered books they had taken from the shelves. But it was not, as Mandarikā imagined, one of the four volumes that constituted the foundation of their faith, but rather an instructional manual entitled *The Kāmasūtra of*

Vatsyayana (a sūtra, like a thread, strung together a number of ideas; kāma, of course, was desire; and Vatsyayana was the monk who had written it). They were rushing through its pages, not for knowledge of god, be it direct or indirect, but rather for information that might be of use to Dattaka during his pending rendezvous with the Princess Dhruvādevī.

"Listen to this," Mitra said with excitement, and read from one of the pages: " 'The ways of enlarging the liṅgam.' "

"I am not interested in enlarging my liṅgam, you stupid brother. I want to know what to say to her."

"Just listen. This is bound to be useful: 'When a man wishes to enlarge his liṅgam, he should rub it with the bristles of certain insects that live in trees, and then after rubbing it for ten nights with oils, he should again rub it with bristles as before. By continuing to do this a swelling will be gradually produced in the liṅgam, and he should then lie on a cot and cause his liṅgam to hang down through a hole in the cot.' "

Mitra turned to Dattaka with great earnestness. "Do you think it would work?"

"I think it is the silliest thing I have ever heard," Dattaka replied. "Furthermore, you are brahmācārin—you should not even be thinking about women."

"I am devoting myself to my studies," Mitra replied. "I am practicing my Sanskrit, reading this to you." He grinned at his own joke. But then his face fell and he sighed. "The fact is, little brother, I can think of little else but women." He flipped another page, and a smile crept back across his lips as he read, " 'If the liṅgam is rubbed with the following things, namely the śāvara kandaka plant, the jalaśuka plant, the fruit of the eggplant, the butter of a she-buffalo, the hasti-carma plant, and the juice of the vajrarasna plant, a swelling lasting one month will be produced.' One month!" Mitra said with wonder.

"And the following month it drops off like a rotten banana."

They laughed so hard that they were rolling around on the floor, holding their stomachs.

"Before someone hears us," Dattaka said, "try to find the part about winning a woman's affections."

Mitra turned the narrow leaves with their rows of fine Nagari script and tiny, detailed illustrations. While Dattaka had learned some Sanskrit from his older brothers, Mitra was presently immersed in its study, along with related subjects, such as prosody, meter, grammar, and etymology, every morning with his guru before going off to the silk stall. All important treatises were written in Sanskrit since, while there were many Prakrits, that language of the holy books was the one tongue shared by educated people throughout the land.

"Let's see," Mitra said, thumbing through the pages. " 'On making acquaintance with the woman . . .' Well, you've already done that. Ah, here we are. 'After a girl has become acquainted with a man . . . and has manifested her love to him by the various outward signs and motions of the body, he should make every effort to gain her over. But as girls are not acquainted with sexual union, they should be treated with the greatest delicacy, and the man should proceed with considerable caution. . . .' "

"Particularly if the girl is to marry Prince Rāma," Dattaka murmured to himself.

" 'When the intentions of the girl are known, and her bashfulness put aside . . . an interchange of clothes, rings and flowers should be made.' "

"Ah," said Dattaka. "That's good advice. I'll bring her a pretty ring. Perhaps Sarasvatī might give me one she has tired of."

Mitra continued: " 'In this the man should take particular care that the things given by him are handsome and valuable. He should, moreover, receive from her a mixture of betel leaves, and when he is going to a party, he should ask for the flower in her hair, or the flower in her hand. He should dispel her fears, and by degrees get her to go with him to some lonely place, and there he should embrace her and kiss her.' "

Mitra grew so excited that his voice wavered, and he grinned and poked Dattaka in the ribs with his elbow.

"I don't know," Dattaka said warily.

"Wait. There's more." Mitra was exploding with gaiety. " 'And finally, at the time of giving her some betel nut . . . or making an exchange of flowers, he should touch and press her private parts—' "

"Dattaka?"

It was Sarasvatī, standing at the curtain.

Mitra hurriedly hid the book behind his back and rolled his

eyes up toward the ceiling, an expression he construed as conveying innocence.

"Where is Nanā?" she said. "I must talk to her."

"Away on one of her walks," Dattaka replied. "She said she would not be back until late." He saw his sister's face fall, and knew from the redness of her eyes that she had been crying. While he loved all his brothers and sisters, he felt something special for Sarasvatī. She was, like himself, an outsider, not one of Yāmunī's brood.

"What have you got there?" Sarasvatī asked Mitra, noticing that he was holding something behind his back.

"Nothing."

"Come now, let me see. Otherwise, I'll tell Father."

Mitra sighed and showed her the book for an instant, and went to place it back in the bookcase.

"What book is that?" Sarasvatī asked. Though the name of it was carved into the cover in beautiful calligraphy, it meant nothing to her. Being a woman, she had never learned to read.

"It is . . ." Mitra hesitated. "Pāṇini's famous Sanskrit grammar."

"Oh, really?" Sarasvatī raised an eyebrow. "I have heard that it is an excellent sūtra, but of such complexity that only the wisest brāhmaṇas can fathom it. And yet my two little brothers peruse it with ease. I am so proud of you."

"Well, you know, it's nothing," Mitra stammered.

"Read me some?" she pleaded. "Just a few lines, so I may hear the sound of it? I can understand some Sanskrit if the sentences are simple and the compounds brief."

Mitra shook his head. "It's really boring. Why don't I read you some of the *Rāmayāna* instead."

"Oh, please, Mitra. I must hear Pāṇini's grammar. I would do you any favor in return."

"Would you give him one of your old rings?" Dattaka asked.

Without a word, Sarasvatī slipped a small brass band with a brownish garnet off her little finger and handed it to Mitra, who, irritated, passed it on to Dattaka.

She took the book from him and leafed through the pages, puzzling over the writing and admiring the illustrations.

"How wonderful," she went on, "to be able to read these

marks. What a universe of ideas must be revealed!" Her brow wrinkled, and she added. "They seem very sensual drawings for a grammar."

"I guess," Mitra mumbled.

"This part here," she said, tapping the page with a long fingernail. "What does it say?"

"Uh, well . . ." Mitra hesitated.

"Yes, dear brother," Dattaka said. "Read it to us."

"You mongoose," Mitra said to Dattaka. He took the book and reluctantly began to read: " 'If a man, after anointing his liṅgam with a mixture of the powders of the white thorn apple, the long pepper and the black pepper, and honey, engages in sexual union with a woman, he makes her subject to his will.' " He finished his recitation in a very soft voice, closed the book, and looked down at the floor. For some time, nobody spoke a word.

Then Sarasvatī looked at them, puzzled, and said, "Well, I am surprised to find Pāṇini's grammar both simple and amusing. I hope you will read me more soon."

In the past, Dattaka had always eaten in the kitchen with the women and children, but now that he was only a week from his initiation, Govinda decided that he would join the men for pūja and dinner. This was a great honor, particularly since they had a guest that evening, a wizened, bent old man named Dakṣa. He was a citizen of extraordinary power, head of the silk guild, a personal friend of the king, and a frequent visitor to Govinda's home.

The pūja chamber was a small room of whitewashed clay walls and cow-dung floor. Ghee lamps had been lighted to supplement the single fading beam of sun that came through a window near the ceiling shaped like an upturned scallop shell. A small, exquisitely carved stone image of Viṣṇu occupied a niche in the wall. Fresh flowers had been arranged on the altar, as well as a brass urn of sacred water, recently retrieved from the Ganges.

While Dattaka, Viśvāvasu, Mitra, and their guest, Dakṣa, knelt facing northwest—the last with a great deal of pain owing to his stiffening joints—Govinda took a sip of the water, then cleansed his hands with it, then sprinkled some on the ground as he knelt along with them. He was a big man, barrel-chested and short-limbed, who moved clumsily among the sacred objects yet treated them with reverential delicacy. He had a round face that radiated the pleasure he found in every part of his life, from bartering down a caravan leader on a shipment of silk to surprising a brāhamaṇa with an unusually generous contribution to the temple. His eyes were small and round and rested in wrinkly sacks of flesh, and he wore a narrow mustache on his upper lip, which he smoothed with his thumb during reflective moments.

For some time all of them practiced a kind of prāṇayama, or breath control, to further purify themselves for the pūja. Dattaka, who had never done it before, grew light-headed, and noticed that the outlines of various objects in the chamber had grown remarkably sharp, the colors unusually vivid.

After reciting a mantra begging forgiveness for his lapses, Govinda performed nyāsa, the act of transferring the spirit of Viṣṇu from the stone idol into his own body. He touched himself six times—on the forehead, the upper arms, the chest, and the thighs. Dattaka noticed the beatific expression that came over his father's face and hoped that someday he, too, could experience the presence of that magnificent god within his own flesh.

It lasted only an instant. Then the god-spirit returned to its stone image, and the knowledge of eternity left Govinda's eyes. With a trace of sadness, he intoned the gayatri, the most ancient and holiest of prayers:

"Let us dwell on the beguiling splendor
Of Savitar the sun god,
That he may inspire our minds."

Before leaving the chamber, they offered burning incense, holy water, and tulasi leaves to the stone image, and finally a bit of the dinner they were about to eat. Govinda laid the image down on a silk pillow, to sleep the night.

As soon as they had quit the solemnity of the pūja chamber, Govinda clapped his hands together and said, "Let's eat!" and shouted to the women to bring out the food.

Anusūyā, Yāmunī, and Mālatī appeared with brass bowls, scoured until they gleamed butter-gold, filled with bean broths, flavored rice, fried breads, and, in honor of their guest, hacked chunks of a haunch of gazelle that had been roasting over the fire all afternoon.

The men sat on cushions surrounding a straw mat, and the women went from place to place, serving little portions of each dish on their clay plates. Normally they ate from banana leaves, but tonight, in honor of their guest, they had bought a set of plates. After dinner, the plates would be smashed, the entire set, for they were not glazed and thus absorbed the liquids and in a few days became smelly and unsightly.

While only five men were present, six cushions had been set out, six clay plates, six brass bowls of water. The sixth place was in memory of Govinda's dead son Virata. Although the period of mourning was long past, Govinda insisted on keeping up the practice. He said that the boy lived forever in his memory and to cease setting a place for him would be an act of unforgivable rudeness.

"Normally we never eat meat," Govinda said to his guest, as he grabbed a shred of roasted gazelle with the first three fingers of his right hand and popped it into his mouth. He continued to talk as he chewed. "Once a year, perhaps twice, in honor of a guest like yourself."

Dattaka and Mitra exchanged glances. Meat somehow found its way into the brass serving bowls at least once a week. But their father was fond of the fiction of his own piety, and they were fond of him so they never made a point of it.

"I am flattered," Dakṣa said. He chewed some of the greasy meat and grinned with pleasure, revealing teeth that were mostly ivory. "But how shall I dispel this bad karma of having forced you to partake in the slaughter of animals?"

"It's simple," Govinda said, through a mouthful of food, without a shred of cynicism. "Every year I give three cows to the brāhmaṇa up the street and he expiates me. This year I'll have him say a mantra for you, too."

"That's very thoughtful," Dakṣa said.

"Many vaiṣyas," Govinda went on, referring to his own class, "are lax about their worship, but we are as rigorous as brahmāṇas. All my boys are brahmācārin. Viśvāvasu studied the Vedas from the age of twelve, four hours a morning, every morning for eight years. Ask him a question about the scriptures. Go ahead, ask him."

"Oh, Father," Viśvāvasu objected, "it's been so long, I barely remember anything."

Viśvāvasu was twenty-nine, Govinda's oldest son and the most closely involved in the silk business, to the extent that they were nearly partners. While Govinda was loud and forthright, Viśvāvasu was quiet and shrewd, like Yāmunī, his mother. He also resembled her in appearance, tall, slim, and languorous, with her high cheekbones and long eyes.

"And Mitra," Govinda continued, "has been studying for two years. How he loves the holy language."

"That's right," Dattaka said. "He was practicing his Sanskrit just this afternoon."

"You mongoose," Mitra muttered under his breath.

"As for Dattaka"—Govinda reached across the mat and cuffed the boy affectionately on the cheek—"he begins his studies next week. He will be the best scholar of them all. What a quick mind he has, and a compassionate nature! I wouldn't be surprised if he became a holy man."

"Not if he has to give up girls," Mitra whispered.

Dattaka ignored his brother's jibe. He was watching Dakṣa. What a peculiar affection he felt for this shriveled old man, whose spine curled with arthritis and whose eyes gleamed with wit. At times like this he had the peculiar sensation that the discussions of the silk trade were a ploy, that the real reason Dakṣa came to visit was to observe him. Sometimes, in an attempt to make reality fit this unlikely and admittedly egotistical hypothesis, he imagined that Dakṣa was his true father or, more likely, his grandfather. Yet since he could not work up nerve enough to ask, his connection with the old man had to remain, for the time, a matter of speculation.

"How lucky I am," Govinda exclaimed, beaming at the boys, "to have such fine, righteous sons to say śraddhā for me after I am gone! Is that not a man's greatest blessing? Remember the tale of the ancient seer, Jaratkāru? While journeying around the world, he came upon some men hanging by their feet from a rope, above a well. A rat was gnawing through the rope. How surprised he was to learn that these men were his forefathers and that he had left them to this terrible fate by refusing to marry and bear a son to say śraddhā for them!

"After all," Govinda went on expansively, "what are the pursuits of this life, what are a man's three goals? Dharma, artha, and kāma. Righteousness, wealth, and pleasure. And I have them all in abundance! As for dharma, we uphold the law, we perform the sacraments, we study the scriptures, give presents to the brāhmaṇas, honor our forefathers, refrain—for the most part—from eating meat or harming any living soul. As for artha, I have, through my own industry and that of my sons, turned my little silk stall into the busiest in the state of Magadha or anywhere else along the Ganges. And kāma? Just regard my two lovely wives: the first plump and gay, the second lean and languorous; the one quick and direct, the other slow and teasing; a girlish type who giggles and shrieks, and a leopard who growls and leaves the print of her claws in my side. Yes, Dakṣa, I am as content as a man could be."

After dinner, the women cleared the food and brought around a box of betel quid. The men lay back on their cushions, chewing the spicy concoctions to aid digestion. After an appropriate interval of time, Dakṣa called for a wooden chest his śūdras had brought along. Govinda's servants brought it in and set it down in front of the old man. He opened the lid and took out the most exquisite piece of silk any of them had ever seen. Its weave was so fine, its color so brilliant that it seemed like sunlight itself made liquid.

"The Golden Fire," Dattaka exclaimed.

"Exactly," Dakṣa said.

"But I thought it was just a story," Mitra said, "like the urn that never empties of ghee."

"Would that it were," Dakṣa said with a smile. "Until recently the Chinese have only been able to produce it in small quantities. Now, however, more and more of it is finding its way into our land. Everybody who has seen it wants it. Already trade is beginning to suffer because of it."

"You are friends with the king," Viśvāvasu said. "Have him put a tariff on it, or bar its import altogether."

"We would simply hurt ourselves," Dakṣa replied, "for much of the silk we buy from the Chinese we sell again at a profit to the

Yavanas, when the monsoon winds carry their great vessels to our shores."

"Is it true," Mitra asked, "that their ships can hold five hundred tons?"

"Twice that," Dakṣa replied. "They are like great wooden whales with sails, and hundreds of slaves to pull the oars if the winds die down."

"Have you ever sailed on one?" Mitra asked, his eyes wide with admiration and wonder.

"When I was young." Dakṣa smiled. "I sailed to Arabia, and to the Kingdom of Axum, where I saw black men with two heads, and to the wonderful city of Alexandria, which was so vast and laden with riches that it made Pāṭaliputra seem like no more than a resting place on a public road."

Now all three sons were leaning forward, hanging on his words.

"But that was long ago," Dakṣa continued, "when I was a boy and I feared nothing. When you are young, you believe that you shall live forever. But when you grow old . . . Ah, when you grow old, even a fall to the gutter threatens your life."

"In other words," Viśvāvasu pressed, "to restrict trade might help our silk farmers, but only at the expense of our wholesalers?"

Dakṣa nodded. "The Chinese would simply use the ports to the south of our empire and divert their wealth to our enemies. That is why Samudra Gupta is so eager to wed his son to the Princess Dhruvādevī—in order to secure the ports on our eastern coast. Even though they are open to the elements and not the best harbors, they are better than nothing."

"Why must the Chinese stop here at all?" Mitra asked. "Why couldn't they sail around the tip of our land all the way to Arabia? Or take the overland routes to the north of the Himalayas and through the empire of the Kushans?"

"The sea is cold and wild in the south. Sea monsters dwell there, mammoth and sharp-toothed, which can rip a vessel in half as a saw rips wood. As for the overland routes, they become more hazardous as the nomads to the north, the savage Hunas, grow ever bolder."

"Is it true," Govinda asked, "that they have overthrown the emperor of China and captured the capital?"

"There seem to be many nomad tribes, all of them intent on destroying what great things man has accomplished throughout this world. In the south of China, according to my reports, there is little change. They continue to live in their slow, orderly, precise fashion, worshiping their forefathers and creating objects of great beauty. But in the north, the dharma is rent, and all is confusion, chaos, and killing."

"The nomads will never reach Pāṭaliputra, will they?" Dattaka asked with concern.

"We'd crush them," Mitra said, slamming a fist into an open hand. "Our elephants would trample them. Our cavalry would outride them, and our archers would send them running."

Dakṣa smiled at the boy, but made no reply.

"So, what are we to do about this Golden Fire?" Viśvāvasu asked.

"Make our own," Dakṣa replied, "and make it better."

"But what is the secret of its exquisite texture?" Viśvāvasu wondered, taking the cloth from Dakṣa and feeling it with his fingers. "So many factors influence the quality of silk. Is it the result of the weather, or the terrain in which the silk is cultivated? Is it because the moth is of a special breed, or the mulberry tree that it feeds upon is of a different color? Is it some special property of the liquid in which the cocoon is soaked before it is unraveled, or another thing altogether that I have not even dreamt of?"

"That is what we must learn," Dakṣa said, "if we are to survive."

After dinner, Sarasvatī waited by the front gate for Nanā to return from her walk. The air had grown cool, and the moon had risen over the hill where the palace stood, outlining its high ramparts and gilded finials. The street was almost empty at this hour but for a few neighbors sitting on their verandas, several foot soldiers out for a night of gambling, an empty bullock cart bouncing along the cobblestones. In the gables of the homes along the street, songbirds had buried their beaks in their breasts in preparation for night. Parakeets hung by their feet like skeins of dyed silk on the drying rack.

As soon as Nanā's familiar form appeared at the corner, Sarasvatī ran to greet her. Nanā wore, as always, a great black uttarīya that covered her entire body, and a sheer black veil across her face, so that only her beautiful eyes could be seen. No kohl outlined those eyes, nor did ornaments grace her body. She seemed to be in mourning, yet who—or what—did she mourn? She had never married or had a family, she claimed. She denied being Dattaka's mother or any relation. Beyond that, she would tell nothing of herself. She had arrived at Govinda's home eleven years ago with the infant baby in her arms, guarding him as a lioness guards her cubs, silent, aloof, and ferociously protective. For six years she had barely let him out of her sight; then, when Dattaka had reached the age when a child must learn independence, she had begun to leave him for ever longer periods and go walking by herself at all hours of the day and night. She was a most unusual woman.

"Oh, Nana, I am so glad to see you," Sarasvatī said, hugging her and letting go of the tears she had been saving all day. "Yāmunī said I would never marry, that no man would have me. Mālatī said I should join a monastery rather than be a drain on the household."

"There, little one," Nanā crooned in her wonderful rasping voice. "First of all, you are no drain on the household. Your father is a rich and generous man, and he loves a home filled with women. As for marriage, if you wish to marry, you shall."

"Oh, Nanā, do you know of a potion or a mantra to cloud a man's mind?"

Nanā was a storehouse of common sense and arcane wisdom and an authority on lovers and their behavior. Sarasvatī sincerely believed that, even though she was a woman, Nanā held the answer to questions that would puzzle the wisest of gurus.

"You shall marry without potions or mantras," Nanā replied, laughing. "But come, I am tired and hungry from my wanderings. Bring me a bowl of curds, and we shall sit on the veranda and talk."

A while later, they knelt together on cushions on the veranda, sipping curds, enjoying the cool night. The street was dark and deserted, the moon the saffron shade of a monk's robe. Even for women of wealth, women with servants, this late hour, when the children were in bed and the housework done, was the only time for themselves.

"Nanā," Sarasvatī asked, "where do you go on your walks?"

"Everywhere and nowhere."

"And what do you look for?"

"Someone I once knew. And swore I would find again."

"A man?" Sarasvatī asked.

"A very special man."

"I do not even bother looking. No man would have me."

"The problem is," Nanā replied, "that you will have no man."

"You mock me," Savasvatī said with hurt in her eyes, and made a motion as if to leave.

"Stay where you are," Nanā said, with a sudden sharpness that was not to be ignored. "If you would listen for once, you could break the habits that make you so miserable. I once heard a holy man say, 'A man will renounce his home, his belongings, even his family. But the last thing he will never renounce is his misery.' This may be the wisest advice I have ever heard, and you would do well to heed it. I have been to the bazaar with you. I have seen men cast longing looks."

"One or two might tarry with me. But none are serious."

"Men are always serious. Three at least would ask for your hand in an instant, if you were to give them the slightest approval."

"But I am so old."

"You are a maiden?"

"Yes," Sarasvatī said shyly.

"And Govinda would pay a fine dowry, though he hates to part with you."

"This is foolish talk. No man would want me. The gods left their sign on me, they have marked me for my evil." She indicated her crooked thighs, her bowed legs.

Nanā smiled. "Believe me, dear Sarasvatī, there is no evil in you, nor has there been in past lives, except perhaps the evil you do yourself. Do you wish to marry?"

"No man would—"

"Answer me!"

"Yes." She looked down at her hands. "Yes, I would marry."

"Then listen carefully to what I am about to say."

"You will tell me about potions and mantras?" she asked eagerly.

"I have no magic for you, sweet one. What I give you is an exercise of the will, simple in concept yet difficult to implement as the disciplines of the yogī. You must convince yourself of what I told you tonight. That you are no evil thing, despite what you see as your defects."

"That would seem simple enough."

"To undo a lifetime of belief?" Nanā laughed. "It is as simple as changing the course of the Ganges, or making Mount Meru stand topsy-turvy on its snowy peak. Yet all things are possible if one has sufficient desire." She yawned and stretched. "And now I think we have had enough talk for one night."

6

Several days later, a wandering monk appeared in the garden of the Govinda home.

Nanā was watering the flowers at the time. By opening a wooden spigot in the tank, she allowed a stream of water to flow along a conduit, through an ingeniously constructed series of ditches that led down the hillside, to each plant and tree and bush, more or less in the quantity required. Her task was to walk along beside the ditches with a stick, dislodging stones and clods of earth that clogged the water's path, and occasionally to kneel to help the water along by paddling it with her hand. She loved watching the dry earth turn black and soft, and bubble as it drank up the water with a soft murmuring sound, like an infant makes sucking at the breast.

It was only after she had returned to the tank and shut the spigot that she saw him watching her from the jasmine grove. He must have crept in the gate while she was occupied. Had he been a real monk, she would have been delighted, for monks always came with fascinating stories of their travels to far-off lands, occasionally even with messages from distant friends. And few activities bestowed such virtuous karma as the offering of hospitality to a wandering monk. Yet almost subconsciously she noticed a dozen incongruities, not one of which disproved his monkhood, but all of which taken together made a convincing argument against it. While most Buddhist monks were of the class called vaiśyas, he had the reddish skin of the kṣatriya, the powerful build. His crouch was not the relaxed crouch of a humble man resting, but tense, like that of a predator waiting to strike. And his eyes were not those limpid pools that came from years of meditation but rather the cold squint of one who has killed and would kill again. He held his staff and begging bowl like a sword and shield.

To make matters worse, for one of the few times she could recall, she was nearly alone in the great house. The other women had gone early to the bazaar to buy food for the celebration, Govinda and Viśvāvasu were at the silk stall, and Mitra was studying at the home of his guru, as he always did in the morning. The only person within shouting distance was Dattaka, who was in the house, drawing. The pretend monk must have been observing their movements for some time, waiting for just this moment. Now he would murder her and Dattaka, steal Govinda's treasure, and be gone by the time the rest of the family returned.

Her mind working frantically, she looked around for something to use as a weapon. Wooden stakes had been hammered into the ground to support a flowering bush. They were fragile, but if she was quick, she might plunge one into his eye socket. She waited, pretending to be unaware of him, and when he was a few steps away, she pulled one out of the dirt and, holding it like a dagger, spun around on the balls of her feet, ready to strike.

He dropped his bowl and staff, and flung himself at her. With his great size and weight, he wrestled her to the ground in an instant, and lay on top of her, holding at bay the hand that gripped the stake. Yet he could not subdue her. Her spirit was indomitable.

"Stop," he gasped, "before you kill a king."

Instantly she recognized the voice and, ceasing her struggle, stared down at him with wonder. "My lord, is it you?"

He let his head fall back and lay on the grass, gazing up at the sky, trying to catch his breath.

"Aye, Sutanukā, it is none other."

"Here I am called Nanā," she warned him lest anyone overhear.

"Still, the nursemaid fights like a man," he said, rising to his feet, brushing off his robes.

"I took you for a thief," she replied. "You look so different with shaved scalp."

"In other words, without my crown I am indistinguishable from a common knave?"

"No common knave. But no monk either. The light of a warrior shines too bright in your eyes."

"Ah, Sutanukā, how I have missed you! Let me gaze upon your face once again."

He reached for her veil, to pull it away, but she seized his wrist and stopped him. "Have you forgotten, my lord? My face is not the face you knew. Many years ago, when you gave up your son, the gods disguised me so that I might go with him and protect him."

"The pox. I had forgotten. Is it very grave? Does nothing remain of your beauty?"

"What remains of my beauty lies beneath the skin."

"Then, like a buried seed, it grows, for though I can see only your eyes, they seem longer and more beguiling than ever."

"My lord is most gracious. Would that we could sit on that swing all morning and improvise kāvya as we did in days gone by. But, knowing my lord, I imagine there is a fine, strong, brave young man he wishes to see. . . ."

"Oh, Sutanukā, is he truly thus, fine and strong and brave?"

"He is all that you would have hoped for and more. Even though he has had no instruction in the use of weapons, he drew his brother's bow one day and shot a single blossom from an aśoka tree at five hundred paces. And though he is ignorant of the art of statecraft, he has reconciled wars between Govinda's two wives with a few soft words. His religious training is not to begin until next week, yet sometimes when he gazes at an image of Viṣṇu, his expression becomes rapturous, and tears stream from his eyes. At those times I cannot help but remember the prediction Vahara Mihira made at his birth. He is indeed a cakravartin."

"I must see him at once! I can wait no longer!"

"Then see him, but begone just as quickly, for every instant you spend here jeopardizes his survival. I shall go back to my work in the garden. You shout the cry of a wandering monk. When he answers the door, beg some food from him. Say only what a monk might say to the young master of a house, and then be on your way."

"This was my plan precisely."

She looked around and, seeing that they were unobserved, lowered her head to his feet. "Wherever I am," she whispered, "whatever I do, I am your servant, my lord."

Dattaka was sitting on his bed in the second-floor chamber he shared with Mitra, drawing a picture of his beloved Dhruvādevī, when he heard the cry of a begging monk from downstairs. At such times in the past he had always rushed to the door, eager to share his food with them and partake, in turn, of their holy radiance. But today he simply lay on the bed, hoping that Nanā would tend to the visitor.

The cause of his melancholy was a visit, the previous day, of Dhruvādevī's handmaiden with a message that the princess and her grandmother would be bathing in the Ganges on Friday at noon. If Dattaka waited in the grove behind the abandoned Śiva shrine, the princess would attempt to find him and lose her. The prospect of such a meeting filled him with excitement but also a curious lethargy. He wished to do nothing else than lie there on his bed, his open box of charcoals beside him, trying to capture on palm-leaf paper the elusive essence of his beloved princess. What a difficult task it was! The form of her face had come easily enough, the eyes with only slightly more trouble. But the mouth! The distinctive pout that seemed to say everything of who she was, appeared as fresh in his imagination as if she were standing before him. Yet try as he might, he could not transfer it to paper. He would sketch it in lightly, rub it away with his fingertip and try again, until paper and fingertip both were black with carbon. Then he would crumple the paper with frustration, hurl it against the wall, and lie back, exhausted from his efforts.

He looked around the room at the toys of his childhood—the bamboo sword and shield, the wooden soldiers Govinda had carved for him, the toy flute, the clay horse on wheels. With the event of his initiation and his first rendezvous with a woman, he felt beyond such playthings. For an instant he saw a future filled with wonderful possibilities, like a train of royal barges, all decked out with banners and garlands, with merry courtiers and trumpeting musicians, glimpsed at a bend of the river.

There, again, the cry of the beggar. Why didn't Nanā attend to it? Irritated at anything that drew him away from his beloved labor, he pulled himself off the bed and made his way through a floor cluttered with the debris of childhood to the window.

Directly beneath him he could see the shaven circular skull of the monk, like a full moon reflected in a tank.

"Just a moment," he shouted, and ran down the staircase two steps at a time.

He ran around to the kitchen, pulled back the heavy drape that hung from a pole, and found himself standing in the shadow of his visitor. The towering monk was so at odds with the quiet, gentle, spiritual presence Dattaka had expected that for an instant he was frightened. But then the man stooped, so he was face to face with the boy, and looked into his eyes, and a great soft grin spread across his face, allaying all Dattaka's fears.

"Candra," he whispered.

"The moon?" Dattaka asked, for it was a common enough word in Sanskrit that he knew the meaning.

"The moon"—the monk hesitated—"is my companion. I wander by night, you see, and sleep during the day."

"That is a curious custom," Dattaka said. "I had not heard of it. Are you of a special order?"

"You might say that."

"Well, come inside. You must be very tired and hungry from your travels. I know there is a kettle of bean broth on the hearth, and a curry, and some fried bread left over from last night's dinner. Will that do?"

"I am overwhelmed by your generosity," the monk said, bowing deeply.

Dattaka held the curtain aside so that the monk might pass before him. He seated him in a corner, away from the heat of the hearth, and brought him a bowl of curds to satisfy his thirst, for the day had already grown very hot.

The monk drank deeply, then wiped his mouth with the back of his right hand and said, "What is your name, boy?"

"Dattaka. And I am no boy. Next week is my initiation."

"Pardon me, I meant no offense. You are obviously a man—I was too weary from my travels to notice. Why do they call you Dattaka, the Adopted One? Are you not the son of he who owns this fine house?"

"No. My real father was a warrior, like yourself."

"I do not know what you mean. I am a simple monk—"

"The scars on your left wrist. They are the scars the bow string makes when a warrior lets loose an arrow."

The monk glanced at his left wrist, at the row of scars, and smiled at the boy's astute perception. "I was once a warrior," he admitted. "But now I care about nothing but achieving enlightenment, for myself and all sentient creatures. Tell me more about your father."

"He was a brave and noble kṣatriya. He lived without fear and died on the battlefield fighting the Śakas for our great king."

"And so he almost did," the monk whispered.

"What did you say?" Dattaka asked.

"I said, 'What a shame he did.' "

"But my foster father is a kind and generous man, and very clever in business."

"Well, that is the way of the vaiśya, is it not? To understand the buying and selling of things. How is it written in the hymn to the Puruṣa, the cosmic man? 'When they divided the Puruṣa, into how many parts did they arrange him? What was his mouth? What were his two arms? What were his thighs and feet called?' "

Dattaka completed the quote without hesitation: " 'The brāhmaṇa was his mouth, his two arms were made the kṣatriya, his two thighs the vaiśya, and from his feet the śūdra were born.' "

"You are not yet brahmācārin and yet you quote the Vedas."

"I listen carefully when my older brother studies. And sometimes I hear my father perform pūja. I have a good memory, that's what Mitra says. Father says I might be a holy man. I am good at selling silk too. But I think I am best as a warrior. My brother Mitra and I have wooden swords. We duel often, and I always win."

"You do not hurt him, I hope."

"Oh, no. I would lay down my life for him. He is the best brother anyone ever had. He is teaching me to read."

"He sounds like a very good brother indeed."

Dattaka took a banana leaf from a shelf and spooned a little rice and bean broth and curry onto it. He gave it to the monk, along with a piece of cold fried bread, then sat down a few feet away and watched him eat.

He had just finished when they heard the sounds of women's voices at the front gate.

"I must be gone," the monk said. He was so tall that when he rose he bumped his head on one of the sacks of cooking pots that hung from the roof beams.

Dattaka urged him to stay. He insisted that his mothers

would be disappointed that they had missed the opportunity to share in the virtuous karma of being hospitable to him. But the monk was adamant.

"I'm sorry the food did not agree with you," Dattaka said, having walked the monk to the edge of the garden.

"Food given in charity tastes like the soma of the gods."

"Then why are there tears in your eyes?" Dattaka asked.

Unable to answer, the monk fled.

Later that week Sarasvatī burst into Nanā's little room on the third floor, nearly in tears. "I cannot make a decent chignon! And look at my nails—they are bitten to the quick! They look horrid! I just want to die."

"It is good to let a lover wait," Nanā said. "It teaches him patience."

Sarasvatī blushed. "What lover? I have no lover. I am on my way to the jeweler's stall, to see if he will mend a broken earring."

"Then why this fuss about your chignon?"

"My hair is horrible. The texture is ruined from too many years of wearing it in a braid."

"There, there. Hair is not so easily ruined. And even then life renews itself—new strands grow to replace the old."

A big black mynah in a cage by the window suddenly cocked its head and cried out, "Her red lips mock the ruby's brightness, and pearls pale beside her skin's whiteness."

"You see?" Nanā said. "Even my mynah thinks you are beautiful. But sometimes we must use our art to improve upon nature. Come sit here."

Sarasvatī lowered herself, cross-legged, on a wooden bench while Nanā busied herself with a tray of little bottles, jars, and boxes, set on a wicker stand that was shaped like an hourglass. Working slowly and methodically, she unraveled the hair, brushed it out, and rubbed it with oil. Then she made a part and rerolled the gleaming black tresses so perfectly that they resembled the smooth oval rocks one finds in riverbeds. The wooden chest in the corner yielded a jewelry box Sarasvatī had never seen before. Out poured the ornaments, like grain from a slit sack: combs of tortoiseshell chased with gold to hold the chignon, a strand of the finest pearls to run along the part, a single sapphire to hang over that spot on the forehead called the tilaka, a necklace of gold plates, a girdle of pearls and gems, bangles of gold and bracelets of silver. There were even anklets of the sort that Nanā always wore, with tinkling bells.

Sarasvatī gasped. "How did you ever come to own such splendid ornaments?"

"Once I had use for them. Now only the spiders use them to anchor their webs."

"But I cannot wear them. They are fit for a princess."

"Then be a princess."

Finally, she brought out a flat ebony case containing extraordinarily thin slivers of ivory shaped like fingernails, and a little jar of tree gum to hold them in place.

"These are far better than real nails," Nanā explained, gluing them in place over Sarasvatī's own torn nails. "If you need to do something with your hands, you simply peel them off."

"They look just like my own. Oh, Nanā, you are so clever."

"This lover you are not going to see," she said, a little while later. "As I reckon it, you have not seen him every day this week. On Monday you say you are going to walk by the river and pick China rose. When you return there is a roselike blush to your cheeks and a light in your eye—but no flowers. Another day, you go to the bazaar to buy fruit. You come back with no fruit, except the grape-red mark of a lover's bite upon your neck."

"There is no fooling you."

"Then do not try."

Sarasvatī's face broke into the most radiant smile. "How heavenly to be able to talk about him! I worried that my breast would burst from keeping it secret. He is the most wonderful man in the world. So handsome and sophisticated. And he truly seems to like me."

"Life's bitter meal," the mynah croaked, "has but one sweet, the joy of lovers when they meet."

"Why shouldn't he?" Nanā demanded. "You are lovely and full of grace and kindness." She stepped back a few feet and examined the young woman critically. "Some kohl on your eyes, I think, and a little lac to bring out the color of your lips."

She applied the kohl with a stylus, from a mother-of-pearl box, tracing the girl's upper and lower lids, making the lines longer and longer until they reached nearly to her ears.

"I've wanted to tell you since the day we met, but he made me swear to keep it secret."

"Oh?"

"You see, there is a problem."

"If there is only one problem, then the gods adore you. Let me guess. He is of a lower class."

"But how did you know? Nanā, you are a sorceress after all. You read my mind—it cannot be otherwise."

"Dear, sweet thing. We invented the system of classes so that lovers would have insurmountable obstacles that could be surmounted."

"But it is against the grain for a woman to marry down. Men may marry down, but women must marry up."

"Up, down. What difference? Govinda will take him into the silk business. When he grows rich enough, a curious thing will happen. His friends and neighbors will suffer a memory loss. They will forget that he was ever śūdra and believe that he was always vaiśya. You yourself will have difficulty recalling that it was ever otherwise. Now keep your mouth still."

Nanā spread just a touch of red paste, from a tiny silver jar, across her lips.

"Go like this," she said, rubbing her upper lip against her lower.

Sarasvatī couldn't stop chattering on about him. "He is very clever. He works at the palace, as a barber to the king."

"Oh, really?" Nanā stopped in the act of applying a beauty mark to the young woman's shoulder and gazed at her steadily. "What is his name?"

"Dūṣaka. Isn't that a lovely name? Is something wrong?"

Nanā put down the black pencil.

Dūṣaka, the Vaidya's servant. She herself had gotten him the job at the palace.

She turned her back on Sarasvatī, walked to the window, and gazed down at the garden, where weeks before she had encountered the king disguised as a monk.

Suppose Rāma had learned of the king's masquerade?

Might he then try to infiltrate the household in order to learn what held such interest for his father?

And might he employ Dūṣaka for just such a task?

Such was the conversation that ran through her head while she gazed out the window. But when she returned she said simply, "I once knew a man named Dūṣaka. But it must have been another."

"And he is handsome, too," Sarasvati chattered on. "Well, not handsome in the way of other men. His chin slopes too much, perhaps, and his skin is very dark. But I think the way he looks is perfect."

"I'm sure he is perfect in every way," Nanā agreed, trying to maintain a positive tone of voice. "Now hold still while I fix the knot of your vasana."

A man could respect the dharma, and practice kāma to exhaustion, yet if he did not procure artha, he had not succeeded in fulfilling the three goals of life. And there was no better way of demonstrating the extent of his artha than to install a steam bath.

Govinda and Viśvāvasu were standing by the half-built steam bath in the garden, arguing with the stonemasons, when Nanā approached, her black robes flowing behind her. They all fell silent at the sight of her. Even after all these years Govinda did not know what to make of her. She pulled him away from the others without a word of explanation and dragged him to a lonely corner of the garden. Viśvāvasu followed a few steps behind, since whatever concerned Govinda concerned him, too.

"There is trouble, sir," she whispered, angrily.

"I know there is trouble," he replied with his usual bluster. "I am paying those stonemasons ten paṇas a month to build my steam bath, and at the present rate it will be ten years before they finish." That was his way of dealing with problems, to make a joke of them. "First it was the rains. Well, of course I do not expect them to work during the rains. I am not a slave driver."

"Govinda is always fair with those who work for him," Viśvāvasu agreed.

"Then they take a month off to build a steam bath for Ajita, my competitor, who has the silk stall next to mine! Can you imagine? The nerve! So I fire them and hire these masons, who built the fine Śiva shrine by the Ganges—and they build me a steam bath that looks like a temple! It may be a good shape for worship, but—here, see for yourself." He held up some plans on a silken scroll. "No place to lie down!"

"It must be wider," Viśvāvasu agreed. "They will have to dig up the foundation and start all over again."

"I fear my problem is graver than yours," Sutanukā said, having waited impatiently for them to finish. "You have noticed the change in Sarasvatī? That she walks around the house humming and that her feet seem to tread the air instead of the earth?"

"Now that you mention it, she has seemed light-hearted."

"She has a lover."

"Well, it's about time." Govinda grinned and winked at Viśvāvasu.

"This is nothing to celebrate. But how can I explain my fears? They involve those things I have sworn not to reveal."

"Things pertaining to Dattaka?" Govinda asked, suddenly concerned.

"So it is exactly, sir. This man of hers—I know him from long ago. He has no integrity. He is of the lower class and would ignore dharma altogether in order to pursue artha and kāma."

"They are the ones who cannot be trusted," Govinda agreed.

"He may have sold himself into the service of another," she went on. "His declarations of love may be no more than a means of infiltrating your home, sir."

"Again and again you say *may*. Is all your anxiety but suspicion? Is there not one shred of evidence to support it?"

"There is not," she admitted.

"Then you will excuse me for hesitating to call the royal guard," Govinda went on sarcastically, "but time and again I have seen my wives convince themselves some harmless beggar was a bloodthirsty burglar, and the man delivering grain, a murderer of little children. It is the nature of women, when left alone, without some project to keep their imaginations in check, to turn every creak into a criminal's crowbar prying at the mortar."

"I, too, hope that my fears are unfounded," Nanā said, controlling her anger, "but considering the special circumstances surrounding Dattaka, might it be prudent to take some kind of precautions?"

" 'The special circumstances surrounding Dattaka,' " Govinda said, mimicking her. "Again and again I hear this, yet no one would share the secret of these circumstances with me. After all, I am the head of the household—it is the sweat of my brow that pays for this magnificent home, the sharpness of my wit that keeps so many relatives well fed and handsomely dressed."

"Sir, no one belittles your talent, industry, or generosity. But I must remind you that when you agreed to take Dattaka and myself into your home, you agreed also to live in ignorance of our true past."

"I know, I know! I know the cursed rules. I have lived with them for ten years. That he must refrain from bathing in public. That his father was a noble kṣatriya killed by the Śakas in battle. That I am a distant uncle. That beyond that his background must never be discussed."

Govinda looked away, and when he turned back, his face was tragic. "Can you for once imagine how I feel? I, who have grown to love this little stranger as I love my own sons? Yet always knowing that he was not my own, that he had been given to my trust like some precious treasure liable to be reclaimed by its rightful owner at any instant. You and Dakṣa know the secret of his origins. But I, his foster father, am to be kept forever in ignorance."

Nanā, who had never seen Govinda thus, was deeply moved. She suddenly understood that his gruff, boisterous, joking manner concealed a nature so fragile that without this armor it would not otherwise survive even the gentle skirmishes of everyday life.

"You must take some precaution," she said. "I would hire mercenaries to guard the house. For a few months only."

"No, no, no. It would attract too much attention. Did I not swear, when I adopted the boy, to avoid any act that might draw attention?"

Nanā doubted his motive. While he was generous to a fault, he was also a great miser, for he had grown up in poverty and the habits of childhood are the hardest to shed. He loved to purchase the luxuries, the steam baths that might never be completed, but the necessities, such as a few paṇas to retile the roof, were as difficult to extract from him as tusks from an elephant.

"Father," Viśvāvasu said, "I have a thought. There was a time, in my boyhood, when we dueled frequently with blunted swords. With some practice we grew to be fair swordsmen."

"Excellent swordsmen, I'd say."

"Let us take down those blunted swords again and practice in the garden each evening. In a few weeks, I wager, we will be the equal of any kṣatriya."

It was the secret belief of every class (particularly the newly rich merchants of the vaiśya class) that given the opportunity, they could perform the work of any other class as well or better. For just this reason the sacred writings warned again and again, lest class barriers deteriorate and anarchy reign, that it was better to do the work of one's own class poorly than another's well.

And so, at dusk on subsequent days, while the women were preparing the evening meal, Govinda and Viśvāvasu would appear in the open section of the garden near the tank, wearing breastplates of layered leather and thick turbans and carrying their old swords, the blades blunted by light wooden scabbards. They crossed their weapons at an angle, clicking them together thrice in salute, and began to duel. Govinda, heavy on his feet, grunted with effort as he lunged and then retreated to catch his breath. Viśvāvasu was shrewd, full of surprising feints and parries, as though they would compensate for his ignorance of even the most basic techniques of swordplay.

Gradually, a crowd would assemble, Mandarikā and her children cheering their father, Mitra and Dattaka admiring both men and imitating their movements from the sidelines. Once dinner was prepared, Sarasvatī, Mālatī, and Govinda's wives would join the party. As the audience grew, the dueling grew more dramatic, the swordsmen leaping and shouting and falling to their knees, and even feigning wounds to please the crowd.

Everyone was impressed except Nanā, who had spent years of her life in the company of real warriors and knew the difference. She never watched for long, for the sight of their mistaken self-confidence created an anxiety that was more than she could bear.

After a few evenings of it, she made up her mind as to what she must do. When everyone was asleep, she visited Dakṣa's home. She recounted Sarasvatī's story to him—omitting Dūṣaka's name to spare him impalement lest she were mistaken and it all turned out to be no more than an odd coincidence. The old man, equally concerned, went directly to the palace and told the king, who was grateful for being awakened. The following day, when the stonemasons arrived for work at Govinda's home, their number had grown by four. They apologized to Govinda for the delays and explained that they were adding men to their crew so they might work around the clock, day and night, to finish the steam bath that much sooner. Govinda was so pleased that he did not reflect on the unusual size and brawn of these men, nor that their skin had the reddish tint of the kṣatriya, nor how they watched with amusement when the two men of the house dueled with their blunted swords. After all, it was not unusual, in this evil Kali Age, to see warriors become workers, and brāhmaṇas, servants.

Nanā, however, noting all these things and sensing the king's hand at work, slept better.

Her only concern now was Sarasvatī.

The Śiva shrine at the bend of the Ganges was a squat, flat-roofed structure with four stone columns in front. The walls were decorated with carvings of Śiva and Parvatī, and their son Gaṇeśa, the remover of obstacles. Intricate floral patterns had been worked into the door jambs. That it bore an uncanny resemblance to Govinda's steam bath was no coincidence for the same stonemasons had, years before, refurbished it. In fact, it differed from that other structure in only one regard: it had been completed.

In other times pilgrims had come from afar to visit it, for this had been a holy site, a caitya, for as long as anyone could recall. Brāmaṇas had lived in simple huts nearby, interrupting their prayers and meditation to care for the idol who resided in the shrine, bathing it and feeding it and putting it to bed at night. Then, however, the temple had been looted by vandals, the image stolen, the altar defiled to such an extent that the brāhmaṇas had thrown up their hands in despair of ever restoring its purity and, shouldering their few possessions, had wandered off into the forest in search of other means of serving the dharma.

Now the shrine, overgrown with vines and creepers, and the mealy yellow fungi that can appear overnight during the rains, existed as a refuge for lovers. Duṣaka had taken Sarasvatī there on their first meeting. She had approached it cautiously, laughing with tension and excitement, as though the spirits of the brāhmaṇas who once cared for it might at any instant reach from behind a stone and lay a cold hand on her bare ankle. With Dūṣaka's encouragement, they had trod the stones of the veranda, dry vines cracking underfoot, and passed through the dark doorway into the tiny room that had been the residence of the idol. Here it was cold and damp. Sarasvatī, who was almost naked, shivered, making her ornaments jingle. Dūṣaka put an arm around her and pulled her close, so that her breast pressed flat against his side. They stood like that for some time, thrilling to the sensation of each other's flesh. Sarasvatī grew aware of her nipples shrinking, hardening. Dūṣaka kissed her, and touched her body with authority he had gained from experiences with shopgirls and handmaidens at the court. Anyone trained in the sixty-four arts would have found his technique appalling, but Sarasvatī, who had been kissed by only three men in her life, thought him the subtlest of lovers. He slipped his hand beneath her vasana and, locating the cleft of her yoni, pried apart the lips and worked his finger into the opening. Though the sensation was more odd than erotic, she threw back her head and moaned as Nanā had instructed her. Then she made the mistake of opening her eyes, which by now had adjusted to the darkness. A thousand bats hung like folded black parasols from the ceiling. She screamed and ran outside.

Dūṣaka chased after her, thinking this a bit of love play. He caught her in a clearing of high grass and pulled her gently to the ground. Lying beside her, he covered her with kisses. Beams of sunlight shot through the foliage, dappling their bodies. Songbirds sang in counterpoint to the hymns of the pilgrims wading in the river. Panting with excitement, he undid the knot of her vasana and pulled off her silk belt, so that she was naked except for her ornaments. Her figure was pleasing as long as one ignored the awful geometry of her thighs.

"Don't," she said, "not here. Someone will see."

"We are alone. There's no one about. Look for yourself."

She shook her head, and set her mouth in a firm line of resistance.

He tried half-heartedly to force her legs apart, but she crossed them and locked her ankles. He rolled away from her and sat up in a sulk. "You don't like me," he complained.

"But I do." She came up behind him, crawling on her knees, and put her arms around his neck. "I like you *too* much. Dūṣaka, be reasonable. How long have we known each other? Only a week."

The purple head of his liṅgam had slipped from the side of his vasana and, like some sleepy rodent peering from its burrow, was appraising her with a single slitty eye. She resisted the urge to reach down and pet it.

Slowly, Nanā had said.

"Then why won't you enjoy kāma with me?" he said.

"I want to do it first with the man I will marry." Like a prescient playwright, Nanā had quoted the entire exchange beforehand, preparing Sarasvatī for every argument.

"Perhaps I am that man." He turned to her hopefully.

"Perhaps."

"Then . . .?"

"When we know for certain."

"By the eyes of Śiva," he muttered, and turned away from her.

"Dúṣaka, don't be angry."

"What do you expect? You tempt a man, you entice him, then you turn your back on him without a thought to his discomfort!"

This last comment convinced Sarasvatī that Nanā was a sorceress, for how else could she have known the words he would speak? (She never thought that her present predicament had been reenacted more often than the *Rāmayāna.)* And so she did precisely as Nanā had instructed her. Still kneeling behind him, she pressed her breasts against his back, and began to lick his ear and whisper certain sibilant syllables known to excite passion in lovers. He grunted with irritation and made as if to pull away, but stayed where he was. She reached for his liṅgam, which, drooping, had vanished beneath the folds of his clothing, and was pleased to see how promptly it stiffened between her fingers. This was a power over men she had not known that she possessed. The head of it grew fat and red as a soma mushroom. When she brought her pursed lips to it, he groaned. After a few moments of this, the stalk began to pulse, his body to jerk. Surprised and frightened, she pulled away, and the ejaculate squirted over her face and chest like an anointment of ghee upon a sacrifice. Dūṣaka smiled at her, lay back, rolled over, and fell asleep almost instantly. Naïve as she was regarding life, love, and men, she found this adorable. She wiped herself clean with leaves, pulled on her garb, kissed him on the neck, and fell asleep curled up beside him.

She woke to the sound of voices and shook Dūṣaka till he woke, too.

"Go away," he muttered, rolling onto his other side.

"Somebody's here."

He heard it, too, and sprang to his feet, trying to cover his naked groin with his vasana, which had come completely undone.

Sarasvatī straightened her necklaces and bangles, which were all awry.

Then they crept back to the shrine and, hiding behind a corner where the shrubbery was particularly dense, peered in the direction of the voices.

Two children, a boy and girl, sat with their backs to them, side by side on a rock, talking with the solemnity of priests. Beyond them the ground sloped away, turning eventually to the heavily trodden mud banks of the Ganges and the silty waters where the pilgrims waded.

"I spend the days in my chamber," the girl was saying, "gazing at the beautiful picture you drew of me. I need you as the lotuses need the moonbeams. Yet I must marry another. There is no hope."

"Don't say such things," the boy pleaded.

He turned his head slightly. Sarasvatī, seeing his face, gasped with surprise. "Dattaka!" she whispered.

"You know him?" Dūṣaka asked.

"He is my little brother."

"Well, I recognize the girl," Dūṣaka boasted. "I have seen her around the palace. She is Dhruvādevī, Prince Rāma's bride-to-be."

"Shhh." Sarasvatī put a finger over her lips. "Let us listen to their conversation."

"I could not go on living," Dattaka said, "if harm came to you. Your are in my thoughts day and night, like a mantra."

"Then run away with me!" the princess exclaimed, taking both his hands and beaming with exultation. "Let us give away all we own, dress like beggars, and trek to Mathurā with our few belongings tied in a sack thrown over our shoulders."

"I must be at the silk stall tomorrow. And next week is my initiation ceremony."

"How dare you talk that way! You are mere kṣatriya and an orphan at that. I am a brāhmaṇī and a princess of the great Śālaṅkāyanas. I offer to give up my kingdom, and you refuse to miss a day in your nasty silk stall!"

"Do not be insulted, sweet princess. Some feel the dharma a heavier weight than others. I don't know why it is, but a sense of duty overwhelms me and guides me in all I do."

"And have you no duty to me, the woman you love?"

Crouched behind the corner of the shrine, Sarasvatī laughed despite herself at this ten-year-old girl referring to herself in such a way.

Dhruvādevī looked around. "What was that?"

"A pheasant beating through the brush," Dattaka guessed, "or a monkey up to mischief." He strained to see toward the shrine, then shrugged his shoulders and turned back to her. "Of course I have a duty to you. I would give everything to take you as my wife. But I cannot turn my back on my family and my duties. I cannot."

"If you do not run away with me," she said pouting, stamping her little foot, "I shall fast until death."

"Then I would mourn you the rest of my life and hope for an early death that I might join you in the Land of the Forefathers."

"But you would not stop me?"

"Not if you are so determined."

"And what if I threatened to drown myself in that holiest of rivers that runs below? Would you not save me?"

"You ask such hard questions! I have taken an oath never to bathe in public—but I'm sure if I broke it to save your life, the gods would forgive me."

Dūṣaka, kneeling by the edge of the shrine, whispered, "Why must he never bathe in public? I have never heard of such a rule."

"There are many mysteries about Dattaka," Sarasvatī whispered back. "He appeared on our doorstep when he was but an infant with his wonderful Nanā—she is the one I talk of all the time."

"The one with the mynah?"

She was pleased. He had been so bored before, but now he

was obviously intrigued. She felt the entire focus of his attention on her and her alone.

"We swore never to say or do anything that would draw attention to him," she went on, "or speak of the unusual circumstances that brought him to our home." She hesitated, and smiled at him warmly. "Of course, I can speak to you about it. You are practically a member of the family, are you not?"

"Practically a member of . . ." he repeated her words, searching for their meaning, which all of a sudden grew clear. "Yes, of course," he agreed, smiling nervously. "A member of the family. We'll be married soon. It's really just a question of time. I'd need a promotion," he mumbled, "a raise in salary. Perhaps next month. But it grows late, I must be getting back to the—"

He reached for the stone molding that decorated the shrine, thinking to pull himself up from his squatting position, but it came loose in his hand, putting him off balance, and he fell face forward, grunting with surprise.

For an instant the children were as tense and alert as deer surprised while feeding.

"Someone's there," Dhruvādevī said, looking back at the shrine with panic.

"Come on!" Dattaka cried and, grabbing her hand, ran into the forest, passing in and out of the diagonal sunbeams that filtered through the foliage. In a few moments they had vanished behind the black vertical lines of the tree trunks.

Two days later, Dattaka had an unusual experience while returning from another of his rendezvous with Dhruvādevī. It happened as he was crossing the wooden bridge that spanned the moat, on his return to Pāṭaliputra. It was nearly dusk and the bridge was crowded with those who would enter or leave the city before the tall timber gates were barred for the night: chariots, palanquins, men on horseback, a group of monks on pilgrimage, a procession of camels with heaps of goods lashed to their humps. He could feel the bridge shake each time their hooves hit the boards. The sun hung low over the hills, red and swollen, and the stench of the moat burned his nostrils. He saw three men approaching him: one slight, with a curl over his forehead; another, squat; the third, tall and handsome. Judging by their elaborate makeup and long fingernails, they were dandies, and from the way they wove back and forth along the bridge, bumping a monk in this direction, frightening a camel in the other, they were drunk on toddy, very drunk. They made unseemly propositions to an old woman on a litter, then laughed uproariously among themselves. They asked a monk if he could be hired to slaughter a goat for their evening meal, and nearly fell to the boards with gaiety. They made little progress with their crossing until they noticed Dattaka. Then they started toward him with the sly nonchalance of pickpockets.

Dattaka, absorbed in thought, half noticed them and moved clear of their path. They swerved toward him, and again he moved out of their way, until he was almost at the edge of the bridge. They passed close by him, and one of their number, the squat ugly fellow, veered sharply, slamming into him from the side.

"You! Watch what you're . . ." Dattaka managed to say before the impact flipped him over the railing and he tumbled to the water below.

It was cold and putrid, shallow enough that his heels dug into the mire. The slick ripply streamers of vegetation seemed to twine about his legs. He kicked and struggled and fought his way toward the murky light until, sputtering, he broke the surface in the middle of some lily pads. Treading water, he looked up and saw three heads—the three men responsible for his predicament—gazing down at him from the railing of the bridge. They didn't look drunk anymore, but dead sober and very attentive. Yet they made no effort to assist him.

People began shouting to one another, and a moment later men on the bank were tossing him a rope, helping him up the steep, slippery incline to dry ground, and trying to determine if he had been hurt in the fall.

"His hair . . ." someone whispered. Dattaka reached up and, touching the wet strands plastered to his forehead and temples, realized to his dismay that his turban had been pulled off by the rushing water. He was doing that which he had vowed never to do—bathing in public. Bare-headed. All he could think about was to cover his head as quickly as possible. He begged a rag from one of the men and wrapped it into a turban, making sure every bit of his hair was tucked beneath it.

Then, having recovered his wits, he ran back to the bridge, intending to give the three drunks a lecture about carelessness and regard for others. But there was no sign of them. The people assembled there could offer no information about where they had gone, nor could they even distinctly remember seeing them. Puzzled and angry, Dattaka continued home.

He found Nanā in her small attic room, her mynah bird perched on her shoulder, eating seeds from her open hand. Even though she was alone and expecting no one, her veil was fastened about her face. He had never seen her without it.

"What happened to you?" she asked, taking in his bedraggled appearance.

"Some drunks knocked me into the moat."

"My poor dear. Let's put you in dry clothes." At times like this, she was no different from a mother.

"Nanā, you don't understand. I was *in the water*."

Fear crept into her eyes. "But you were wearing a turban?"

"No. It came off. I borrowed this rag when I climbed out. Nanā, what is it about my hair that I must keep secret? Why do you always rub that black oil into it after I bathe?"

"How many people saw you? What did they say? Here, let me look."

She pulled the turban off his head and made a sad sound in the back of her throat.

"I'm sorry," Dattaka said. "I tried not to go in the water, but the man pushed me so hard—"

"What did he look like, this man?"

As he spoke, Nanā selected a bottle of black oil from a tray of cosmetics and, sitting him on the bed, shook a few drops onto his scalp.

"Why make such a fuss about my hair?" he insisted.

"Some things it is safer not to know," she replied, massaging the oil in with her fingertips.

"Why should there be danger? What does it matter? I am but the son of a kṣatriya who died in the service of the king. I have done nothing wrong."

She sighed and sat down beside him. "Have you never suspected that there was more to the truth than that?"

"I have wished it were so," he admitted. "Yet I imagine all men have such yearnings. Consider kings who go to such trouble carving their words on stone columns, and the poor fools who scribble Sanskrit stories in hope of a moment's glory. Nanā, tell me. If I am not who I think, who am I then?"

"You are nothing. Nothing but the most precious jewel in mankind's golden crown. No, do not ask me to explain. I tell you this because circumstances have begun to change. Were we astrologers, we would bemoan the treacherous conjunction of the planets, and were we palmists, we should tremble to perceive the disastrous intersection of lifeline and destiny. Be thankful for eleven years of peace and prosperity with the generous Govinda, for I sense those years are at an end."

"But how do you know?"

"A clue, a coincidence, a suspicion. A conspiracy of ill omens and baneful dreams. Bees building a hive outside my window and cats crossing my path. Only this morning I saw a dove land upon the roof."

"And yet to me the world has never seemed so full of wonderful omens! Today by the Śiva shrine, I felt a holy presence. I saw blue jays, all to my left, and my right eye began to throb. The trees seemed suffused with a golden light, and a beautiful music came from the air."

The mynah bird on Nanā's shoulder cocked its head and cackled, "The clarity of man's intellect dies when clouded by a pretty girl's lamp-black eyes."

"Yes, the world is all aglow with light," Nanā replied bitterly. "My little one has his first taste of love. Is there not trouble enough without you going off every afternoon with Prince Rāma's bride-to-be?"

Dattaka looked at her with surprise. "Then you know."

"I and everyone else in Pātaḷiputra. Your brother Mitra keeps a secret as well as my mynah." She reached up and patted the bird.

"My youth will not return to me," the bird squawked. "The Ganges flows ever onward to the sea."

"If only you had picked some other girl. . . ." she said.

"I didn't pick her. Nor she me. We were lovers in other lives." He grew excited, recounting their speculations on this popular topic. "We can almost remember the circumstances. In one life I was a humble goatherd, she a simple mountain girl—"

"And in another, you were a prince, she a princess stolen from your side by evil savages from the hill tribes."

"How did you know?"

"I have heard it before, a hundred times at least. We would believe that the gods plan our lives, that all is ordained according to some cosmic scheme, and we are not simply feathers tossed about by the wind. Well, I will tell you this, my little friend." She was angry now; she had never spoken to him thus. "If you insist on continuing to meet with her, you will hasten the disaster as surely as if you chose to throw rocks at Prince Rāma when he rode by on his elephant. Do you understand me?"

"I am not afraid of Prince Rāma," Dattaka said.

"Be afraid!" Nanā nearly shouted at him. "He would kill you with less thought than he would crush an insect underfoot."

"He would have to catch me first. I am as quick as a squirrel."

"You foolish, foolish boy." The anger went out of her, and she took him protectively in her arms. "There is wisdom in your heart, but the blood of the kṣatriya boils in your veins. See the princess if you must—but do your old Nanā one favor? Be careful. Be very, very careful."

"Who's there?" Prince Rāma cried anxiously, hearing a clatter outside the door.

Yājñavalkya had taught him that a prince was never so vulnerable as in his bath, and Rāma suddenly saw his own plump body lying in the splendid golden tank, the shiny island of his stomach rising above the water, as an irresistible temptation to an assassin's knife. Usually he had guards attending him, but that afternoon he had sent them away so that he might be alone with his new servant, the handsome teenage boy who was presently lathering him. What attracted the prince was not his youth or his coquettish smile, but rather the unusually bright blush of his cheeks, the coin-sized circles of color. He was eager to use the piercing instrument on them.

"Three drunken rowdies," replied a voice, and without waiting for permission, Kubera, Nandana, and Karabhaka came staggering into the bathing chamber, arm in arm.

His three childhood friends were grown men now. Kubera, slim and effeminate, tweezed his eyebrows and spent hours arranging his hair to fall in a cascade of curls down his forehead. He tilted his head to one side when he spoke and let his hands dangle from his wrists as though they were damp rags.

Nandana looked like a toad. He had hardly any neck and his eyebrows made a solid bar across his forehead. His prodigious strength had only increased with the years. Sometimes, for amusement, he would fight an elephant bare-handed, wrestle it to the ground, and kill it with a two-handed blow to the temple—a trick he had perfected for the pleasure of Rāma.

The king's young cousin Karabhaka had grown tall and handsome, and wore a thin mustache. Though he seemed to like women no more than any of his friends, he delighted in seducing them and leaving them with their maidenhood gone or, better, with child. He had neglected all his studies of warfare and statecraft and devoted himself instead to collecting gossip, in order to raise the reputation of one man and damn another, depending on his whim. Mockery dripped, like dew, from every word he spoke.

"How dare you interrupt me like this?" Rāma hissed at them. He was embarrassed at being found in a state of excitement, with the tip of his liṅgam piercing the water, like an otter's head.

"News such as we have cannot wait," Karabhaka said.

"Even for handsome young servant boys," Kubera added, smiling seductively at the teenager.

"What sort of news?" Rāma asked skeptically.

"We three arch spies," Karabhaka said, "have learned why the king impersonates a monk."

Rāma dismissed the servant boy with a pat on his firm rump. Then he lay back in the tank and addressed his visitors: "Well? And why does he?"

"Such information is valuable," Kubera said.

"Don't toy with me," Rāma shouted, half rising from the water, "or you shall find yourself in the dungeon with rats gnawing your flesh."

"I thought we were friends," Kubera said in a soft mocking voice. "We've known each other since we were little boys. We played together in the palace gardens—I played with yours and you played with mine."

"Disrespectful tart," Rāma said. "You shall go to the dungeon for that." But already Kubera's clowning was eroding his anger.

"Who's down there these days?" Kubera inquired. "Are there some of those handsome political dissenters? Perhaps a yogī who can turn his liṅgam into an iron bar?"

"Methinks he would make a vacation out of it," Nandana said. "What a scurrilous piece of trash that Kubera is."

"But an excellent spy," Kubera said.

"I'll be the judge of that," Rāma said. "Tell me what you have learned."

"We would tell you at once," Karabhaka said, "and negotiate with you afterward. But then you might say, 'I knew it all the time.' "

"Scoundrels, all three of you!" Rāma declared, but now he was smiling. "Well? What will you have from me? My wealth? My ornaments? My sexual favors?"

"We've had the last," Kubera muttered. "It was hardly worth the effort."

Karabhaka and Nandana laughed.

"Well?" Rāma said.

"Kubera would like," Karabhaka began, "the fortune you won from him last week. Nandana wants a position of importance in the army. And I would like a house especially built for me on the royal hunting grounds."

"And is there nothing else?" Rāma asked sarcastically. "A golden palace perhaps, or a bullock cart filled with diamonds? What about a hundred thousand Yavana slaves?"

"No, thank you," Kubera said. "They're too short and they smell bad."

"And if this information of yours proves to be worthless?" Rāma asked.

"It shall be worth what we ask for, and ten times that," Karabhaka assured him.

So Rāma agreed.

And they told him about knocking Dattaka into the moat, and about the honey color of his hair where the water had rinsed out the dye.

And the prince, once he had finished destroying the bathing chamber, hurling the water urns against the walls in a sheer white rage, agreed that it had been worth every paṇa.

Then he set about concocting a plan for revenge.

7

Young as Dattaka was, he had learned this truth about the relativity of time: the more you dreaded an event—specifically, the marriage of Princess Dhruvādevī to Prince Rāma—the more quickly it approached. It seemed as though only a day or two had passed from the moment he first set eyes on her in front of the silk stall to the day when he pressed his face to the wall surrounding the palace gardens to watch, through a chink between the timbers, the festivities that signaled the beginning of her life as Rāma's bride.

Earlier in the week, Dattaka had witnessed a procession of one hundred elephants, so pale as to be nearly white, with gilded tusks, embroidered blankets over their rounded backs, and nets of jewels across their heads, trudging down the Royal Way to the palace, followed by fifty chariots drawn by teams of white stallions, and several hundred bearers all in bright silks. A stranger standing beside him pointed to an imposing figure atop the palest of the elephants and whispered that it was the king of the Śālaṅkāyanas, come to Pāṭaliputra for his daughter's wedding, and that the other elephants were being ridden by his queens and ministers and courtiers.

All week the bazaar had buzzed with gossip about the celebration. Dattaka overheard a goldsmith bragging about how he and his sons had helped renovate the ancient palace of Candragupta Maurya, that it would make a comfortable home for the Śālaṅkāyana tribesmen during their stay. A few days later, three Śālaṅkāyana queens visited the silk stall—obviously acting on the recommendation of the princess—and bought out half the inventory. A friend of Govinda's, stopping by the house, told about a quail fight he had attended the night before where a dozen Śālaṅkāyana lords had arrived en masse, comporting themselves as properly as if they were in a temple, even when they bet wrong on three fights in a row.

The morning of the wedding the conch had sounded from the highest turrets of the palace, and messengers had run through the streets, declaring it a public holiday and posting decrees that told of the glorious union soon to take place. Bands of musicians serenaded from second-story balconies. Vendors appeared hawking snacks and sweets, little trinkets to memorialize the day. The usual assortment of snake charmers, conjurers, jugglers, bards, and acrobats emerged like beads of sweat on the brow of a reveler. Dattaka felt that of all the city's inhabitants, he alone was miserable.

Now, peeking through the chink in the wall, while the crowd behind him, believing as crowds do that to move a hair's breadth closer will somehow enhance the pleasure of the event, threatened to crush him, Dattaka could see the gay throng of courtiers garbed in splendid ornaments, milling about to the sound of vīnās, while servants passed among them with golden bowls filled with fruit and nuts.

Open-sided pavilions of red and gold silk, banners flapping from their gilded posts, had been erected upon level stretches of the palace gardens. There was the marriage pavilion, a curtain separating the groom's half from the bride's, and there, the altar where the nuptial fire would be kindled. Brāhmaṇas, under the direction of the Purohita, were positioning the ritual millstone to the west of the fire, along with the sieve of roasted rice. The jar of holy water had been placed to the northeast of it, the pile of hardwood close behind it.

In another pavilion, actors were performing a play by the great young poet Kālidāsa. The stage was barren of scenery and props, as was the custom with Sanskrit drama, the actors indulging in elaborate mime to indicate when they were riding in a chariot or caught in the rains. A curtain in the rear of the stage hid the actors until their entrance, as well as the musicians who played between acts and accompanied their songs.

There were so many sights to see! Yet all Dattaka longed for was a glimpse of Dhruvādevī. Their last meeting by the Śiva shrine only two days before had been fraught with sadness. The wedding preparations were well under way by then and the princess had only managed to slip away through cunning and bold-faced lies. Though she spoke of stopping by the silk stall after the marriage, and he of coming to the palace on some excuse, both knew in their hearts that they would never again see the other. They spoke little, and spent much time gazing into each other's eyes and listening to the sounds of the birds and the pilgrims singing by the river. She no longer suggested that they run away together, nor did she threaten to fast until death if he did not agree, for she had suddenly lost faith in the fable of her own freedom. When the sun touched the treetops and she finally embraced him, the iron earring he had yanked off the thief in the bazaar pressed into his breastbone and caused a sharp pain above his heart. Tears washed the kohl into dark trails down her cheeks.

By pressing his head close against the timbers, so the rough wood left its mark on his cheek, he could make out the ancient palace of the Mauryans, where the Śālaṅkāyanas had been housed for the wedding. A silhouette passed back and forth across a third-story window. Could that have been the room where Dhruvādevī was dressing? Did she have any time during that flurry of preparations, of royal visitors, and gifts, and intricate ritual, to remember the boy who worked at the silk stall?

It seemed unlikely.

He grew ever more miserable, little suspecting that in the very chamber he was watching with such a heavy heart, oblivious to the ministrations of her mother and grandmother and handmaidens, Dhruvādevī reclined on a wooden divan, gazing out her window at the great crowd pressing against the palace wall and wondering if Dattaka was among them. The more she wondered about it, the more certain she grew that his love for her was a passing thing, easily defeated by the obstacles that karma had set between them. Oh, perhaps he would moon over her for a few days, but then he would be distracted by his initiation ceremony. During the following years, while he was brahmācārin, he would abhor all thoughts of women. By the time he was ready to marry, she would be an old hag discarded by Rāma for a younger queen, a prisoner of the harem for the rest of her days.

Dhruvādevī yawned and stretched. She had a terrible itch behind her left ear but she dared not scratch it for fear of disturbing her coiffure or her makeup or the drape of her vasana. They had been preparing her since well before dawn for this, the most important day of her life, and every detail of her appearance had to be perfect. Now all that remained was for her mother, who was being adorned in a chamber down the hall, to arrive and paint the golden mark upon her forehead that all brides wore and tie the yellow woolen cord that was to bind her wrist for the next three days, until the marriage was consummated.

"Her mother cannot see her like this," her grandmother announced to the assembled handmaidens, aunts, and female cousins. "From the look of her, she awaits a funeral, not a wedding." She turned to her granddaughter. "Your mother has come all the way from Bhabanesar for this occasion. She will be here any moment. Can't you manufacture a single smile for her?"

Dhruvādevī grimaced, less a smile than the expression of someone who has just swallowed sour milk.

A few of the handmaidens laughed at the face, but Nāsatyādevī silenced them with a glance.

"Would you smile, Grandmother," the princess said, "if you had been washed and rubbed and brushed and braided and decorated like some prize elephant?"

"You are a princess. You have certain responsibilities. Sometimes the mantle is difficult to wear, but there are many privileges."

"I don't want privileges!" Dhruvādevī shouted, having had enough of it all. She rose and stamped her foot on the tile. "I don't want to be a princess. I'd sooner be a beggar than marry—"

Nāsatyādevī slapped her very hard across the face, abruptly silencing her. The handmaidens cowered in terror.

"You hit me," Dhruvādevī said in surprise, touching her cheek with her hand.

"The future of an empire rests on what you do today. You will act in accordance with the dharma or I will beat you so hard that you will never leave this room."

"Yes, Grandmother," Dhruvādevī said softly.

"Now smile," Nāsatyādevī said. "Show me how joyful a woman looks on the day of her marriage."

Dhruvādevī managed the smallest of smiles. Then she burst into tears and threw herself, face down, on the divan.

"I don't know what to do with her," Nāsatyādevī said, throwing up her hands in despair.

"My lady," began a handmaiden named Yamī, "if you will

excuse me for speaking, I have heard they have a fine vidūṣaka in this palace, a dwarf who can bring a smile to any face with his wordplay and clever tricks."

"Then call a porter," Nāsatyādevī ordered, "and have him brought here this instant—for I am at my wit's end."

When, a short time later, the dwarf arrived at Dhruvādevī's chambers, the princess was lying on the divan with a pillow over her head, and her grandmother was pleading with her to remove it lest she suffocate.

"Her mother will be here any moment," Nāsatyādevī explained to the dwarf. "You must do something."

"Leave her to me, my lady," the dwarf said, bowing deeply. "Victory shall be ours!"

At the dwarf's insistence, the grandmother, aunts, cousins, and handmaidens were escorted from the room. When the dwarf was alone with the princess, he touched her bare shoulder and whispered, "Princess?"

She withdrew her head from beneath the pillow and gazed at him with amazement. "You are very small," she said.

"It is my profession," he replied.

She stood up and faced him. They stood eye to eye, precisely the same height.

"You are no taller than I. Yet you are a grown man. How did you come to be thus?"

"I bathed in water too hot and shrank."

"Truly? No, you jest!" She thought for a moment. "It must be that an elephant fell on your head and compressed you."

"That it is indeed," the dwarf agreed, "for I have all the fine qualities of normal men but in a smaller space."

"And to which of the four classes do you belong? Are you brāhmaṇa, or kṣatriva, or vaiśya, or śūdra? Or do you dwarfs have a special class to yourselves?"

"We are of the brah class," the dwarf replied.

"The brah class? But, how fascinating! I have never heard anyone speak of it."

"Were we full height, we would certainly be brāhamaṇas, but being only half height, we must content ourselves to be brahs."

Dhruvādevī laughed and clapped her hands with delight.

"What an excellent jest!" She looked around to make sure that the chamber was empty. "Would that I could marry you instead. How I hate this awful state of Magadha, where there is no sight of the sea! I have no friends here, no family. Oh, dwarf, I want only to go home. Please help me go home. . . ."

Again her voice was lost in tears.

"*This* is your home," the dwarf said softly. "True, it is far from the sea, but it is very near the Ganges, which, flowing as it does through Śiva's hair, from heaven to earth, to the underworld, is greater than any sea. As for friends, I am not the only one. There is another, a boy who sells silk. . . ."

She turned to him, with an expression as much of joy as astonishment, then caught herself and pretended to be puzzled. "I know not what you mean."

"Princess, we have no time to be coy." His voice grew serious. Now that she was feeling better, he hurried to tell her what she needed to know before her grandmother returned. "Do not worry about Prince Rāma. He has no interest in you, or any other young woman. He loves only his mother, the mahiṣī. He will practice kāma with you once or twice, out of curiosity, and then leave you be."

"So I can spend the rest of my life a prisoner in the harem."

"After your marriage you will be more free than before, for you will no longer be under the thumb of your grandmother and your nursemaid. The harem is not the prison you might think. The old brāhmaṇa who watches over the queens is doddering, and the Yavana women who guard the doors have no concept of dharma and duty. Do you imagine that one king, who is most of the time so exhausted from his myriad duties that he falls asleep over his dinner, could satisfy so many women?" The dwarf grinned mischievously and shook his enormous head. His voice dropped to a whisper. "There are secret passages beneath the palace. Some of them lead to sites far beyond the city walls, groves where lovers can rendezvous without fear of interruption."

"You would show me these passages?" she asked, sniffing, drying her eyes.

"With pleasure." The dwarf gave a small bow. "I would even help you get messages to a certain boy who works in the silk stalls.

But only if you dry your tears and make yourself ready for your wedding. All the people of our glorious city are gathered below, waiting for a glimpse of you."

Dhruvādevī wiped her eyes. "But why would you do all this for me?"

"I have reasons," the dwarf said, suddenly shy. "From the moment I laid eyes on you I have—but no, I cannot go on."

"Please do," the princess insisted, suddenly fascinated.

"I shall! But no, why bother! There is no hope for me. You love another."

"You mean to say . . . ?"

"Mine has been a lonely life. We dwarfs are not long-lived. It is unlikely that I shall see ten more autumns upon this green earth. Thanks to the grace of my lord, Samudra Gupta, I have tasted kāma with many women. But never with a woman I truly loved. If I could experience that, just once, then I could go on to the Land of the Forefathers in peace."

"But I am a maiden."

"You shall not always be so."

"Dwarf, *if* you help me see my love, and *if* kāma is truly as wonderful as the poets say, and *if* that is all you need to die in peace, then I will certainly try to accommodate you, once at least."

The dwarf bowed deeply.

After he left, Nāsatyādevī and the rest of the entourage returned. The old woman was chagrined to see her granddaughter's makeup smudged and her chignon pushed out of shape, and ordered the toilet begun all over again. But at least the princess was smiling.

Thank goodness for the dwarf.

Dattaka stood at the fence until his legs ached, and his stomach rumbled with hunger, and the pressure of the crowd made him worry that the texture of the timbers would be permanently impressed upon the front of his body. When he felt he could not bear it another instant, he heard the musicians strike up a joyful air, and the wedding processions appeared, stepping in time to the cymbals and drums: the bride's party marching from the south of the garden, led by her father and dozens of cousins and nieces who were bridesmaids; the groom's from the north, his three best friends marching beside him, one holding a white parasol over his head to shade him from the sun, the others swinging yak-tail fly whisks. The prince had a drunken stagger, but most of the audience was so overwhelmed by the splendor of the procession, the sparkling jewels and richly brocaded robes of silk, that they failed to notice. Reaching the pavilion, the bride's party sat to the south of the curtain, the bride herself directly beside it; the groom's family on the opposite side, in mirror image. The Purohita muttered mantras, while his assistants drew aside the curtain. Still bride and groom were not permitted even to glance at each other.

Then the king of the Śālāṅkāyanas, an imposing figure with a long silk uttarīya draped over his shoulder, rose and drew his sword from its scabbard. Standing over his daughter, as though to behead her, he touched the point of his blade to her scalp and declared his intentions of giving her, wholly and completely, to Prince Rāma of the Guptas. He sprinkled his hands with water from the Ganges, a gesture signifying that a gift, once given by him, could not be taken back.

Shakily Prince Rāma rose, and swore to treat her with piety, to secure dharma, artha, and kāma for her, and to form with her a single being. Or so he tried to say, but stumbled over the formula and had to be prompted several times by his friends, who could barely refrain from smiling, and even by the Purohita. The king of the Śālāṅkāyanas pretended not to notice, but those who knew him well could see that he was not amused.

Receiving permission from the Purohita, bride and groom turned to see, for the first time, the mate with whom they would share the rest of their lives.

Dattaka could bear it no longer. He drew away from the wall and fled through the crowd.

The princess, wishing to make the best possible impression—even if it was only a marriage of convenience, it was still a marriage—had rehearsed a hundred times how she would turn to face him and gaze lovingly into his eyes. She had imagined him the worst conceivable monster so that the reality could only be an improvement. But her preparations were for naught: it was not his malformation that startled and disturbed her so much as his eyes, which were like those of a scaly thing found hiding in a dark well or beneath the mossy cornerstone of a temple.

She immediately got hold of herself and put on her well-practiced smile. But in that unguarded instant, Rāma had caught a glimpse of her terror. He did not seem to mind. He simply smiled back at her. Something about the smile fascinated her, as she had once been mesmerized by the sight of a man whose head had been crushed, like some soft fruit, under the front leg of an elephant. Though the sun was hot enough to make her sweat beneath her heavy silks, she found to her amazement that she was shivering. She wanted to run, weeping, to her grandmother's lap. She wanted to return to her wonderful country by the sea, where the cold gray horizon seemed the very border of the earth. She wanted to sit with Dattaka on the broad flat stone by the Śiva shrine, and hold his hand, and listen to the devotional songs of the pilgrims bathing below in the Ganges. Yet thousands of people were watching. The very future of her land depended on her comporting herself impeccably throughout the remainder of the ceremony.

Later she remembered only isolated moments. Prince Rāma and her father offering ghee and rice to the nuptial fire. Knotting together the corners of their garments and circling the fire in the auspicious clockwise direction. Her touching the millstone with her right foot that she might be as steadfast as a millstone. Her intoning the sacred verse by which their people had been wed since the dawn of time:

"I am the song, you are the verse, I am the sky, you are the earth.
Come let us marry and give children to the world,
That we may be victorious, and live a hundred autumns."

And taking the seven steps:

One step for food
Two steps for strength,
Three for artha,
Four for good fortune,
Five for children,
Six for the seasons,
And in seven steps be my friend!

Her friend? She glanced at him, and he smiled back at her. At such times, she noticed that the cleft of his upper lip widened and she could see the base of his teeth, the moist pink gum. She wanted to scream.

The Purohita was sprinkling them with water from the Ganges. The members of the wedding party were throwing rice at them. Mantras and more mantras. Sacrifice after sacrifice, until the smell of burning rice and ghee grew sickening. The heat was insufferable. She felt faint, as though her knees would buckle. The beaming faces of relations, grotesque and distorted, circled her like demons. And always him, the cleft in his lip like an infant girl's yoni. Oh, to get away from him with his falsely smiling eyes!

And then, mercifully, it was over. She found herself sitting on an elaborately carved bench at one end of a great hall filled with wedding guests. So many friends and relatives, so many strangers. Enormous golden bowls of food had been set on tripods, and musicians wandered between the columns, playing festive songs. She recognized the tall, handsome man, gazing at her with such concern, as her father and wished she could reassure him. But ritual demanded she remain seated there and silent until nightfall. (At that time she and her husband would go outside and gaze at the Pole Star, a symbol of their fidelity, and then she would be permitted to talk.) The space beside her on the bench, where her husband should have sat, was empty. One of the Gupta porters explained apologetically that sudden urgent business had required Prince Rāma's attention but that he would rejoin her soon. She smiled and nodded, and praised the gods for having created the custom of the mute bride. If only she could endure the next few hours, it would be night, and she could climb into bed with her stuffed rag doll and close her eyes and pretend it had never happened.

Rāma and his friends Karabhaka, Nanda, and Kubera were in his apartments, stripped of ornaments, blackening their faces and bodies with pitch, until they were so dark that they resembled the very lowest of the caṇḍāla. Oddly, there was no laughter, no cynical quips, no gossiping. They worked with a quiet intensity unusual to them. Presently they heard a knocking on the door, and Dūṣaka entered carrying five vasanas he had dyed black in the privacy of his own quarters.

"What's this all about?" he asked, puzzled.

"We have an errand," Rāma replied.

"What sort of errand?"

"A dark errand."

"And no need for me, I suppose." Dūṣaka looked down at the floor. He was the outsider, the child denied a place in the ritual.

Rāma stopped what he was doing and looked at Dūṣaka affectionately. "Little monkey, how many vasanas have you dyed for me?"

"Five," the barber replied.

"And how many are in this room?"

Dūṣaka's brow wrinkled in thought. Then he beamed. "Oh, thank you, Prince Rāma. I shall do my best, I swear. Victory shall be ours."

"The silly thing cares not where we go or what we do," Kubera remarked.

Dūṣaka defended himself as he, too, began to cover his skin with pitch. "Whatever Prince Rāma chooses to do will be an act of splendid karma. I consider it an honor to share in that karma."

"He is a good little monkey," Rāma said, leaving a thumb-smear of black on Dūṣaka's cheek.

Govinda was sitting on a pile of cushions in his corner of the main room, chewing betel quid and reading a collection of poems he had purchased at the bazaar that afternoon. Anusūyā, across from him, spun flax on a small wheel that she held in her lap. Now and then she looked up and smiled lovingly, if a trifle anxiously, at him, and inquired, "Still no sign of Dattaka? I worry for him. It's growing late."

And Govinda would laugh and reply, "He's probably singing under some little girl's window, just as I did at that age," or give some other reassurance, for he had unwavering faith in Dattaka's ability to take care of himself in any situation.

And she would turn to Viśvāvasu, who was sitting cross-legged at a low desk on the other side of the room, poring over the days' receipts, calculating credits and debits on an ingenious little device given him by a Chinese merchant, a wooden frame with a number of wires stretched parallel across it upon which beads were strung, and say, "Viśvāvasu, dear, go look for him. See that he's all right."

Then Govinda would chide her for being such a worrier, and reassured, she would return to her spinning.

Indeed, the peacefulness that evening was such that one imagined the entire earth free of discord, even the cat and the mouse making a truce and lying down together to warm themselves in the cool night. The responsibilities of evening pūja were past. Mandarikā was upstairs, putting her children to bed. Yāmunī and her mother, Mālatī, had retired to their chambers. Nanā was on one of her walks, and Mitra was keeping out of trouble—for the moment.

"It is so quiet!" Anusūyā said.

"That is because Father sent away the stonemasons," Viśvāvasu explained, clicking the beads of his calculating device. "He said to them, 'It is a festival day. Stop your blasted hammering and go celebrate.' "

"I will not have people working on a festival day," Govinda said. "After all, I am not a slave driver."

"And they would not go," Viśvāvasu continued. "Never have I seen such stubbornness. Father grew angrier and angrier. Finally, he threatened to call a guard and have them arrested." Viśvāvasu laughed to think of it.

"That got them going," Govinda said. He yawned and stretched. "How excellent I feel on this, the eve of Dattaka's initiation. I have hired the finest priest in Pāṭaliputra, a brāhmaṇa of exceptional purity, with a voice like thunder. How go the preparations for the feast?"

"All is ready," Anusūyā replied. "The relishes have been prepared, and a huge kettle of ghee waits on the hearth, for frying. First thing in the morning we shall visit the bazaar for fruits and vegetables."

She made it sound so simple. Like some consummate diplomat, she never let him know of the endless labor involved in running the house or of the constant bickering between the wives.

"I must be the happiest man on earth," Govinda said. "What have I done to be so blessed with wonderful wives and children and excellent good fortune? Perhaps in a former life I practiced austerities in the Himalayas or saved the life of the Buddha."

"I would not be surprised," Anusūyā replied. "There is something of the holy man about you. I am happy I met you in this life, for in the next I am certain you will be an unbearable snob of a brāhmaṇa."

Govinda laughed.

"If you feel good, Father," Viśvāvasu said, looking up from his calculating machine, "I will make you feel even better. Never have our earnings been so great. We have more capital than we can put back into the stall. It is time we thought about expanding, investing, starting another business. Perhaps we should sponsor a caravan. That's where the real profits lie. I met a man last week who had bought a third share in a caravan to—"

"Quiet," Anusūyā said, straining to hear. "I think it must be Dattaka. Thank goodness he's home."

"What?" Govinda said. "I heard nothing."

For a moment they were all silent, attentive.

Then a sudden crash, a splintering of wood, as though a timber had been rammed through the back door. The air grew charged. Govinda and Viśvāvasu locked eyes.

"The swords," Viśvāvasu whispered.

Govinda, who was closer to the chest in the next room where the weapons were kept, rushed to get them. When he returned, five men in black vasanas and turbans, their skin blackened with pitch, were standing at the far end of the room. Each held a short, crescent-shaped sword.

Govinda tossed one of his swords to Viśvāvasu, who caught it by the hilt and held it ready.

"What do you want?" Govinda asked the men in black. Despite his efforts, he could not entirely control the trembling of his voice.

"The boy," one of them replied. "The son who is not a son. Give him to us now and no one will be harmed."

His voice was thin and whistled when he spoke, as the air escaped from a tea kettle.

"Boy? There's no boy here. All my children are grown."

"For every moment you make me wait," the man with the whistling voice said, "you will suffer the more."

"If it's money you want, I'll give you money. I've a fortune in jewels. I'll hand them over right now."

"The *boy!*" the man said angrily. "Another instant and one of you will die."

"We'll see about that," Govinda said. "Viśvāvasu, come, let victory be ours!"

And with a bellow worthy of a bull elephant, he leaped at them, sword swinging. Viśvāvasu charged from the other direction.

Anusūyā flattened herself against the wall and watched with terror as her husband and son fought off the housebreakers. The seven of them moved back and forth around the room, lunging, parrying, retreating, and attacking again, smashing all the furniture and tearing down every curtain in the process. At first Govinda and his son had the advantage, for the others did not expect them to be so well prepared. The householders attacked with wonderful bravado, and while they were still no experts, they had benefited from their practice. First Govinda fought off one, then he scratched a second and knocked the sword from the hand of the third. Viśvāvasu kept his opponents busy, too. Had the numbers been equal, victory might well have been theirs, but they were outnumbered better than two to one. And the housebreakers, while no expert swordsmen, were young men with endless stamina. Each one that was fought off came back with new vigor, while Govinda grew more fatigued, the slice of his blade slower and less carefully directed.

Suddenly Govinda groaned. Viśvāvasu looked over at him and saw his father hunched over, his face twisted in pain, clutching his side as though to hold closed the sudden wound, the blood coursing from between his fingers.

"Father!" he cried.

Govinda slumped to the floor.

That moment's inattention was time enough for another of the men in black to slip behind Viśvāvasu and slash fiercely at his neck. Viśvāvasu's head, held by a hinge of skin, rolled onto his chest, while blood spurted from the open pipe of his neck. His body shuddered and lurched, and he fell with a thud, eyes rolled up toward the ceiling.

Anusūyā slid down to a crouching position and held her face in her hands. She couldn't stop screaming. After the housebreakers had run upstairs, she threw herself across the bodies and clung to them as though she were a shipwreck's survivor and they the driftwood that would keep her afloat.

One of the housebreakers was dispatched to the kitchen to make a fire, while the others searched for the children. Finally, in the gables behind Nanā's loft, the space used as a granary, they found the rest of the family huddled behind the sacks of rice and beans like frightened mice. The old woman, Mālatī, woken by the clashing of the blades, had not even had an opportunity to cover her bald head with a shawl.

The first housebreaker grabbed Nipa and Nanda, the second took Pinaka. They tucked the children under their arms as they would screaming pigs and carried them downstairs. The third threatened Mandarikā, Yāmunī, Mālatī, and Sarasvatī with his sword, while the fourth was left with the unenviable task of subduing Mitra. The boy bit him and clawed him, broke away, and ran down the stairs, screaming for help. The fifth housebreaker—Whistling Voice—who was waiting at the bottom of the stairs, grabbed Mitra and bound his wrists with the boy's own silk belt.

The children were carried into the kitchen, and the women, wrists bound with their belts, were made to march along behind them, prodded by an occasional prick of the sword in their backs and buttocks. Mitra lay bound in the corner while the housebreaker who had captured him fed logs into the hearth. The flames leaped almost to the ceiling, and the ghee in the huge black iron kettle bubbled furiously.

The one with the whistling voice addressed them when they had all been gathered into the kitchen: "This is your last chance. Which one has the honey-colored hair? Tell me and I will spare the rest."

"Spare them! Spare my children!" Mandarikā wailed.

"I am the one with the honey-colored hair," Mitra said. "I will come with you, but you must let the others go." He could barely control his voice.

"We shall see if he is telling the truth," Whistling Voice said.

They forced Mitra to his knees and made him bow his head. Then, protecting their hands from the heat with folded cloths, they tipped the black kettle of ghee so that the scalding liquid poured over Mitra's head. His scream was high-pitched and piercing. Where the oil touched his skin, it turned cherry-red and cracked, and erupted in blisters. Mitra grabbed his head in his hands, curled into a ball, and rolled on the dung floor, screaming.

"I cannot bear this squealing pig," Whistling Voice said. "Put him out of his agony."

The short housebreaker swung his sword and Mitra's head rolled away.

Yāmunī fainted, and Mālatī gasped for breath, as though in a seizure.

"Bring the next child," Whistling Voice demanded.

"But they are too young to be him," another housebreaker objected.

"So it would appear. But perhaps some sorcerer has laid down a veil of enchantment to delude us."

"They are what they seem," Mandarikā pleaded, "little children who have done nothing wrong. Do what you like with me—I shall be gracious and obliging—but if you have a drop of pity in your heart, leave them be."

"What a kind offer," Whistling Voice said, reaching out to pinch one of her dark nipples. "But before I can enjoy myself, I must be certain about these children."

Nanda, the youngest, died instantly. No sooner did the ghee touch his scalp than he shivered and fell limp from a combination of fright and shock, and a weak heart that no one knew he had.

The twins were less fortunate. They screamed and writhed for an eternity before the sword saved them.

Then Whistling Voice ripped off Mandarikās' vasana, threw her to the floor, and raped her while his friends whispered encouragement. Her eyes seemed to have turned opaque. It was as though the ātman had already departed and what dumb flesh remained neither saw nor felt nor comprehended. As the leader ejaculated, he spread his large hands around her throat and strangled her. She did not resist; to the contrary, she seemed to welcome it.

The tall one raped Yāmunī, who was still unconscious, while another of the band forced himself between the legs of her frail old mother, joking all the while about her ugliness, her hairlessness, her lack of teeth. Afterward, the daughter died cleanly, by the sword, but the mother was forced to feel her head turned until her neck cracked like chicken bones in the jaws of a jackal.

Only Sarasvatī remained, crouched in the corner, sobbing hysterically. Apparently there was something special about her, for the housebreakers exchanged knowing smiles. They deferred to one of their number who had been holding back, reluctant to join them. In time he gave into their crude coaxing and forced her down, pulled apart her legs, located the opening of her yoni, and tried half-heartedly to penetrate it.

His companions watched critically. "He is as limp as a wet rope," one of them remarked.

"He needs our help," the tall one said, moving toward her.

"I need no help!" he shouted at them, anger flaring. He rubbed his hand in the mixture of ghee and blood that covered the floor, then made a fist of it and plunged it into her yoni.

The ripping of the dry, delicate skin could be heard above her gagging.

Blood ran down his arm.

"Observe," the tall one said, "how he now grows hard. A virgin's blood is the best aphrodisiac."

Reluctant no longer, the assailant pulled out his fist and forced himself between her legs, jamming in his liṅgam. For an instant their faces were inches apart. Their eyes met.

"Dūṣaka," she whispered.

He turned away and went at her with a blind fury groaning as the muscles in his liṅgam began their automatic pumping.

Then, quickly, he stood up, his organ hanging wet and limp by his thigh.

"Now kill her," Whistling Voice said, handing him a sword.

He took the sword and stood over her weeping, shivering form.

"Kill her," he insisted.

He raised the sword.

"How dare you!" The voice came from behind them.

There, at the entrance to the kitchen, was a small woman dressed all in black, with a black veil across her face. She carried a lighted torch to find her way, for it was late at night, and she had been wandering the streets as was her practice. Something about her voice, a steel-like inner strength, stopped them cold. Her very presence was a reprimand.

"You dogs," Nanā whispered, viewing the carnage. *"You filthy dogs. Get out!"*

She came toward them, thrusting the torch as though it were a sword. The tall housebreaker wrested it from her hand, but the floor was so slick with ghee and blood that his feet slipped out from under him. No sooner had the torch touched the floor than the oil-soaked dung burst into flame. A crackling, dancing, yellow wall of fire sprang up between them. In an instant the air was filled with billows of thick black smoke. Nanā lifted Sarasvatī across her back, though the girl was bigger and at least ten pounds heavier, and carried her out through the main room. Anusūyā was still there, crouched over the bodies of her husband and her husband's son, rocking and weeping.

"Follow me!" Nanā shouted above the crackle of the fire, and Anusūyā obeyed, though she hardly seemed to know what she was doing.

Within minutes the neighbors from up and down the street—every able-bodied man between sixteen and sixty—came running with buckets and urns and whatever else they could find that might hold water. They knocked down the fence in their haste to get into the garden. They made a chain from the tank to the house and passed the buckets back and forth, shouting to one another to work faster. It was the rare occasion when brāhmaṇa stood shoulder to shoulder with śūdra servant, and thoughts of purity and ritual were subordinated to concern for fellow man. Sometime later two elephants, owned by a rich man up the street, were maneuvered alongside the tank and put to work spraying water from their trunks. But the proximity of the fire made them so skittish that in the end they caused more damage than good, trampling the garden and breaking the fruit trees.

Nanā, Anusūyā, and Sarasvatī huddled together in the street while their home was consumed like so much dried tinder. Great chunks of flaming embers were swept up into the night sky by the waves of rising heat, like newly born stars rushing to meet their brothers.

Soon, of Govinda's excellent house, only a few charred beams remained, and the beginnings of a stone steam bath that would never be completed.

* * *

For the second time that day, Princess Dhruvādevī had been bathed and rubbed with oils, her hair brushed out and dressed (though this time in a simpler style more suitable for rati), her face and body made up in such a manner as to emphasize her childish innocence yet also enhance the seeds of her adult sexuality. Unlike the makeup she wore during the wedding, these were rati cosmetics, prepared from edible foodstuffs—dried beet, rice flower, ginger root, cinnamon, and nutmeg—ground and blended to subtle shades and flavors, so a lover might be encouraged to put his mouth to all parts of the body.

Her wrist was still bound with the cord of yellow wool that her mother had tied there.

The nuptial bed, a wedding gift from the king, was a splendid raft of chased gold, with upended elephant tusks at each corner supporting a canopy, a tapestry of the young Krișņa, playing his pipes and courting seven milkmaids. Dhruvādevī lay on the south side of the bed, her slim, naked, girl-child body drowning in the goose-down pallet, the mountains of pillows. A sheet of green silk patterned with diamonds and vines was all that covered her. A wooden staff made a furrow beside her, the line that custom decreed Prince Rāma could not cross for three nights. How wise those ancient brāhmaņas had been to make such a law! Else the new husband, overcome with passion, might try to enjoy rati with his bride while they were still virtual strangers and poison her mind to the practice forever.

But Prince Rāma was a strange sort of man, who seemed to pay little heed to the dharma. All through the wedding festivities, for example, the princess had sat alone and silent on the wooden bench, waiting for his return. When the stars appeared, Rāma was still gone, and she could not go outside with him and view the Pole Star, the unmoving point in the heavens that was such a powerful symbol of fidelity. Even if theirs was a marriage of form, still these rituals were the pearls that one strung upon the bare cord of life, to lend it beauty and meaning. Her mother often reminisced about how she and her father had gazed at the Pole Star when they were married, and Dhruvādevī wanted to enjoy the ritual too so that she could tell her children about it. Also, it was humiliating to be treated thus in front of the guests. She didn't care so much for herself, but she grew ever more concerned for her father, who, each time he looked her way, wore an expression of restrained fury.

It was this disregard for the dharma that led her to suspect Prince Rāma might try to enjoy rati with her this very night rather than wait the prescribed time. And they had not yet even exchanged a few words of conversation! It was no wonder that, even though exhausted, she had lain awake for hours awaiting the return of her husband and fretting over what he might demand of her. As she had assured her mother, she knew all about the subleties and variations of rati that men enjoyed with women. She had been told by the courtesan who instructed her, and again by her mother, and again by her grandmother, and yet again by one of her more precocious handmaidens, that it would be very painful the first time, that she should plead with him to go slowly and be gentle, and that she should try to relax and concentrate on her most pleasant memory in order to totally ignore what was going on. The memory, she had decided, would be that of herself and Dattaka sitting on the broad flat stone behind the Śiva shrine. If that didn't work, she would think about shopping in the bazaar. While the thought of Dattaka sometimes made her miserable, the thought of shopping always filled her with pleasure.

And so she had lain there, unmoving, arms by her side, gazing at the tapestry overhead and contemplating her own initiation into the society of Woman, when finally, after many hours, she heard the sound of footsteps in the corridor. The tapestry covering the doorway was pulled aside. Torchlight in the corridor presented the silhouette of a familiar figure.

"My husband—is that you?"

"Yes."

"You were away so long. You missed the Pole Star. I hope your business was not unpleasant."

"There was a certain satisfaction to it."

He walked to the side of the bed where she lay and crouched beside her. Now that he was closer, she could see that he wore no ornaments, that his hair was in disarray, that his skin was covered with an oily black tar. He had several fresh welts on his body, and a bandage around his shoulder was soaked with blood.

"My husband," she gasped. "You have been in a fight. Let

me attend to your wounds. Once, after a campaign, I watched the vaidyas dress my father's wounds, and I am certain I can stop the bleeding and ease the pain."

"But the problem, little one, is that I don't want to ease the pain. All I want to do, right now, is enjoy rati with my new bride."

"Then so it shall be, my husband."

Yet he remained crouched where he was. "They have instructed you," he went on, "in all the ways that men and women couple?"

"I do not know if I have learned all the ways, for knowledge, in those subjects of importance, seems a road with no end. I am versed in many."

"Well put, little one. And were you instructed in all the varied forms of the embrace, the kiss, the scratch, the bite, the vocalizations, the striking, the playing of roles, and the mouth congress?"

"I know not what you mean by 'the striking' and 'the playing of roles.' I suspect that we who live by the sea do not engage in such practices. Otherwise, I am familiar with the catalogue."

"Ah, it is just my misfortune to have one so selectively trained, for role play is my favorite."

"Then perhaps the prince shall teach it to me. I am a willing student. Anything I can do to enhance his enjoyment of rati will give me delight."

"We shall see how willing a student you are. Good intentions are one thing. But rati, as I enjoy it, requires a most refined sensibility, which I am not certain can be learned, but must be acquired over many previous lives. Tonight we will have a test."

The wall behind the bed was faced with sheets of silver embossed with figures of lovers twined together in every imaginable embrace. Prince Rāma, reaching down, pulled one of the lovers by the ankle, and the form swung up, cunningly hinged at the head, to reveal a secret compartment. From this he withdrew a wide flat box of carved ivory. Inside, it was lined with soft cloth and divided into compartments, each of which held a different device. Some of them resembled the instruments vaidyas used in surgery, wooden-handled and iron-tipped, while others looked like the metalsmith's tongs or the carpenter's wedge, though smaller and more beautifully finished. Rāma removed one and held it up before her face. It was a very long, sharp needle set in a wooden handle.

"Did they teach you about this?" he asked kindly.

She shook her head.

He turned it over in his hands, running his fingers lovingly along the length of it. "It is called a piercing instrument. You see, there are parts of a woman's body that may be pierced by a skilled lover without making the blood flow or causing harm. The cheeks, for example. The nipples. The soft parts of the nose, and the ears. The lips of the yoni. There is even—and a friend of mine who is a connoisseur in these matters swears to it—a manner of penetrating the abdomen so that the point emerges from the rear, without injury. In time, a woman of appropriate temperament, with the proper tutelage, may grow to find these piercings delectable. She will not be satisfied by anything less."

Dhruvādevī nodded with interest. "Such pleasure is difficult for me to imagine. I must trust my husband's experience and wisdom in such matters."

Prince Rāma took her hand and turned it palm up. With extraordinary delicacy, he inserted the point of the piercing instrument into the knot of the yellow cord that Dhruvādevī's mother had tied about her wrist early that morning and pulled it open. The cord dropped off.

"Now you are all mine," he said.

"I am yours," she agreed, mesmerized.

"We shall begin with the piercing of the cheek, for that is generally considered the most pleasurable." He raised the instrument and placed the tip of it against her soft young cheek.

"But one moment, my husband, while I make my toilet. Then, when I return, we shall pass the night learning to use this and the other devices in your ivory case. For now that we are husband and wife, it is my duty to bring you kāma, of which, wise men agree, rati is the most important part."

She rose from the bed and wrapping the silk sheet around her like a gown, walked slowly to the entrance. Then she bolted, running full speed past the puzzled guards, down the corridor and the sweeping staircase that led to the ground floor, out across the garden to the ancient Mauryan palace, where her father was still in residence. There she stayed the night. In an audience the first thing next morning, the king of the Śālaṅkāyanas informed the King of Kings that the marriage was annulled and that Dhruvādevī would be returning home with him that day. Samudra Gupta pleaded with him to reconsider. He gave his oath, sworn by the sacred Garuḍa seal, that Princess Dhruvādevī would have her own chamber in the harem with the finest appointments, that she would be mahiṣī, and that she would have no obligations toward the prince other than the occasional public appearance. He then gave the Śālāṅkāyana king a gift of a thousand cows, a hundred elephants, two golden palanquins, and a bangle with a diamond as large as a human fist. Grudgingly, the Śālāṅkāyana king agreed to leave his daughter in Magadha. But, he declared, if Prince Rāma ever so much as touched her, he would form an alliance with enemies of the empire—including the Śakas—and lead a campaign against the Guptas that would not end until the Ganges turned red with blood.

Never before had Dattaka stayed out after dark. He knew that Govinda and his mothers and Nanā must have been frantically worried about him, but after the spectacle of Dhruvādevī's wedding, he could not bear the prospect of seeing them. He could tolerate no company but his own, and that simply because the alternative—self-destruction—would have deprived him of his treasured melancholy. He wandered the streets of the city, pitying the people celebrating, drinking toddy, singing to the rhythms of the wandering musicians, for being so simpleminded as to be happy. As for himself, he would never be happy again. Although he had barely reached the age of initiation, lifelong renunciation seemed the only course left open to him.

He left the city by the main gates and walked along the Ganges until, in time, he reached the overgrown Śiva shrine. He sat cross-legged on the broad flat stone where he and Dhruvādevī had once sat together, and watched the sky grow dark, the campfires of the cowherds appear along the horizon, the stars emerge like a dusting of diamonds. The Pole Star, overhead and unmoving, seemed the axis of the universe. Right now Dhruvādevī and Prince Rāma would be standing in the palace garden, gazing at it together while the rest of the wedding party cheered. Then they would certainly face each other and kiss. Dattaka tortured himself, as spurned lovers often do, with the thought of her soft pouting lips pressed to the prince's cleft deformity. In the hills, a jackal howled in frustration over the fine fat cows just beyond its reach.

In time the boy rose and started back to the city. He had been brooding for so many hours that he did not realize it was closer to dawn than dusk. Although he was alone in the dark, he had no fear of tigers; although he was barefoot, he was not concerned about snakes. He would have welcomed a death of drama and struggle, or so he believed. As he neared the gates, he noticed a flickering yellow light reflected by the mist, the kind of light made by a burning house. Unless contained, it might spread to other buildings and destroy whole neighborhoods, if not the city itself. A familiar proverb, attributed to the Buddha, stated that Pāṭaliputra had three enemies: fire, flood, and dissension among friends. All the men in the neighborhood would have banded together by now to stop the fire. Since it was in the area of his own home, Govinda, Viśvāvasu, and Mitra were certainly helping pass the buckets. He quickened his step so that he might join them. In a way he felt thankful, for the fire might distract his father from his lateness and save him from punishment. While he was indifferent to death from snakebite or a tiger's attack, the thought of his father's anger frightened him.

Even when he reached the street where he lived and saw the charred foundations of what had been his home, the ragged fragments of walls, the fallen joists, the caṇḍālas loading the bullock carts with the blackened remains of bodies, he still denied it and tried to convince himself that, confused by the feeble light of dawn, he had turned down the wrong street or had approached the right street from the wrong direction. But then he caught sight of Nanā running toward him, eyes brimming with despair, and in his heart he knew that the worst had come to pass.

"Victory be yours," Vasubandhu grunted, as he lowered his great weight to the floor in order to kiss his king's feet. "Excuse me for disturbing your tranquillity."

That he dared disturb Samudra Gupta at this time in the afternoon, which the monarch regularly put aside to compose kavya or play the vīṇā, left no doubt that he had news of the greatest importance: news regarding the murder of Govinda's family, the burning of his house.

"Prince Candra is unharmed," he said at once.

"Thank the gods for that."

"Sutanukā, too, survived."

"May victory be ours," said the king.

"They are both in Dakṣa's protection. Govinda's eldest wife lives too, and so does his daughter. All the rest are dead."

"I have caused naught but tragedy to this poor innocent Govinda and his family. May Viṣṇu reward him in future lives."

"I'm sure he shall, my lord."

With the king's permission, Vasubandhu pulled up a cushion and sat down facing him, his crossed legs appearing oddly insubstantial beneath his great belly. He wiped the sweat from his forehead with a piece of silk.

"Our spies," he continued, "have confirmed your suspicions regarding the identity of the housebreakers."

"Then it was . . ."

Vasubandhu spoke the name for him, to spare him the pain: "Rāma." He lowered his eyes, unable to bear the sight of his lord's face, flushed with rage.

"He will pay," the king whispered. "He will pay and pay again. I have been too lenient too long. If he insists on raping and murdering like a barbaric Huna, then he shall be treated as such." The king's voice grew louder, trembling with anger. "Let us see how brave he is without the veil of night and a mask of lampblack. Let us see his courage when confronted with his crime in the light of day. He believes he shall rule the empire of the Guptas? Well, when I am done with him he shall be fit to rule none but the toads and lizards!"

"Very good, my lord," Vasubandhu said. "I applaud your decision. Shall I have the guards send for him?"

"Yes, at once."

"Guards!"

"Wait," the king called, reaching out a hand.

"Yes, my lord?"

"Review the facts for me, so that I may have them at my call when he arrives."

"He vanished after the wedding, right before the massacre. Later one of my spies saw him return to the palace via a tunnel, his face blackened, his feet red, as though he had gone wading in an ocean of blood."

"Yet—yet if his face was black, then it might have been another. For a black face in a black night is well-nigh invisible. Is that not so?"

"Yes, but—"

"And the fact that he left after the wedding proves nothing."

"That detail in itself, perhaps. But taken within the context of the event—"

"Suppose some enemy of the Guptas wished to weaken us from within. Might this not be the perfect opportunity? Somehow he discovers that the prince has arranged a little innocent gaming with his friends, to celebrate his wedding. He contrives to frame him by allowing our spies to see a gang of men resembling them, dressed as assassins, dripping blood."

"It seems far-fetched."

"Or what if Rāma *was* responsible," the king went on, hardly seeming to hear his minister, "but his attack on Govinda's house, no more than coincidence? Naught but mischief that got out of hand."

"Mischief? The cold-blooded murder of men, women, and children?"

The king's voice grew cool, logical, as though explaining calculations to a schoolchild. "Let us say the prince drank too much, and grew randy. His friends had heard tell of a pretty daughter at Govinda's home. They went to investigate. The daughter, seeing what handsome fellows they were, invited them to enjoy kāma with her. Govinda came upon them, mistook Rāma for a burglar, drew his sword. The daughter cried rape, as women do in such situations, to remove the blame from herself. Rāma had to defend himself. One thing led to the next."

"My lord, it is a piece of fancy."

"You say I deceive myself?" the king bellowed, turning suddenly savage. "I am the beloved of Lord Viṣṇu. I see the world as it is—it is you who are deceived, you with your cursed Buddhism. Begone from here! Get your fat butt away from my chamber!"

Vasubandhu rose and started to leave. Just as he reached the tapestry, Samudra Gupta called to him. "Wait!" His voice softened. "Old friend, forgive me. They are not my words, but the words of a demon. How my head throbs!" He closed his eyes and massaged his silver temples.

"I have done what no man has done before," the king

continued, after a time. "I have conquered kingdoms and forged alliances, made our balance of trade the envy of the rest of the world. Raised the arts to a level of beauty and refinement previously unimagined, and in all other ways spread peace and prosperity throughout the kingdom. Yet, faced with the anger of one son toward the other, I am like the śūdra who, afraid of making a wrong move, stands awkwardly in the corner, kicking the dung with his feet."

"Oh, my lord," Vasubandhu said, shaking his head. "You are nothing of the sort."

"How my head aches! It is more than I can bear. Have them make me a potion to ease the pain."

"Yes, my lord," Vasubandhu said, rising. "And while I am at it, shall I also summon the prince?"

The king hesitated a long time before replying. "Yes. Send the prince."

Rāma took his time answering his father's summons. When he arrived, ornaments hung all over him like icicles. He barely lowered his head in salute. "Victory, Father. You wished to see me?"

"My son, we must talk."

"It is always a pleasure. As a child I longed for your company, but you were so busy. Now when you offer me an audience, I think: better late than never."

"I spent time with you when you were a child. At least, I intended to. There were so many other matters, consolidating the empire, war with the Śakas . . ."

"I thought you despised the sight of me."

"No, no! My child, I loved you then as I love you now. If only my love for you were not so intense, my task might be less difficult."

"And what task is that, dear Father?"

He regarded the king with limpid black eyes, as large and innocent as an infant's.

The king glanced at his son's soft body. "You have fresh wounds."

"A duel to defend your honor. Overhearing one of the guards whispering that you had grown weak and old, I challenged him and dispatched him to the five elements with a few thrusts of my blade." He looked down at himself. "Most of these cuts are superficial. This shoulder wound hurts when I raise my arm. I keep a compress on it at night."

"You must not duel," the king said. "Your life is too precious."

"My father's honor is more precious."

The king glanced down at his son's hands. The nails of the right hand, usually nearly as long as the fingers themselves, were broken off short, and one had been ripped off altogether.

"And your nails?" the king inquired.

"A cart was rumbling through the streets with a wooden image of Viṣṇu in the rear lying upon a bed of straw. It hit a bump and the image bounced out of the cart. As chance would have it, I was only a few steps away. I dove for it and caught it just before it would have shattered against the cobblestones. My nails caught on the carriage wheel and broke, but I paid it no heed. All that I cared about was protecting the image from the impurity of the street. After all, Father, Viṣṇu has blessed you with his protection and boundless good fortune. It was the least I could do in return."

"The night of your wedding," the king said, "you vanished for several hours. Where did you go?"

"Oh, Father, it makes me blush, but I suppose I must tell you the truth. Frightened by the prospect of practicing rati with my new bride, I visited a pub and drank toddy until my fears vanished. Alas, our wedding night was a sham. She thought I meant to hurt her. Women believe I am as evil as I am ugly."

"Perhaps in time she will overcome her fears."

"I hope so, Father."

He stood there silently, waiting for his father to speak.

Finally the king said, "Is there nothing else you wish to tell me?"

Rāma appeared to consider the question with care. "Only that I love you," he said at last.

A massive pyre had been constructed quickly at the expense of the silk guild and under the supervision of Dakṣa. It sat at a corner of the burning ground, like a crude house of dried timber, so tall that the caṇḍālas had to hoist the bodies across their backs and climb ladders to reach the top. The dead were laid out upon a carpet of black antelope skins, first the children—Nanda, Pinaka, Nipa, and

Mitra, who had been so brave—then Viśvāvasu and Mandarikā, Yāmunī and Govinda, old Mālati. A brāhmaṇa of exceptional purity sacrificed nine cows, one for each of them. The three ritual fires were ignited all at once, and the mourners watched with anticipation to see which flame would reach the corpses first. The air was deathly still, with not a hint of a breeze. The smoke streamed straight up, three dark ribbons against a light gray sky. They converged as perfectly as trained temple dancers, a portent of supreme good fortune. All seven of them would surely be liberated from the bondage of karma, the cycle of eternal rebirth.

Dattaka stood apart from the rest of the mourners and guild members, along with Anusūyā and Sarasvatī. He did not cry. None of them cried. They seemed like sleepwalkers, dazed, glassy-eyed, hardly responding when friends and family came forward with words of sympathy. Nanā watched them with concern, intervening when it seemed that too many mourners were crowding them, demanding too much of them. She knew from experience that dealing with sympathetic friends in the wake of a crisis could be as stressful as the crisis itself.

The instant the flames reached her husband's body, Anusūyā's eyes flew open, as if she had been suddenly slapped awake. "Govinda!" she screamed, and ran toward the pyre. The air rippled with waves of heat. The whole world seemed immersed in molten glass. The brāhmaṇa had secretly ordered the caṇḍālas to leave a ladder standing so she might avail herself of it if she came to her senses in time. Could she climb the rungs in this searing heat, weakened as she was with grief? Nobody considered stopping her; to the contrary, a feeling of relief passed through those gathered below. The stamina she exhibited then was certainly a gift from the gods, a reward for a life of courage and kindness. She climbed quickly up the ladder, walked through the flames with the joyful expression of a young bride taking the seven steps, and, lying down at her husband's side, allowed the fires to consume her.

The brāhmaṇa began a new series of mantras to speed the passage of her ātman and to celebrate her courage and love for her husband. She had made the final, ultimate sacrifice of the satī, the virtuous wife.

* * *

Dakṣa insisted that Dattaka, Sarasvatī, and Nanā sleep in the guest quarters of his magnificent house. It was customary, after a member's death, for the guild to assume responsibility for the welfare of the family, and Dakṣa felt that duty particularly strongly because of his friendship with the king. He made it clear that the orphans were to stay with him for as long as they liked, for the rest of their lives if they so desired. Since he lived alone and had many śūdra servants to care for him, they would be little imposition.

During the night Dattaka awoke, screaming with terror. In moments a dark form was beside him, rubbing his hands and whispering soothing words.

"Nanā?" he said. "Is that you? I had the most terrible dream."

She was all dressed and had the smells of the night on her, as though she had just returned from one of her endless walks. Poised on her shoulder, yellow talons dug into the black cloth of her cloak, was the mynah. He tilted his head at Dattaka and the moonlight caught in his glass-bead eyes. Aside from a few scorched feathers, he seemed intact.

"He lives?" Dattaka asked, amazed that anything so frivolous as a poetry-quoting bird could have survived the conflagration.

Nanā smiled. "Tonight I walked by the ruins of the house. I saw something dark, hopping among the charred ruins. Thinking it was a rat, I grabbed a stick and made ready to strike at it. And then I saw it was my mynah. Alas, he no longer flies, nor does he speak. Yet I thank the gods for his company."

She sat down on the edge of the bed and, allowing the mynah to climb onto her finger, offered him to Dattaka. Dattaka sat up, took the bird on his own finger, and stroked his scorched feathers.

"I am glad he lives," Dattaka agreed. "Even silent, he comforts me."

"I think I prefer him without his endless versifying."

"How did he learn so many quatrains?"

"He was once the property of a poet. This poet, like all of his profession, could find nothing to do with his time that might profit society, so he spent it drinking toddy and teaching his bird verse."

"And was he in love with you, Nanā? Did he give you the mynah as a token of his passion?"

"He owed me money," she said sourly, "and he gave me the bird in payment of his debt. That is why I call him Suvarṇam, which is Sanskrit for 'gold.' "

Dattaka laughed.

"Do you wish to go back to sleep?" Nanā asked.

"I would talk a little more, if you do not mind."

Nanā smiled. "I would like nothing better. When I am alone, there are only the voices of my past, reminding me of my mistakes. How do you fare?"

"There is a great emptiness in my heart."

"You worry me," Nanā said, "and so does your sister."

"Sarasvatī? What of her?"

"She is not as strong as you. She lies on her bed but does not sleep. She makes no response when I speak to her, and when I lift her hand, it is limp and cold. In fact, I suspect she has retreated to a chamber of the soul where none can reach her."

"Perhaps she has a demon in her."

"Many demons," Nanā agreed. "The death of her family, the betrayal of her lover. We must make up for all of them. Can you help me do that?"

Dattaka simply gazed at her without replying. His thoughts were elsewhere. Finally he said, "The killers wanted me, didn't they?"

Nanā nodded.

"And had they found me, they might have let the others live?"

"Such limbs of logic bear no fruit."

"Who are they?" Dattaka asked. "You must tell me now, for I shall have my vengeance on them. I shall see them die at the blade of my sword, every one of them."

"One lone boy who does not even own a sword? Those who would kill you are men of wealth and power. Heed my words: tend to your own survival and let the gods attend to the vengeance."

"Then you know who they are! Tell me at once."

"Tomorrow Dakṣa will talk to you. He will tell you what you must know to survive."

"Then at least tell me about myself," he pleaded. "Who am I that I would drive men to such ugly acts?"

"This, too, must be Dakṣa's decision."

"And what of my initiation? Will it ever take place, or will I spend the rest of my life an outsider? For then I should have climbed on the funeral pyre too, and immolated myself along with all those I loved."

"Dakṣa shall decide."

"For all the power you impart to him, his name might be Viṣṇu instead."

"As far as your life is concerned," Nanā said, "he is indeed the god of your fate. If you live, it is by his cunning and mercy."

Dattaka lay back in bed, making a pillow of his hands, and gazed at the ceiling, considering this last remark with a troubled expression. Nanā reached out and smoothed his hair, as mothers do.

"Nanā," he said, "can I ask you something?"

"Anything, my dear."

"Is it true that in ancient times a widow was not expected to die on her husband's funeral pyre? Is it true that she was allowed to remarry and live as before?"

"Many practices were allowed in ancient times that are forbidden in this evil Kali Age."

"I once overheard a Yavana who was visiting Father say that the brāhmaṇas made a widow burn herself so she would not steal her husband's money and poison him while he was alive."

"Dattaka!" Nanā was appalled. "How can you believe such stories? Can you imagine Anusūyā behaving thus with Govinda? She loved him so. And no one *made* her take to the pyre. It was her own decision."

"But she loved Sarasvatī, and me too. And we needed her more, because we are still alive and aching with loss." His voice became strained, as though he was going to cry. "So why did she do it, Nanā? Why did she kill herself?"

"Because that is our custom."

"But *why* is it our custom?"

Nanā sighed. "Why do our people do any of the things they do? Why do we pierce our earlobes? Why do we walk clockwise around the deity? Why do we wake in the morning and go to sleep at night, and stroll upon our feet instead of our elbows?"

"Then she killed herself for no better reason than that it was what she had seen others do?"

"A widow's lot is a hard one. She must sleep on the ground

and keep out of sight. She is a bad omen to all but her own children. She cannot attend the weddings of her daughters or join in festival days. And if she lapses from her asceticism for even an instant, she imperils her husband's spirit, for though he is no longer flesh, their destinies are still intertwined. But if she throws herself on his pyre, she dies as she lived, by her husband's side, and gains the most excellent karma, to benefit herself and her children for hundreds of generations to come."

"But why did she kill herself?" he insisted, as though he had heard not a word of what she had said. "I needed her more. She was my mother, she was all I had left. Who will take care of me now? Who will cover me at night and cook my supper? What am I going to do, Nanā? I cannot live without her. I must have her back! I must!" He kept saying these last words over and over again, and suddenly he was pounding her with his fists, and crying, and gasping for breath. She put her arms around him and held him very close, frightened for him, at the depth of his rage and anguish, and concerned too for her own safety, for his strength was considerable. But then he went limp and rested against her, suddenly very much a small boy, his body racked with sobs. She held him for a long time before he fell asleep. Then she laid him gently down and pulled the covers up over him, kissed him on the forehead, and tiptoed from his chamber.

The next morning Sarasvatī was gone. One of the servants reported seeing her leave Dakṣa's house before dawn, heading for the main gates of the city. By questioning street sweepers and vendors, Nanā and Dattaka traced her journey down to the river. By the time they reached the bank, a band of pilgrims were dragging her limp body to dry ground. Her long black tresses clung to her face and neck and shoulders, and her skin was gray and green, as though it had absorbed the color of the water, like fabric in a vat of dye. A holy man, the only one bathing there at that early hour, had seen her walk to the banks. Thinking her another pilgrim, he made no effort to stop her, that is, not until she crossed from the shallow part of the river to the center, where the currents were swift and deadly. As soon as he realized her intentions, he called to her, but she paid him no heed. Alas, he could not touch her, for to touch a woman would have been to incur the worst impurity. Only the fact that her body had lodged between two rocks had stopped her from being swept out to sea.

Standing on the shore, in a ring about her body, those pilgrims who happened to be present agreed that there was no finer way to die than to drown in that holiest of rivers.

Dakṣa called Dattaka into his sanctum, a chamber in the rear of the house where he retired every evening to chew betal quid and review the day's business. He sat on some cushions behind a low desk of polished rosewood, which he used to write upon, and motioned Dattaka toward a cushion facing him. Surprised by the texture beneath his bare feet, Dattaka looked down and saw that the rug he trod upon was the entire skin of a tiger, head and all, its mouth propped open in a fierce grimace. Other animal skins were stretched across the walls in lieu of tapestries of paintings, so that their stripes and spots, their varied textures and grains, might be displayed to the best advantage.

"You are surprised to see animal skins?" Dakṣa said, amused.

Dattaka nodded as he sank down cross-legged on the cushions. While he was not often shy, he felt intimidated by the presence of this old man who sat on the king's privy council and exercised such influence over the commerce of the country.

"I didn't expect . . ." he began. "What I mean is, a man of your purity. . . ."

Dakṣa cackled with merriment. "I have no purity! I mock the gods."

"But you are so kind. You cannot pass a beggar without dipping into your purse. And yesterday, when we were homeless, you took us in as though we were your own children."

"I wanted to help you. I have very much, and others have little."

"Then you enforce the dharma."

"I do what I like."

"I don't understand."

"We have much to talk about tonight, but we would do well to know each other better before we begin. While I was a frequent visitor to your home, I always listened more than I spoke. As a result, I learned a great deal about you, while you learned only a little about me. So I will tell you a story I am fond of telling in the hope that you may better understand who I am."

He paused to take a betel quid from a brass box. His ivory teeth were dyed orange from chewing them. He offered one to Dattaka, but the boy shook his head.

"In my youth," he went on, "I believed that man could achieve moksa, liberation from this painful existence. I traveled all around the world looking for a great guru to help me achieve this end. I searched the hot sultry jungles of the Dravidians and climbed the snow-capped peaks of the Himalayas. One day I met a great forest hermit, a man with beautiful eyes and white hair that reached to the ground, who had lived in a hut for forty years eating nothing but roots and berries and had never known a woman. I sat with him beneath a palm, delighting in his darshan, when suddenly a coconut fell from the canopy of leaves overhead and cracked his skull. With his legs still crossed in the lotus manner, he rolled over backward, dead."

Dattaka drew in his breath with dismay.

"At that very instant," Dakṣa continued, "I had a great insight."

"Yes?" Dattaka said.

Dakṣa leaned forward and raised one eyebrow. "It was as simple as this: Alive is alive! Dead is dead! Pleasure is pleasure, and pain is pain! Life's only illusion is to believe things other than what they are!" He cackled with glee and, leaning even closer, added in a whisper, "I would have human skins stretched on these walls, but then who would visit me?"

Dattaka just sat there with his mouth open, not knowing what to say.

"You are very quiet for a young man with so many questions," Dakṣa remarked.

Realizing this was the opportunity he had been waiting for, the boy plunged ahead. "I must know who killed my family. I will not sleep until I have vengeance upon them."

Dakṣa smiled. "Then you will grow very sleepy."

"Do not mock me. I am young, but my sword is quick, and my arrow can pierce the mango fruit at five hundred paces."

"Would that all your enemies were mangoes. Those agreeable fruit neither flee, nor fight back, nor plot against you while you sleep."

Dattaka stood up. "I will leave now," he said, the resolve of his politeness crumbling abruptly. "You seem to have no purpose but to ridicule me as you ridicule the lives of those animals whose skins are stretched across your walls."

"Sit down," Dakṣa ordered. "You cannot afford luxuries like pride. Step out my door, child, and you will go to the five elements by nightfall."

"I don't care," Dattaka said.

"If your responsibility were only to yourself, I might allow such foolishness. But the future of the dharma itself may rest on your survival."

"Is that what Nanā meant when she said I was the brightest jewel in mankind's golden crown?"

"Forget such notions of grandeur. For the moment we must concern ourselves with getting you out of Pāṭaliputra, out of Magadha, out of the land of the Sons of Bharata altogether. I have considered many plans since last night, but one pleases me most, for it accomplishes two ends. As you may recall, your father and I had been concerned about the influx from China of that silk called the Golden Fire. We secretly planned to send a few of our bravest men to that far land, to learn the secret for us. You will be among them."

"You want me to go to China?"

"Yes."

"But . . ." It seemed like such an impossible scheme, he didn't know where his objections should begin. "It is so distant! How will I find my way? And what of my return? I fear I will be eaten by one-horned horses or drowned in the sea. No, I cannot go, it is out of the question."

"I have financed a caravan, and you will travel with it. There will be sixty bullock carts, a dozen guards on horseback, and the finest land pilot in the state to guide you. He has made twelve trips to China already and knows the routes the way you know the path from doorstep to hearth."

"But when I arrive in China—what then? I neither speak nor understand their strange language. How will I find their silk farms?

And if by chance I do, and they discover me snooping about, they will certainly kill me, for I understand they guard the secret of their silk production every bit as carefully as we do our own."

Dakṣa nodded. "So they do. Their silk farms are veritable fortresses, protected by high walls and patrolled by savage dogs. But no door will be barred to you, for you will arrive tonsured and dressed in saffron, and quoting the words of the Buddha."

"Excuse me?" Dattaka said, completely baffled.

"You will go disguised as a Buddhist monk, in the company of a half dozen other false monks. The Chinese, you see, are starved for Buddhism. They adore it and cannot get enough. Surely you have seen them visiting our city, buying up statues of the Buddha and scrolls of his sayings to translate into their own tongue. As a Buddhist monk, you will gain access to all the finest homes. And in time, if you keep your eyes and ears open, you will learn the secret of the Golden Fire."

"But—I cannot!" He threw up his hands in despair. "I know nothing of Buddhism! I am a Viṣṇuite."

"You will learn. You will leave for the great Buddhist monastery at Nālandā this very night. There you will study the teachings of the compassionate one, as well as Chinese and any other skills you may need for your journey. Of course, the monks at Nālandā will believe that your desire to learn Buddhism is sincere. They will know nothing of our plan. So say farewell to your homeland of Magadha, for it shall be years before you again set eyes on its rice paddies and rolling hills."

"But . . ." Dattaka hesitated, his mind so crowded with misgivings that he did not know which to voice first. "But what of my initiation?"

"There is no time."

"I must be initiated!" Dattaka pleaded. "Otherwise, I will wear no sacred thread. I will be excluded from my class, and from Āryan society. I will be no better than the loathesome caṇḍālas who cart the bodies to the burning grounds. I will be nothing!" Tears welled in his eyes.

"Ritual does not make a man a warrior or a priest," Dakṣa said softly.

"I cannot go."

"You cannot stay."

"There is someone who keeps me here."

"If it is Nanā you worry about, she may go with you."

He shook his head glumly. "Another."

"One who wears an earring of glass and iron around her neck, though she owns pearls and diamonds beyond number?"

Dattaka looked at the old man suspiciously, not daring to hope.

Dakṣa let his thin lips relax into a smile. Without a word, he lifted a trembling forefinger, as knotty and twisted as a twig, toward the entrance to the adjoining chamber.

Not knowing what to expect, Dattaka rose and approached the room. He was filled with apprehension. He pulled aside the tapestry and saw a dwarf sitting on cushions, throwing the dice. His partner, a young girl, sat with her back toward the entrance, engrossed in the game.

"Thank the gods you've arrived," the dwarf said noticing the visitor. "One more roll of the nuts"—so the dice were called, for in Vedic times nuts had been used in their stead—"and I would be ruined."

The girl turned. It was Dhruvādevī. Her smile upon seeing Dattaka was so radiant that it seemed to illuminate the chamber like a tiny sun. She rose and took a step toward him. For a time they stood there, gazing at each other shyly.

"Never again will we be parted," he said, moving to her side and grasping her hand. "And when we return from China, years hence, you will take a new name and live as my wife."

"Wait," she said hurriedly, "you misunderstand. I cannot go with you tonight."

"Tomorrow, then?"

"Never. I must stay here, at the palace, with my husband the prince."

The pain spread over his face, as the blood of a wounded man soaks the gauze. He let go of her hand, and his voice, when he spoke again, was dark with accusation.

"Then why did you come here?"

"To see you one last time before you left. Oh, Dattaka, do not hate me. What choice do I have?"

"You could go to China with me," he said, the words sounding foolish even as he spoke them.

"I am the wife of Rāma Gupta. My duty is to him."

"Go, then," Dattaka said angrily. "Go to your husband the prince and bother me no more!"

"I risked my life to see you this last time. Let us be happy so that the memory of tonight may sustain me through the sad times to come."

She reached for his hand once again.

He drew away from her. "You didn't have to marry him." His voice was twisted with pain. "You could have run away. Now you are his princess forever."

"Dattaka, please!" she cried.

He would not hear her.

"I will go now to Nālandā," he told Dakṣa, turning his back on the princess, "or any place else you wish to send me. Nothing more holds me to this life."

8

The Vaidya touched the cheek of the man from whom he had successfully removed a gallstone three days before, drawing it out through a minute incision in the anal canal, a process requiring the utmost dexterity and patience. The patient's flesh was as hot as hearthstones. He tried to hide his disappointment from the students gathered around the bed; it would not do for them to learn, so early in their studies, that their "wise" teacher was himself only a neophyte stumbling about in the dark. For every healing trick he learned, a hundred new problems defined themselves. And, as always, the problem that irked him most was the fever. It was indeed a demon sworn to plague him, to torture his patients and mock at his attempts to fight back.

He showed his students how to swab parts of the body with clothes soaked in cold water and described how, if the heat grew excessive, the patient might be carried to the river and immersed up to the neck for brief periods of time. As he lectured, he thought of another fever long ago, that of Queen Sāvitrīdevī, whose passing had set in motion the chain of events, of "causation," as the Buddhists like to say, that had resulted in his coming here to the great monastery at Nālandā.

Nālandā had begun hundreds of years ago as a simple Buddhist monastery, commemorating a holy place, or caitya, where some of the Buddha's ashes had been buried. Over the centuries, nourished by an influx of scientists, philosophers, scholars, and pilgrims from all over the civilized world, it had grown to a great city, a "university" where government was democratic and class distinctions were abandoned. Freethinking, discourse, and dialogue of all kinds were encouraged. Physiology, astronomy, mathematics, logic, and epistemology were taught, as well as the sacred books of the brāhmaṇas. Since the Buddha had laid emphasis on the healing arts, the Ayurvedic sciences received special attention. The greatest vaidyas of the land came there to practice and teach. Every medicinal herb known was cultivated in the gardens, and the hospital that had been erected, a hall of baked bricks, with whitewashed walls and dung floors, and many windows to let in the sun and air, was one of the finest.

The Vaidya had never been so happy. The adoration of his patients had always made him uncomfortable—the grateful women offering themselves for kāma, the men pressing gifts upon him, the students deifying him. Here, his individual identity was submerged within a brotherhood whose sole aim was to improve the welfare of man. There was no glorification of individuals. Even the abbot took a turn in the kitchen. The work had no reward but the pleasure of its own execution.

"Our greatest problem," he told his students, as they moved toward the exit of the hospital, having finished their round of patients, "is the fever. If only we knew whence it arose, or its cause, thousands of lives could be saved. My own teacher, a vaidya of great experience, taught me that the fever was a result of the samana, the wind that fans the fires of the stomach, sending those fires out of control. Yet my own observations have led me to doubt this. Fever appears least frequently when the wound can be cauterized with heat. Why should the application of heat reduce the heat of the body? It also seems that the cleaner the surroundings, the less the likelihood that the fever will attack. This, too, is a mystery. Perhaps someday one of you will find the answer."

A monk appeared at the end of the hall. His shaven head was as smooth and brown as a nut. His cheeks were sunken. His expression was grave, while his pupils were aflame with an inner light. At first sight, one might have thought him a young man, for there were few wrinkles on his face, and his stride showed the formidable energy of youth. Yet there, on second look, was the wisdom and suffering of a lifetime—or several, if one believed in the transmigration of the soul. Like the others, he wore an underrobe, a robe, a cloak, a cloth girdle, and a belt, all patched together from old rags and clothing donated by the laity and all dyed a brilliant saffron, an auspicious color for the spiritual life. Simple rope sandals protected his feet from the heat of the ground. No ornament or special vestment distinguished him as the abbot of the grandest monastery on earth. In the Buddhist order, or sangha as it was called, there was no rank but seniority of ordination, and the position of abbot, chosen by consensus among the rest, was more a convenience for expediting business than anything else.

When he reached the Vaidya, he lowered his head and pressed his palms together in namaste. "Brother, if you are done with your patients," the elder monk began, "then perhaps you have time for me."

"I am never done with my patients," the Vaidya replied with a small smile, "but I always have time for you, Brother Yāsa."

The distant sound of drum beats, four in a row, and two blasts of the conch indicated the time for the morning chores. The monks dispersed quickly. Their schedule was strenuous, and every task, from meditation to cleaning the latrines, had to be executed with the utmost attentiveness, for attentiveness was the principal path to enlightenment.

The Vaidya walked beside Brother Yāsa into the courtyard, where mango groves shaded them from the blinding sun. The walls were decorated with frescoes of blissful bodhisattvas dispersed with geometrical precision throughout their heavenly domain. A karṇikāra tree trailed golden blossoms, and blue lotuses with wide-open calyxes floated on the surface of a stream that wound through the grounds, crossed here and there by wooden footbridges with delicate latticework railings. This courtyard, with its beautiful sights and smells, all calculated to aid patients in their recovery, was one of eight annexes that had been added, over hundreds of years, to the original courtyard and stūpa.

Even from where they stood, the Vaidya and the abbot could see the top of the stūpa, the repository of a share of the Buddha's ashes. It was a vast, creamy-white hemisphere set on a huge pedestal, like an egg in an egg cup, girdled with terraces that could be reached by steps, and topped with a ceremonial stone umbrella and a golden spire. A smaller stūpa occupied each corner of the courtyard, corresponding with the four points of the compass, each containing the remains of a monk of outstanding piety. A great brick wall, three stories high, surrounded the courtyard, containing within its colonnade the simple chambers where the monks lived.

"I wish to talk to you about the group of pilgrims that arrived last night," Brother Yāsa said, inviting the Vaidya to sit with him in the shade of a mango grove. "A young boy and a woman. People of wealth, I would guess, for they travel with many bearers and bodyguards."

"It sounds not at all an unusual group," the Vaidya said, wondering why his friend had bothered bringing it to his attention. Wealthy parties frequently came visiting from Pāṭaliputra to view the stūpas, hear a lecture, leave a few paṇas for the purpose of accumulating merit. The trip took only four days by foot, due southwest, along good roads with many inns and rest stops.

"They brought fine silks and jewels for our treasury," the abbot went on. "Now that the state is cutting back support, such gifts are welcome."

"Then accept them. What is the problem?"

"I . . ." He hesitated, and smiled. "Does it amuse you that I, the abbot, who am supposed to be the most venerable and wise of this monastery, always bring my problems to you?"

The Vaidya shrugged. "It is the mystique of my profession. Because I know a few tricks of healing, and after more patients than I care to recall have perfected a thoughtful manner of listening, people assume I know all the answers. If anything, I am like the bowl of the vīṇā, which makes louder the plucked string; at times I can help a man understand that he knows that which he knew all along."

"The problem is the woman. I doubt her sincerity."

The Vaidya shrugged. "All are skeptical at the beginning. When they hear the beauty of the Buddha's teaching, then they become sincere."

"I fear I am not making myself clear. Let me tell you what happened and you will better understand. No sooner do they arrive than the woman insists on a private audience. She tells me she is greatly concerned about the boy in her charge, for he is listless and sleeps poorly, and seems interested in nothing. Then she asks if we have a great vaidya here who might care for him. Well, I reply, we have many great vaidyas, and one of them will certainly take him as a patient. But this is not enough. She insists that there is a special vaidya, a mahāvaidya, whose reputation has traveled as far as Ujjayinī, a short man with a nose—you will excuse me for saying this—like a fig."

"A fig?" The Vaidya reached up and felt his own nose. Then he laughed. "I suppose she means me. Well, I will be happy to see the boy. I can always fit another patient into my schedule."

"You miss my point," the abbot continued. "Though she claimed to be concerned only in the boy's recovery, I could not help but think that she had some special, personal interest in you, for her words grew quick when she spoke of you, and her hands trembled, and a certain light gleamed in her eyes."

"I cannot imagine why such a woman—" Suddenly he broke off and paled, and his features underwent a remarkable transformation. "What did you say her name was?"

"The others call her Nanā. Her true name I did not ask."

The Vaidya's eyes opened wide, and he reached out and grabbed the abbot's wrist. "Describe her!"

"She wears a black veil."

"But what of her form? Is she slight and slender, and graceful as a deer?"

"She is all those things."

"No, it could not be," the Vaidya whispered, shaking his head. "Not here. Not after all this time."

"I will not pry," the abbot said. "Your life before you came to Nālandā is your own business. But, knowing that you wish with all your heart to achieve enlightenment, I must remind you that emotional entanglements will bind you to the wheel of rebirth for ages to come. Consider this please, and then tell me if you wish to see her. Otherwise, I will send her away."

"Send her away," he said quickly, and immediately changed his mind. "No, you must not! I could not deny the boy my healing skills. Or is it my own selfish desire to see her once again? If indeed it is her. For all I know, it might be an old patient come to complain about some growth I cut away ten years ago. Oh, why did I ever allow myself to become involved with one such as her! I should have stayed in bed that fateful night with the covers pulled over my head."

"Will you see her?" the abbot pressed.

"Oh, I don't know. I don't know."

"You must give me an answer."

"Yes. No! Yes." The Vaidya, realizing how foolish he must have seemed, forced himself to be decisive. "This evening, in front of the great stūpa, before the final meditation."

A public place was best, and between meditations, so he might have an excuse to leave if necessary.

Satisfied, the abbot returned to his cell.

For some time afterward the Vaidya remained seated on the stone bench beneath the mango trees, musing over the workings of a karma that would reunite would-be lovers with monastic halls.

The Vaidya had climbed to the highest of the wood terraces that circled the stūpa so he could have a view of the entire courtyard and catch the first glimpse of her approach. The setting sun had left him in the monument's chill shadow and painted the two smaller stūpas facing him a warm pink. He rested his elbows on the fretwork railing and wished that he were somewhere else, anywhere else, rather than here, listening to his heart drum with anticipation. For the first time since his arrival at Nālandā, his tranquillity had been shattered. He found himself craving betel quid, and chewing on his nails, a habit he had abandoned in his youth. He prayed this mysterious woman in black would be Sutanukā; he prayed with equal fervor that she would be someone else.

He could recall no personal struggle as intense as that following the vow of celibacy he had taken upon entering Nālandā. While previously his pursuit of kāma had been confined to an occasional dalliance with a sophisticated older woman who had once been his patient, or with the pretty maid who brought him special herbs that only grew in the south, now that he was forced to abandon it once and forever, his imagination ran wild. During meditation he would imagine the most lascivious scenes involving buxom dancing girls and concubines in number. And always Sutanukā was among them, leading him on. It had been such a problem that he had considered leaving the monastery. But Brother Yāsa had told him that such experiences were commonplace. He need only sincerely wish for the urge to leave him, and in time it would fall away, like the skin of a snake when it grows dry and useless. The abbot had been right. Within a year, his meditation was no longer disturbed by thoughts of women; a few years more and the erotic dreams, the waking to find his pallet damp with his ejaculate, even those became a thing of the past. So he had thought he was over it forever, the impulse that lowers men to the level of dogs and makes them slaves to the lingam's single desire to rid itself of semen. Yet now, a decade later, he felt the stirrings, as strong and disruptive as when he'd been a young man.

Śiva, deploying his lethal third eye, had burned the pleasure goddess Kāma to ashes when she had attempted to disturb his meditation atop Mount Kailāsa. And during his meditation beneath the bodhi tree, the Buddha had managed to ignore the efforts of Māra's three voluptuous daughters—Desire, Pleasure, and Passion. The Vaidya knew too well that he was neither the God of Ascetics, as Śiva is sometimes called, nor the Sage of the Sākyas.

The fact that Sutanukā was the most beautiful woman in Magadha might alone have tested his will; that she was also cultured and witty, a charming companion, and an expert in the art of pleasing men seemed unfair. And if all that were not enough, there was one thing more: he loved her still.

Now he saw through the dusk the figure of a woman all veiled in black, crossing the courtyard. Though her face was hidden, her stride was familiar, as was the easy grace with which she climbed from terrace to terrace. By the time she reached him, his heart was racing and the blood was drumming in his ears.

"Victory to you, sir," she said, her palms pressed together in namaste.

He had expected her to sound like Sutanukā and was shocked by the low, rasping timbre of her voice. Yet the cadence was familiar. How puzzling!

"You are the visitor from Pāṭaliputra?" he managed to get out. "The abbot said you wished to speak to me."

"I have traveled here with a boy named Dattaka, who has a sickness of the soul. Perhaps you, who are known as the greatest vaidya in the land, can help him. A band of thieves . . . Why do you stare at me so?"

"Forgive me, but you remind me of a woman I once knew. Continue, please."

"As I was saying, a band of thieves massacred his family and burned down his home. The loss of those he loved did him great harm. There seems to have been a death within him, too."

"How could a boy not be harmed by such an awful event? But children are resilient in a way that we are not. Send him to my chamber in the morning, after meditation, and I will do what I can for him."

"This unworthy woman thanks you from the bottom of her heart," she said, prostrating herself before him.

When she rose, he looked at her eyes—all of her face that showed above the veil—and compared them with his recollection of Sutanukā's eyes. But the latter had lined her lids with kohl while the former used none. Never before had the Vaidya appreciated how great a change a touch of makeup might cause in a woman's appearance. The pitting of the skin around her eyes—smallpox scars?

Then he understood.

The rasping voice, the veils, the change of profession.

It was Sutanukā indeed. Sutanukā stricken with smallpox. What use had a king for an ugly gaṇikā? He had dismissed her, and she had found a position with one of the city's wealthy families, caring for their children. The family had been killed, and she had come to him for help.

"Again you stare at me!"

"Excuse me, but I cannot get over how you remind me of that woman I mentioned before. Are you quite sure we have never met?"

"With all respect, the Vaidya must be mistaken. I would never have forgotten such a meeting, however brief."

The Vaidya nodded thoughtfully.

The sun had dropped behind the hills. Quite suddenly it was dark, and the sky was glistening with stars. The Vaidya bade the woman goodnight and returned to his small, barren chamber, his heart overflowing with joy.

The Vaidya was sitting on the floor of his chamber, darning his robe in the bright morning light, when a slim, handsome boy drew aside the tapestry across the entrance.

"I am Dattaka," he said. "I was told you would teach me about Buddhism."

At the Vaidya's permission, he entered and prostrated himself.

The Vaidya glanced down at the boy's back, then looked again. There, on his left shoulder blade, was a birthmark shaped like a cobra. The Vaidya shivered with fear and awe at the wondrous patterns woven by karma upon the loom of his life. Eleven years ago he had delivered an infant with that same strange, auspicious mark in precisely the same place. Supposedly Candra Gupta II had been killed by a rattle filled with virulent scorpions. Yet here was a lad of eleven autumns, an orphan judging by his name, whose skin bore the reddish tint of the kṣatriya and whose face was a youthful—and pleasanter—version of Samudra Gupta's scowling countenance.

"What are you doing?" Dattaka demanded, as the Vaidya reached forward and rubbed a lock of the boy's hair between his fingers. A black oily substance came off on his thumb and index finger.

"The texture of the hair can tell us much about a boy's health."

So the Vaidya said, but his mind buzzed with questions. Why had they counterfeited the young prince's death? And colored his hair to make him look like a normal boy and sent him to grow up with a normal family in the city? Was it just coincidence that, but for him, the entire family had been slaughtered? The Vaidya's heart went out to the poor boy, orphaned twice.

"You have grown into a fine young man," the Vaidya said, unable to resist complimenting the both of them.

"You knew me when I was a child?" Dattaka asked, puzzled.

"I—no, of course not. I was thinking of another. I am old, and my mind wanders." To an eleven-year-old, the Vaidya knew, anyone beyond the age of twenty seemed mature, and a man approaching fifty years, ancient.

He proceeded to ask the boy some questions about himself, his foster family, what games he enjoyed, and which festival days were his favorites, less for the answers themselves than to observe his behavior while answering. From Dattaka's listless manner, the rings beneath his eyes, the dullness in his gaze—as though he had drawn a membrane across it for protection as certain reptiles do—it was apparent that the three doṣas had been thrown into an imbalance, the phlegm dominating the wind and the bile, causing a tamasic condition. He was reasonably certain he could return the boy to health. But first he would have to make friends and win his confidence.

"Do you know the story of the Buddha?"

"I think so." His voice was scarcely audible. "I mean, I don't know. My foster father was a Viṣṇuite. He could quote the holy books and argue about the meaning of the subtlest verses. I was going to study the holy books too but . . ." The boy became agitated by the memory and broke off.

The Vaidya did not press him. He began in a soothing voice: "The Buddha was born of the Śākya tribe that lived at the foot of the Himalayas. That is why he is sometimes called Śākyamuni—the muni, or sage, of the Śākyas. His mother, Mahāmāya, the queen of the tribe, dreamt that the guardians of the four quarters of the universe came to bathe her and a wondrous white elephant with a lotus in his trunk entered her side. It was a very auspicious dream, the wise men of the tribe agreed. Her son would be an avatāra, or a cakravartin." The Vaidya hesitated. "Do you know what those words mean, 'avatāra,' 'cakravartin'?"

"The avatāras were the incarnations of Viṣṇu," Dattaka said. "The fish, the tortoise, the boar, and all the rest. The brāhmaṇa who taught my brother Mitra used to say that the Buddha himself was just another incarnation of Viṣṇu."

"The Viṣṇuites would gobble up faiths as a whale does little fishes," the Vaidya said ruefully.

"As for the other word, I know it not."

"As an avatāra is born on earth to guide men spiritually, so the cakravartin will lead them politically. It is at best a shaky distinction, as the spiritual and the political are so closely intertwined that they are nearly one and the same. King Śuddhodana, the Buddha's father, did not want his son to become either of these things, so he confined Siddhārtha—that was how they had named him—to a wonderful palace, where all signs of human misery had been erased. The young prince was surrounded with beautiful objects and scintillating company, yet he was not happy.

"One day while riding in the park in his chariot, he spied a creature the likes of which he had never seen. He asked his charioteer as to the nature of this repulsive beast, and his charioteer replied that it was a man who had grown old and enfeebled. Siddhārtha was deeply disturbed to learn that men grew old."

"How did the old man get into the park?" Dattaka asked. "It would have seemed a simple enough task to keep him out."

"A very good question. In fact, it was not an old man at all, but one of the gods, disguised as an old man, determined to help Siddhārtha become the Buddha."

"Oh. I see."

"Next he saw a sick man, covered with pox, shaking from the chills."

"Another god?"

The Vaidya nodded. "Siddhārtha's charioteer told him that this was disease, another cause of human suffering."

"I would not be surprised if that charioteer were also a god," Dattaka said to himself.

"And finally they passed a procession carrying a corpse to the burning ground. As in the other instances, his charioteer explained that this was death and that it claimed all men at the end of their lives. The discovery that he himself would someday die disturbed Siddhārtha most of all."

"But as he began to despair, he saw a sign of hope, a wandering monk in saffron robes, wearing a blissful smile. At that instant he recognized this future as his own future."

"I'll wager his father wasn't very happy," Dattaka said.

"Well, not at first perhaps. But he was a wise man. He knew there was a time for a father to let go of his children."

The Vaidya fell silent, thinking of his own students back in Pāṭaliputra and how they had wept at his departure. He cleared his throat and continued. "Siddhārtha went out into the world and wandered about as a beggar. Then he lived in the forest and studied the Upaniṣads with a great teacher. Finally, he joined with five other ascetics and tried to find liberation through fasting and mortification of the flesh. In time he realized even that path led nowhere."

"What did he do?"

"He sat down to meditate beneath a pipal tree, making a solemn vow that he would not stir until he had solved the riddle of human suffering, even if it meant his death. He sat for forty-nine days. Oh, it was not easy. He was tempted by all sorts of demons and devils, passions and illusions. But he ignored them all. And finally he came upon the great truth."

"Can you tell it to me?"

"The great truth cannot be told. Every man must realize it for himself, through meditation and a proper way of life. In time, if you remain here at Nālandā, you will study the Four Noble Truths and the Eightfold Path, which will serve as signposts for your journey. For the moment, I will tell you this much: out of ignorance arises imagination, thence self-consciousness, thence Name and Form, thence the Six Senses, thence Contact, thence Feeling, thence

Craving, thence Attachment, thence Becoming, thence Rebirth, thence all manifold ills to which the flesh is heir."

"I am not sure I understand," Dattaka said.

"If you did, you would be the Buddha," the Vaidya said, laughing, and sent him away to ponder what he had learned.

More and more during the following days, Dattaka looked forward to visiting the small, hot cell, so damp that moss grew between the bricks. He loved the smell of the Vaidya's moist body, the odor of incense still clinging from the meditation hall, and the fragrance of the karṇikāra tree that bloomed just outside the window. He could have sat forever on the mat facing him, watching the motes dance across the diagonal slash of light that entered from the single high window, and listening to him teach.

After several sessions, Dattaka felt comfortable enough to confide in the Vaidya. He spoke, haltingly, of the princess who had married another, the loss of his family, his aborted initiation, and his exile from Pāṭaliputra. When the boy's grief was such that he could no longer speak, the Vaidya embraced him and held his shaking shoulders until his sobs subsided.

Confessing was like peeling the layers of an onion, working ever deeper toward a core of shame. In time Dattaka revealed that he had come to Nālandā under false pretenses. It was all part of a plan, so that he could learn to play the part of a Buddhist monk convincingly and travel through China unharmed.

"But why would you want to travel through China?" the Vaidya asked.

"To steal the silkworms that spin the Golden Fire and bring them back to the Land of the Sons of Bharata."

"Silkworms?" The Vaidya scratched his head.

"They are very valuable to certain people," Dattaka confided.

"Buy why not send someone more experienced in deceit?"

"My sponsor, the good Dakṣa, would accomplish two purposes: get his silkworms and also have me far away so I would be safe from those who killed my family. You see, it was me they were after. Had I been there, the rogues would certainly have spared the lives of Govinda, and Mitra, and the rest. Now you understand why the death of my family is my fault."

His voice had grown softer and more sorrowful until now he could hardly be heard. "What I don't understand," he went on in a whisper, "is why they want to kill me. I have not violated the dharma. I have taken nothing that was not mine, nor have I harmed anyone. What a puzzle it is!"

A puzzle to Dattaka, but suddenly obvious to the Vaidya: the massacre was Prince Rāma's work. Candra's existence posed another threat to a succession already jeopardized by deformities of character and body. Who else could benefit from such a fine boy's demise?

"So I have come here in deceit," Dattaka said shamefully. "Beat me, or insult me, or throw me out if you like. Surely I deserve no better."

The Vaidya squeezed Dattaka's shoulder. "What brings a man to the Buddha is of no matter," he said, "so long as he comes, and listens, and learns."

Vāmana had been promising to visit Princess Dhruvādevī for days, but some business had always intervened. Had she been deflowered and abandoned by her new husband, as the dwarf had anticipated, he would have found time for her sooner. But since, according to the pervasive rumor, she was still a maiden, he felt no urgency. It was another rumor that finally brought him there, the rumor of her failing health.

Entering her chambers, he was alarmed to find her resembling the children beggars held up when the wealthy pass in their carriages. The skin of her chest was stretched across the ridges of her ribs, and her wrists were as thin and fragile as saplings. Though she smiled when she saw him, it was a fleeting ray of sun that comes between the rains. Rarely within the walls of the palace had he seen so sad a child. He trundled out the very best from his repertoire of jokes and tricks, those that in the past had pleased even the most difficult audience, but to no avail. Finally sensing the uselessness of it, he gave up his forced merrymaking and, sitting beside her, spoke to her sincerely, as a concerned friend. Why wasn't she eating? What was wrong? What might he do to help?

She replied that she had simply lost her appetite, as she had lost the desire to play, or learn, or do anything other than lie in bed. There was nothing wrong, nothing that a visit from Yama, the god of death, wouldn't cure. The dwarf could help her by bringing her a good strong poison.

Alarmed, the dwarf went directly to the king, who was

equally concerned. Whether he cared about the princess or not, he was unquestionably anxious about attracting her father's ire and precipitating war with the Śālāṅkāyanas. He ordered the dwarf to do whatever he felt necessary to make her eat, even if it involved tying her to a rack of the sort they used in the inquisition chamber, opening her throat with a funnel, and trickling in milk and honey and rice water.

Obviously such extreme measures would only aggravate the situation. The dwarf visited the vaidya in town, a sensible young man known as Kaṅka, who, after hearing all her symptoms, prescribed inhaling the smoke produced by burning churrus. It would, he assured the dwarf, both restore her appetite and improve her mood.

Now the problem remained of how the dwarf would approach the princess with this delicate matter. After a time, he thought of a plan. He knew of a queen, a certain Vinatādevī, from whose chambers the sweet smell of churrus issued regularly. She had lived in the harem nine autumns, long enough to know the techniques of keeping the wolves of boredom at bay; yet she was young enough (barely eighteen) to approach the precocious princess as a friend.

She was unusual in other regards as well. For one, she was something of a weed in the king's garden, tall and angular and lacking both the full bosom and the round hips that were the trademark of feminine beauty in the Land of the Sons of Bharata. For another, she frequently stole out of the harem to attend quail fights and cockfights and to drink in the pubs, alongside the men, like a common prostitute.

She was not a special favorite of the dwarf. Still, she was civil enough when he explained Dhruvādevī's plight and asked her to befriend the girl and share some churrus with her.

At the dwarf's encouragement, Vinatādevī sent a messenger to Dhruvādevī's apartments asking if she might come to visit that evening, for no other reason than to make conversation and pass the time enjoyably. She knew that at night people were more easily swayed to do that which ran cross-grain to their nature. Dhruvādevī sent back a noncommittal, "As you like."

Vinatādevī arrived at Dhruvādevī's chambers with a present, a small bronze brazier, beautifully engraved with images of lovers practicing kāma, as were often found on temple walls. Dhruvādevī examined it admiringly, too embarrassed to admit that she had not the vaguest idea how it might be used. Vinatādevī found such grown-up manners amusing in a ten-year-old child.

They sat on cushions, and one of the princess's handmaidens brought them a tray of sweet, chewy sesame balls and cups of sugarcane syrup flavored with lemon and ginger. Two musicians, hidden in an alcove, plucked at their vīṇās and sang softly to entertain them.

For a time neither the woman nor the girl spoke. Vinatādevī sipped at her cane syrup and examined the princess with a bold eye. The princess sat perfectly still, chin raised, practicing her haughtiest expression and staring straight ahead as though she were all alone.

In time the queen, having learned from the dwarf how the princess missed her home by the sea, began to speak of a journey she herself had made to Śiśupālgaṛh several years before. The princess, despite her determination to remain aloof with someone she considered slightly below her in station, was delighted to hear talk of the city she knew so well. Within minutes, she was chattering as freely as she would have with a lifelong friend.

Now Vinatādevī guided the conversation in a different direction so that Dhruvādevī might learn that they had shared similar marital plights.

Samudra Gupta had married Vinatādevī following the death of his golden-haired, blue-eyed Sāvitrīdevī as one rushes to the bazaar to buy a new monkey after one's own pet has died, lest the vacuum created by the creature's absence becomes unbearable. And, just as the new pet always proves a disappointment, failing to live up to the fine qualities of its predecessor, so this queen was a disappointment to the king. In time she became no more than a reminder of Sāvitrīdevī's death and the awful incidents surrounding it, the repercussions of which seemed as though they might spread for all eternity, like the ripples of a stone dropped in a pond. The king grew to dread the sight of her, and the other queens, sensing his disfavor, shunned her also.

Dhruvādevī listened, intrigued. Eventually she felt comfortable enough to ask Vinatādevī about the purpose of the brazier. In response, the queen ordered one of her handmaidens to bring it back filled with hot embers. The handmaiden returned and set down the brazier on a low table between the queen and the princess. Through little openings cut out so as to outline the lovers engraved on the bronze, the embers could be seen glowing within.

Vinatādevī opened a box of chased gold and removed from it what looked like a large fruit pit, at once black and oily.

"What's that?" the princess asked.

"Churrus," the queen replied. "A most wondrous substance."

"Is it animal, vegetable, mineral, or other?"

"Would the gods give us a wonderful gift like churrus if it required the slaughter of an animal?" she asked rhetorically, and shook her head.

"Like all good things," she went on, "it is vegetable, growing from the earth. A certain caste of śūdras living in the state of Nepāla devote themselves to its preparation, walking naked through fields of especially resinous hemp and allowing their bodies to be covered with the sticky exudation, then scraping it from their skin with knives, mixing it with secret powders to make it burn better, smell sweeter, and enhance its effects, then rolling it into balls between their palms."

"Its effects?" the princess asked with interest. "And what might they be?"

"Trust me," Vinatādevī said, "that they will be pleasurable."

"At the palace of my father they would, on certain festival days, in particular Śiva-rātrī, the birthday of Lord Śiva, make a drink of hemp by infusing it in milk and water. They would drink it and become very gay."

"This is like that, yet different," Vinatādevī said, pinching off a piece the size of an almond.

She had no sooner placed it on the burning coal than it began to smolder. The smoke rose in a thin blue thread, straight and narrow as the rope the magician climbs to reach heaven.

"How sweet it smells," the princess exclaimed. "Would that I could wear such an essence."

"Then you would certainly affect men's minds."

Vinatādevī showed the princess how to hold a straw made from a hollow reed above the brazier and suck in the smoke, then hold the smoke in the lungs for as long as she could bear without fainting.

"The smoke crawls up the straw," Dhruvādevī observed, "as Śeṣa the snake king crawls up Gaṇeśa's trunk in a storm."

Again and again the princess tried to do as she had been shown, but, unaccustomed to the tickling smoke, exploded in a fit of coughing every time.

The queen could not conceal a certain irritation at the sight of so much good churrus going to waste. Presently, she took back the straw, filled her own lungs with smoke, then leaning over and pressing her own lips to those of the little girl, gently blew the smoke into her mouth.

Dhruvādevī immediately understood and emptied her lungs before each smoky kiss, the better to inhale the smoke. They kept this up for some time, until the bit of churrus was burned to a white ash.

"Well?" Vindatādevī asked. "Do you feel unusual?"

Dhruvādevī shook her head. "I feel nothing out of the ordinary." She giggled. "Perhaps we should inhale some more."

"From the looks of you, you have inhaled quite enough. Your eyes are red as aśoka blossoms, and you slur your speech like a drunkard."

"Nonsense!" the princess snapped. "I am in perfect control of my felicities. I mean, my facilities." She giggled again. "Where have the sesame balls gone?"

"In your stomach," Vinatādevī replied. "Shall I have your handmaiden bring more?"

"What we need," the princess said, "is a great roasted dolphin stuffed with mango and honey—it was my father's favorite dish at banquets—then shark boiled in coconut milk, and crab curry, and flounder with tamarind, and crisp samosas filled with roe, and a great tray of rice with saffron and almonds—"

"It is late, but we could wake the chef, and beg him to—"

"I beg no one!" Dhruvādevī replied. "I am the princess of the Śālāṅkāyanas! I will order him to go to the kitchen and make us a feast with every sort of fish that swims in the sea or lies upon the ocean floor or crawls upon the beach! And if he refuses, I shall ask the king to cut off the top of his head and drop a ball of red-hot iron on his brain."

"That will certainly persuade him," Vinatādevī agreed. "But first let us try asking him politely, for while authority born of fear bears quick fruit, it sows the seed of rebellion."

"But first let us inhale a little more smoke of the churrus," the princess suggested.

What began that evening soon became ritual. Vinatādevī would come to Dhruvādevī's apartments with her churrus, and they would sit together, inhaling the sweet smoke, eating, listening to the musicians weave their subtle improvisations, telling each other of their pasts (for their presents held little interest, and their futures even less), suffering fits of giggling that left them lying on the floor, their stomachs aching, and eventually tiptoeing down to the kitchens and waking the chef who required no threats, being rather flattered by their attentions and amused by their eating habits.

Each night the kisses by which the smoke was transferred grew longer and more passionate. Once Vinatādevī probed the princess's mouth with her tongue and, when she was not rejected, made free with her hands on the girl's small, thin body. Dhruvādevī, having missed the opportunity to test her new-learned skills on her husband, gained some satisfaction trying them now. They made her friend Vinatādevī happy, and that was good; yet for herself they meant no more than the recitation of some obscure Vedic verse learned by rote. What the young princess enjoyed most was the quiet time after the passion was spent, when she could lie still in Vinatādevī's arms, as she had once lain in her mother's arms, and remember the sound of the sea, the crashing of the waves against the cliffs of her homeland.

When the Vaidya was sufficiently familiar with Dattaka's problem, he began a program of treatment that consisted, like all Ayurvedic cures, of three parts: "Purify, pacify, and remove the cause," as he enjoyed telling his students.

In order to purify, he ordered the boy massaged twice a day with medicinal oils and rice boluses. He himself administered the Purge to the Head, burning drops in the eyes and ears that cleansed the nadis and brought forth copious tears, relieving the body of the numerous poisons.

To pacify, he gave Dattaka a mixture of herbs that would strengthen his nervous system, and another mixture to allow him to sleep at night, for rest was among the most universal and beneficial of cures. At mealtimes, all food was sattvic and rajassic, spicy and sweet, to directly counteract the dull tamasic qualities of his body.

As for removing the cause, while it was impossible to undo what had been done, he hoped to change the way Dattaka perceived it. First in importance was to convince him that he was not responsible. Even if the men who had carried out the massacre had indeed been searching for Dattaka, as the Vaidya suspected, the boy could no more be faulted than could a cow take the blame for the existence of ritual sacrifice among the brāhmaṇas.

Whenever Dattaka alluded to his own guilt, the Vaidya would say in a gently mocking but kindly voice, "My, how important you must be!" or, "I always thought such events were ordained by a man's karma." In time, Dattaka understood.

One last element of the therapy involved assigning Dattaka a task of responsibility by which he might reestablish his self-worth. With permission of the abbot, the Vaidya gave him what was possibly the most important job in the entire monastery: minding the clepsydra, the water clock that regulated all activities. Beginning well before sunrise, Dattaka would sit in the lotus position, perfectly motionless, beside a brass basin of water in which floated a small copper cup called a kapala yantra. As water seeped into the cup through a small hole in its bottom, it would sink and strike the bottom with a muffled clanging sound indicating that forty-five minutes had passed since the last clang. That was precisely the time the cup took to fill. Then Dattaka would bang a great drum as loudly as he could, to signal the time to the rest of the monastery. He would retrieve the cup from the bottom of the basin, empty it, and float it on top again. The second time it hit the bottom, he would bang the drum twice; the third time, three times. The fourth time, he would bang four times, blow two blasts on the conch shell, and play a drum roll. Then the cycle would start all over again. Thus the day was divided into four equal divisions, as was the night.

When he was not overseeing the clepsydra, he did other chores, such as gardening, cooking, and washing. And of course, since it was a Buddhist monastery, he meditated. At first, being a child and a novice, he was not permitted to enter the great hall where the hundreds of monks sat in long rows concentrating upon their own breath, for fear he would disturb them with his fidgeting. Instead, he was confined to an antechamber where he could, if the pain of crossed legs grew unbearable or the desire to scratch an itchy nose irresistible, satisfy the urge without disturbing others. To the surprise of the monk who had been assigned to monitor him, the very first time he meditated Dattaka remained perfectly still for the duration, not even stretching during the brief periods set aside for that purpose. The monk was so impressed that he told his brothers. In a few days everyone wanted a peek at "the little one who sits as still as a stone."

By the end of the week, the abbot decided to make an exception to the rule and allow Dattaka to meditate in the great hall. The other monks, at first wary, were soon convinced by the boy's impeccable behavior during the long hours of sitting. In a few weeks he had earned the respect usually reserved for monks of many years' experience and unusual piety.

As soon as the gong sounded that marked the end of meditation and the final sūtras were chanted, Dattaka rose on aching legs and bowed to his pillow in thanks for the comfort it had provided. He bowed to the statue at the end of the long meditation hall, a life-sized Buddha of black stone with tendrils of incense drifting about its base, and joined the procession of monks shuffling out to the courtyard. His feet having turned numb, he worried for the first few steps that he might fall over. But then circulation returned and his step grew confident.

He had to strain to keep his eyes open, the sun was so bright. The courtyard was filled with monks running to relieve themselves, or to get to lessons or chores. The heat rose off the paving stones in waves, making the immaculate white domes of the stūpa shimmer as though they were underwater.

This morning Dattaka was excited, for he had arranged to meet Nanā, whom he had not seen for two entire weeks, here in the courtyard. Catching sight of a bit of black robe rounding the monument, he ran to her with open arms. How good it felt to embrace her once again, she who was so close to him. But then all the sounds around him, the scuffle of sandals and swishing of robes, came to a sudden stop. Self-consciously, Dattaka pulled away from Nanā and looked around. All the monks were staring at him. Recalling that he too was a monk, with shaven head and saffron robe, he quit his embrace that instant and, mortified with shame, bowed to them all in namaste.

When he looked back at Nanā, she had her hand over her face, concealing not tears, as he had first feared, but laughter.

"How funny you look," she said, "bald-headed."

"But I am a monk! This is how a monk must look!"

"Forgive me," she added quickly, seeing how much she had hurt him. "I am behaving like the crudest of śūdras. In fact, I am laughing with pleasure to see you so handsome and healthy."

"And not at my bald head?"

"No." But then she had to add, "Not entirely."

"Oh, Nanā! Well, whatever I am today, it is the Vaidya's work. He is a very great healer. He took the grief from my shoulders as though it were naught but a mantle."

"Then you grieve no more for Govinda and Mitra and all the others?" she asked in wonder, for rare was the night when she did not weep for them.

"I think of them every moment," Dattaka admitted. "Sometimes I see them as clearly as a painting: Nipa, Pinaka, and Nanda playing in the garden, Mitra studying his Sanskrit, Govinda looking over some piece of silk with a deep frown upon his face. Other times they are in the background, like the singing of monks you overhear when you walk by the Ganges. But they are always with me. What is gone is the poison that woke me from my sleep and turned my thoughts as black as tamarind. Do you understand?"

She nodded.

"Nanā, I think this school called Nālandā must be the most wonderful place on earth. Do you think . . ." He hesitated. "What I mean is, I know I promised Dakṣa I would go to China but . . ." He tried again. "What I am trying to say is, do you suppose I could stay here? I would give anything to be a monk, like the Vaidya and his brothers. When I sit with them in the meditation hall, I feel that I am not alone. They are the new family the gods have given me to replace the family that I lost. Oh, please, can't I stay?"

"Did you tell the Vaidya of your wishes?"

"Yes."

"And what did he say?"

"He was delighted. He said he must ask the abbot, as a formality. But he assured me there would be no problem."

Nanā shook her head. "You have a debt to Dakṣa," she said sternly. "When you had no one, he took you in and cared for you. And for many years before that, he watched you from afar and helped Govinda with his business so that you might lead a life of comfort."

Lest she see his disappointment, he turned away from her and pretended to watch some monks working at the base of the stūpa, repainting the fretwork railing a brilliant red. After a time he turned back to her. "Nanā?"

"Yes?"

"I don't want to go to China."

"The unknown," she said, "is always frightening."

"What if I never return? What if I die in that foreign land, with no brāhmaṇas to pray for me?"

"The gods will care for you. Of that I have no doubt."

"Do you know what the trip is like?" His eyes opened very wide. "I made friends with a Chinese monk, and he told me all about it. First one must cross a thousand deltas to reach the sea, then sail past a place called the Columns of Copper, and wander among the Ten Thousand Mountains, and penetrate the Iron Gates. There is an endless desert where human bones are strewn like fruit pits in the marketplace and water is more highly valued than pearls. And even upon reaching China, the trip is only half done, for those who seek silk, this same monk tells me, must then cross the Purple-Colored Barrier, a great stone wall as high as Mount Meru, built to hold off the invaders, and traverse the entire land of China, the northern part where now the cruel barbarians rule and all is in chaos, and sail along a river called the Yellow River, until they finally reach the easternmost sea that borders the very edge of the world, and a land called Lin-tzu, for there, and only there, do the Chinese grow their silk."

"It may seem long and difficult now, but you will find excitement and adventure along the way. No doubt many men will become your friends, and women will teach you how kāma is worshiped in foreign lands. When you return, the secret of the Golden Fire will make you a very rich man."

Again Dattaka was quiet for some time. She was surprised to see him so thoughtful, for she recalled him as an impulsive, daring child.

"What greater wealth could there be," he said finally, "than the Four Noble Truths? What treasures could vie with the Eightfold Path?"

"You must go," Nanā said. "When you return, then you may join the sangha." Of course, she knew, even as she said it, that it was a lie. He would return to meet his death, or he would return as king. But never would he be a simple monk. Never.

"You have been more than a mother to me, prudent and wise, selfless in your attention. In the past when I acted against your advice, I was always sorry. Yet when I did as you told me, in time I always saw the wisdom of your orders. I wish to stay here as much as I have ever wished for anything in my life. Yet if you advise me to do so, I will join Dakṣa's caravan. I will be a false monk if I cannot be a real one."

She took his head in her hands and kissed his brow. "Thank you, little one."

"And what of you, Nanā? What will become of you?" He grew shy. "Might you come to China with me?"

She laughed. "I am too old for such adventure. No, I do not know what I shall do. I suppose, since karma has braided a garland of our destinies, I will bide my time, waiting for your return."

"But who shall care for you in the meantime?" he asked with concern.

"Do not worry, little one," she reassured him. "Nanā knows all the woman's tricks of survival."

Meanwhile, the Vaidya visited the abbot in his chamber. He sat down on a pillow opposite him, folding the end of his robes neatly around his knees as one would wrap a package, and waited while the abbot finished a letter he was writing. Even with several ghee lamps to illuminate the work, the abbot still had to lean forward until his nose nearly touched the page.

"Now, my good friend," the abbot said, rolling the letter closed and sealing it with wax, "what brings you here this evening?"

"News of the happiest sort. The boy called Dattaka, who came for a short visit, has changed his mind and decided to stay. He asks if he can join the sangha."

"Tell me about him. I know little, but I have heard rumors of a life shrouded in mystery and frequented by violence."

"The truth is more remarkable than anything you might suppose. I myself am well suited to tell it, for I brought him into the world." The Vaidya lowered his voice. "This Dattaka is none other than Prince Candra of Magadha, the son of Samudra Gupta!"

Assured, after knowing him for these many years, of the

abbot's confidentiality, the Vaidya recounted Dattaka's story as he had pieced it together from his own experience and what he had been told by the woman called Nanā.

The lines on the abbot's brow grew deeper as he learned of the killing and destruction that were the fruit of Rāma's wrath. When the Vaidya had finished, he shook his head. "The boy must not stay here. He cannot join the sangha."

"What?" The Vaidya was astounded. He could not believe what he was hearing. "But why not? He is perfect in meditation. He is impeccable in his chores. He understands the Eightfold Path and the Four Noble Truths better than some who have been here a decade."

"Yes, yes. I understand that he is spiritually precocious. The problem is this. By keeping him here we encourage our own destruction. Perhaps we have sealed our fate already, I do not know. But I know this: if not for a history of tolerance and a few highly placed Buddhist ministers in his cabinet—I speak mainly of Vasubandhu, the brilliant philosopher, who endures the king's insults in order to ensure the survival of our faith—Samudra Gupta and his stern Purohita would happily have us outlawed. He has said on countless occasions that the true faith of the Land of the Sons of Bharata is the faith of the brāhmaṇas, that the true ritual is the ritual of sacrifice, that the true god is He who is called Viṣṇu. Prince Rāma is twenty-four years old and eager to take the throne. As the Buddha is known for compassion, so is the prince famous for his lack of it. If half the stories I hear of him are true, he is a villain to rival Ravana, the demon king of Laṅka. Imagine him inheriting his father's dislike of us, as well as the throne—and then learning that we have sheltered his most hated enemy."

"We have never denied anyone the Great Vehicle," countered the Vaidya, coming as close to anger as anyone had ever seen him. "Dattaka will be the first ever turned away from our door. He is so happy here. And he has been turned away from so many homes."

"Would you give him the Great Vehicle if it meant the end of Nālandā?" said the abbot. "Would you educate one monk at the peril of ten thousand? Would you risk the end of all the good works we have done, the cloistering of scholars and philosophers, the vaidyas we have trained, the lives we have saved in our hospitals? The studies you yourself have done toward finding a cure for the fever?"

The abbot sighed and continued, "Old friend, do not despise me. My interest must be the good of the sangha."

"You do us a terrible disservice," the Vaidya said. "He is special, perhaps an avatāra. He is the heart and the soul of Buddhism, come to breathe life back into the dharma. If we protect him, the bodhisattvas will see that we are done no harm. But if we turn him away, we prove that we are no different than the Viṣṇuites; we reveal ourselves to be nothing more than a hollow, self-important institution whose only purpose is propagating its own existence."

"Those are strong criticisms, Vaidya. I fear that in a moment of anger you mistake a boil for a tumor. You would burn the shrine because a gatepost displeases you. Go to your chamber and meditate. Recall your Buddha nature, the face you had before you had a face. Next time we talk, you may speak those words again if you choose. Otherwise, we shall pretend they were never spoken. Goodnight."

A few days later, while crossing the courtyard on his way to mind the clepsydra, Dattaka was intercepted by a messenger, who told him he had visitors waiting by the stone arch that stood in front of the monastery's main gate. This sort of arch, with gently sloping sides and several lintels across the top, was known as a torana and was a symbol of welcome and victory throughout the Land of the Sons of Bharata.

Dattaka knew at once that these must be the people who would take him to meet the caravan. He had almost convinced himself that Dakṣa had forgotten him or that the venture had been postponed for lack of funding. The prospect of leaving Nālandā was like waking from a wonderful dream to a cold gray dawn. His first impulse was to run and hide until the visitors had left and he could return to his meditating, and his lessons, and minding the clepsydra. But his sense of obligation to the dharma was greater than ever, and it bade him behave as Nanā and Dakṣa would have liked.

Returning to the barracks that had been his home the last few weeks, he gathered the few belongings permitted a monk—a begging bowl, a razor to shave his head every month, tweezers to keep his body free from hair, a clipper for his nails, a curved tin scraper for his tongue, a twig of the neem tree to clean his teeth, some gauze to filter his drinking water, needle and thread to mend his robes, and a priceless copy of *The Questions of Menander,* which the Vaidya had given him—into the center of a piece of cotton, tied the corners together, hung the bundle on the end of his walking stick, and, resting the stick across his shoulder, made for the gate of the monastery.

There, beyond the gate, standing in rank by the torana, was a patti of soldiers—not a strict patti of elephant, chariot, horsemen, and foot soldiers as was employed in war, but rather a loose one, consisting of seven foot soldiers, and three men on horseback. Could so many men have been sent to accompany one small boy? It seemed unlikely. There must have been some mistake. "Victory," Dattaka said, approaching the nayaka who appeared to be in charge.

"Forgive this worthless orphan for speaking, but have you seen anyone who might be waiting for me? My name is Dattaka."

"I have not seen myself," the nāyaka replied in a deep rumble of a voice, "for I have no mirror. But I have seen them." He pointed to his soldiers. They all laughed.

"I am Sambhu, of the silk guild's standing army," the nāyaka continued. "Dakṣa has sent me and my men to accompany you to Campā, where the caravan is being outfitted. We will stay by your side all the way to China lest any rogue or highwayman seeks to trouble you, and if Viṣṇu wills it, we will return to see the rolling hills of Magadha and the silty water of the Ganges." And he added under his breath, "If not in this life, then in the next."

"You mean all of you were sent here just for me?" Dattaka asked in amazement.

"In truth, Dakṣa said, 'Take a few weeks off, my boys. Go hunt and gamble and find some long-eyed woman with hips that shake the earth when they walk.' So we told him we would, but then we crept off to this Buddhist place so we could meditate instead."

This time Dattaka laughed, too. He liked this Sambhu, with his gentle sarcasm. He reminded him of Govinda.

He was an unusually tall man even for a kṣatriya, with a belly from too much eating and so many battle scars that his skin resembled a map of roads and rivers. He had a touch of the wildman in his eyes, a flat lopsided nose from having been too often broken, a coarse beard, and teeth with spaces between them, like the boards of a weathered fence. Perhaps a trip to China in the company of him and his soldiers might not be so bad. For the first time Dattaka found himself looking forward to the adventure rather than dreading it.

"Well, little master," Sambhu said, "have you forgotten any last detail?"

One of the horses, a white Nejd stallion, threw back his head, pulling at his reins, impatient to be off. "Easy," the horseman said. "Easy."

"There are two," Dattaka said, "to whom I would say my farewells."

Nanā and the Vaidya were waiting by the torana. Dattaka prostrated himself before the Vaidya, then embraced Nanā for the last time. Eyes filled with tears, he finally drew away from them, swung his stick over his shoulder, and indicated to Sambhu that he was ready to go. The nāyaka called to his men and they started down the long road into the valley, the soldiers on horseback going on ahead, kicking up a plume of dust, and those on foot following, surrounding Dattaka like a guard. Once, and one time only, Dattaka turned to look back. That was the last they would see of him for many, many years.

In time the Vaidya turned to Nanā and said, "And what of you? Will you find another child to care for?"

"I have been thinking," she began slowly, "that rather than caring for one, as I have done in the past, I should like to care for many."

"And how would you do that?" the Vaidya replied innocently enough.

"I wish to study the healing arts and become a vaidya." She looked him in the eye, bold as a man. "I should like to be your student."

The Vaidya laughed. "You could not stay here. You would have to become a nun and shave your head and give up all those things that women adore."

In response, Nanā drew back her shawl and pulled the veil from her face. Her head was shaven clean, her skin so pitted it had the texture of coarse cereal.

"I gave them up long ago," she said softly. "All I ask is a reason to go on living now that he is gone."

"If that is all you ask," the Vaidya replied cautiously, beginning to realize that this was no impulse on her part, as she might have him believe, but rather part of a carefully planned strategy, "then I will comply. But ask no more of me, woman, or you will find yourself expelled from Nālandā."

"Do not worry about me," she said, her voice grown haughty and resentful at the very implication. "My behavior shall be impeccable. Worry for yourself, Vaidya, for of the two sexes, it is men who are weaker of will."

The Vaidya stared at her in amazement. Then he turned and went back to his patients.

She followed at a distance, her head lowered in respect.

On several occasions during her visits to Dhruvādevī's chambers, Vinatādevī asked about the iron and glass ornament the princess wore about her neck. At first Dhruvādevī was secretive, but after she had come to trust the older woman, she decided to confide in her.

"But you must promise you won't tell," she said. "Swear by Śiva and Śeṣa, by Parvatī and Gaṇeśa, for of all I own, what I am about to show you is most precious."

Vinatādevī swore.

Dhruvādevī ran to her great golden bed and removed two pieces of palm-leaf paper from under the pillow. One was a drawing of herself, immature in technique but surprisingly deft in the way it had caught her character, her pouting mouth, her haughty expression, and the fearfulness that lay behind it. The other picture, of a young boy, was far cruder but showed hours of dogged labor, particularly in the border of the interwoven lotus blossoms that framed his face. What little pleasure Dhruvādevī had found in the solitary days following her marriage had come from exercising her memory in order to draw this picture of Dattaka.

Recognizing immediately that these were pictures of lovers drawn by each other—such mutual sketching being a common practice among the upper classes—Vinatādevī did what was expected of her and paid a host of compliments to the boy's character as conveyed by the drawing, as well as the artist's skill. (Actually, because of a problem getting his eyes level, he looked slightly intoxicated.) Encouraged, Dhruvādevī told her new friend all about her child lover, how she thought about him always and would never give her heart to another.

Never, the queen pointed out, was a long time. She regarded the pictures, one after the other, with a sympathetic smile.

Then she looked at the tapestry across the doorway and her eyes widened with fear: There was Rāma Gupta, arms folded across his chest, observing them coolly.

"Pray do not interrupt your conversation for me," he said with mock concern. "I am but a husband waiting to visit his wife. Yet you regard me as though I were a housebreaker."

"Forgive me, noble prince," Vinatādevī said, prostrating herself before him, "but that is how I identify those who come on tiptoe, unannounced and uninvited."

"Vile-tongued whore," he hissed, his voice whistling through the slot in his lip like steam escaping a kettle. "I would see you writhe on the stake for that."

"May I remind the prince that my lord is Samudra Gupta and that he deals harshly with those who would abuse his property."

Prince Rāma scowled, but could think of no response. He turned to Dhruvādevī, demanding, "And what of you? Why do you gape at me so?"

The princess recovered her wits and prostrated herself. "Forgive me, beloved husband, but you have been away so long that I thought you an apparition."

"*I* have been away? My bride, I must be confused. It was you, I thought, who fled our bedchamber on our wedding night."

"Pity me, beloved husband. I am only a child. The prospect of kāma frightened me."

"Yet you have no fear of kāma with a woman."

Dhruvādevī blushed. "It is the way of the harem."

"In time you will plead for my instruction in kāma, as the monk pleads for the wisdom of the mountain sage."

He turned to Vinatādevī and said, "I would be alone with my wife."

As she was leaving, he added, "But show me those pictures first."

"What pictures?" she said.

"The ones you slipped, a moment ago, into the pearly web of your girdle."

"I know not what you mean."

"Do not be coy with me. Overheated, my temper will flare like a ghee-soaked torch."

"There was one picture only, a drawing I made of the princess."

She withdrew it from her girdle and offered it to him.

Prince Rāma raised an eyebrow. "I did not know you had such skill with the charcoal. Now show me the other, for I saw you hide two pictures."

"You were mistaken, noble prince."

"Give it to me, or I shall make you undress, here and now."

"A man makes a woman undress for one reason only. When your father learns of this, he will not be pleased. The *Dharmaśāstras* say that a son and a father shall not share—"

"Begone with you, my patience is at an end!"

After she had left, he bade his wife rise and said, "You should not keep company with such women. She speaks and behaves like a man, and violates the dharma at every step."

"But she is a good companion to me," Dhruvādevī answered shyly.

"A good companion? *A good companion?*" He pointed his finger accusingly. "Look at you! Eyes red as a demon's! Half asleep even when you are awake. Slurring your speech and staggering like a warrior who has taken too many blows to the head. Only ten autumns on earth and already ruined for any task more complex than combing your hair."

Dhruvādevī started to cry. She buried her face in her hands in shame.

"Good for nothing but making my life miserable," Rāma went on, oblivious. "I'm referring, of course, to the way you ran from me on my wedding night. Everyone knows about it. The whole court tells the story and mocks me behind my back. You have made me a laughingstock, a figure to be ridiculed."

"I'm sorry," she whimpered. Her shoulders rose and fell with her sobbing, and her words were almost unintelligible.

He stared at her a long time. "Are you really?"

"Yes. I really am. I never meant to embarrass you. I was so scared."

To her surprise, he put his arm around her and offered her a piece of silk with which to dry her eyes. "Do not take all the blame," he said. "The trouble on our wedding night was as much my fault as yours. I was impulsive and foolish to suggest such a sophisticated form of kāma to one as young and inexperienced as yourself."

"The piercing instrument frightened me. I would have tried any other form of kāma to please you, but that—I could not."

"If only I had been more patient," he said, "I might have won you over. For years I have longed for the companionship of marriage. How ashamed I was to have failed."

His confession touched her, for she recognized the same sensations she herself was experiencing. In the flattering light of the ghee lamps he did not seem as ugly as he had before. In a way he reminded her of her father, King Jātadhāra, who was always imagining that the people of his court were whispering about him or plotting his fall. And, like Jātadhāra, Rāma would someday be king, the greatest king in the land, the King of Kings. Thinking of the power she might then command—if she held his favor—made her head spin. Even despising him as she did, could she not still play the wife and lighten the weight of her own guilt, the sense of her own shame? Her instructors in kāma had said on many occasions that surviving as a queen was often a question of pretending and that if one pretended hard enough, one might fool even oneself.

"If you really truly feel thus," she went on, "perhaps we can try being husband and wife again, for I know it is my duty."

"Perhaps," Rāma agreed. "After all, there is more to marriage than kāma. This night, for example, I have the weight of the world on my shoulders. How it would help me to discuss it with someone like yourself."

"Then please, my husband, do so. I will try my hardest to be of assistance."

He sat down cross-legged; she knelt behind him massaging his shoulders in a way she had been taught most pleased a husband, while denying her revulsion at the touch of his clammy skin. It was easy to deny even the baldest facts when one had inhaled sufficient churrus.

"I am going to tell you something," Rāma said, "that very few people know. You may be displeased with me as a husband, but if you are interested in maintaining peace in the Land of the Sons of Bharata, you will keep it in the strictest confidence. Do I have your word? Very well, then. Eleven years ago one of the queens bore an infant, a brother to me, named Candra. The old astrologer predicted that the infant would grow up to be a cakravartin—a universal emperor. My father, jealous and afraid of losing the throne, hired assassins to kill the baby. When they failed, my secret agents, in order to keep my infant brother safe from harm, placed him in the home of a trusted citizen, a silk merchant named Govinda."

Upon hearing the name, she drew in her breath sharply. "Did they call him Dattaka—the Adopted One?"

"Yes, that was his name."

"I know him!"

"I thought you might, for he worked at the stall where you bought the silk for your wedding dress."

"Yes, that's right."

"And so perhaps you can help me. I feel he is old enough that the king would not dare try to kill him again. I want to bring him back to the palace, so he can live here with me."

"Dattaka? Here, at the palace?" Dhruvādevī's entire face lit up with joy. Seen through the mist of churrus smoke, such wonderful events appeared less suspicious than they might to a more sober and analytical mind.

"You must try to understand my loneliness," Rāma went on. "I never had other children to play with when I was a child. They shied away and called me demon because of my deformity. How wonderful, I used to think, to have a little brother or sister."

"But what of succession?" Dhruvādevī said. "Wouldn't a brother be a rival for the throne?"

"Ah, you're a clever thing," Rāma said admiringly. "Yes, a little brother would be a rival. We would certainly be jealous of each other, and quarrel now and then. But I think that with patience and understanding, we would work out a way of dealing with the problem. Perhaps I, as the elder, would rule seven years, and then he would rule seven, and then I seven again. Or perhaps we would both rule at once from twin thrones carved from a single piece of stone. There is no problem to which wise and loving men cannot find a solution.

"Alas, all my plans and dreams came to naught. The evening before I was to invite him back, vandals burned down the house where he was living and slaughtered the family that had adopted him. He fled. And now I cannot find him. Imagine my grief." Tears spilled from his great brown eyes.

"Dakṣa and Vāmana helped him escape," she said. "They will know where he is."

Rāma shook his head thoughtfully. "I fear they are not to be trusted. They are my father's bosom friends. Perhaps their escape plan was in truth a murder plan."

Her face filled with anguish. "Oh, no! And I, thinking they were his friends, helped them."

"There is much to learn about the intrigues of the Gupta court," Rāma cautioned her. "More often than not, those who seem trustworthy are the betrayers, while the betrayers are the ones to be trusted."

"I begin to understand," she said softly.

"Tell me all you can remember. If we work together, perhaps my brother's life can be saved."

Now, her smooth brow furrowed with thought, she began to recount the events of the evening at Dakṣa's house, where she had seen Candra for the last time.

When she told him they were sending his brother to China, Rāma's face became a tragic mask.

"Wait," Dhruvādevī said. "He was going somewhere else first—to one of the Buddhist monasteries. I can't recall why."

"Which monastery?" Rāma pressed. "You must remember."

"I cannot," she said sadly.

"Was it Bodhgaya? Rājagṛha? Sārnāth? Vaiśali?"

"No."

"Was it Kuśinagara? Lumbinī? Śrāvastī? Sankasia?"

"No."

"Sañchi? Ajanta? Amarāvatī? Ellora? Nāgārjunakoṇḍa?"

"No, no, no!" She stopped massaging him and made her hands into fists. "You confuse me with all your names. If you would only be quiet for a moment so I could think!"

Rāma waited, patient and silent.

She shook her head with frustration. "It is no use. I cannot remember." Tears began to well in her eyes. "He will probably lose his life because I cannot remember a silly name."

"Perhaps tonight it will come to you in your sleep. Sometimes that happens when we sincerely wish to recall a name. Keep a piece of palm leaf by the bed so you can write it down."

"Rāma," she said haltingly, "I am sorry. About Candra—and about everything."

"So you finally understand the goodness behind my evil lip," Rāma said. "What a shame you did not perceive it earlier, before you complained to our fathers and drove a wedge between us."

"But if I remembered the name of the monastery, and if I learned to enjoy the"—she hesitated and swallowed—"the piercing instruments, then might I be forgiven?"

"Perhaps," Rāma conceded. "It is never too late to hope. But now I must go. My duties are many, my time little."

Just as he reached the door, she screamed, "Wait! Nālandā, that was it! Nālandā, Nālandā."

Rāma turned to her and smiled.

Part III

THE DEMON KING OF MAGADHA

9

Sitting on his throne that morning and listening to the petitioners' unusually niggling and trivial requests (any matters of sufficient complexity or importance to make them of interest were diverted to the king), Prince Rāma could not help but reflect on the disappointing nature of his life thus far. Though he had reached the age of thirty-two autumns, he had yet to partake in any of the glory he felt was his destiny.

His palace, for example. He cared not that the ancient structure had once belonged to Candragupta Maurya, the noblest king of the land, and that his own father had drained the treasury restoring it to its original grandeur for him. All he could focus upon was its diminutive size.

And then the question of his military career. In his daydreams he found valor warring with the Śakas, gained the adoration of his subjects, and lived to hear his exploits recounted by the bards. In his real life, the kingdom was at peace, his subjects seemed terrified of him, and the great poet Kālidāsa, whose kāvya *Śakuntalā* was considered the finest work ever penned in the perfected language, had taken a thousand paṇas as first payment for an ode nearly two years ago and had yet to present him with a single śloka.

His wife, Dhruvādevī, with naught to do but smoke churrus and eat, had grown so fat that she no longer had the shape of a woman. If her presence in the harem was not irritating enough, every month for the past eight years, with the regularity of the waxing moon, she visited him in the throne room to ask if anyone had yet found Prince Candra.

And of course this was his greatest frustration of all. Prince Candra still roamed the world, free as the ātman that has left the body. The assassins Rāma had sent to Nālandā to bring back his brother's head had brought back only reports of how they had missed him by days. The small army he had dispatched to locate Candra in China had been mistaken by the Chinese for an aggressor force and annihilated. Various spies and false caravans sent with the same purpose had vanished or returned with contradictory stories: that Candra was long dead and buried, that he had become a high-ranking adviser to the emperor of that strange land, that he had already returned to the Land of the Sons of Bharata, that he had been seen selling clay pots in the land of the Parthians. At the very thought of his brother, Rāma's pulse would quicken, his heart beat savagely, his complexion darken. Without even knowing it, he curled his hands into fists and made as if to tear the air between them. Ah, the frustration, the maddening frustration! With all his power he could not seem to even touch his young brother, regardless of how he tried.

Another petitioner came forward, a potter of the vaiśya class who had been accused of killing a cow that belonged to a brāhmaṇa. A local board of magistrates had convicted him on the slim evidence of a bone—purportedly a cow bone—found in his hut, and had sentenced him to give up all his property to the brāhmaṇa as well as to spend a month, head shaven, garbed in the skin of a cow, wandering with the herd. It was a rather old-fashioned punishment but not, in Rāma's eyes, overly severe. Now that the vaiśya had served the sentence, he would have the prince reverse the verdict and clear his name so that he could once again practice his trade. He said that the bone in question belonged to a killer tiger he had slain to protect his village, not a cow, and that any man learned in the biology of animals would attest to the fact.

Prince Rāma, bored beyond relief, struggling in fact to keep his eyes open in the face of this droning, endless account, took the bone, promising to have it examined yet having no intention of doing so, and told the page he would see the next petitioner.

Ah, what grandeur might be his if he could be king! Candragupta Maurya was not much older than Rāma's father when he ceded his throne and starved himself to death in the manner of the Jains. Viśamitra, whose story is told in the mahākāvya known as the *Rāmayāna,* willingly renounced his throne to lead the life of a wandering ascetic. Why couldn't Samudra Gupta do the same? The measures need not be so extreme. He could enter the stage of life known as vānaprastha and take his favorite queen to a little hut in the forest to beg alms and practice austerities. How rewarding such a spiritual existence might be for someone getting on in years!

But no, Samudra Gupta was determined to retain the sandals and white parasol until he was doddering, while Prince Rāma was made to live in this little palace like a child in a playhouse, spending his time determining whether a bone belonged to a cow or a tiger.

As if his frustration were not sufficient, the page announced that Princess Dhruvādevī had arrived and requested an audience. That was all he needed to complete his awful day.

He made a languorous motion with his left hand, so that his many rings glittered and his long nails cleaved the air, and said that she was to wait. Determined to make that wait as long as possible, he gave the remaining petitioners such a share of his time and attention, such a thorough and sympathetic hearing, that each decided on his own that the "cruel prince" rumors they had heard were nothing but the propaganda of discontent Buddhists and Jains.

Only when every last plea had been heard, every last dispute decided, only after the prince had ordered a goblet of imported Yavana wine to quench his thirst and a plate of figs to ease his hunger, only then did he have the page show in the princess.

Though she was eighteen autumns, the age when most women enjoy a smooth simple beauty, like the sketch that has yet to be worked over with the crosshatch of life's triumphs and tragedies, only her face showed it. Somehow her face had remained thin and extraordinarily lovely, with long eyes, a finely chiseled nose and chin, and, of course, the pouting lips that would now be better described as sensuous. The rest of her had grown grotesquely fat. Her breasts and belly were like grain sacks bulging over the top of her golden girdle, her legs inverted cones, deeply dimpled at the knees, her arms like sausages between her tight-fitting bangles. She less walked than waddled.

It was a difficult condition to maintain, requiring a life of total indolence as could only be found at the palace, an appetite artificially stimulated by churrus as well as unlimited amounts of sweets to sate it, and, finally, no desire to appear otherwise.

Prince Rāma felt pleasure seeing her thus reduced in beauty and agility. Perhaps now that people whispered about her behind her back and made up vicious nicknames, she would begin to understand the tragedy of his life, too.

"Yes," he said wearily, as she reached his throne and struggled to prostrate herself before him.

"Excuse this unworthy woman," she began in that whining voice that irritated him so, "but I was wondering—is there any news of Prince Candra?"

Why did she do it! Why did she badger him so? Was there no way to make her stop?

Suddenly the simplest solution in the world occurred to him. Why hadn't he thought of it years ago?

"Yes, I have heard about him," he said in measured tones. "He was killed by demons in the Nāga Hills." And, for effect, he added, "They tortured him to death and ate his flesh."

She gazed at him with such horror that it was all he could do to stop himself from laughing. Then he had another inspiration. He picked up the cow bone, tiger bone, whatever it was, and handed it to her.

"All that remains of him." This, as if wiping a tear from his eye.

She took it stupidly, absorbing its dry, grainy texture, yet not seeming to understand completely what it was. Bit by bit comprehension crept into her eyes. She screamed, dropped it on the tiles, and ran from the room, the flesh of her thighs slapping together.

Rāma laughed until he was short of breath. He rose at once and hurried to the steambath, where he had planned to rendezvous with his three friends, Nandana, Kubera, and Karabhaka. How they would enjoy hearing of this!

Princess Dhruvādevī fled to her chambers, threw herself on her splendid wedding bed, and lay there weeping, trapped by its four upturned elephant tusks as surely as any prisoner in a dungeon. Her handmaidens, who had seen her like this many times before, did not bother trying to comfort her. One went to fetch Vinatādevī, another filled the little bronze brazier with hot embers, and a third ran to the kitchen to alert the chef. The sweet smoke, they were certain, would turn her tears to laughter, as it always did.

But when Vinatādevī arrived with her golden box of churrus,

Dhruvādevī shook her head and continued to cry. "I will take nothing but poison now, for he is dead and I have no wish but to join him."

She went on to tell about her meeting with Prince Rāma, and the bone.

"Well, this is an odd coincidence," Vinatādevī said, "because just as Prince Rāma gave you evidence of his death, I will give you evidence of his life."

"What evidence?" Dhruvādevī asked, raising her head and regarding the queen through teary eyes.

Vinatādevī excused herself and returned minutes later with a chest of ebony, no larger than an altar stone, braced with brass bands and cornerpieces.

"One of the porters left it with me," she said, placing it on the bed, "when he could not find you."

This was not exactly the truth.

In fact, the queen had run into the porter several days ago, while he was searching for Dhruvādevī. Overwhelmed with curiosity and a certain sense of foreboding, she had bribed him to give the package to her instead. If this were a present from a suitor, she would know about it, for her love for the princess burned hot as ever. How could a woman defend herself if she did not know the identity of her rivals? In the privacy of her chamber she had opened it and, recognizing the contents as well as its import, had hidden the chest, vowing never to show it to Dhruvādevī lest it mean the end of their love affair. Yet now, seeing the princess so distraught, she realized, with the pleasure one feels when surprised by one's own higher instincts, that her concern for her lover exceeded her own self-interest.

The princess wiped her eyes, took the chest on her lap, opened the latch, and pulled back the lid. She reached inside and took out two garments of yellow silk, a fabric so fine and lustrous that the light seemed to dance across its surface like flames. It was a quilted jacket and pants, sewn in the "Asian" style, such as she had wanted for wedding garb long ago. Her brow furrowed as she examined the exquisite quality of the silk and the sewing.

"The Golden Fire," she whispered.

The chest contained nothing else, no note scratched on palm leaf or clue carved in the wood to reveal who had sent it.

"Whom shall I thank for it?" she asked Vinatādevī.

"I can think of only one man who could have sent it."

"No, no." Dhruvādevī shook her head. "It could not be."

"Tell me, then. Who else knew of your desire for such a garment, made of such wondrous cloth?"

"You, for one."

"Well, it is not from me. Who else?"

"No one else."

"Exactly. It is from him."

"You would not toy with me? Not in a matter of such importance?"

"Have I ever before?" Vinatādevī asked.

Dhruvādevī searched her friend's eyes for any clue that this might be a trick and, seeing naught but sincerity, explored for the first time the thought that Dattaka might still be alive and thinking of her—enough to have ordered this exquisite suit of clothes. The rush of feelings was more than she could bear.

"Are you all right?" Vinatādevī inquired with concern.

"I am—" She could barely speak. "I am . . . Oh, there are no words!" And she rocked back and forth, laughing and weeping, rubbing the cloth to her cheek, even pressing it to her lips. "The Golden Fire," she murmured. "I wanted it so badly that I threw a tantrum right there at the bazaar. 'Grandmother,' I said, 'If you do not let me wear an "Asian"-style costume to my wedding, then I will not be married at all. I will starve myself to death!' "

She gazed down at her body and a sad expression emerged from the strange mixture of laughter and tears. "I do not look like a woman who could threaten to starve herself, do I?"

"You are perhaps a little heavy," Vinatādevī conceded. "But men like that in a woman."

"Had I known I would see him again I would have taken better care of myself." She lifted her breasts in her hands, then slid her palms down her hips. "I am like an elephant. I am despicable. How could I have ever allowed this to happen? How I must have hated myself to bury myself under so much food and drink! Certainly he will hate me, too."

"If you gained the weight, you can lose it."

"Will you help me? Will you remind me of my beautiful Dattaka every time I reach for a cake or candy?"

Vinatādevī hesitated. Finally she said in a soft voice, "Though it means losing the only person I have ever loved, I will help."

Dhruvādevī was holding the jacket in front of her, measuring the length of the sleeves against her own arms, hardly aware that her friend had spoken. "Now, tell me where I can find him. I must see the man he has turned out to be. I cannot bear to wait."

"Alas, I do not know."

"But you received the package," Dhruvādevī insisted, and added, "Why do you look away?"

"Some bit of dust in my eye," the queen lied. Then, turning and assuming a brusque tone of voice lest her true feelings be seen: "You were asking about the package. The porter delivered it."

"Then let us ask the porter, for presents of such splendor do not simply appear from the heavens."

While waiting for him to arrive, Dhruvādevī made a half-hearted attempt to pull on the pants. They would go no further than her knees. As for the jacket, it stopped at her shoulders.

"There is a tailor I know who could alter them," Vinatādevī offered. "His stitches are so fine, you would not know where cloth had been added."

"*Something* must be altered," Dhruvādevī agreed sadly, abandoning her efforts.

The porter, a boy of sixteen, blushed to find himself in their presence; he twined his fingers as he spoke, and studiously avoided their eyes. Responding to their questioning, he said that the present had been left at the gatehouse, examined for poison or death-dealing devices as was the procedure, and passed on to the porter for delivery.

Beyond that, he knew nothing. Satisfied, they dismissed him.

"If there is one man," the princess said to Vinatādevī, "who would know about this costume"—she held it in her lap now, caressing it as she would a pet kitten—"it is Dakṣa, the guild head. Let us steal out of the harem and follow the tunnels beneath the palace to his home, that we may unravel the mystery this very night."

* * *

Though the two women arrived quite late, Dakṣa agreed to see them immediately. Vinatādevī and Dhruvādevī, ebony chest clutched to her bosom, followed the śūdra servant into the bedroom and bowed beside the bed.

Dakṣa lay on his back, barely able to raise his head. In recent years arthritis had skewed him out of shape, had warped and shrunk his body until it looked, there beneath the sheets, like the remains of some small, broken toy. His skin, mottled with age spots, was drawn taut across his skull; his eyes, though rheumy, still sparkled with intelligence. His hair was no more than a thin fleece at the temples.

"We are sorry to disturb your sleep," Dhruvādevī began.

"I do not sleep," he said. "I know not day from night. My body is a bed of red-hot coals; my ātman, the Yogi who tries to lie upon it without having learned the trick of it."

"What about churrus to ease your pain?" Vinatādevī suggested.

"I must keep my senses. I am head of the most important guild in the land. Furthermore, I am dying. I can hear Yama's chariot rattling down the street. For ninety-three years every brahmaṇa and holy man, Buddhist and Jain, has been telling me what happens when the body goes to the five elements. Now that I have an opportunity to see for myself, I do not intend to miss a moment of it."

"Thank you for agreeing to see us," Dhruvādevī said.

"I thought you would be beautiful," Dakṣa said frankly. "I hoped the sight of you might give me joy. As it is, you only worsen my affliction. But since you are here, speak your piece."

Dhruvādevī felt tears in her eyes. Indeed, he was right, there was little of the princess left in her. Still, she pulled herself up to her full height and addressed him in her proudest voice: "Sir, I am Princess Dhruvādevī of the great and noble tribe of the Śālaṅkāyanas, mahiṣī to Prince Rāma Gupta, the heir to the throne of Magadha. And my companion is Queen Vinatādevī, twelfth bride of Samudra Gupta, King of Kings. Please do not address us in such tones."

Dakṣa appeared intrigued, if not humbled, by her revelation. "So you are the princess who came here years ago? Dattaka's little girl friend. Look at you now."

The dry clicking sound in his throat might have been laughter.

"Let us bring this unfortunate audience to a close as soon as possible," Vinatādevī said. "Tell us what we wish to know, and we will be gone. We have no desire to be abused by one so ill-mannered as yourself. If not for your advanced age and decrepit state" (and well-known friendship with the king—but she couldn't say that), "we would see you taken to task for your insolence."

Dakṣa was cackling now. Saliva bubbled at the corners of his mouth and ran down his chin, but he did not raise a hand to wipe it away. "Such vanity in creatures of such trivial accomplishment. As queen and princess you have no duty but to appear attractive, and you cannot even manage that. Ah, it does amuse me. This life is so full of entertaining things, I could live a thousand autumns and never grow bored. Now, what is it you wish to know?"

Dhruvādevī could barely keep back the tears, his words hurt her so. She opened the black chest, took out the suit of yellow silk, and held it close before Dakṣa's face. "Where does this come from?" she demanded.

Dakṣa stared at her, but said nothing.

"Tell me where it comes from!" She held the cloth closer.

Still, nothing.

"Tell me, you son of a barren whore!" she exclaimed, jamming the cloth against his face as though to suffocate him. He made a muffled groaning sound and his body began to twist and turn beneath the sheets.

Vinatādevī pulled her away. Dakṣa was gasping for breath, mouth gaping, eyes bulging, skin a mealy blue-gray.

"By the eyes of Śiva," Dhruvādevī exclaimed, "I have killed him—or nearly. Let us get help."

They called his servants, who, moaning with distress at their master's misfortune, pulled back the sheets and massaged his misshapen body, hoping to encourage the flow of the doṣas, and gave him camphor to inhale. When his breathing again became even, and some color returned to his fingers, they ordered the women to leave and never return.

"Let them stay," Dakṣa murmured in a tremulous voice. "We are not done with our talk."

The servants objected, but he insisted.

"I should not have teased you so," he said when again they were alone, "but you knew as well as I whence the suit came."

"Then it was Dattaka?"

Dakṣa nodded. "He tends the farm where the Golden Fire is made."

"And where is the farm? Tell me at once!"

"But I cannot. Silk is secret. And the Golden Fire is a special secret. If people knew its origin—whether it was the floss off a tree, the web of a spider, or the fur of a one-horned horse spun ever so fine—they would sell the secret to the Parthians, the Yavanas, the Kushans, the Arabians. And that would be the end of the silk trade that brings so much gold to the coffers of Samudra Gupta."

"But I have no interest in selling silk! I would swear silence upon the Garuḍa seal. Be reasonable, old man."

"There is another, more important, matter," Dakṣa continued. "I speak of those who would see him harmed. If you so much as sent a message, it might mean his life. Even your coming here tonight places him in the gravest jeopardy. Suppose Prince Rāma's spies have followed you?"

"Do you think I am so naïve? Rāma has told me that Dattaka is his brother and that those who plot against him are none other than you and the king."

"Little girl," Dakṣa replied wearily, "he is indeed Rāma's brother. On that point and that alone are you correct."

"I do not believe you."

"You had better believe me, for it was I, Dakṣa, who watched over him the years he lived with Govinda, and I, Dakṣa, who took him in after the massacre, and I again who sent him to learn the manners of a monk, and, yes, I again who arranged an entire caravan to guide him out of harm's way. And I'll wager that even such ninnies as yourselves can guess who has taken care of Candra since his return. That's right, old Dakṣa. But if you think I will reveal his whereabouts to such fools as yourselves, who mistake me for his assassin while supposing the most evil man in the land to be his benefactor, you are mistaken."

"Prove that what you say is true!" Dhruvādevī dared him.

"I need prove nothing. I am old and sick. Now go away and let me die in peace."

"I would believe him," Vinatādevī whispered to the princess. "Being at the end of his days, what reason has he to lie?"

"If you really love this Dattaka," Dakṣa said, "then leave him alone, for your bumbling explorations will certainly mean his end. Just as you have nearly caused his death in the past, you will certainly achieve it this time around. Now please depart, for I suspect my next guest, Yama, is waiting in the street. And, as beauty elevates the spirit, I fear that looks such as yours will send my ātman to some land of dreadful darkness."

It seemed to the members of the court as though Dhruvādevī had vanished and a slim, sylphlike creature of breathtaking beauty had taken her place, for all transformations have the appearance of magic when the labor involved is concealed: the agony of the silkworm as it turns into a moth, the years the conjurer spends perfecting his tricks, the million revisions of the storyteller as he refines his "effortless" prose.

Yet her labor was no less than the labor of those just mentioned, for she had to deny herself her two greatest pleasures: eating, and the churrus that stimulated her appetite beyond control. Many was the night she struggled till she cried out from the pain of it, and only a supreme act of will stopped her from calling for her brazier or creeping down to the kitchen. As the promise of God's grace gives the holy man strength to deny earthly pleasures, likewise the thought that her efforts might result in her regaining Dattaka saw her through.

She sought the advice of certain gaṇikās and handmaidens at court who were known for their artful application of makeup, their skill in shaping a chignon. She hired the best jewelers to find emeralds that matched her sea-green eyes, pearls her teeth, rubies her nipples, and to make a set of ornaments that would be the envy of every man and woman in the land.

Oddly, her placid beauty gave no hint of the ever increasing turbulence that beset her soul. For hours she would sit and wonder about the kind of man her child-lover had become. Such adventures as he had experienced traveling to China must have made him very knowledgeable. She, on the other hand, having spent year after year in the harem, felt as hollow as a dried seed. Whatever would she talk to him about? What did she have to say?

She began taking an interest in affairs of state, paying close attention when the ministers spoke, and even questioning them during banquets and other occasions when the harem was permitted to mingle with the rest of the court. She arranged to meet with artists and poets and to listen to them discuss art (though most of these conversations were less about aesthetics than gossip and backbiting). If she gained anything from these encounters, it was a sense of surprise at how much she herself knew regarding a variety of subjects, and what sharp wit and good common sense she possessed.

Another new practice she took up at this time, in the desire to further "deepen" herself, was painting. At first she tried to paint the charcoal sketch she had once made of Dattaka, as well as the view from her window, and a portrait of her friend Vinatādevī. None were a success, for she found herself unable to capture a likeness. Since she loved mixing the colors, she abandoned life studies and passed the hours simply painting bright patterns on cloth for her own amusement.

Several distinguished brāhmaṇa bachelors, not realizing that this sylph was the same creature as Rāma's corpulent princess, inquired whether she was promised, that they might meet her—chaperoned, naturally—in the garden. But once they learned the truth they quickly turned their interest elsewhere. The great poet Kālidāsa, catching sight of her through a chink in the palace wall one afternoon, wrote an ode to her, likening her to an apsaras, those nymphs who dance for the gods. In a brief time word of her beauty had spread throughout the land. That the true extent of her reputation be understood, one should consider the following: a coalition of artists from the distant city of Mathurā actually petitioned Prince Rāma for one hour with his wife, to paint and sketch her that they might have notes to refer to when attempting to depict the perfection of the goddesses.

Rāma denied the petition. This new interest in his least favorite bride brought him no pleasure. While he had felt her grotesque fatness almost an act of sympathy toward himself, he found her new beautification an affront. Whenever he heard rumor of her newfound charm, he ground his teeth and murmured to himself, "How fair would she look if I used the piercing instrument on her sweet face, or the wedge, or the scissors?"

* * *

One night Dhruvādevī visited Vinatādevī's chamber. "Dear friend," she began, "tonight I must go and search for Dattaka. Only the gods know when we will meet again."

"I suppose I should be grateful for the few years we had together. But oh, I shall miss you!" She embraced her, and held her tight. Then she cleared her throat. "Enough of this! We are like sentimental old ladies! Let us turn to more practical matters. Just how do you intend to escape?"

"By the tunnels, as we have in the past."

"What of Rāma's spies?"

"Until this moment I have mentioned my journey to no one. Nor have I laid in provisions, or fashioned a walking stick for myself, or done anything else that would suggest my leaving. I will depart at that hour midway between dusk and dawn when even the most vigilant grow drowsy."

"And how will you travel?"

"Alone. By foot."

"Dressed thus?" Vinatādevī began to laugh.

"And why not?" Dhruvādevī demanded.

"Because you will be robbed and raped before you are five minutes beyond the city walls."

"Then what do you suggest?"

"Dress like a beggar. Or better, a widow! Yes, that's it. No one will trouble you if you dress like a widow. Wear white and rub yourself with ashes and mat your hair."

"Ugh. I could not bear it. Matted hair!"

"You'd best do as I say. Now, how do you intend to find him? Do you plan to wander from home to home, asking, 'Have you seen a handsome young man named Dattaka?' "

"Do not mock me so! You sound like that horrible old man, Dakṣa. In fact, I have given it some thought and made some inquiries—all very discreet, mind you—and devised a sensible plan. We know that Dattaka is in charge of a silk farm. As it happens, there are silk farms close by. They lie to the south, near Nālandā and Rājagṛha. I will travel there first, asking directions as I go, for they are only a few days' walk and the way is safe. Like the most cunning spy, I will penetrate their fortifications and, assuming the guise of a silk worker, learn all I can of the whereabouts of my love. If I do not find him there, at least I will find those who know of him and can guide me further in my search. Perhaps it is only a matter of weeks before he holds me in his arms. Or perhaps years may pass and my hair turn gray before I lay my tired head on his shoulder. I care not, for I have made up my mind. Only the prospect of finding him makes my life worth living."

Dhruvādevī paused, trying to gauge her friend's reaction to what she had just said, and continued, "You are thinking, How will this poor sheltered princess, who has never been without a dozen handmaidens to wait upon her, ever survive beyond the harem walls? Admit it."

"I was thinking nothing of the kind," Vinatādevī lied. "You will do excellently. You will triumph in all your ventures. Victory will certainly be yours. But let us hire a good brāhmaṇa to say some mantras for you nonetheless, for your health and safety, and the likelihood of us someday meeting again."

Emerging from the dank, mossy cave that was the terminus of the tunnel that had been her escape route, Dhruvādevī felt a momentary elation: she had succeeded in her bold escape. She touched the place in her girdle where she had hidden a bag of gold and silver paṇas, a gift from Vinatādevī. How comforting, the weight of the coins! What information she could not gain by her own cunning, she could surely buy. It was only a question of time now, she assured herself, before she and Dattaka were reunited.

But soon afterward, as she inched her way through a moonless night barely more bright than the cave, clutching the ebony chest to her bosom, stumbling on the ridges left by cart wheels and the pits made by ox hooves, never quite sure if she had reached the road to Nālandā or had wandered off it to fall in some farmer's irrigation canal and drown, elation gave way to anxiety, anxiety to fear.

For one like herself, who had spent half her life in a harem being pampered like a parakeet, to be suddenly stripped of protection and transported here was something for which she was wholly unprepared. While the romantic plans she had concocted were one thing, the reality, as is so often the case, was something else. Except for the trip from her homeland to Pāṭaliputra these many years ago, she had never been beyond the city walls, or wholly alone, or forced to walk outdoors at night. Even the most familiar night sounds—the chirp of the cicadas, the gulp of the bullfrogs, the whoo-whooting of the owl—were mysterious and terrifying to her. All the stories she had heard about lonely pilgrims being attacked by tigers, bitten by cobras, murdered by highwaymen, and eaten by demons came back to her. Every shadow seemed a wild beast crouching, every sound the creak of a rapist's sandal. Sweat began to trickle from under her arms, and she found herself chanting the gāyatrī to herself, over and over, very quickly.

Dismaying thoughts overwhelmed her. Just how angry would Prince Rāma be when he learned that she had gone? Might he send his soldiers after her? And if they captured her, might he then finally have an excuse for meting out the kind of punishment he had so long wanted to inflict upon her? She recalled their wedding night, Rāma's blackened, bloodstained face inches from her own, his mouth a slash of white, the piercing instrument held tight in a hand that trembled with anticipation, the sharp point just touching her cheek.

Had she really given up a comfortable, secure position in the harem as well as the love of a kind woman, all in the hope of finding a man whom she had neither seen nor heard from since childhood? And all because she had received a present that *might* have been from him? She must have been mad! Yet she had no choice now but to continue with this disastrous folly, for to turn back would most certainly be to feel Rāma's wrath.

So long as Rāma lived, she could never turn back.

The clink of a pebble was as startling as a thunder clap. "Don't hurt me," she cried out. "Please! I'll give you everything." But then she saw the vertically irised, luminous green eyes of a house cat staring up at her. "Oh, kitty," she gasped, holding her hand to her chest, "don't scare me so!" She squatted right where she was, simply trying to regain her breath, while the cat meowed and rubbed back and forth against her calf. "A widow and a cat," she mused, when she had calmed down. "Aren't we a pair of bad omens."

Presently she heard the sweetest sound she would ever hear, that of farmers in their huts singing the ancient prayers, those same ones she remembered her own father singing. And then dawn came, as it comes to even the worst of nightmare-ridden nights. The sun rose over the hills and she became aware of bamboo groves at the roadside, and fields of wheat and millet extending in every direction, guarded by hollow-eyed, sun-bleached buffalo skeletons raised on wooden poles. In the distance she saw entire families moving through rows of sugarcane, singing as they slashed at the tall stalks with their sickles or waded knee-deep in the warm muddy water of the rice paddies, their vasanas pulled up around their groins to stay dry. Man and bullock labored together to keep the water moving along the irrigation canals by means of buckets on balance poles, water screws, and other ingenious devices. As the sun rose higher, the air grew rich with the odor of cow manure, of baking earth, of things green and growing.

Now that it was day, she began to feel the heat and see the dust swirls of travelers approaching on cart and horseback. Soon the top of her scalp grew as hot as fried bread. Her throat tickled and her skin burned from the ashes she had rubbed all over herself that she might appear to be a widow. Seeing a farmer squatting in the shade of his tank, sharpening his sickle on a whetstone, she left the road and approached him. "Good sir," she began, "I have been walking a long time. Could I take some water from—"

"Whatever," he said, waving his hand to indicate that she should do as she liked. He rose quickly and turned his back to her, pretending interest in the sickle.

So this is how it feels, she thought, to be the personification of bad luck.

Carefully putting down the ebony chest, she dipped her veil in water and wiped her eyes and face with it, then arranged it across her forehead to keep herself cool. She didn't suppose it could make her look any worse than she already did, with her matted hair and ash-streaked skin. There was a wonderful freedom in knowing that.

At noon she stopped at another hut and offered a few kakinis to an old woman squatting by a spinning wheel, in return for a bite of food. The old woman was also a widow and quite friendly. Her mouth contained one single tooth. She invited Dhruvādevī inside and gave her lentil broth and bread. The princess, having never glimpsed the inside of such a hut before, was astounded by the poverty. An oil jar, a water jar, an iron cooking pot. A few bags of barley and dried beans hanging from the bamboo roof poles, to keep them from rodents. No bed or other furniture, except for a mat laid out upon the ground. An image of Śiva drawn upon a scrap of cloth was the extent of decoration. Even the old woman's cloak and vasana were patched from scraps of old cloth. Had Dhruvādevī been told of subjects living thus in the great kingdom of Magadha, she would have believed it a jest.

All afternoon Dhruvādevī pressed on, bearing the slights and insults of those she passed on the road. A group of boys threw stones and shouted for her to get out of sight. Although they were common śūdras, she found herself fighting back tears. How could people be so cruel? When next she saw a widow, she would feed and shelter her for a month.

The sun set but she could find no farmer who would lend a corner of his floor to sleep upon. No one wanted to share in her dreadful karma. A traveler she met on the road, an ascetic of great spiritual attainments, or so he declared himself, with white beard and hair to his shoulders, offered to make camp with her and remain on the lookout while she slept. As for himself, he explained, he had transcended such physical needs. His fire drill soon kindled a blaze in a pile of dried grass and sticks that they had collected. Even though the earth was hard and rocky, her exhaustion was such that she fell asleep in moments. The last thing she recalled was the ascetic sitting in the lotus position before the fire, his eyes rolled up so that only the whites showed; he had told her that he intended to meditate all night.

When she woke again, he was lying on top of her, pulling her knees up to her chest and apart, that he could force his stiff liṅgam into the part of her that no man had ever touched. She managed to scream once, very loudly, before he clapped his hand over her mouth. They rolled over and over in the dirt, struggling. She bit him and thrust her knee into his groin, but he clung like a tick. As a last resort, she set them both rolling toward the remains of the fire, hoping he would be beneath her when they reached the still-glowing embers. He was. Screaming, he let go of her, leaped to his feet, and began to dance about, clapping at his back with his palms and crying for water.

Now she heard horses' hooves and shouting, and saw against the starlit night the indistinct shapes of a band of horsemen leaving the road and descending upon her.

Pity me, she thought, half hysterical, another gang of highwaymen to finish the work this scoundrel has begun. But then, when they drew closer, she recognized the pennants of Samudra Gupta flying from their staffs. They leaped from their mounts, ten of them, and held the miserable fraud at swordpoint while the nāyaka in charge of the detail, a tall swaggering fellow, approached the princess and, saluting her, asked the nature of her complaint. Weeping hysterically and gasping for breath from her exertion, she told them.

"Lies, all lies," the ascetic swore, and explained that it was really she who had tempted him with lascivious words and gestures while he was trying to reach samadhi.

The nāyaka asked the ascetic to recite the yāmas and niyamas, the rules of conduct by which a yogī lived. The ascetic knew not a single one. Then the nāyaka asked him to quote a few slokas from the *Bhagavad Gītā*, and when the cur failed at that as well, the nāyaka, convinced of his guilt, drew his sword and chopped off his head with a single stroke. Holding it by its long white hair, he placed it at Dhruvādevī's feet.

"My apologies," he said, "in the name of my lord, Samudra Gupta, King of Kings, that such a crime could take place on one of his highways."

Then he looked at her more closely and his mouth opened in surprise. "Ah, I did not notice before, in the darkness and confusion, that you are a widow!" His voice was not unkind. "That explains it. This crime is but your karma punishing you for lacking the courage to burn alongside your husband, as would a virtuous woman."

Her rage was like a seeping acid. She was about to tell them her true identity, recite her pedigree in her most cutting tone, and threaten them all with loss of their noses, as was her wont, when a warning sounded in her mind:

Your life may depend upon the success of your deception.

Instead, she swallowed her rage, took a breath, and said, "I am grateful you happened along when you did."

"In fact, we are searching for a young woman. Princess Dhruvādevī, the wife of Prince Rāma. She vanished this very night—kidnapped, we fear. Have you seen anything suspicious?"

"No," Dhruvādevī replied, her heart beating wildly. "I am

but a poor, unfortunate widow making my way south to visit my children."

They offered to accompany her to the nearest hut, but she declined, and did not breathe easily until the clatter of their hooves was lost in the sounds of the night.

The next night she slept behind a farmer's tank, and the night after that, curled in the tall grass of a mango grove. It was not until the fourth night that she found an inn where the proprietress was willing to put her up, and then only on the condition that she sleep with the animals, in the walled courtyard. At least she would be safe and well fed.

When the proprietress brought the evening meal—potato curry, lentil broth, and rice heaped on a palm leaf—Dhruvādevī asked if she knew anything of the silk farms said to be nearby.

The woman, who was about forty-five autumns, thin and shrewd, and of some wealth judging by her ornaments, replied that Samudra Gupta guarded his silk farms as carefully as he did his wives. (Was it coincidence, that turn of phrase?)

Carefully, so as to avoid revealing the sack of coins she carried in her girdle, Dhruvādevī brought out a single silver paṇa.

Accepting the money while gazing in the other direction, as if that made a bribe less offensive, the proprietress told of a village named Viṣādaḥ, a half day to the south, where lived a caste that sent their daughters to work on the silk farms. There she might learn the secrets of silk, where and how it was grown—for a price.

"I am no spy!" Dhruvādevī said. "I am but a poor widow trying to find my son, who works with the silk somewhere in this part of the country."

Her face covered with ashes, she could pass for a woman with a grown son.

The proprietress was staring at Dhruvādevī in the most disdainful way. Feeling she had to do something to gain the woman's respect, the princess opened the ebony chest and took out the outfit of Golden Fire.

"See? He made this suit for me."

It had the desired effect. The proprietress could do naught but gape at the beauty of it, shimmering in the dusk's last light. She reached out to touch it and the princess, enjoying her advantage, pulled it away.

"If I allowed everyone who wished to caress it the privilege, it would soon be ruined."

"Then sell it to me," the proprietress said. "I will give you any amount."

"It is not for sale."

"I will give fifty silver paṇas," the proprietress said, "and let you sleep in a fine soft bed inside."

"Then you are a scoundrel, for it is worth a thousand paṇas at least. And you could find no bed for me before and said I must sleep with the animals."

"A thousand paṇas!" She thew back her head and laughed. "What are you? A princess in disguise? Keep your silly silks." She snorted with contempt and went back to the inn.

After the conditions in which she had been sleeping, the courtyard was an improvement. The proprietress had supplied her with a blanket, which, smoothed over a pile of hay, made a soft and cozy niche. As for the animals, they kept to themselves. The two cows seemed like cunning sculptures, and the half-dozen chickens were perfectly content with their perches in the lower branches of a small tree. The only creature that caused her concern was an elephant belonging to one of the guests, tethered to a metal ring in the courtyard wall by a chain just long enough to let her reach, with her trunk, the remote corner where Dhruvādevī slept.

When the mahout came down at bedtime to see that his elephant was being properly cared for, he assured Dhruvādevī that she had nothing to fear. Baby—so he called the elephant—was the soundest of sleepers, and even if the beast remained awake, and sought to explore the courtyard, baby was as harmless as a Jain. Perhaps there was one gesture for which the young widow might be on guard, the mahout continued after a moment's reflection: if she woke during the night and found the trunk wrapped round her arm. Elephants, he explained, were fond of pulling sugarcane from its roots and sometimes, in their extreme nearsightedness, had been known to mistake the arm of a sleeping woman for a piece of cane and yank it right out of its socket.

Dhruvādevī curled into a ball, arms and legs tucked beneath her, ebony chest clutched to her bosom lest the proprietress should try to steal it while she slept—though as it turned out, she slept hardly at all. In the morning every joint ached, every muscle throbbed. The simple job of standing up seemed as difficult, as painful as assuming the most complex pose of the yogīs.

The following afternoon, stopping for water by the hut of a reasonably amiable farmer, she asked of the village called Visadah. As luck would have it, he had a daughter living there whom he had been planning to visit for weeks. This made a perfect excuse. He offered to walk the distance with Dhruvādevī and show her the precise location.

It was not really a village; rather, a dozen mushroom-shaped huts of mud over bamboo surrounding a stone Śiva liṅgam that was smooth from being touched by so many generations of hands.

The farmer's daughter was out behind her hut, cultivating her vegetable garden with her husband. She was less pleased to see her father than Dhruvādevī would have expected from the glowing way he had spoken of her, and set to quarreling with him almost immediately over a bull he had promised them but had never delivered. When, during a lull in the fighting, Dhruvādevī asked about neighbors who worked at the silk farms, the farmer's daughter replied peevishly that the silk workers lived in barracks at the farms, as though it were a fact known to even the simplest dunce. A moment later though, apparently regretting her rudeness, she recalled a worker named Caturikā who had been visiting the village every evening to care for her mother, who was sick with a demon.

"How will I know her?" Dhruvādevī asked.

"She has dozens of colored patches sewn to her vasana—it is a sign of her caste."

Dhruvādevī found a comfortable place in the shade of a bamboo tree and knelt there, waiting. She could not help but continue to observe the bickering between father, daughter, and son-in-law, most of which had to do with money or the lack of it. It came to her as a revelation that poor people, whom she had always imagined to be carefree and jolly—for so did they appear to her when they came to the palace on one errand or another—were for the most part miserable. She had imagined, as young people do, that she knew most everything about life; but at that moment she had an inkling of how little she really did know, and it humbled her.

At dusk, among those returning from the fields and trails,

she spied a pretty though weary girl of about her own age, wearing a colorfully patched vasana.

"Excuse me," Dhruvādevī said, catching her by the shoulder, "but I have traveled far to talk to one like yourself."

"I prefer to think there are none like me," the girl said with a smile, turning to face her, "but I am probably mistaken."

She was dark-skinned, with a round face, large eyes that seemed to take pleasure in everything she saw, and a heart-shaped mouth eager for any excuse to smile. She was short of stature, with breasts, as the poets say, "too heavy for her slender waist to bear." She wore a vasana of orange silk, patched in the peculiar manner of her caste, bangles of bronze, and a modest necklace of aquamarine and amethyst. Her name, she said, was Caturikā.

Dhruvādevī, having introduced herself, asked if they might talk a moment.

"They say widows are bad luck," Caturikā remarked, in such a manner as to make it clear that she was altogether serious, "but I am so weary with my life that I would welcome even bad luck over its monotony."

And, more sincerely: "In truth I am pleased to have a visitor, and look forward to hearing what news you may have of the world outside this small village. But first I must visit my mother, who is very old and needs my care. Will you wait?"

An hour later Caturikā came out of her mother's hut, sweating from the heat and looking even wearier than before.

"How is your mother?" Dhruvādevī asked.

"She barely knows me. At times she calls me by her sister's name, and at other times, thinking I am her mother, she pleads with me to take her down to the river to play. Ah, but old age is a sad thing."

Caturikā led her to a mango grove and, before kneeling down beside her, plucked a fruit whose skin showed the blush of ripeness. When they were comfortable, she cut some slices with a dagger that she kept in her girdle, gave the slices to Dhruvādevī, and kept the pit to suck on herself.

The first thing Caturikā wanted to know was whether Dhruvādevī had ever visited Pāṭaliputra. Had she seen the palace? Had she overheard any gossip about the royal family? Was Samudra Gupta as noble as they said? And was the Prince Rāma as cruel? And the Princess Dhruvādevī—was she so beautiful that men who laid eyes on her could never love another?

Dhruvādevī was so shocked by this line of questioning, it was all she could do to go on chewing the mango pulp. Was this Caturikā one of Rāma's spies, questioning her that she could report back to him?

She looked closely into those large, guileless eyes. No, it could not be. The answer was simpler: she was young, and impressionable, and the life of the royal family with all its excesses of artha and kāma, its scandalous cruelty and beauty, made her own dull life bearable. Never would Dhruvādevī have believed that lower-class girls in country villages spoke about her as though she were a character in the *Rāmayāna*. If only she could have told Caturikā that the widow sitting beside her was Dhruvādevī herself!

In appreciation, the princess gave her a few choice tidbits supposedly overheard at the bazaar by a friend of a brother of a porter to the king: that Prince Rāma loved young men more than he did women, that the king suffered from terrible headaches, and—why not?—that the beautiful Princess Dhruvādevī had been kidnapped by some foreign king who would have her for his harem. (What a good story that was!)

Caturikā was as grateful as if she had been given a hundred cows or a bag of diamonds. If palace gossip was a valuable commodity—which apparently it was—Caturikā was rich. Dhruvādevī could imagine her doling it out slowly among her friends for months to come.

Now Caturikā insisted on knowing about Dhruvādevī.

"My name is Dhurā," the Princess said, using the Sanskrit word for "burden" that so closely resembled her own name, "and I once lived in a far-off land and worked in the silk farms there. Then my husband died. Lacking the courage to lie beside him on the funeral pyre, I gained the scorn of all who had been my friends. I fled to the state of Magadha, where I had relatives, and lived with them for a time. But they were poor and feeding me was a burden. In time I decided to go out and fend for myself. I heard there were silk farms here, near Nālandā and Rājagṛha. Last night I stopped at an inn, and the proprietress mentioned a caste of silk workers who lived in this village."

Caturikā nodded. "I am of that caste. Once this whole village was ours, but then some of us argued and moved away, and others died of a plague. Now there are farmers living here, too." She lowered her voice. "They are very stupid people. Sūdras. You know? I live at the silk farm, in the barracks. It's just a little way from the village."

"You are not married?" Dhruvādevī asked with wonder. "But you are so pretty, with such a fine figure!"

Caturikā shrugged. "As you know, most silk work is better done by women. Since there is no work for the young men, they move away. I do not believe there is an unmarried man among us under sixty, unless you count the farmers—and who would want to marry one of them?" She paused to suck at the mango pit. "What kind of work do you do with the silk?"

"I . . . well, I don't know exactly what you call it here. It's the very first part of the process." Dhruvādevī pretended to be searching for the word.

"You mean unraveling?"

"Yes, that's it. I'm an unraveler."

"Well, what a coincidence! That's what I do, too. See?" She held out her fingers, and Dhruvādevī saw that they were red and covered with blisters. Then she looked at Dhruvādevī's hands and her eyes opened wide in wonder. "But your hands are so smooth. Never have I seen such smooth hands. And your nails are so long! How can you be an unraveler and have hands like these?"

Dhruvādevī thought quickly. "I have not worked for many months."

"Or else you are a goddess sent to earth to test my kindness."

Dhruvādevī laughed. "I am no goddess. It just happens that my hands heal quickly."

"Well, I had better be kind to you just in case," Caturikā said with that same teasing smile. "So, my fellow unraveler, tonight you will stay with me in my mother's hut, and tomorrow I will take you to the silk farm and find you work, for I know production is greater than ever, and they need girls desperately. But tell me, do you have a sample of your work to show Maitreya, the foreman? He is less easily impressed by word than deed."

Dhruvādevī thought for a moment. Then she opened the

ebony chest and brought out the suit of Golden Fire. "This is some of my work," she said, unfolding it before Caturikā.

Caturikā took it, gave it the most cursory inspection, and returned it. The spark of pleasure that had been dancing in her eye all afternoon vanished, and she grew suddenly subdued, withdrawn. And so she remained all evening, much to Dhruvādevī's confusion.

At first Dhruvādevī mistook the silk farm for a fortress, for all around it were walls of the tallest timber, mortared so that nothing could be seen within. Soldiers stood on the ramparts, their tall, brawny figures outlined by the first pale light of dawn, their long bows ready to repel suspicious visitors. Again she had slept badly, disturbed by the sounds of Caturikā's mother coughing and muttering. Now, as they approached the gate, her mind turned anxiously to what might be expected of her. What was unraveling anyway? Might she fool the foreman by watching the other girls and doing as they did? There was nothing that a girl of the lower classes could do that a princess could not—or so she tried to reassure herself.

The guards at the gate seemed to know Caturikā well and inquired after her mother. Caturikā introduced Dhruvādevī, explaining that she was an unraveler from far away who was looking for work. A discussion ensued about whether the *Dharmaśāstras* permitted a widow to work, and if so, whether the inauspiciousness of having one present would doom the entire enterprise to endless bad luck. It soon became apparent that neither guard had ever read a word of any śāstra; these well-intentioned but illiterate men were simply imitating the earnest discussions they had heard among brāhmaṇas. Finally, they decided that the decision must be left to Maitreya the foreman—a fact the girls had known all along.

Though Dhruvādevī had worn silk since birth, she took the fabric so much for granted—as one always does with the familiar—that she had never speculated as to its source. And so she entered the fortress half expecting to see some kind of exotic sheep or goat, whose long sheer fleece could be spun into silk thread. Yet all she saw, at first, were rows of trees, and peculiar trees at that, tall and round-topped, with long shiny leaves and small clusters of berries a pale pink in color. Women used long poles with hooked ends to pull the youngest leaves, which they stored in wicker baskets.

Beyond the orchard, which was several acres in size, she could see the cloth roofs of pavilions where many more women were working over broad bamboo trays. There were also scores of braziers streaming smoke into the clear blue sky, although what function they served she could not tell from such a distance. Their smoke reminded her of the smoke of the churrus, and she wished, for the thousandth time since leaving the palace, that she could retreat into some small space and inhale its sweet smoke until the real world grew as ephemeral as a dream. In the same area as the pavilions and braziers, were several large buildings of timber and sun-dried brick—barracks for the workers, according to Caturikā—and a few smaller huts, which served as administrative offices.

Caturikā and Dhruvādevī, reaching the entrance to the hut belonging to Maitreya the foreman, waited for him to look up from a book in which he was carefully inscribing figures.

"Yes? What do you want?" he said, finally raising his eyes. Though he spoke the Prakrit of Magadha, he put on the refined accent of the brahmaṇa, and in every other way tried to present himself as a person of breeding.

He was fifty autumns, with a puffy, jowly face and small red-rimmed eyes. He stood with his fingers laced over his big belly, and when he walked, the belly went first, like the servant who clears the way for his master.

"I bring with me," Caturikā said, "an unraveler from a far-off land."

"An unraveler, eh?" Maitreya walked to the entrance so he could better see her face. "How fast can you undo a cocoon?"

"Oh—" Dhruvādevī gazed thoughtfully at the ceiling of the hut. "As fast as the next. A little faster when I'm in practice."

She kept her hands concealed in the folds of her white cloak in what she hoped seemed a casual manner, so he would not question the smoothness of her fingers as Caturikā had the day before.

"Well," he went on, "we need unravelers. What we don't need," he continued, taking in her white clothing, her tangled hair and blackened skin, "is the bad luck of a widow."

"I think perhaps," Caturikā began uncertainly, "the customs are different where she comes from. I think they wear ashes and jata"—that was what they called the matted hair—"and the white vasana after surviving a famine, to thank the gods."

Dhruvādevī glanced over at Caturikā. What a good friend to tell such stories for her! She would have to find an opportunity to repay her.

"Oh?" Maitreya looked undecided. "And how long before you can pretty yourself up? I like my girls to look pretty."

"Soon," Dhruvādevī said, smiling so as to give him an idea of how attractive she might become.

After all, if she no longer needed to travel, why further endure the lot of the widow? And if by good fortune the gods had actually guided her to the silk farm where Dattaka worked, it was her obligation to look as beautiful as possible for him. If he were at another silk farm, well, ashes were always easy to come by. She could already feel the cool, cleansing bath, the tug of the hairbrush.

"Well, then," Maitreya said, nodding, "we'll give you the test."

"Test?" Dhruvādevī asked, experiencing a sudden stab of anxiety. "And what test is that?"

"To see how fast you unravel. And if you can unravel at all. Of course, you are an honorable woman. But there are those less honest who would sneak into our silk farms and learn the secrets we have been guarding for centuries. So whenever a new person comes from the outside, we test them. If they say they are an unraveler, we make them unravel."

"And if they cannot unravel?" Dhruvādevī asked with an awful sinking feeling in her stomach.

"Then," Maitreya said, staring her in the eye, "we know they are spies, and we execute them. Now come along and we'll get things ready."

A brazier was set up in an isolated corner of the silk farm and a brass basin of water left to heat on top of it. Maitreya watched it, and when the water reached a rolling boil, he opened his fist above it and dropped in a dozen fuzzy, pale golden objects that looked like swallow's eggs but were somewhat smaller, perhaps the size of the last joint of a woman's small finger.

Dhruvādevī, sensing that she was supposed to possess an

intimate understanding of what she now observed, and that her very life depended on a convincing performance, sustained a knowing expression, nodding every now and then and making approving sounds in the back of her throat. She kept glancing over at Caturikā, hoping for some kind of hint to the meaning of this unfathomable ritual, but none was forthcoming. Although the day was hot, a chill passed through her. She intertwined her fingers over her stomach as Maitreya did, to conceal the degree to which her hands were shaking.

Another man arrived with a device that looked something like a spinning wheel, but far more intricate in design, with a brass ring suspended on an arm, and a bobbin cleverly mounted to spin and rotate at the same time.

Maitreya handed it to her and said, "Begin!"

She looked at him, and at Caturikā. "I cannot," she said.

"And why is that?" Maitreya demanded.

"Because—"

"Because," Caturikā said, "she is left-handed, and it is a right-handed wheel, as anyone can see."

"Yes, of course," Dhruvādevī said. "I cannot unravel on a right-handed wheel. It is impossible."

"Find her a left-handed wheel," Maitreya ordered the man who had brought the first wheel. Clearly the foreman's patience was running thin, for he muttered something to himself, questioning whether a widow could possibly be worth this amount of trouble. He said he could waste no more time—he had his accounting to finish—but he would return in a short while to observe her progress. Thrusting his belly forward and folding his fingers across it, he departed.

"If we hurry," Caturikā said in a low voice, "I may be able to show you something of the unraveler's art before he returns."

"Yet by helping me you jeopardize your own life, too."

"It's true. What a fool I am." She smiled. "But you know such excellent gossip, I could not bear to see you go to the five so soon."

Caturikā knelt beside the brazier and, with one deft motion, lifted a cream-colored egg from the boiling water.

"How did you grab the egg?" Dhruvādevī asked in wonder.

"Not so loud! Do you want to be caught? Look, you have to hold your hand like this. See? And it's not an egg, you silly goose. It's a cocoon. The silk worm spins it."

"Worm? Cocoon?"

"Oh, you really don't know the first thing, do you? Now look closely."

She held the cocoon between the thumb and index finger of her left hand and delicately ran the nail of her right index finger up and down the side until the end of a thread came loose, as fine as the strand a spider spins, but much, much stronger.

Caturikā threaded the strand through the brass ring of the unraveling machine and, keeping hold of the thread's end in her right hand, dropped the cocoon back in the boiling water. The water kept soft the natural glue that held the cocoon together, she explained, permitting it to be unraveled. Now she did the same with three other cocoons, and once all four threads had been led through the ring, she tied the ends of them together, her tiny fingers working so fast it seemed like magic, and fastened them to the bobbin. Then, kneeling, and taking the strange device in her lap, she began to spin it in two ways at once, with such perfect control that it seemed a child's game. The threads from the four cocoons slipped through the ring and then twined together beneath her fingers, producing one perfect silk thread, which wound up on the bobbin.

"You'll tell Maitreya that you found you could use the right-handed wheel after all."

"Will you be done soon?" Dhruvādevī asked, looking nervously over her shoulder.

Caturikā shook her head. "Each cocoon holds enough thread to reach from here to the gate of the farm and back. While the silkworm spins it in four days, the unraveling takes a week at least. Do you think you can do what I am doing, now that I have started? Starting is the hard part."

"Let me try." Dhruvādevī knelt alongside her and took the device in her lap. She managed to turn it the way Caturikā showed her, but the silk did not twine smoothly and, bunching up on the bobbin, had to be unwound and wound again.

"I'd better do it myself," Caturikā whispered, quickly taking it back from her. "Then I'll give it back to you, and you can say you did it. Perhaps that will allow you time to escape."

"How did you know I was lying?" Dhruvādevī asked, as Caturikā resumed her work.

She snorted. "Your hands. Time cannot heal the unraveler's hands. No woman who does any sort of work at all has hands like yours. Obviously you are of the twice-born. And then you said you had made the thread for that suit you carry about in your ebony case."

"Why do you doubt it?"

"Because *I* made it."

"What?" Dhruvādevī gasped.

"There, I've worked quickly. This is a respectable amount of unraveling. Now, you take it, but don't spin any more! Just hold it in your lap and pretend you've just finished."

"What did you mean when you said you made the suit of Golden Fire?"

"No time to talk now. If he asks you to do more, say you've hurt your finger. Understand?"

"I understand perfectly," came a voice from behind them.

So intent had they been on their deception that they had failed to notice Maitreya stealing up from behind.

"I understand," he continued, "that you are both spies, as I've suspected all along."

"Do not treat me so roughly!" Dhruvādevī protested, as the guards bound her to a stake set out in the middle of an open space. "I am a princess."

"And I am the king of China," the first guard said, giving a brutal hitch to the rope across her breasts, so that she cried out with pain.

"You will die for that!" Dhruvādevī shouted. She weighed death here against the possibility of torture at her husband's hands and, finding the former more repellent, or at least more imminent, chose to let the truth about herself be known. "He is Rāma of Magadha and he will not see one of his wives treated thus. Contact him at once! I command it!"

The guards laughed and went about their work.

"Please, be quiet," Caturikā said, disgusted.

"But I really am a princess of Magadha."

Until this time Dhruvādevī had believed that the success of her disguise was the result of her masking her regalness and that once she cared to reveal it, people would recognize it as surely as they would the sun emerging from behind a thunderhead. She had thought that she had only to slip into her regal voice and make a pronouncement, and she would be obeyed, as she had always been in the past. But now she saw that despite all she had been told about her own goddesslike nature, she was, without ornaments and makeup and a beautiful chignon, indistinguishable from any other woman. This came as a shock.

When the guards had gone, she tried to struggle free from her bindings, but even the slightest motion made the ropes cut deeper into her and the rough stake scrape her back. The top of her head grew hot as a hearthstone, as did her nose, and her shoulders, and the incline of her breasts. The precious moisture of life trickled from beneath her arms and between her legs. At first she worried about her lovely smooth skin, unoiled, blistering like old whitewash; then she simply worried about staying alive.

"If only this had been the right silk farm," she whispered to herself. "If only Dattaka had been here, it all would have been different."

"He will be here soon enough," Caturikā said, "but we will die nonetheless."

"Dattaka? *My* Dattaka?"

"I speak of the manager of our silk farm, a fine, handsome man, one of the twice-born. No one you would know."

"But he must be the one! You see, we were childhood sweethearts. Perhaps he loves me still. We will certainly be saved, and you will be well rewarded for bringing us back together."

Caturikā'a laughter was a dry rattle in her throat. "You fool! Dattaka is as wise and graceful as Krișṇa. He has no use for you. Anyway, he loves another."

"I don't believe you."

"The suit of Golden Fire, the one you certainly stole. He ordered it made for her, his true love."

"But I am she!"

"Just as you are an expert unraveler."

But what was the point of arguing?

Dhruvādevī's eyes grew dry and her vision light, as though

the sun were exploding. Translucent shapes swam in the air before her. She recalled something Dattaka had once confided to her about an older brother—Virata, was that his name?—being burned at the stake. Was this how it felt, the pain, the humiliation?

The sequence of events grew unclear. At one point Maitreya was there, questioning them. Over and over she pleaded her innocence and the innocence of Caturikā. Then he was showing her the suit of Golden Fire, demanding to know where she had stolen it, and she was screaming that it was hers, and he must give it back, he must, he must. Another time, a horde of red ants had climbed all the way up her left leg and were penetrating her yoni, and she was screaming with pain and disgust. And then she recalled seeing Caturikā slumped against the ropes and being untied and dragged away, unconscious.

At some point she too lost consciousness, for when she woke again it was night and she and Caturikā were in a pit too deep and steep-walled to climb out of. The bottom was muddy and smelled of urine and feces. Overhead she could see a square of glittering stars. Caturikā was huddled in the corner, weeping.

"What now?" Dhruvādevī asked.

Caturikā continued to weep.

In the morning the head of a guard intruded upon the square of sky above them. "Which one of you first?" he inquired gruffly.

"For what?" Dhruvādevī asked.

"The executioner's sword." He drew his index finger across his throat. "Well? Be quick, for Yama waits just past those trees."

Without hesitating, Dhruvādevī reached up. The guard grabbed her wrist and pulled her out of the pit as easily as if she were a rag doll. They marched her to the clearing where stood the stake she had been tied to the day before. All the workers of the silk farm had been called together to watch, a warning to those who would sell the secret of silk to foreign agents. The women with the patches of bright silk sewn to their vasanas lent a gay air, as though they were gathered for a festival. A guard stood in the center of the clearing, swinging his broad, short sword, rehearsing his strokes according to the classic pattern.

Though she was shaking inside, Dhruvādevī tried to be brave, to walk forward with a bold step and a level gaze. Was it all to end here, surrounded by strangers in this remote place, with her wearing the widow's whites? She, the future queen of Magadha, passing to the five without a brāhmaṇa to chant for her. As she approached the executioner, she was amazed by what a bright and lovely day it was. The sky was clear and the sun glittered off the shiny leaves of the mulberry trees as though they were the little mirrors sewn to a piece of fine silk. Yama, as is too often the case, seemed the least likely of guests.

She was made to prostrate herself and stretch out her neck so that it was an easy target. Everything grew silent. Even the crickets stopped their chirping. All she could hear was someone whispering the gayatri for her, and for that unknown person her heart filled with gratitude. She heard the executioner draw in his breath as he raised his sword for the fatal blow.

Then came the sound of hoofbeats.

"Wait!" she screamed.

There, far off by the gate, a figure on horseback moving in their direction.

Any reprieve was welcome now that she stood at death's door. The rider could be a courier sent to save her by Rāma, or Vinatādevī, or even her own father, the king of the Śālaṅkāyanas. She kicked at the guards, and bit them, and scratched with her nails, much to the delight of the audience, who cheered as though they were attending a quail fight. It took three of the burly men to subdue her and stretch her out on the ground. One of them held her ears in a painful grip and forced her face into the dust. She writhed and squirmed with such force that the executioner hesitated to lower his sword for fear of dismembering one of her captors by mistake.

The hoofbeats grew closer and came to a stop almost on top of her.

"What's this?" the rider of the horse said. It was a voice at once familiar and strange.

The guard had so tight a grip on her head that she could see nothing but the earth beneath her. The dust stung her eyes.

"Welcome, my lord," she heard Maitreya say. "While you were gone, this makebelieve widow appeared. We found out she was a spy, so she proved bad luck to no one but herself. You are just in time to witness her execution."

"She fights like a tiger," the voice said, with what seemed admiration.

She tried to speak, to plead her innocence, but breathed in dust and choked on it. She felt as though the guard, if he did not loosen his grip, would tear her ears off.

"She claimed she was an unraveler," Maitreya said, "yet she could not unravel a single cocoon. Furthermore, she had stolen the suit of Golden Fire whose making you yourself supervised with such care. Perhaps you would question her yourself."

"I would like to do that," the new voice replied.

She heard Maitreya ordering the guards to let her up, and felt the grip on her ears loosen. She raised her head and rose with all the dignity she could find in her battered and sun-blistered body.

There before her, atop one of the magnificent white stallions called Nejds, was a slim, fine-boned young man of extraordinary beauty. His black hair was a tumble of curls, and his eyes were black and deep as wells. Yet there was no mistaking the straight nose and flared nostrils, nor the proudly jutting chin, nor—and this most striking of all—the way he squinted at her, as though trying to see the woman beneath the matted hair and ashes and dreadful white cloth.

She stood facing him, tall and erect, determined to manifest, despite the circumstances, all the royal bearing of a Sālāṅkāyana princess. Then she smiled and, reaching into the bosom of her cape, brought out a simple iron and glass earring that she always wore around her neck on a golden chain.

A long silence ensued. Those who stood in the audience whispered to one another, wondering what could be the meaning of the strange gesture.

"I will take her back to my home for questioning," the man on horseback announced finally.

Leaning way over in the saddle, he grabbed her around the waist and pulled her up to the saddle, so she sat in front of him. Then, holding her tight so she would not fall off, he clicked his tongue and snapped the reins. The white Nejd galloped toward the front gate of the farm, weaving between the mulberry trees, whose leaves glistened like the scales of a silver fish.

10

At first Samudra Gupta had found it difficult to defecate. In time he grew aware of a pain in his bowels, an ache at first, like the ache of muscles overtaxed, but growing more severe by the month. Probing the sensitive area to the left of his groin with his fingertips he discovered a shape, small, round, and hard, like a mango pit embedded in the muscle. When he tried to relieve himself, blood streamed from his anus. Soon the mango pit had grown to a fruit, and the pain had become something terrible and primordial. At night he had a recurring dream that he was a woman giving birth. When, after hours of labor, he succeeded in expelling it, the midwives held up a monstrous squirming thing the color of cayenne, slick with fluid and grasping at the air with its claws. And one of them—in the dream it was usually Sutanukā—would say, "Such are the children born to men."

He called Vasubandhu and the Purohita to his bedchamber to announce that his death was near. Unable to kneel, he lay propped up on pillows. He had told no one but them, for as jackals circle a wounded deer, so do the enemies of a king prey upon his weakness.

The Purohita, an old man now but still straight and clear-eyed, and possessed of an alertness and mental facility that put younger men to shame, pleaded with him to call the great Vaidya, the mahāvaidya who now resided at Nālandā. Surely he could remove it with his knife.

Cut it out of me as he cut Prince Candra from Sāvitrīdevī's belly, the king thought. Yes, I would now turn to him for help. So does Time make all things their opposites, turning kings to beggars, beggars to kings.

But when he finally spoke, what he said was, "I will suffer the death my karma has provided. What we must discuss now is succession. Come morn I will send you, my mahāmantrin, to the silk farm where Prince Candra resides. You will tell him his true identity—surely by now the seed of royalty has manifested itself, and it should come as no great surprise—and bring him back to the palace. I have still a few months before this *thing*"—he touched the lump in his groin—"destroys me. That should be time enough to train him in the rudiments of kingship. Then, when I pass to the five, you two shall stay close beside him and let him benefit from your invaluable wisdom and experience. I have no doubt he shall be a worthy king."

He fell silent and lowered his gaze. The other two waited, neither daring to speak the thought that preoccupied them both. Finally, Vasubandhu, taking the duty upon himself, uttered the painful question: "And what of Prince Rāma?"

"*Exile*." The word was like a sword slash.

After they had gone, the king sat for some time, staring at the floor. Never had he felt so alone, so sad and afraid.

Finally he sent for Prince Rāma.

When Rāma arrived he bowed to his father, but then, instead of sitting down opposite him, wandered off to the gaming board and, leaning over it, began to move the pieces about in a most speculative way. For a time the king watched his son arrange the figures of gold and iron, ivory and crystal, into the classical formations; kākapadī (arrayed like a crow's foot), sarpasarī (moving like a snake), sarvatobhadrā (all-auspicious), and the like.

"As you war with yourself upon the gaming board," he said finally, "I have been warring in my mind."

"So I see," said the prince, "for while you smile and speak in a gentle voice, as though nothing were wrong, a pallor of the skin, a cold sweat, and fleeting grimaces betray your pain. You must refrain from these conflicts, Father, for they are the source of your misery, I am certain."

"The battle has ended," the king said. "After so many years, I have reached a decision."

"What a coincidence. For I have been consulting with Yājñavalkya, our minister of war and peace. And I, too, have reached a decision." He chuckled. "But we are as coy as maidens. Why this indirect, mysterious style? Surely the king and the prince hold nothing secret from each other."

"If you wish, for once in your life, to speak openly and honestly," the king said without smiling, "I should welcome it."

"Oh, Father! You are displeased with me tonight. Will you take the rod to me? No? Well, no need. I shall speak honestly, I swear it. But I must have a drink to loosen my tongue. What about some of that dark red wine we were sent by the Yavanas?"

They called for wine. Then, after a long period of silence, unexpectedly and without preamble, the king said, "It was you who twice tried to kill Prince Candra."

Prince Rāma, taken so by surprise, appeared disarmed for one of the few times the king could recall. But then he recovered his wits and, assuming a weary and pathetic look, nodded. "I can no longer deny the accusations. I was a child then, made envious by my brother's beauty—for everyone spoke of how perfect he was—and by the astrologer's predictions of his future grandeur. Now I am older, I am a man, a warrior. Were he still alive, I would cherish him, for only now do I understand the importance of familial loyalty, and of keeping the Gupta dynasty strong and united. Is that why you called me here tonight, Father? To tell me that Prince Candra still lives? If that is so, then tell me at once! No news could bring me more happiness."

"He lives," the king replied.

"How wonderful! But then he must return to the palace. He can watch over things while you and I lead our army against the Śakas. Yes, Father, the time is right—so says Yājñavalkya, for that was the subject of our discussion. Our cavalry matches theirs in number, while in elephants and chariots we have the advantage. Furthermore, he believes that I am of a perfect age to lead them. With my youth and prowess, and your age and valor, victory will be ours—of that there can be no doubt."

"There will be no war with the Śakas," the king said quietly.

"But, Father, we must! Think of how we will flourish with free access to the western seaports. The gods themselves encourage us to go forth and conquer, and make ours the greatest empire of the civilized world!"

Just then a serving girl arrived bearing two glass goblets and a decanter of blood-red wine on a brass tray. Moving with the stylized grace of a dancer, she placed the tray on a low table with brass top and teak legs, poured the wine, and backed out of the chamber.

"You have tried to take your brother's life," the king began, his face impassive, yet his voice trembling ever so slightly. "Your treatment of the Princess Dhruvādevī has nearly resulted in a war between ourselves and the Śālāṇkāyanas, whom we hoped to make allies by the union. You have kept a network of spies since you were a child and encouraged disloyalty to me at all levels of service."

"But, Father, as I just said, I was a child then, jealous of my brother's perfect face and body. If at times my ugliness has driven me to perform evil acts—"

"There shall be no further discussion," the king said, cutting him off. "In the morning you are to be banished. Never again are you to walk the roads of the Land of the Sons of Bharata."

"B-b-but, Father!" Rāma's voice cracked. Tears welled in his eyes.

"This has been the most difficult decision of my reign," the king said truthfully. "I would sooner bear the karma of sending one hundred innocent men to their deaths."

"Where will I go?" Rāma said, weeping openly now.

"There are many places you may live. Our people have made communities among the Parthians, the Chinese, the Yavanas. Ah, my son, my son, do not grieve so! I cannot stand to see it. I love you to the bottom of my heart—yet I must do this for the good of my people."

"Think how they will speak of me," Rāma moaned, "for gossip loves nothing so much as tales of the great who have fallen. Think of the kāvya in which I shall be vilified past recognition. I will become a monster to be used by parents to frighten little children into obeying the dharma."

"My darling son, I swear to you, I will have it known that you died courageously, saving my own life from assassins. And those few who are party to the truth will keep your secret or face death."

"Ah, Father, you are so just. Would that the gods could have formed me more in your image. Turn aside now, Father, so that I can dry my eyes, regain hold of my feelings, and face you once more as a man."

The king rose and, turning his back to his son, walked the length of the room. When he returned, Rāma did appear to have regained some control over himself.

"I would sit here and sip this excellent wine for a moment before I retire," Rāma said. "Perhaps I will live among the Roman Yavanas." He made as if to be lighthearted and gay. "Any people who make such fine wine must certainly appreciate kāma. Will you drink a toast to me, to my future among the barbarians?"

The king, saddened beyond words, lifted his glass to his lips. Yet as it passed before the torchlight, he thought he noticed a certain murkiness, and hesitated.

"Is something the matter, Father?"

"This wine—" he began.

"Do you fear that, during the moment you looked away, I poisoned it? Do you believe that I am so evil I would kill my own father, the king, the most perfect incarnation of the dharma?"

"Of course not," the king said shaking his head.

"I understand if you no longer have any trust, or regard, or love for me. In truth, I have earned your suspicions. Do not drink the wine. I do not deserve a toast."

"To my firstborn," the king said stubbornly. "With his quick wit and courage, he cannot fail to find greatness in foreign lands."

Then he raised the glass to his lips and, making his point, drained it to the dregs.

"Ah, Father," Rāma said, "Even now you think of my feelings. I shall miss you so very much."

"And I," the king agreed, "you."

"Let me kiss you good-bye," Rāma said.

He stood up and embraced his father, and kissed him, absorbing the heady smell of wine and betel quid, the feel of his coarsely bearded cheek, wet with tears.

The sky above the palace's golden spires was gray with dawn when the cramps woke the king. He extricated himself from the bedding and managed to walk a few steps before the next cramp, like a steel wire cutting his gut, dropped him to his knees. He could not gather enough breath to shout for help. In desperation, he rolled onto his back and kicked, infantlike, at a pedestal supporting a statue of Viṣṇu. (Forgive me, he prayed.) The crash of stone upon the tiles brought the guards running.

Some of them panicked when they saw their beloved king lying amid the rubble of his god, his face as white as the fragments of stone that surrounded and covered him. They lifted him tenderly to the bed and would have called a vaidya had he not stopped them. The time for vaidyas was long past. The Purohita, and the mahāmantrin, they were the ones he called for between the spasms that racked his body. His vision blurred, and waves of icy coldness radiated along the spiderweb pathways of his nerves.

Vasubandhu arrived short of breath, fat jiggling, filled with fear by what the guards had told him. He rushed to the side of the king's bed and knelt there, watching with heartbreak and horror as the great conqueror squirmed like a fish washed aground. The same panic seized him as had taken the guards, panic over the loss of the king and the anarchy that might follow in its wake.

"I am here, my lord," Vasubandhu said, taking the king's hand.

"Ah, good, wise minister of mine. You counseled me well, and I mocked you in return. Do you forgive me?"

"There is nothing to forgive. I am sure I deserved what little mockery you meted out."

Another spasm arched the king's back like the bow he once drew and made it appear that his eyes would burst from his skull.

"Is it that thing that grows in your bowels," Vasubandhu asked, when he was quiet again, "or might it be poison? For I have seen men poisoned, and they suffer as you suffer now. If this be so, then tell me the name of the villain and I will see his head on a pike, like a victory banner."

"What difference?" the king muttered. "It is done. Only myself to blame." He gasped from another stab of pain. "We all spend our lives laying the foundations for our death."

"No, you must not talk so. You cannot die. We need you."

"I have only a few breaths left—do not make me waste them arguing over what is obvious." He seemed about to insult Vasubandhu in his usual manner, but stopped himself at the last instant.

"Yes, my lord," Vasubandhu said humbly.

"Now listen closely. Forget those plans of last night. We thought we had months—but we have only minutes. Disaster is nigh, and we must move quickly to forestall it. My cousin Aryaka, governor of the state of Kosala, must take the throne until Prince Candra can return."

"And what of . . .?" But he didn't have to mention Rāma's name.

"Have the guards seize him at once. Let them treat him as they would a conquered king, with the greatest respect and honor. See that he is exiled to the farthest corner of the world and then be always alert for his return. He must never rule the Land of the Sons of Bharata, for he will lead my people into the darkest depths of the Kali Age, the way of the fishes, when the strong eat the weak as they fancy, and the dharma rots like a fruit unpicked."

"Might it not be safer to imprison him, or . . ." Vasubandhu hesitated.

"Whatever he has done, he is my son."

"And if he tries to seize the throne by force?"

"Then use force to stop him! Candra must be king! Do you understand?" Unexpectedly, the king raised himself from the bed and sinking his fingers into Vasubandhu's plump shoulder, drew him very close. *"Candra must be king."*

"Yes," said the minister, astonished by such strength in a dying man.

The king let go of Vasubandhu and lay back on the bed, his eyes glazed, his voice drifting off into reverie: "Only the thought of Prince Candra, of his purity and kindness, brings me peace. If I could once more see his dear face! To die without ever knowing your son is a tragic thing indeed. Thank the gods for those few minutes we spent together in Govinda's kitchen many years ago. Perhaps in another life my son and I will have a thousand cool afternoons together, to walk and play, and speak of so many matters"—the king smiled—"of the ways of women, of poetry and painting, of how best to prepare for battle. Purohita? Where is my Purohita?"

"Here beside you, my lord."

The holiest of brāhmaṇas had arrived moments ago, having rushed from the temple where he had been performing morning pūja. Now the mahāmantrin moved aside so that the Purohita could kneel close to the king's head and hear his voice, which was growing ever fainter, like the hymn of a pilgrim beginning a long journey.

"Is it you, my teacher?" the king whispered. He was staring straight at him, but seemed not to see. "I have so many questions, so many doubts. Are we really more than our flesh? Do we truly survive our deaths?"

"Do you not recall that part of the *Bhagavad Gītā* that we studied when you were a child, in which Kriṣṇa tells Arjuna not to grieve for that which is imperishable?"

"But I was always such a poor student. Could you not remind me?"

The Purohita began to chant in a low voice:

> "Never was there a time when I did not exist, nor you, nor the lords who rule us, and never shall we cease to be.
>
> Just as the ātman that dwells within the body passes through childhood, youth and old age, so at death it merely passes on to a body of another sort. The wise are not deceived by this.
>
> That which is nonexistent can never be, and that which exists now can never cease to be. No man can change the Changeless.
>
> Just as he casts away his worn-out clothes, and dresses in new clothes, so does the ātman discard worn-out bodies and take on bodies that are new.
>
> Weapons cannot cut this soul, nor fires burn it, nor rains drench it, nor the breezes blow it dry.
>
> For it is eternal, all-pervading, unchanging, immovable. The same forever and ever."

The Purohita reached down and gently closed the king's eyes. Then, in a whisper, he completed the passage:

> "Knowing this, we should not grieve."

Having recited several mantras to aid the ātman in its passage, the Purohita prostrated himself, rose, and fled from the chamber, shielding himself from grief by concentrating on the complex funeral preparations that would have to be begun immediately. A group of ten soldiers was waiting in the hall. The nāyaka in charge approached the Purohita, pressed his palms together in namaste, and explained in a most respectful manner that he had been ordered to arrest the holiest of the brāhmaṇas for having conspired against, and participated in a plan to assassinate, Samudra Gupta, the King of Kings and Lord of the Land.

"By whose orders?" the Purohita said, in a chilling voice.

"Prince Rāma," the nāyaka replied, barely able to hide his shame.

"Lay one hand upon me," the Purohita said, "and your karma shall blacken like a corpse on the pyre. You yourself shall be born again as an earthworm, never to see the light of day, and your wives and children and children's children shall return as lice and maggots for a thousand lifetimes to come."

The nāyaka, terrified by the Purohita's prediction, gestured for his men to hold back. After a brief though agonizing interval of reflection, he said, "You are to remain in your quarters until you receive further orders." Then he added, sheepishly, "Your Most Excellent Holiness."

Vasubandhu, emerging from the chamber moments later, saw the soldiers massed in the hall detaining the Purohita and, instantly comprehending the situation, ducked back into the king's chamber, hoping to reach one of the secret exits concealed by the tapestry behind the king's bed and escape via an underground tunnel.

But his weight interfered as did the fragments of the shattered Viṣṇu statue that littered the floor. He was not halfway there before the guards seized him and dragged him to the dungeon, where, in the brief time since the King's death, those ministers, advisers, astrologers, and concubines who were loyal to him had already been assembled. They sat in their dank, dark cells like the lowest of criminals, wondering if the coup would succeed and if they would ever see the light of day again.

At dawn the conch sounded from the highest parapet of the palace, announcing the death of a king. Yet even before the people of Pāṭaliputra could adjust to the idea that Samudra Gupta was dead, before they could mourn him and march in his great funeral procession, criers were appearing throughout the city, announcing the consecration of Prince Rāma.

Rāma permitted the old Purohita, kept under a kind of house arrest and now simply another brāhmaṇa with graying topknot, to oversee the king's funeral, as long as it was held in quiet in order not to "cast a pall of gloom"—those were his words—over the coming festivities. They would be the responsibility of the new purohita, Prince Rāma's childhood friend Kubera, who was, after all, a brāhmaṇa and knew most of the important mantras by heart.

The following days were hectic with preparations. Three hundred śūdra laborers, working under the guidance of a skilled architect from Mathurā, raised a pavilion in the public gardens using the curious style reserved for temporary structures. The sectional platform, as well as the pillars that rose from it, were of wood dressed to resemble stone, while the only real stone was used in the altar that would hold the sacred flame. Overhead, a canopy of red, green, and golden silk undulated with the breeze. A temporary throne, carved from the wood of a fig tree, stood upon a tiger skin in the center of the pavilion. Gems, bars of precious metals, art objects, and jeweled weapons from the royal treasury were heaped together at one end of the platform, while in another part, gifts from the populace, garlands, roasted grains, bolts of cloth, urns of ghee and perfumed oils, formed a second mountain.

The fearful subjects would buy the favor of their new king.

The night before the consecration, the streets throughout Pāṭaliputra were swept clean. Aloe and sandalwood were piled along the sides of the Royal Way, where the procession would pass, so they could be ignited and sweeten the air with their smoke. The torana at the gate of the city was draped with garlands; more flowers, woven together so cleverly that they might have been mistaken for tapestries, brought color to the facades of the whitewashed buildings. Ropes of pearls and colored stones were hung from the balconies, along with strips of gaily painted linen. Silk banners flew from the gilded spires of the palace. Any structure left unadorned seemed intolerable as a woman without her bangles.

By dawn the Royal Way appeared to be a solid mass of humanity. Dense as it was, the vendors managed to make their way through, hawking their wares, their garlands and trinkets. The acrobats managed to find room to stand atop one another's shoulders, and the musicians, to strum their vīṇās and sing, for a kākinī, a hymn to one's favorite god. Dozens of eager faces filled the windows overlooking that broad street. The supports of one balcony, overburdened with onlookers, cracked, and the structure, like a dinghy overcrowded with sailors, fell on the wave of spectators below. Miraculously, no one was killed.

Now the crowd grew still as the sounds of trumpets and drums approached. The procession appeared in the distance, marching down the cobbled road to the palace, raising dust devils in its wake. First the musicians, dressed in bright silks, then Prince Rāma's golden chariot, the prince standing in the center, garbed in dangling earrings, a dozen necklaces, and twice that many bracelets and rings and bangles. His handsomest young porters surrounded him, one holding the white parasol, another making patterns above his head with the royal fly whisk. As he passed, the crowds cheered, and those on the balconies threw rice and roasted grains and flowers. The royal mahout followed atop the state elephant, a splendid beast near-white in color and huge, with gilded tusks, a headdress of beaded pearls and emeralds, and a blanket of silk brocade. Another animal handler led a splendid white bull with a golden collar and gilded horns, all bedecked with garlands of yellow blossoms. Next came the queens of the harem riding in howdahs strapped to the backs of fine elephants, demurely peeking through the curtains at their subjects. Important brāhmaṇas, ministers, and members of the guard followed, carrying banners and royal insignia. Maidens of the court came last, strewing flowers in their wake.

As the procession passed, the people fell in behind it and followed it along the length of the Royal Way, past the piles of burning aloe and sandalwood, whose sweet smoke rose like columns supporting the celestial pavilion of the sky. When it arrived at the palace, so many people crowded into the public gardens that scarcely a plant or bush was spared.

Prince Rāma disappeared and returned sometime later, stripped of ornaments and makeup, wearing only the initiatory garment, a pure white cloak.

The attention of the great crowd turned to Kubera, who, taken with his new position as purohita, went through the customary offerings with considerable panache, though occasionally forgetting some bit of mantra or ritual. When this happened, a knowledgeable brāhmaṇa stationed in the wings for just this purpose would prompt him in a whisper. At first Kubera was grateful, yet finally he became so annoyed by these constant corrections and interruptions that he turned to the brāhmaṇa and hissed, "Oh, be silent, you silly whore's son, I am the purohita and I'll do it however I want!"

Finally, he picked up the vase carved from the wood of a fig tree, supposedly filled with purifying water collected from the Ganges and all the other sacred rivers, streams, pools, and wells throughout the Land of the Sons of Bharata; but, having neglected this ritual item until the last instant and not wishing to have his oversight discovered, as well as thinking it might be a good joke on Rāma, Kubera had filled it instead with his own urine. Before an audience of thousands, in an atmosphere of hushed and reverential anticipation, he poured the water into four vases arranged to correspond to the compass points.

Rāma dropped his cloak and took a ritual bath in the pool beside the pavilion. Having been dried by his servants and dressed again in his white cloak, he mounted the pavilion and received a bow and three arrows from the new purohita, that he might enjoy victory in all four directions. Then, ever so seriously (far too seriously, Kubera thought), he turned to face the four compass points, establishing himself as ruler of the world for all the six seasons.

Prince Rāma, now King Rāma, returned to his wooden throne and the purificatory rites began. The brāhmaṇas and other dignitaries, an endless line of shining bald domes and topknots, filed past him one by one, dipping their hands into the wooden vase and sprinkling the king with the water. Meanwhile, Kubera, fulfilling the duties of the purohita, used the hollow horn of a black antelope to spread the water all over the king's body.

"What is this stuff?" Rāma whispered, like the ventriloquist who talks for his puppet, neither moving his lips nor altering his pious expression, nor in any other way letting on that he was the speaker. "It stings where there are cuts in my skin and has the smell of pee."

"It *is* pee," Kubera whispered, also acting as though he were not really speaking. "I forgot to collect the right waters so I filled it with my pee instead."

"You knave," Rāma said, still stony-faced, and staring forward, but in a voice trembling with rage, "I'll cut off your balls for this."

"But you forget," Kubera went on, barely moving his lips, "I am the purohita. Even my pee is purifying."

Hours later, when every important personage in the state of Magadha—or so it seemed—had paid tribute, the new king mounted the state elephant and, heralded by trumpets and drummers, again marched through the city, this time showing his might with a procession of five hundred soldiers on horseback and a thousand foot soldiers, their turbans like a river of white lotuses.

At least a hundred thousand subjects of all castes and classes—even non-Āryans, caṇḍālas, and the like, though these unfortunates were naturally confined to a narrow section of gutter so as not to contaminate the others with their impurity—had gathered in the flower-strewn central square of the city to view the new king. Despite their fear of him, it was a festival day, and life was so burdened with misery that nothing must stop one from enjoying a festival day.

A cheer filled the air when, from beyond the rows of drummers and trumpeters, the bejeweled elephant appeared, his coarse hide as white as the narrow limed houses surrounding the square, his great feet crushing blossoms like the presses used to make perfume. The procession slowly circled the square in the auspicious clockwise direction, allowing everyone a good view of their new king.

Suddenly the cheers began to subside. The sky grew dark. King Rāma, shielding his eyes with his hand, looked heavenward from his high, rocking, pitching ship of a throne, and to his dismay, saw a chip of the sun disappear, as though some demon had taken a bite from it. It grew darker still, dusklike although it was only midday and cold. With a great flapping of wings, the birds that nested in the eaves of all the roofs of the city rose as one, filling the sky like ash. The crowd gasped and murmured and began to mill about.

Rāma recalled the cryptic words of Vahara Mihira when he had gone to join the rest of Samudra Gupta's followers in the dungeon. The old astrologer had turned the milky orbs of his eyes upon Rāma and murmured, "Make yourself king, but even the sun will hide its face in shame."

The sky was dark, the sun a crescent sliver. Rāma shivered from the cold as well as fear. The royal mahout, straddling the elephant's neck, tried, by cooing softly and prodding with his golden hook, to keep the beast distracted from the bizarre turn of events. Sweat poured from beneath his turban. A chorus of distressed whinnying came from the ranks of horses behind them, an anxious clatter of hooves on cobblestones, the sounds of riders struggling to keep their mounts under control. Rāma forced himself to keep his gaze straight ahead, knowing how improper it would seem for a king to look back in fear; yet fear was what he felt, a fear like nothing he had ever known. The responsibility of punishment, long neglected by his father, was being assumed by the gods, and with a vengeance.

Then it was blackest night. The air grew icy and from nowhere a wind came whistling, whipping the banners that topped the buildings and making whirlwinds of petals that stung the skin and caught in the eye. Despite himself, Rāma looked up and saw that the sun was no more, and in its place was a fiery bangle, a sun all hollow in the middle to herald the coming of a hollow king. The tapestry of pleasure seekers had unraveled into ten thousand screaming faces streaming through the square. Horses threw their riders and charged, trampling people underfoot. What they feared worst had come to pass, the darkest night of the Kali Age, the extinction of the dharma. Anarchy had arrived, mātsya-nyāya, the Time of the Fishes, when the powerful ate the weak. The elephant, unable to resist the excitement in the air, rose on his hind legs, bellowing. King Rāma tumbled from his saddle of cushions, fell the long distance to the earth, and, banging his head on the cobblestones, lay there as though dead.

The finest vaidyas pronounced Rāma's injury no more than a momentary loss of breath. Later, luxuriating in the steaming perfumed water of his bath, he sent for the new astrologer, a friend of Nandana's. According to him, this eating up of the sun was the fault of the moon and not to be taken too seriously. One heavenly body simply "eclipsed" another, he explained, demonstrating by passing a mango set out for a snack in front of a shiny brass plate. Though Rāma did not understand, he was relieved to learn that the sun had returned and was shining as strongly as ever. Even if the gods disapproved of him, they had not reached the point of reducing the world to perpetual darkness. After the bath, a young masseur with firm buttocks and a taste for pain further improved his mood, and by the time he entered the throne room, whatever fears he had entertained regarding his rule were long gone.

Still, the event left him with a lingering uneasiness. He was concerned that so many had witnessed his fall, a moment of supreme humiliation. Karabhaka, his handsome childhood friend who was now mahamāntrin, reassured him that because of the darkness and confusion, far fewer had noticed it than Rāma would have imagined. Nonetheless, Rāma ordered a patti of guards to find those who had seen the fall and put them to death. Saving one last piece of business for himself, he went down to the stables where the elephants lay sleeping in the straw and plunged his sword hilt-deep in the left eye of the beast who had betrayed him.

The mahout entered at just that moment. Witnessing the beast's great white body in its death shiver, the blood bubbling from its pierced eye, he flung himself upon it weeping with loss. A mahout, it must be understood, loves his elephants as he does his children. Then, mad with rage, he went for the king.

Rāma regretted having to kill him also, for he was an excellent mahout, and with a war to be fought mahouts were more valuable than ever.

Returning to the throne room, Rāma signed into law his first official act as king: an order freeing all prisoners. This was a tradition that had existed since Mauryan times and before, and one to be respected. All those who had been loyal to his father were followed after their release from the dungeon and retaken prisoner upon reaching the palace gates. This fleeting taste of freedom, this little bit of hope dashed at the last instant, had a peculiar piquancy to it that gave Rāma an almost sexual pleasure.

Among the other edicts signed into effect that day was one outlawing Buddhism. What a sign of weakness his father's tolerance had always seemed to the prince! From this point on, all Buddhist monasteries were the property of the state. Recalling that the great university-monastery at Nālandā had once sheltered his brother, Rāma ordered that a small army, a gulma, be dispatched for that destination as soon as the rains had passed. The senāpatis would drive out all its inhabitants—violently if they refused to go peacefully—and begin preparations so that the king might use it for a hunting lodge and stalk deer and boar upon its grounds.

So ended the first day of Rāma's reign. On the second day, he burned alive seven men of questionable loyalty and impaled three more for plotting against him. By the end of the week he was performing nearly fifty executions each day, all in public in the main square, and all by the most colorful means. One prisoner's head was squashed like a grape beneath the front foot of an elephant, another prisoner was torn apart by bullocks, a third buried to the neck and left in range of a hungry bear. Those whose ears and noses had been cut off as punishment for lesser crimes became so commonplace that people no longer gave them a second glance.

Rāma's reign of terror seemed to have no bounds; yet in fact it did. Much as he would have liked to do it, he stopped short at executing Vasubandhu, the old purohita, Vāmana the dwarf, and other popular members of Samudra Gupta's council of advisers. His reasons were simple: what power he wielded came from the military, who supported him because he had promised war with the Śakas just as soon as the rains had passed. He worried that the execution of these beloved ministers might turn Yājñavalkya and the other senāpatis who controlled the army against him.

In return for the loyalty the military had shown him, Rāma signed into law a restructuring of the kingdom's economy. Taxation of crops and cattle, of handcrafts and cloth, of the iron mines as well as the jewel mines, and of the ever precious salt, of gambling, of inheritance, even of the work the prostitute performed on her back, all these were raised to an almost ruinous rate, as were tolls, import duties, and passport fees. And rather than using a portion of this substantial wealth as Samudra Gupta had done, to feed the armies of beggars, to buy up grains in preparation for times of famine, to maintain the highways—miserable as they were—and keep them reasonably free of thieves, it was now diverted to two new projects. One involved the procuring of ten thousand horses in order to double the size of the cavalry in preparation for war; the other, the building of a new palace for King Rāma where the old Mauryan palace had stood, a structure all of stone and three times the size of his father's, a monument to endure over the ages and show the world a thousand years hence the greatness of King Rāma Gupta.

While Rāma was about it, he changed his harem, too. Since he already had four wives who would soon be capable of bearing him an heir, and his love for that sex in general was none too great, he decided that all his future wives should be young men. There was no precedent for this novel innovation in the *Arthaśāstra* or the Laws of Manu or any of the *Dharmaśāstras*, for the love of man for man was not common in the Land of the Sons of Bharata as it was, for example, among the Yavanas, both Greek and Roman. However, the new purohita and mahāmantrin, promised that they, too, could enjoy kāma with these young men, gave their hearty approval, and Rāma deemed that sufficient.

In order to find worthy candidates, Rāma held contests, svayaṃvaras. But rather than appealing to the nobler instincts of the men by involving them in bouts of target shooting and other exhibitions of skill in which the kṣatriya took pride, as did the svayaṃvaras of epic times, he debased the events by forcing them to compete for their lives, wrestling to the death with wild animals, or pummeling each other with brass-spiked leather gloves or other barbaric weapons. A thousand paṇas was awarded to the victor, as well as a place in the harem. But these positions seemed to offer little permanence. As soon as the new brides fell from favor—often after only one night—they were deprived of their beautiful ornaments and silks and kicked into the gutter.

In short, the people realized that their darkest expectations had been justified. The dharma was gone. Virtue, purity, dreams of sanctity, and the hope of salvation were things of the past. A new title for this evil ruler came to be heard, whispered in the shadows of the stalls at the marketplace and in the taverns late at night: the Demon King of Magadha.

11

Dattaka spoke not a word to Dhruvādevī as they galloped out of the silk farm, though admittedly there was no way to make oneself heard over the drumming of the horse's hooves. Desperate to divine his intent, she tried even to decipher the silent code of the arm he held about her waist.

His home was only minutes away, surrounded, like the silk farm, by timber walls. The guards saw them coming, swung open the gates, and bowed as they galloped through. The grounds within the walls had been artfully cultivated. Stone paths wound between flowerbeds, past groves of shade trees and a pool with islands of pink lotuses floating upon it. The half-dozen whitewashed buildings included stables, a steam bath, servants' quarters, and a kitchen. The main house was four stories tall, with a spacious veranda surrounding the ground floor, balconies on the upper floors, and a barrel-vaulted roof of clay tile.

The servants prostrated themselves as he drew his steed to a halt and lowered Dhruvādevī to the ground. No sooner had he himself dismounted than a stablehand appeared to lead the horse away. To Dhruvādevī's dismay, Dattaka barely glanced at her. He left her in the care of three servant girls and started for the main house.

The servants undressed her and took her to the steam bath. Dhruvādevī, who had been dreaming of a bath for weeks, did not protest. After she had worked up a good sweat, they poured water over her with wooden ladles, rinsing away the stinging ash. The skin beneath was raw and pink, and she was appalled, not only by the red welts where the ropes had bound her and by the sun blisters on her nose and shoulders and breasts, but also by the bruises her body had suffered from being manhandled by the guards. She looked up suddenly and caught the maidservants eyeing her critically.

After a bath in the pool, they took her to a chamber in the main house and, laying her down on a table, spread cool oil on her skin and massaged her aching muscles. At first they considered cropping her hair short, so tangled had it become in jata; but after hours of painful and tedious work they managed to remove the snarls and oil it and arrange it in a chignon so it was nearly as fine in texture, as luxuriant in its blackness as it had been before her "widowhood."

Were his plans truly but to question me, Dhruvādevī thought, would he put his servants to so much trouble?

They covered her welts and bruises with cosmetics, and disguised the blisters as best they could. They applied lac to her palms, soles, and lips, outlined her eyes with kohl, and skillfully painted that mark known as the tilaka on her forehead. Then they brought out a chest of ornaments and decorated her as though she were a statue in a shrine. Finally they dressed her in the suit of Golden Fire, the very same one she had been lugging about in its ebony chest all this time. She thought she had lost it forever at the silk farm, but apparently someone had been sent back for it.

Afterward, the servant girls stood with their hands on their hips admiring her much as builders admire a sturdy shed they have just completed. Then they led her to a chamber where pillows were piled on the floor and brass trays of fruits and nuts had been set out on low bamboo tables shaped like hourglasses. Before she could seat herself, Dattaka was standing at the door. The servant girls giggled and backed out of the chamber, leaving them alone.

They stood facing each other. For the longest time neither said a word.

"Dattaka?" she inquired in the faintest voice, for to speak in even normal tones might have shattered this frail dream of a world as though it were crystal.

"I am happy to have you as a visitor in my house."

He was painfully stiff and self-conscious.

"And I," she said, "am happy to be here."

"Would you care for something to drink? Some fruit perhaps, or nuts?"

She laughed. "But my stomach is so aflutter, I could not eat."

"Mine, too." He smiled. "It has been a long time."

"Indeed it has."

"You must have wondered who had sent you the suit of Golden Fire. You had probably forgotten about me years ago. After all, what importance could a childhood flirtation have to a woman like yourself, a princess of Magadha."

"No importance whatsoever," she agreed. "That was why I gave up everything I had to wander around the countryside, searching for a man who might have been dead or living oceans away."

"Do not joke with me now," he pleaded. "I have battled a dozen Chinese warriors single-handed, but never have my palms sweated so." He held them up so she could see.

"If what you fear is that one day has passed in the last eight years when I did not think of you and your journey, and worry about you, and imagine myself in your embrace, then rest easy."

"So much for the eight years, but what of today? What of this moment?"

"Though this handsome man is a stranger, he also knows the geography of my very soul. So certain I am that my destiny is by his side that I would give him the pleasure that even my husband has been denied."

And then they were in each other's arms, holding each other as though the force of their embrace might merge them into one being.

Dattaka pulled away from her. "No, we must not. What of your husband?"

"He is no husband. He loves only young boys, and his caresses satisfy only when they bring a cry of pain."

"But the dharma—"

"I have lived long enough by the law of the brāhmaṇas. Now I must follow the law of my heart."

"It frightens me," he said, "passions so strong, that come so suddenly."

"Have no fear," she said soothingly. "The gods guide us in all we do. Once, years ago, I dressed in the wrong garment and married the wrong man. Look!" She smiled and turned around so he could admire her. "Finally, I am dressed in my wedding suit of Golden Fire. And finally"—her voice grew very soft—"I am marrying the man I truly love."

She came close to him and taking both his hands in hers, began to recite the ancient words by which their people wed: "I am the song, you are the verse, I am the sky, you are the earth."

"Come let us marry," he went on, "and give children to the world, that we may be victorious and live one hundred autumns."

Now, standing alongside each other, they took seven steps across the chamber.

One step for food,
Two steps for strength,
Three for artha,
Four for good fortune,
Five for children,
Six for the seasons,
And in seven steps be my friend!

Then she faced him and, gazing into his eyes, whispered, "Now let us do what we could not when we were children."

As suddenly as a maiden becomes a woman, the season called Grīṣma, with its unbearable heat, gave way to Varṣa and the clouds began to gather, the rolling gray thunderheads, and merge until the entire sky resembled the roiling steamy surface of a demon's kettle. Wandering monks and beggars appeared at the door of Dattaka's home in ever greater number, asking for a space in the stables or permission to build huts of salvaged sticks and bricks and palm leaves. None were denied. Meanwhile, Dattaka's servants grew busy caulking the roof and securing the shutters, laying in stocks of beans and grains, dried and pickled vegetables, sesame oil and ghee. The preparations were completed just in time, or so it seemed, as it did every year; as the last of the cows was being herded into the barn, the heavens burst like a lanced boil and the rains began.

Activity at the silk farm ceased, as in most trades, for space was insufficient to move work indoors.

Dattaka and Dhruvādevī found themselves with an eternity of afternoons to talk and worship kāma to the pleasant drumming of the rain on the tiled roofs.

Some have argued that the Āryan's sophistication regarding physical love was the result of being housebound three months of the year. Whether or not this is true none can say, for we each bear witness to only the briefest slice of time and pass to our children what knowledge we can in the hope that they will behave in less foolish a manner. But it can be stated with certainty that Dattaka and Dhruvādevī, during those months they were trapped together by torrents of rain, found an intimacy and sensual understanding rare among men and women.

Hour after hour they delighted in each other; they drank of each other's presence like nomads rescued from a desert of loneliness.

Were these perfect days pages in a book, the thread that bound them would have been Dattaka's accounts of his trip to China. Dhruvādevī found them as entrancing as any tale spun by poet or bard, and all the more extraordinary for their being true. He told her of the caravan, its stubborn camels and constant bullocks, the noble caravan leader, the land pilot who would lie in the foremost cart all night watching the stars overhead and shouting directions; the caravan guards who would sometimes grow drunk and rowdy, and need to be tied up and dragged behind a cart till they sobered. He told of sailing down the Ganges on great barges and marching alongside the river called Son of Brahmā; of fighting off attacks by the savage hill people while passing through Assam; and of hunting a herd of one-horned horses in order to sell their appendages to the Chinese, who, believing them to be aphrodisiacs, were willing to pay any price.

And then he spoke of his years in China, masquerading as a Buddhist monk, spreading the word of the Compassionate One while working his way ever east toward the entrepôt of Lin-tzu and the secret of the Golden Fire.

One day, all alone and ravenously hungry, he had come upon what seemed to be a fortified orchard and, finding fingerholds between the bricks, worked his way to the top of the wall, hoping that within it he might discover some delectable fruit. What he saw, peering down from the top of the wall, filled him with excitement: hundreds of workers with long hooked poles pulling the youngest leaves off the highest branches. From visits he had paid to the silk farms as a boy, in the company of his father and brothers, he knew that these were mulberry trees and that their new leaves, finely shredded, were the only food suitable for infant silkworms. He had passed other silk farms in his travels through China, but never one so heavily fortified; that led him to believe that he might at last have come upon the secret of the Golden Fire.

But he speculated no more, for at that instant he was seized by guards and taken to the local tribunal to be questioned by a Chinese magistrate in silk robes and slippers, and a queer black hat.

Dattaka swore that he was but a bhikṣu, as the wandering Buddhist monks were called, hoping to find a piece of fruit to sustain his hunger. The magistrate, unconvinced, was about to order him tortured, when Dattaka pulled a handful of jewels from a concealed pocket in his saffron robes, diamonds and emeralds, sapphires and rubies, that he had hidden away for just such an occasion. A legitimate Chinese official would never have accepted his bribe, but the magistrate was one of the barbarian tribe that had seized power during that time of political upheaval in the north, and was corrupt in every bone.

One bribe bought his freedom, while another purchased the secret of the Golden Fire. The wonderful thread was spun by a special strain of silkworm. Having wrapped the tiny eggs that the Chinese official had given him in a piece of linen soaked in cold water, Dattaka started on the long journey back to his homeland. Years before, Dakṣa had instructed him in this technique; as long as the silkworm eggs were kept cold, they would last indefinitely without hatching. But allow them to warm to the temperature of the human body and they would hatch in a matter of days, making all his work in vain.

By his own ingenuity and daring and the grace of the gods, he managed to preserve them throughout the long and hazardous journey back to Magadha. Dakṣa, delighted to see his dream fulfilled, offered Dattaka a position as manager of the largest of the silk farms, as well as a share of the earnings. Were he to accept, he would become a very rich man. Yet he refused. During all his years in China, he had entertained one dream, to return to Nālandā and study the teachings of the Compassionate One at the feet of the kind old man they called the Vaidya.

And so, having fulfilled his obligation to Dakṣa—this was about two autumns ago—he had left for Nālandā. Yet when he reached the monastery's great gates and asked to be accepted into the sangha, the abbot refused without explanation. He would not allow him to visit his beloved teacher, the Vaidya, or even to set foot within the walls. Astonished and humiliated, Dattaka departed.

Having been denied the life of his dreams, he turned to the life of his past, and accepted Dakṣa's offer. In time, as predicted, he grew extraordinarily rich and built the fine house where he now lived. Yet he found no pleasure in his achievements. The darkest depression lay over him. At times his despair grew so great that he contemplated taking his own life with poison, or wading into the Ganges, to die as his sister Sarasvatī had these many years past.

Why had they rejected him at the sangha? What was it about him that brought death and disaster to those he most loved? Obviously it was of a piece with the rules regarding coloring his hair, and the edict against speaking of his past. Endlessly he sifted through the clues, trying to make sense of things. Time and again he turned to Dakṣa for the key that would unlock the door to his past, but the old man was silent, as always.

At this point in his storytelling—and it was a point he returned to often, like a man with a treasure who could not recall precisely where he had buried it and walked the same ground over and over again, searching for a stone, a marker, a bit of turned-up soil—Dhruvādevī would distract him by rubbing her lips across his cheek, or playing with a lock of his hair, and lure him into more kāma.

For she knew the answer.

Rāma himself had told her.

Dattaka was Candra, and Candra was prince of Magadha.

She had but to pass along the knowledge and the mystery of his existence would be solved in an instant. He would finally know who he was. What a service to perform for a lover! Each day she swore to herself that she would do just that come the morrow. I will allow myself just one more day of this blissful life, she swore to herself, and then I will tell him. It is not fair that I know and he does not. If ever he learns that I withheld such a precious secret, he will never forgive me. Thus did she argue with herself. Yet the days became weeks, as they do for the procrastinator, and the weeks months, and still she said nothing.

Why did she hesitate? Why did she put it off so?

Though she deceived herself with a hundred artful answers, the truth was lodged like a splinter in her heart: Samudra Gupta was an old man, and when he died, the throne would pass to a prince the likes of whose evil the land had never witnessed. Were there a good prince, he would be obliged to wage a battle for the throne. If Dattaka was defeated, she would lose him; yet if he succeeded, if he vanquished his brother and became king himself, then she would lose him too, for a king is the property of his subjects and a stranger to his wives. Her only certain victory lay in maintaining his ignorance.

Given circumstances sufficiently adverse, even the most perfectly trimmed ship of love will run aground.

Over the months a hundred little differences, viewed through the lens of their isolation, seemed to attain monumental proportions. After making love at night, for example, Dattaka, knowing he would fall straight to sleep, would arrange the chamber so it would be precisely as he wanted it when he awoke. Dhruvādevī, on the other hand, invigorated from kāma, would rise from the big rope bed, dress, and dash through the rain to the cooking shed, where she would satisfy a ravenous appetite with whatever was left over from dinner. This scandalized the servants, who, as provincial śūdras, had never witnessed such eccentric behavior in a woman. They talked, and the talk got back to Dattaka.

Following her late snack, she would return to the bedroom, throw her sopping clothes all over the tile floor, make a drawing of Dattaka on a piece of palm leaf, or practice the vīṇā, which Dattaka was teaching her to play, or stumble her way through a story in the *Jātakas*, or the more difficult *Questions of Menander*—she was good with languages and could read a bit of Pali—and finally climb into bed beside him. When Dattaka woke in the morning, the chamber appeared as though it had been sacked by Hunas.

As time passed, he found this less and less charming. On several occasions he asked her to adhere to his schedule. She tried—half-heartedly, it seemed to him—but the old habits refused to die.

Meanwhile, she grew less and less patient with his introspective ramblings regarding his true identity. Reminders of her deception, they pricked constantly at her conscience. She wanted to scream at him, "Be silent! Do not torture me so!" But then she would have had to explain everything, and that she could not do.

Her decision to withhold the truth, made to free them, became instead a prison of her own design.

The rains that Varṣa were the worst in years. Walking even the short distance to the cooking shed was like fighting one's way through a thousand beaded curtains. Day after day it beat upon the roof, overflowed the downspouts, sought its way through any joint less than perfect. For each crack in the ceiling that began to drip, a brass pot was placed on the floor to catch the water. By the second month of Varṣa the house was an obstacle course of pots. Dattaka told Dhruvādevī that he had hired a singer and a vīṇā player to help pass the time, but in fact he wanted their music to mask the drip-drip-drip, which sound, though he had lived with it a lifetime, now threatened to drive him mad. He was a man who needed physical work, horses to ride, and swordplay, to keep the jackals of melancholy at bay.

Then one morning in the beginning of the third month of their confinement, Dhruvādevī woke with a queasy feeling. She sat up and the chamber spun about her. She just had time to climb from the swaying rope bed and run out to the garden before she vomited. Fortunately, the rain had stopped for a moment, and she could squat in the mud without being drenched. Dattaka appeared at her side with a gourd of water for her to rinse her mouth.

"Get away from me!" she snapped, when he offered it. Suddenly his presence seemed intolerable.

"What is it?" he asked, following her back inside. "What's wrong?"

Her muddy footprints were a string of recriminations on the tile.

"Don't worry, I shan't make a mess of your bedchamber."

That would serve him right.

"I care not about my bedchamber. All I care about is Dhruvādevī."

"Well, that's certainly not how it seems, with all your complaining."

"What complaining?"

She mocked his solemn tones: " 'Dhruvādevī, why must you go to the cooking shed at night, why must you throw your wet clothes on the floor, why must you breath the air . . .?' "

"If you know that I care about these things," he said, hurt by her mockery, "then why don't you heed me? As for a simple thing like going to sleep when I do, you will not even try! And your eating. You eat like a man—no, you eat like ten men! It's a good thing you are mistress to a rich man, for your eating would drive a poor man to ruin!"

"Mistress! You call me *mistress?*" She stared at him in outrage.

Dattaka tried to retract his words. "I meant it only as a figure of speech. Of course you are like a wife to me, you are more than a wife, you are—"

"You called me *mistress!* I, princess of the Śālāṅkayanas, bride to the heir of the throne of Magadha!"

"I thought you said," Dattaka remarked, seeing a chance for counterattack, "that you were not really his bride."

"Apparently I am no one's bride. Apparently I am nothing but some plaything to you, some gaṇikā you will have your fun with and then abandon when . . . when . . ."

Her eyes opened wide and, putting her hand over her mouth, she ran for the door. She reached the garden just in time to squat down and vomit into the flowerbed. The rain was starting again now, dancing on the surface of the pool.

When the spasms had passed, she ran back into the house, where Dattaka was awaiting her. He was so confused by her anger that he could not think what to do.

"What is it?" he pleaded. "What makes you so ill?"

"The gods punish me for leaving my husband—that is why. I have grown impure and now I suffer! Yama will come for me this very day, and I will be born again as a toad or a lizard!"

"My darling, do not say such things!"

"Is it not so? Did you yourself not call me *mistress?*"

"I said that simply because no brāhmaṇa has wed us."

"Yet I do not see you hiring a brāhmaṇa to do the service."

"My love, I would hire a brāhmaṇa in an instant, but you are already wed to another. The dharma says—"

"I know what the dharma says. This"—she spat at him—"is what I think of your dharma."

Dattaka gasped. He wiped the spit off his face with his hand. Then he pointed at the door and said in a quivering voice, "Leave this house and do not return until you can venerate the dharma."

She was astonished, at that instant, by his resemblance to Samudra Gupta: the way he squinted at her, the force of his voice.

"I will leave," she shouted at him, "but I will not return—not ever!"

Clad as she was, without even a cape to protect her, she ran through the rain to the stables, untied a horse, and prepared to mount him. But at the last moment, thinking Dattaka might repent and try to follow her, she untied the rest of the horses, and shouted and clapped her hands, to send them running into the courtyard. That would keep them busy for a while. Now she climbed on the horse, kicked her heels into his side, and galloped to the gate.

"Wait!" Dattaka screamed. He was running after her, but the mud slowed him down. He tripped and fell, and when he regained his feet, he was as black as a demon.

Ignoring him, she dismounted in order to open the gate. She struggled with the bolt, then leaned her shoulder against the wood until the pivots finally turned in their stone sockets. Climbing back on her mount, she galloped away.

She was astonished to see how the rain had affected the countryside beyond the walls of Dattaka's estate. The tributary of the Son that supplied them with water had swollen and overflowed its banks. The hills were an extraordinarily vivid green, and the lowlands had become an interlinking pattern of ponds and pools. Reaching a crossroads, she hesitated, wondering where she should go, the perpetual problem of one who runs away from, rather than to, a destination.

She could not return to Pāṭaliputra, that much was certain.

She thought of the silk farm and Nālandā, since they were both close by, but the former would be deserted and the latter impossibly crowded with bhikṣus from all over the country seeking shelter from the rains.

Then she remembered Caturikā. Her mother's mud hut was only a short ride to the west. She wiped the water from her face, turned the horse and kicked him to a gallop.

The circle of huts was a sorry sight, some of them washed away altogether, others patched with palm leaves and cloth. One hut's roof, having collapsed in two places, resembled a skull, eyeholes turned toward heaven. Men, muddy to the waist, were digging with sticks and picks and shovels, trying to widen a drainage ditch that had already overflowed its banks. Dhruvādevī slipped down from the horse, tied it to a small, twisted tree, and ran to the nearest hut. At least a dozen people, as well as a variety of chickens, goats, and even a cow, were crowded into the dank, gloomy interior. Everything smelled of mildew, and the cooking pots hanging from the bamboo roof beams bore an ugly gray-green mold.

"What do you want?" demanded an old woman, a rasping voice and two eyes shining in the darkness.

"Shelter," Dhruvādevī said.

"What does anyone want during Varṣa?" another voice echoed, sarcastically.

"Haven't you made trouble enough?" Caturikā's face defined itself in the grayness. Sitting beside her, cleaning rice, was her tiny wizened mother. "First you nearly get me executed. Then I hear that you have become Dattaka's lover. Living like a rich woman, but never even bothering to thank me for bringing you together. So do the twice-born reward kindness, I suppose."

"I'm sorry," Dhruvādevī said. "I meant to send you money, but then the rains came and I could not leave the house. Forgive me, please. You were so kind. One day, I swear, I will reward you beyond your dreams."

"This beggarwoman would have us believe she's a princess?" asked the old woman who had first spoke. She seemed the matriarch, the one in charge.

"Well, she is no unraveler," Caturikā said coldly, "and she is too stupid to be a spy. So perhaps she speaks the truth."

While once Dhruvādevī would have pounced on any soul so foolish as to question her royal nature—no less imply that her intelligence was anything other than divine—she now hung her head in shame at her own treatment of Caturikā. Someday she would make up for it.

"Do you bring food?" another voice asked.

"No," Dhruvādevī said. A chicken began to peck at her foot and she gently pushed the bird away. "But I—"

"Then put her out. We've hardly enough for ourselves."

"Please give me shelter," Dhruvādevī pleaded. "Dattaka, my lover, has thrown me out. And I am sick and dying."

"Is it pox or plague?" the old woman said with fear. "For if it is either, away with you this instant!"

"Neither," Dhruvādevī said, "but rather some fatal ailment of the stomach. When I woke this morning, my head spun, my stomach burned, and I vomited twice."

There was a moment of silence that struck Dhruvādevī as particularly odd.

"The nausea," Caturikā said, "has it gone away now that it is noon?"

Dhruvādevī considered her stomach. "Yes," she said, surprised, "it is better. Much better. But I am certainly dying nonetheless."

The women began to laugh.

"Do you find my death so amusing?" Dhruvādevī asked, mightily offended.

"You are not dying, you silly goose," Caturikā said. "That is the sickness of the mixing semens. You are with child!"

"With child?" she whispered.

Now they laughed till the tears ran down their faces and held their sides from the pain, the kinder ones at her innocence, or in sympathy, or in recollection of themselves when they became pregnant with their first child, the crueler ones to see such a haughty figure fall victim to a predicament that knew neither caste nor class.

Dhruvādevī stood there dumbly for a few moments; then she began to weep and ran out into the rain. Caturikā ran after her and dragged her back inside. All the women, regretting their behavior, began to fuss over her; dozens of arms, like a Śiva idol come to life, reached out of the gloom and began to care for her, drying her off, wrapped in a blanket, fixing her hair in a braid so that her back might dry, while voices bombarded her with advice about eating bread to quell the nausea, chewing garlic to keep away the demons, drinking herb tea to quicken the labor.

Dhruvādevī surrendered herself to their charge with an almost luxurious feeling of helplessness.

A few minutes later, over the beating of the rain, they heard horse's hooves sucking at the mud. Dattaka appeared at the door to the hut, soaked, a turban around his head.

"I am looking for the young woman who owns that horse tied outside," he announced to those gathered within.

"Well, you cannot have her," said the old woman. "You who would send the woman who carries your child out into this terrible rain. Begone with you! Scat! Get away!" she came at him, waving a stick, as though to drive off a cat.

"The woman who carries my child?" he said dumbly. His eyes having adjusted to the darkness, he saw Dhruvādevī squatting among them, a blanket wrapped around her shoulders. "You are carrying my child?" he asked.

She nodded.

He gazed at her silently, and in time an odd smile spread across his face. "May the gods bless us," he murmured. Then he knelt before her and said, "If I have said or done hurtful things—" A chicken hopped onto his thigh. He pushed the bird away with a sigh of frustration and began again. "If I have said or done hurtful things, forgive me, for I did them out of ignorance. I know little of the ways of women, or how men should act when they live alongside them. Please, come home with me. I will try harder."

"I beg your forgiveness as well," Dhruvādevī said, prostrating herself at his feet. "I have been selfish and thought of no one's welfare but my own. But now I promise I will learn to care for my husband—and my child."

He took her hand and started to lead her out of the hut; but Dhruvādevī stopped him. "One thing more," she said, screwing up her courage for the request she was about to make. Better do it now, while he was so forgiving and compliant. "Caturikā and her mother—they must come with us. We must care for them as she cared for me. And then we must send food and supplies to the people of this village, for without us they may not survive the rains."

"There are thousands of villages in need of help," Dattaka whispered lest the villagers overhear him. "If we were to send men and food to each of them—"

"A little charity is better than none at all. We have much and they have little. If you so love the teachings of the Compassionate One, do as I say."

Dattaka stared at her as though he had never seen her before. Then he said, "I bow to your wisdom, wife of mine."

In time, the rains stopped, and Varṣa gave way to the season called Śarad. Dattaka left his house and stood in the courtyard, gazing at the clear sky in wonder. After all these months, despite what his experience and common sense told him, he had begun to doubt he would ever see blue sky again. But he did not stand there long, for much remained to be done at the house and even more at the silk farm. While the women servants aired the bedding, checked the provisions for mold, and scrubbed the mildew from the corners, the men repaired the leaking roofs, the cracked downspouts, the parts of walls and balconies that had peeled or broken away. The livestock, let out of the stables and barns, stood for a time stupidly blinking at the sun before wandering off to graze the fresh green grass.

When repairs at home seemed well under way, Dattaka set out for the silk farm. Dhruvādevī, as weary of the house as he, begged to be taken along. Now that she knew she was pregnant, she rode in a palanquin, while Dattaka trotted alongside on his horse.

No sooner had they entered the gates of the silk farm than Maitreya prostrated himself in the mud at Dhruvādevī's feet, begging her forgiveness. He presented her with an entire bolt of Golden Fire, as well as a bolt of an exquisite purple silk with a green border and a dozen belts of braided silk in all different colors. From the way his smile was fixed on his face, one could tell he feared for his life, and he breathed an audible sigh when Dhruvādevī pronounced her forgiveness.

Workers bustled about everywhere, patching the canopies that would shelter the pavilions from the sun, removing the ladders and spinning devices from the sheds where they had been stored, setting up the braziers and scraping the mold off the earthenware dishes, where the cocoons would soon dance in boiling waters. Finally it was time for the making of silk to begin. Tiny silk eggs, preserved in wet cloths for the last three months, were dropped into a vat of water in order that the fertile ones, which floated, might be separated from the infertile, which sank to the bottom. The former were then skimmed off and sewn inside the bright patches that the women wore on their vasanas, that their bodies might warm them to hatching temperature.

Weeks later, when the eggs hatched, the infant silkworms were spread out on a bamboo frame and a coarse cloth covered with shredded mulberry leaves lowered over them, that they could crawl through the weave and get their food. Such was the limit of their mobility. For some three thousand years they had been bred for the sole purpose of spinning silk. As caterpillars, they could no longer walk; as moths, they could barely fly. They simply lay there like fat concubines waiting to be cared for. The only food that would nourish their silk spinning was the leaf of the mulberry tree, and were it left more than an inch away, they would starve to death.

When time came for them to spin their cocoons, they were placed in frames that had been divided by slats into hundreds of tiny compartments. Once the cocoons were complete, the frames were placed in the full sun, that the heat would kill the burgeoning moths before they completed their metamorphosis.

Then finally, the cocoons were dropped into boiling water, unraveled, and spun together so they might then be woven into silk.

"Has it ever struck you," Dhruvādevī once said to Dattaka, "how much we are like them? We pass our lives spinning our beautiful cocoons. Yet if we are to continue to live and grow, we must destroy them."

On a day soon after Rāma's consecration, before the rains had even begun, the Vaidya could be found walking the long, whitewashed brick hall that was the hospital at Nālandā, greeting and examining his patients in his own quiet, modest style, listening sympathetically to their complaints and prescribing routines of massage, herbal medicines, purges, and right thoughts. "Pacify, purify, and remove the cause," as he was fond of saying. A number of students trailed along after him, observing him with rapt attention, thrilled to be in the tutelage of so famous a healer.

Life at the monastery agreed with the Vaidya. If he had aged in the last decade, it was hardly noticeable. If anything, he seemed more youthful and energetic than ever. The peace of meditation, the opportunity to help those who suffered, the excitement of his research, all these things kept him young and vital.

Still, there were difficulties. As the fame of the hospital spread, and the patients arrived in ever greater numbers, the Vaidya found it more and more difficult to give each of them the time and attention he deserved. And so he trained his students as quickly as he could that they could be vaidyas too. But the ratio remained unfavorable, the former group tending to grow ill more quickly and in greater number than the latter group could learn to heal them. Another hospital was being planned, but such ventures required time and money.

Other matters frustrated the Vaidya as well. Though he had been at the monastery seventeen years now, and often left the world behind when he meditated, he had yet to experience the enlightenment wherein the mysteries of life and death are explained. Would that he could penetrate that awesome secret before his death! For as a constant witness to Yama's comings and goings, he had begun to doubt whether man passed this way more than once.

And then there was the question of Nanā. When first she arrived at Nālandā, he had found himself in a state of constant distraction. Finally, he had gone to see Yāsa, the abbot, about having her sent away. The abbot had offered this advice: "If you send her away, you simply avoid the problem. An alcoholic who wishes to stop drinking clears his house of toddy, and makes the local brewer promise to sell him no more. Has he overcome his habit? No, he has become an addict of not-drinking. All he thinks about day and night is not-drinking. One obsession imprisons him to this life just as badly as another. If you send her away, she will still be here. You must confront the matter. That is part of your journey."

Though in time he had grown used to her presence, he had never achieved his aim of feeling as though she were just another student. That her head was shaven, her face scarred, her body hidden in shapeless robes, these things were of no consequence. Whenever she was with him, even under conditions most inconducive to romantic thoughts, in the presence of the diseased and dying, of those misshapen by elephantiasis and goiter and amputation, he still felt a stirring in the deepest part of him. He tried all the monks' tricks: imagining the woman's naked body as a decaying corpse, sitting in a lotus position with his heel digging into the perineum, even the tantric practice of drawing the semen back up the spinal cord. Nothing helped.

She, meanwhile, seemed unaware that he existed in any capacity other than teacher. She had gone about her studies with single-minded determination, soon outstripping in her knowledge and technique those who had started their studies years earlier. Recently he had appointed her his chief assistant, since she was second to none but him, and superior to him in midwifery and those operations that required extreme dexterity, such as scraping the veils-of-age from the eyes of an old man.

Despite her high status, she never missed an opportunity to follow him on his rounds. She stood among the group of students presently observing him, her eyes bright with interest and intelligence, digesting his every word, his subtlest motion. He cleansed his mind of her as best he could and moved along to the next patient, from whose stomach he had recently cut a fist-sized tumor.

"Whenever we perform surgery," he said, unwrapping the dressing, "we run a risk of the fever. From all I can tell, it is an invisible demon that sometimes enters the cut and heats the blood until death results. Five years ago, operating from the premise that the gods would not give us a problem without also giving us a solution, I began to dress the wounds of each person I operated upon with a piece of lamb's wool soaked in a different liquid."

From the corner of his eye, he could see her watching him. Didn't her mind ever wander? She had heard this lecture a hundred times at least, and still she listened as though it were a reading of the Vedas.

"I tried every liquid I could find," he went on, "beginning with those most sacred, cow's urine, and the water of the Ganges, and saving for last those that we most despise, like alcohol."

One of the students laughed. It seemed grotesque pouring alcohol upon a wound.

"I sought to include everything," the Vaidya continued, "for if we trust only that which is recommended by tradition or scripture, we simply repeat the mistakes of our ancestors. Every time a liquid failed to cure the fever, I abandoned it. Yet when the fever did not come, I reused that liquid until it did, for fever is an inconsistent as . . ." ("a lover" he was going to say, but censured himself, for fear of betraying his true thoughts)" . . . the weather.

"Oddly enough, cow urine and the water of the Ganges proved ineffective almost at once, while alcohol, though I've used it only a few times, seems"—he lifted off the lamb's wool—"promising."

To his delight, the scar where he had cut away the tumor was cool and pink in color. Once again, alcohol had kept the fever at bay. He ticked off another mark on a register he kept in his mind, but did not allow himself optimism, for he had too much work to do to waste energy on hopes and disappointments.

"Perhaps," one of the students suggested, "the demon grows drunk on the alcohol and falls asleep."

"Perhaps," the Vaidya agreed.

He heard shouts from the courtyard beyond the hall, strange

at any hour in a place of such quiet and tranquillity, and the sound of galloping horses.

The Vaidya, having instructed one of the students to put a new dressing on the wound, was moving on to the next patient when suddenly the curtain across the doorway was swept aside and a senāpati, wearing a breastplate of layered leather and a sword swinging by his side, marched in, followed by a patti of foot soldiers.

"All bow to the envoy of Rāma Gupta," he shouted, "the King of Kings and Lord of the Land of the Sons of Bharata!"

The Vaidya's students, puzzled and fearful, looked to him for advice.

"*King* Rāma Gupta?" he wondered aloud. It was the first he had heard of it. He shrugged and fell to his knees, nodding for his students to follow his own example. He cared not if one king replaced another, for they both seemed to him equal embodiments of evil. However, he could not help but notice Nanā pale and stagger backward at the news of Samudra Gupta's passing, that she might brace herself against the wall lest she faint from grief and surprise. If he had maintained any delusions about having transcended his desire for her, they were swept away by the stab of jealousy he felt upon witnessing this manifestation of love for the valiant kṣatriya who had been her master so many years ago.

The senāpati broke the Garuḍa seal and opened the scroll. "King Rāma Gupta does proclaim the following: that the monastery of Nālandā is no longer the property of the Buddhists but belongs now to King Rāma Gupta to be used as a hunting lodge, and however else he pleases!"

Those gathered in the hall gasped, almost in one breath.

"That all monks, scholars, priests, bhikṣus, pilgrims, patients, and other men or women presently inhabiting Nālandā be gone by nightfall except for those who wish to stay behind to serve the king and his court.

"That from this time on the practice of Buddhism is forbidden in the state of Magadha and those other states that are feudatory, and everywhere else in the Land of the Sons of Bharata, in order that those who did practice Buddhism can now return to the true faith of the brahmaṇa.

"That anyone found practicing Buddhism after today will be immediately executed by impalement."

Now everyone, students and patients alike, began to talk excitedly with one another. Some of the patients wailed and wept, while others struggled from their beds and, gathering their few possessions to their breast, began to limp or crawl toward the exit.

"You must be gone by nightfall," the senāpati shouted to everyone, rolling up the proclamation and hiding it in his cloak. "All of you!" Then he turned and led his soldiers to the next hall, where he would read the proclamation again.

"What will we do?" the Vaidya's students asked him.

The Vaidya held out his palms. "I do not know. Such a thing is beyond my experience."

"Is there no one we can turn to for help?" another student asked.

"There is one." It was Nanā.

"And who is that?" the Vaidya asked.

"You know as well as I. The man who could be king instead of Rāma."

Now the Vaidya understood. She was so quick, always a step ahead of him. "The last I knew, he was on his way to China."

"That was many years ago. Either he has returned by now, or he has died along the way."

"Assuming he still lives," the Vaidya asked, "where would we find him?"

"That I do not know, but certain possibilities seem more likely than others. Since he is old Dakṣa's ward, he may still be employed in the silk business, as a merchant or financier."

"There are supposed to be silk farms not far from here. We could visit each of them and search for a clue to his whereabouts. But it might take us months!" He gazed at the sorry crowd of patients trudging toward the door. "How long can they survive without our help? And the rains are nearly upon us."

"If the bodhisattvas, in their wisdom, wish for us to find him," Nanā said with certainty, "they will show us the way. We will sleep in caves or beg shelter from farmers. Now let us choose a few of those monks who are most resourceful to travel with us, and be on our way."

Dhruvādevī fell into the habit of accompanying Dattaka to the silk farm every day and found it a welcome diversion. She would stroll about the farm, observing all the different tasks the women did, wondering which, if any, she might master. Caturikā tried to teach her unraveling, but she lacked the dexterity to spin the fine filaments into thread. As for picking the leaves, that appeared dull work. However, there was a shed where women dyed skeins of thread in vats of boiling colors, and that intrigued her. It seemed a more sophisticated version of the cloth painting she had practiced at the palace. She returned there day after day and watched them until she had learned their secrets: how they affixed the skein to a long wooden arm and then boiled it in a mordant to make the dye adhere, how they then dipped it in vats of blue made from indigo, and green from copper, ground gall nut for black, and sandalwood for red, and kept the skein moving so that the dye would take evenly all over.

Recalling how her own people had made a wonderful purple dye from shellfish, she sent a messenger to Kaliṅga to bring back a few baskets of it, as well as to leave a message with her father saying that she was of good health and mind, and missed him and the rest of the family terribly.

Not wishing to cause him undue concern, she had already written a letter telling how Rāma had sent several of his wives—herself included—to spend some time in a country lodge, to quell their complaints of boredom and to relieve himself from having to endure their constant harping. King Jātadhāra's hatred for Rāma was such that he could only be pleased to learn that the distance separating his daughter and son-in-law had increased. In a second letter she mentioned a neighbor she had met by chance, a young man who was of the twice-born, handsome, kind, and who venerated the dharma. She was laying the groundwork so that when the time came to tell the truth, her father would not be too shocked.

The messenger returned with three cartfuls of shellfish as well as a cart of gifts for the princess. The first skein raised from the vat of dye Dhruvādevī prepared from the shellfish was a glorious shade of purple, one that the other dyers had been trying to achieve for years. She found herself a heroine. From then on, more and more of her time was involved in seeking new dyes. She could not eat a piece of fruit without squeezing a bit of its juice on some white linen, nor could she pass an interestingly colored rock without trying to scrape off a bit of its surface.

She discovered that the dust left on grindstones after knives had been sharpened made a somewhat deeper red than sandalwood, and madder a lighter one. Convinced she could find even more vibrant colors, she made long forays into the countryside, where she picked every sort of root, berry, and tree bark, and brought them all back in a basket she balanced on her head.

It was during one of these outings that she spied a train of monks shuffling up the road in her direction. Recognizing them by their shaven heads and saffron robes as Buddhists, and knowing how her husband (for so she had come to think of him) loved the faith of the Compassionate One, she waited for their approach. Were they well mannered and civil, she might please Dattaka by inviting them home for the evening meal.

When they were quite close, the first in the party, a small man with a round little belly and a fig of a nose, bowed to her.

"Victory, my lady," he began. His voice sounded weary, and there was a great sadness in his eyes. "Can you help us? We look for the home of a man named Dattaka."

Suddenly she was on guard. People from the world beyond the silk farm searching for her husband could only mean trouble. Her heart began to race, and even the clear sunny day seemed filled with menace.

"Though I have lived here many years," she began without giving a second thought to the lie, "I know no man by that name. But wait—it does strike a familiar chord. To the south, some fifty or sixty miles hence, there lives a man by that name. Though I could be mistaken."

"That is our ill fortune." He sighed, and sitting down on a rock, wiped his bald head with his sleeve. The others, nine of them altogether, took this as a sign that they were to rest, and sat on the ground surrounding him. "What will we do?" he said, holding his face in his hands. "Dattaka is our only hope."

He seemed so desolate that her heart stirred for him. If only it were something else he desired, money or lodgings, she would have given him all she had. But she could not give him Dattaka—she could not do that.

"What is the problem?" she said. "Perhaps I can be of help."

"The problem," he said thoughtfully. "The problem is, we are Buddhists." From her puzzled expression, it was evident she did not know what he was talking about. "Then you have not heard the latest decree of the Demon King of Magadha?"

"The Demon King of Magadha? Surely you do not bestow

such a dark title on Samudra Gupta. He has his critics, that I know, but he has always been tolerant to those of your sect."

"My dear woman, were Samudra Gupta still king, I should be back in my monastery with my patients rather than walking these dusty roads in search of a man I have not seen in many years."

"Then he is not king?" she said, her heart rising to her throat.

"I regret to say that Yama took him five months ago. The Demon King is his son, Rāma Gupta."

Dhruvādevī gasped and stepped back. Suddenly she felt in very, very grave danger.

"I hope my news did not shock you," the monk said. "Had I known your sensitivity, I would have spoken it more gently. I assumed everyone knew."

"I did not know."

"Among his many edicts on attaining the throne was one outlawing the practice of Buddhism. All monks are to be impaled."

"Yet you wear your saffron robes," Dhruvādevī said with concern.

"Better to be dead than live a life of insincerity," he replied. "Months ago an army arrived at our monastery, Nālandā, and drove us away. Since then we have been homeless, living as bhikṣus, wandering the country far and wide in search of Dattaka."

"And what of your monastery?" she said, wanting to divert the talk away from her loved one.

"Rāma and his friends made a hunting lodge of it." The monk shook his head in grief. "A hunting lodge! From all I hear, they have desecrated everything Buddhist and use the place to practice the foulest perversions."

Now one of his followers spoke, and Dhruvādevī was surprised to see that it was a woman. Her face was horribly scarred from the pox, and her voice was low and gruff.

"They drove out even the sick and crippled. Those who could walk were forced to carry those who could not, and any who moved too slowly for the taste of Rāma's savage senāpatis were slaughtered on the spot. I saw the senseless murder of children in sight of their parents, and old men and women before the eyes of their children. Ah, given the chance I would make them pay, every one of them." She raised her fist, and shook it at the heavens.

"Those who harm others," the first monk said to her gently, "will feel harm themselves. The wheel of karma turns full circle, rest assured."

"I am so sorry to hear this," Dhruvādevī said, "so sorry. I would invite you back to my home, but it is small and we have little food."

"You are very kind even to think of it," the monk with the funny nose replied.

Dhruvādevī hesitated. "This Dattaka you speak of. How could he help—assuming that you found him?"

"This I cannot say," the nun replied, "without betraying a sacred trust. But believe me, he alone is our salvation. Are you certain he does not live hereabouts?"

The woman gazed deep into Dhruvādevī's eyes, into her very soul. In that instant, the younger woman sensed that they knew she was lying.

"It is as I said," Dhruvādevī replied nervously, her voice verging on the shrill. "He lives a hundred miles to the west. Now stop questioning me and be gone!"

And saying this she turned and hurried away from them, so disturbed that she forgot entirely about the plants and minerals she had spent all morning collecting.

"Why do you act so strange tonight," Dattaka asked as they ate their evening meal, "so distant and preoccupied? Is this another symptom of pregnancy, like your sickness in the morning and your craving for chick-pea candy in the middle of the night?"

"Was I being distant?" Dhruvādevī asked. "I had not even noticed. Forgive me, husband dear, if I have been ignoring you, but I met some bhikṣus today and they are much on my mind."

"Ah, bhikṣus. How I once longed for that life! But I am very happy as a householder," he added quickly, "with such a fine wife and a baby on the way."

"You don't have to say that."

"But it's true." He took a bite of curry. "Now tell me about these monks. Did they preach to you?"

"They did," she replied.

"But how fortunate for you! What was the essence of their teaching?"

"The essence of their teaching?" She reflected for a moment. "That every man has a duty in life. And even if that man is ignorant of it, and those around him hide the truth from him, still sooner or later circumstances will force him to fulfill it."

"Wise teaching indeed," Dattaka agreed, picking up a slice of curried potato between the thumb and index finger of his right hand, as manners dictated. "They must have been very fine monks. I imagine they spoke of the Buddha's father and how he kept his son confined to the palace and tried to hide all manifestations of human suffering from his sight. But he saw human suffering and fulfilled his destiny nonetheless."

"And do you think," Dhruvādevī said, toying with a crust of fried bread, "that he was happier for it?"

"It is difficult to think of such a case in terms of happy or sad." For Dattaka, unaware of its relevance, it was no more than an intriguing philosophical problem, like those with which the brāhmaṇas love to toy. "Karma is inescapable for those who have not yet freed themselves from causality. And naturally there was unsurpassed joy in the realization of his Buddha nature."

"What I mean is, do you think he might have been happier if his father had managed to hide suffering from him and let him grow to old age in ignorance?"

Dattaka smiled. "Well *he* might have been happier, but all the rest of us would have been quite a bit sadder, for we should have never heard his glorious teachings."

Dattaka looked at his wife, hoping this quip might have cheered her up, but she seemed even more glum than before.

"So you think," she went on, "that improving the lot of our people goes before the happiness of a special few? Even if what those few have found is more precious and perfect than the very finest ornament of a king? Even if it is so perfect that it glows like a beacon in the darkness of this evil Kali Age? Even if the likes of it are not to be seen again for a million kalpas?"

"Well, it depends," Dattaka said, "on the nature of this precious thing."

"What could be so precious but love?"

He laughed. "I hear a woman speaking."

"Do not make light of me—this matter is as important as life itself."

"I am sorry. I thought we talked in the abstract, to exercise our minds. I did not realize that kingdoms might rise and fall on the outcome of what we decide this night."

"Well they may! So stop your sarcasm and speak seriously."

"All right," he said, dead serious now. "You ask if the love of two people could ever be more precious than the welfare of many. I answer no. There. The subject is closed. Let us talk of other things. Did you discover any new dyes on your outing today?"

Dhruvādevī burst into tears. She rose, ran to the sleeping chamber, threw herself down on the rope bed, and wept into the pillows.

A moment later she felt the bed shift as Dattaka sat down beside her. His hands stroked her luxurious hair.

"I'm sorry," he said softly. "I did not mean to upset you so. Sometimes everything I say is wrong."

"No, it is my fault. I am so selfish, like a little girl. I would let the whole world go to its destruction in order that you and I could live here in our little island of peace."

"Do not worry so, for the whole world is not bound for destruction, at least not at this moment."

She rolled onto her back and gazed up at him, her eyes glazed with sadness. "But it is, my sweet. All things good—your beloved Nālandā among them—have been turned evil."

Dattaka's expression grew hard on hearing this. "If something grave has happened . . ." he warned her.

"Reassure me first," she pleaded, reaching up for him, "for I fear I shall lose you forever. Tell me there is nothing I could say or do that would make you love me less!"

"What is it you know?" he insisted.

"Swear your love for me first!"

"Tell me what you know, woman, and tell me now or you shall regret it."

And so she told him who he was, ever so quickly, as one pulls a tooth to be over and done with the pain.

At first he thought it some poor joke and refused to believe it.

Speaking more slowly now, she recounted the tales she had heard of Vahara Mihira's prediction, and how Candra's wet nurse had died protecting him from a rattle filled with deadly scorpions.

She told how Prince Rāma had disappeared the night of the massacre—her wedding night—and returned very late, face blackened with pitch and spattered with blood. She suggested that Dakṣa had sent Dattaka to China to protect him from Rāma's dagger. And then she gave him the true reason the monks had stopped her on the road.

As she talked on, Dattaka grew ever more pale and disturbed. Seeing this, she broke off and exclaimed piteously, "Now you know what a selfish beast I am! Shall I pack my things and leave this very moment?"

"I do not know," Dattaka said, "I do not know, *I do not know*. You have set my entire world on end. Suddenly all is changed—the moon is the sun, the earth is the firmament. I am overwhelmed! I must have time to make sense of it!"

He rose from the bed and, tossing a cloak across his shoulders, fled from the house.

Dhruvādevī thought of the silkworms struggling to rip open their cocoons. Then she put her head to the pillow and soon was fast asleep.

Footsteps woke her. She opened her eyes, and Dattaka was standing over her, gazing down upon her tenderly.

"Can you forgive me?" she whispered.

"I understand what drove you to wait as you did. Perhaps if you had told me sooner, many men could have been spared their suffering, and much of the pain and sadness in our land could have been averted. This is something we will never know. Yet you did finally tell me, and for that I thank you."

She could not help but notice that her question remained unanswered. Yet she did not press him, for silence was at least ambiguous.

He seemed different, prouder, and somehow aloof from her. It was eerie how much he suddenly resembled Samudra Gupta. She had lost him indeed, but in a way she had never imagined: the man she had known had ceased to exist, and another had taken his place, a prince, a player in the destiny of her land. How quick and thorough a transformation it had been!

He raised her to her feet and, leading her back to the main room, introduced her to the monk and the nun she had encountered that morning. The one with the figlike nose was the great Vaidya of Nālandā, about whom Dattaka had spoken so often. And the woman with the pockmarked face was Nanā, who had raised him from infancy.

Dhruvādevī prostrated herself humbly before them.

"I am pleased that Dattaka has found such a fine wife," Nanā said, raising the princess to her feet and embracing her.

"You are too kind," Dhruvādevī said. "He has told me so much about you. I hope we can be friends." She turned to Dattaka. "Was finding them a terrible task?"

"I knew where you were walking today, so I rode there first. Then, having no idea where the monks were bound, I rode in ever widening circles, stopping at every hut I passed to wake those within and ask what they had seen or heard. In time I found them, my dear friends, sleeping on the bare earth, beneath the shelter of some great boulders."

"When I heard the hoofbeats," the Vaidya said, "I worried it was one of Rāma's soldiers coming to kill us for being bhikṣus. Ah, I have grown to be a very nervous man these past months."

"Not that I have noticed," Nanā said. "His conviction seems never to have wavered for a moment, and his bravery in the face of peril has been the equal of that of any kṣatriya. At the height of the rains we found ourselves caught in a flash flood, swept along like flotsam in the rushing water. Through the work of the benevolent bodhisattvas, we reached a dry perch on the roof of a stone shrine. During the days we were forced to remain there, waiting for the waters to subside, the Vaidya led us in chants and meditations and told us stories of the Buddha and the patriarchs, so that never for an instant did our spirits flag."

It was clear to Dhruvādevī, from the adoring way that Nanā spoke of the Vaidya, that she was infatuated. Yet she seemed sincere about her nun-hood and kept her eyes averted. The princess was intrigued.

"Another time," Nanā went on, "after the rains had ended, we were walking through the foothills when suddenly we saw a tiger perched on a bluff above us. We all cowered with fear, but the Vaidya raised his arms and growled with such ferocity that he scared the tiger away."

The Vaidya smiled, recalling the incident. "I did it all without a thought. It was as though a strange force entered my body."

"The bodhisattvas were watching over us," Nanā said with certainty.

"I am happy," Dhruvādevī said, "that your trials and tribulations are at an end. Now that you have found Dattaka," she went on, dreading the response, "what will you do next?"

"That is for Dattaka to say," the Vaidya replied.

They all looked to him for an answer.

"The silk guild has a standing army of a thousand," Dattaka said. "I will lead them against those forces that occupy Nālandā. If we are successful, then we will march on Pāṭaliputra. An evil king must not be permitted to rule."

"You would war with your brother?" Dhruvādevī said.

"I would," Dattaka replied.

"Then a thousand is not enough. My father has an army of ten thousand, and he loathes Rāma more than any being on earth. Let us send a messenger explaining our predicament. I am certain that once he understands, he will come and join forces with you. Together, my love, I am certain that victory will be ours."

The carcass of a deer was roasting in the middle of the great meditation hall at Nālandā. The tiles in the floor had been pried up, then a pit had been dug and filled with sūtras. Lives of the Buddha, collections of prayers, philosophical discourses, and didactic tales, works on every conceivable subject, from dharma to Ayurveda to kāvya to kāma to cooking—nothing was spared. They made excellent tinder, these books, the palm-leaf pages flaring quickly and brightly, the carved wooden covers burning steadily for many hours and producing a hot bed of coals. Fat hissed as it dripped from the bloody carcass, leaving black spatters on the iridescent ash of knowledge. The pillows where once monks meditated were now piled high so that Rāma's "ministers"—Karabhaka, Kubera, and Nandana—currently vacationing from their tedious duties at the capital, might recline while being fed and massaged by young male servants chosen for their good looks, lithe figures, and large liṅgams. The bells and gongs of the monastery had been pried from their chains and turned upside down so they could be used for mugs for toddy, the great tapestries that once covered the walls shredded to provide napkins for wiping away the grease, blowing the nose, or cleansing the genitals of some messy effusion. They had dressed themselves in saffron robes to enhance the joke of their being there, and now and then, between slicing some hot meat off the carcass with their broad swords or caressing a servant boy, they would rise and, in tones of mock piety, mutter some silly parody of a prayer, lisping so that it sounded like the Pāli many Buddhists spoke.

Now the clap of running sandals echoed through the hall. The three men looked up, not terribly concerned, and saw Dūṣaka hurrying toward them. Thc bumbling śūdra had been placed in charge of the monastery nearly a half year ago, at the time it was seized, as a reward for his excellent spying. It was his duty to see that the gardens were nicely maintained, that provisions were adequate, and that the servant boys didn't become too saucy. He looked frightened.

"An army!" he stammered, as he reached them, "Coming this way . . . elephants and chariots . . . What are we to do?"

"Calm down, calm down," Karabhaka said, with a drunken smile. As mahamāntrin, such matters were his responsibility. "Whose army is it? That's the important question."

"If it is Rāma's army," Kubera said hopefully, "then we will have to spend the night entertaining the soldiers." He leered at the others, and they laughed uproariously.

"And if it is the army of our enemies," continued the squat, muscular Nandana, who was mahāsenāpati of Rāma's army, "then we will have to prepare to fight!" He lifted his sword from the tiles, the blade yellow with fat from the venison, and held it high, while his comrades hooted and cheered.

"By their banners," Dūṣaka went on, still trying to catch his breath, "they are two armies, the army of the silk guild and that of the Śālāṅkāyanas."

"The silk guild and the Śālāṅkāyanas?" Karabhaka grew puzzled. "A curious alliance."

"You don't suppose—" Kubera began with a troubled expression.

"What?"

"I was going to suggest an alliance of Rāma's enemies. After all, it was the silk guild that befriended Prince Candra."

At this statement the sense of gaiety gave way to a certain sobriety. They leaned closer to better hear Kubera, leaving servant boys abandoned and oily slices of venison on the floor, uneaten.

"And Jātadhāra," Kubera went on, "king of the Śālāṅkāyanas, has said more than once that Rāma would look most handsome with his head on a pike."

"Coincidence," Karabhaka snapped, but they could see he was worried. Suddenly sober, he pushed a servant boy off his lap, and rose to face Dūṣaka. "How big an army is it?"

"Ten thousand at least," Dūṣaka said.

"And how many days' march?"

"The distance of an arrow's flight."

"What!" He grabbed Dūṣaka by his neck. "Why didn't you tell us sooner?"

"I was—" Dūṣaka broke off. "I was taking a nap."

"And what of the guards?"

Dūṣaka shrugged. "Gambling."

"Knave!" Karabhaka said and struck him across the side of his head.

Karabhaka started across the meditation hall, followed by Kubera and Nandana. Dūṣaka hobbled after them, still dazed by the blow. Their pace quickened as they crossed the courtyard, and by the time they climbed to the parapets of the wall that surrounded the monastery, they were at a run. The few hundred of Rāma's army that had been left to guard the monastery were arrayed along the parapets, holding their longbows in their left fists, prepared to fire on command. Kubera, Karabhaka, and Nandana peered through a slit in the crenellated wall and saw the valley beneath them filled with chariots and foot soldiers, cavalry and elephants, flying the pennants of the silk guild and the Śālāṅkāyana king. The army had brought great wooden battering rams on wheels to knock down the gates and movable towers to mount the walls, as well as ballistas, catapults, and other instruments of siege.

Nandana ordered Kubera to run along the parapet that circled the monastery in order to determine the extent to which they had been surrounded. Then he called over the nāyaka in charge of the monastery guard, an older man who had served Samudra Gupta with distinction. His left hand was a stump, and an old wound in the knee made him swing from side to side as he approached.

"What shall we do?" Nandana asked.

"Wait," the nāyaka said gruffly. "They'll send a messenger with terms. See, there he is now."

A rider on horseback broke through the line of elephants and rode at breakneck speed to the gate of the monastery.

Nandana leaned over the parapet and shouted down to him, "What do you want?"

"We march on behalf of Candra Gupta," the messenger shouted back, "the true heir to the throne of Magadha! Throw down your weapons and surrender Nālandā or feel our might!"

A distant look crept into the aging soldier's eyes as though recalling some wonderful memory. "Prince Candra," he murmured, an odd fervor to his voice. "The child of the comet lives."

"What shall we do?" Nandana demanded again, panic in his voice, fear mounting with every passing second.

"We stand no chance against an army of that size. Let us throw down our arms and join them."

While Nandana's training enabled him to lead an army though certain familiar situations, he was completely at a loss when faced by the unexpected. At such times he deferred to Karabhaka, who was far cleverer.

"May I remind you," Karabhaka said to the nāyaka, taking charge of the awkward situation, "that your king is Rāma Gupta and that you have sworn to go to the death defending him. Or would you rather be executed for treason?"

The nāyaka looked down, shamefaced.

"Now," Karabhaka said, "what do you suggest?"

"We are outnumbered twenty to one or worse. We will indeed die defending him, and to no point as I see it."

"It is your job to serve," Karabhaka said sternly, "and mine to decide what has a point and what has not."

"But you could hold them off for a time?" Nandana said.

The nāyaka replied that he could.

At this time Kubera returned, huffing, from his run around the parapet and reported in a low voice that, but for the small stūpa to the south that backed against a rocky outcropping, they were completely surrounded.

"Might we order our guards to defend the monastery," Karabhaka whispered to his friends, "while we slip over the wall on a rope and hide in that rocky place until such a time as it is safe to flee?"

"It seems the best plan," Nandana agreed.

"I'm so scared," Kubera whispered. "Tell me we will be all right."

"What about me?" Dūṣaka said. "Can I come, too?"

"If you can find the rope," Karabhaka said.

"I know just where one is," Dūṣaka said, and raced off.

The nāyaka coughed for their attention. "The messenger is waiting."

"Here is my answer," Nandana said, and seizing the nāyaka's longbow and an arrow from his quiver, he leaned over the parapet and shot an arrow into the messenger's heart. The three friends, having crowded to the edge of the wall to watch the reaction, were not disappointed. The messenger gazed up at them with a truly comical expression of surprise, for if there was one inviolable aspect to the dharma of warfare it was that messengers were not to be harmed. He tugged at the shaft, trying to pull it from his chest, then toppled off his horse and lay on the ground, his body jerking in its death throes.

Prince Candra's army, witnessing this dreadful transgression, immediately began to advance, elephants foremost.

"How shall we defend ourselves?" the nāyaka asked anxiously.

"I leave it in your hands," Nandana said. "We must attend to other things." And he and his two friends moved hastily along the parapet.

Dūṣaka was waiting at the appointed place with a long rope that he had already secured to one of the notches in the crenellation. By good fortune the guards had all moved to the parts of the wall that were under attack, and no one was present to witness their cowardice. Dūṣaka went first, to test the strength of the rope. The others urged him to hurry, for already they could feel the impact of battering rams against the gate and hear the splintering of timbers as bit by bit it gave way.

Dūṣaka swung over the wall, slid down the rope, which ended

a few feet short of the ground, and jumped the rest of the way, Kubera followed, then Karabhaka and Nandana. They ran to the shelter of a small outlying stūpa containing the ashes of a particularly pious Buddhist monk who had died young, and crouched behind its low stone wall, planning to hide there until nightfall.

Alas, a very short time later Karabhaka was dismayed to hear Nālandā's guards blowing the signal of surrender on their conches. Peering over the low wall, he saw his own soldiers pushing open the monastery gates and running forward to embrace the opposing army as though they were lost brothers.

While pitching camp, several of the silk guild's mahouts approached the stūpa, thinking its sturdy railing an excellent place to temporarily chain their elephants. Dūṣaka and the three friends, finding themselves surrounded by the great wrinkly beasts, and in jeopardy of being crushed under their enormous feet at any moment, ran from their hiding place with their hands raised in the universal gesture of surrender.

Nālandā having been seized, those four who had briefly been masters of the monastery were each led to a monk's cell and left with a soldier to guard him. Dūṣaka, finding himself in a chamber barely five feet square, with a narrow rope bed and one tiny window, could not help but reflect, despite his essentially nonphilosophical nature, on the capriciousness of man's karma. After all he had endured, the toadying to the courtiers, the social climbing, the favors and the intrigue, he was worse off now than when he had first come to work for the Vaidya twenty years ago.

Sometime later that evening the guard opened the creaking wooden door and allowed entrance to a monk carrying a bowl of lentil broth and fried bread. Dūṣaka had not eaten in hours and fell upon it greedily, sopping up the broth with the bread until the clay bowl was as clean as when it had been made. But when he looked up to thank his visitor, he was surprised to see that the monk, who had meanwhile slipped his robe down over his shoulders, was no monk at all but a woman. Her figure, slim-waisted, with breasts like ripe fruit, was enough to make him overlook her baldness and her badly pockmarked face.

"Forgive me," she said, "but while watching you, this unworthy woman has developed a desire for rati that she cannot control."

Dūṣaka laughed nervously. "I always knew you nuns were a randy bunch. Playing at being ascetics when all the time you were enjoying kāma with the monks. But your voice, it sounds somehow familiar. Is it possible that we have met before?"

"Hush." She put a finger over her lips and glanced back to indicate that no sound must alert the guard to what they would do. Then kneeling in front of Dūṣaka, she untied the knot of his vasana and began to caress his liṅgam and rub her lips along it so as to create a pleasure that was nearly intolerable. It was all he could do not to cry aloud, and groan and weep for mercy. Somewhere in a dark corner of what was at best a dimly lit mind, it occurred to him that this was a woman of extraordinary finesse in the art of kāma; that it made no sense, her being a monk, and even less sense, her being here, practicing her art on him. Yet, as is so often the case with men, his urgent liṅgam cried louder than the voice of common sense.

Presently she eased him down on his back, and lifting her robe, straddled him, impaling herself on his rigid purple stake. Up and down she slid, twisting this way and that.

"Is it pleasant?" she whispered, smiling down at him.

"Ecstasy," he whispered back.

"As pleasant as it was with Sarasvatī?"

"Sarasvatī?" The name jogged his memory. Even as the pressure in his liṅgam cried out for relief, a strange uneasiness overcame him. He felt like the man who tries but cannot recall the dream in which the secrets of life itself are revealed.

"Surely you remember Sarasvatī," she went on in a soft voice, never interrupting the twisting motion of her hips. "She was a maiden, the daughter of Govinda. You seduced her with your good looks and smooth tongue. Then, when you had learned what you wished to know, you abandoned her."

"I knew her not," he lied, now that he recollected it all fell. He wished his semen would come, that he could be done with her.

"Afterward, she drowned herself," the nun said.

"Quiet now," he cried, "for you spoil my kāma."

"I fear I shall spoil it forever," she said, drawing something from her girdle without ever breaking the rhythm of her hips. The moonlight caught on a dagger's blade.

"What's that for?" he asked nervously, praying it might be the key to some new kind of kāma, but knowing in his heart of hearts that it was not.

"This," she whispered, "is for vengeance." She rose slightly, so that his liṅgam popped loose of her. Then she gripped it like a sword hilt and, just as the ribbons of white ejaculate spurted into the air like some brief and ill-conceived fountain, sliced through it at the base. As she rose, holding it in her fist and scowling down at him, she became more than human: she became Durga, the goddess, the woman warrior, the bloodthirsty destroyer of giants.

He looked in horror at the gaping wound between his legs, the dangling viscera and spouting blood. His eyes bulged and his mouth opened wide to scream, but no sound was forthcoming.

"And so is the dharma served," she whispered and, throwing down the severed organ with disgust, fled, silent as a shadow.

Later she visited the cells of Rāma's three friends and dispatched them each in their sleep with a thrust of the dagger. By now her lust for vengeance had been sated, and she merely wished to have it over with. Soon all those who had participated in the murder of Govinda and his family were dead—all but King Rāma, whose death would be the privilege of another.

The Vaidya strolled through the courtyard of the great stūpa, breathing deeply of the fresh night air and stretching his legs after a day of scrubbing floors and making beds. How good it was to have Nālandā back! Her great white stūpa was like a sun that illuminated even the darkest corners of man's ignorance. Though the courtyard was empty now, only a few hours ago it had been teeming. The monks, having heard that Nālandā was liberated, were returning in droves, and the bhikṣus were coming also, to reassure themselves with a sight of it. Even the patients had begun to arrive, some of them limping on sticks, or being carried by friends, or in litters. Many had died from lack of care during their long exile, but a surprising number had survived.

He saw a small, slim figure crossing the courtyard, her round breasts moving beneath stiff saffron robes.

"Where do you come from at so late an hour?" he called to her.

Nanā, who hadn't noticed him before, gasped with surprise. "I might ask the the same of you," she said defensively.

"I was cleaning out the hospital. Word of our victory spreads fast. Already the patients return and clamor for our services."

"Well, I too had unfinished business."

"What is that you hide in your robe?" the Vaidya asked.

"A healing tool," Nanā said noncommitally.

"I notice you come from the cells where the prisoners are kept. Perhaps you have been administering to one of them."

"In a manner of speaking," Nanā allowed.

"Which one is it and what ails him? I am still wide awake. I could take a look at him if you value my opinion."

"I value your opinion more than that of anyone," she replied frankly. "But what problems ailed them I have cured forever."

"I see," the Vaidya said, suddenly beginning to perceive the nature of her night work. There were circumstances, he imagined, when those acts forbidden by the sangha—murder, theft, and the like—were permissible, but they were certainly beyond his experience. He would rather remain ignorant of such things, particularly where this remarkable woman was concerned. Lest she tell him any more about it, he quickly changed the subject:

"There is something I must speak to you about. This afternoon I visited Dattaka—or Prince Candra, as I suppose we should call him now—at his pavilion, to thank him for returning our monastery. He was sitting with his senāpati, planning his march on Pāṭaliputra, where he would do war with his brother Rāma. He told me he would have the best vaidya in the land to care for his men, and just as I was about to reply that I would be delighted to serve him, he asked for you." The Vaidya laughed. "So does the student surpass the teacher, I suppose."

"Nonsense," she said. "He asked for me because he knows that you are too busy here."

"Or perhaps he thinks you would be more courageous in the conditions of battle," the Vaidya suggested. "After all, I am a timid man."

"You—timid? You who would challenge Yama every day of your life?" She shook her head. "How long would such an assignment last?"

"It depends, I suppose, on how long Rāma would fight. I have heard of battles lasting for years."

"We would be apart for a long time," she said. "I would miss your . . ." she hesitated.

"Yes?" he said. "You were going to say?"

"Your instruction."

"By now you know as much as I."

"Well, what do you think?" Nanā asked. "Do you think I should go?"

"Such a decision is between yourself and Prince Candra."

He would have said that the prospect of a future without her stretched before him like an arid desert, but his shyness confused him and he could not find the words.

"I gave him my youth when he was a babe." She laughed lightly, to hide how much it hurt her, the Vaidya's indifference to their separation. "I might as well give him the rest of my days." And she added, her voice cracking with grief despite all her efforts, "I certainly shall not find happiness here."

But before the Vaidya could ask what she meant, she had fled into the night.

12

Those who had known Dattaka would not have recognized him as the young prince riding atop the splendid elephant, for he had abandoned the turban as well as the black oil that had helped keep his secret for so many years and allowed his honey-colored hair to fall loose past his shoulders.

Riding beside him on a second elephant was his co-commander, Jātadhāra, Dhruvādevī's father, a tall man with a brow as craggy as the cliffs above the sea and eyes like his daughter's, dark as the waves. In the style of his countrymen, he wore many necklaces of pearl, and ornaments inlaid with iridescent shells. He was gruff and silent by nature, and ruled his own people with an iron will. While at first he had been suspicious of Candra's youth and inexperience, watching him lead the attack on Nālandā had convinced him of the prince's ability. Seeing the spell he wove over his soldiers—they seemed eager to fight for him, happy to die in his cause—Jātadhāra now deferred to him in all decisions.

Having led his army to the outskirts of Pāṭaliputra, Candra dispatched a messenger with orders that Prince Rāma should either plan to abdicate his throne immediately or prepare to do battle. Soon afterward the messenger returned with a plea from Rāma that they meet and talk before any action be taken.

Candra climbed down from his mount and, in the company of Jātadhāra and their collected senāpati and guards, marched to the meeting place he had chosen, the Śiva shrine overlooking the Ganges. He believed it auspicious, since it was here, many years ago, that he had fallen in love with Dhruvādevī. While they waited by the monument of moss and stone for Rāma's arrival, Candra paced like a nervous cat, his hand flying to the hilt of his sword at the slightest sound.

Yet when finally he heard the trumpets and drums approaching, and saw Rāma's golden howdah bobbing along above the treetops, strapped to the great gray back of the magnificent elephant of state, with hundreds of cavalry and foot soldiers following close behind, Candra grew cool and still, like a lotus pond on a windless day. The elephant vanished from view and some time later he heard a rustling in the underbrush—the path to the shrine was poorly maintained—and Rāma appeared on foot, weighed down with golden ornaments and surrounded by his own guards and senāpati. His dissolute reign had left him plump and soft, with an unhealthy pallor and rings under his eyes.

In this manner they met for the first time.

Rāma smirked, as if the very idea of the slim, diminutive youth, with his bizarre hair, usurping him was laughable. He waited for Candra, who was after all inferior in age and therefore in position, to come forward and prostrate himself. But Candra simply stared at him and refused to move. The minutes wore on and the tension grew palpable. Such an insult warranted imprisonment or death, even under a kind king. Yet, were there any substance to the rumors of Candra's popularity, attempting to arrest him now might prove disastrous.

Frightened by the prospect of so early a confrontation, Rāma smiled and stepped forward, saying, "Dear brother, at last we meet."

In response to a nod from Candra, the guards blocked Rāma's path with crossed pikes.

"Have you come to a decision regarding your abdication?" Candra asked.

"*Abdication?* No, I could not abdicate. If I did, who would rule in my place? A silk farmer?" He laughed and shook his head. "At present, with the country at war, the situation is too precarious to even discuss such matters."

"At war?" Candra asked, knowing this lack of knowledge an exhibition of weakness, but still unable to refrain from inquiring. "With whom does Magadha make war?"

"With the Śakas. Yes—finally! A chance to stretch our empire from sea to sea. If only you were not in such a rush to demand this and that of your poor brother, I would tell you the whole story at our leisure. We have so much to talk about!" He smiled and shook his head over the irony of it. "All my life," he went on, "I've thought, what if little brother had survived? How pleasant to have him to confide in, and share my joys and woes. (It may surprise you to learn that sitting on my throne I am among the loneliest men on earth.)" His brow furrowed with displeasure. "Now that we meet, you have naught but contempt for our shared blood and nothing to greet me with but ultimatums."

"You have declared war on the Śakas?" Candra said, refusing to accept such folly as truth. "Why, you are mad. They are invincible horsemen, and their capital, Ujjayinī, is impenetrable."

"If you would just give me a moment to explain," Rāma said, as though dealing with a fool or a child. "All our feudatories have agreed to fight by our side. With the combined forces of Magadha, of the Parivrājakas, the Ucchakalpas, the Vākāṭakas, the Mālavas, the Ārjunāyanas, and, I hope, of the Śālāṅkāyanas"—he smiled at King Jātadhāra—"we will have an aksauhini army a half million strong! Think of it: fifty thousand elephants, a hundred thousand horses, hundreds of thousands of soldiers!"

"I would sooner have one good senāpati," Candra said, "and a thousand men who believe in what they are fighting for."

"Well spoken, little brother," Rāma said, clapping his hands with delight. "You seem to have inherited all of father's capacity for self-righteous disapproval. But consider this: if your army battles mine now, the damage we do each other will certainly result in our defeat at the hands of the Śakas, and possibly in the end of the Gupta dynasty altogether. On the other hand, if we fight side by side, the better our chance of victory."

"No wonder they call him the Demon King," Jātadhāra said under his breath.

"And if we are victorious," Candra said, "what then?"

"I'm sure we will devise an arrangement," Rāma said casually. "After all, we are both statesmen and familiar with the art of negotiation and compromise. Perhaps you will rule for one year and I the next. Or we might rule together, from matching thrones both carved from the same block of stone." He waved his hands as if sculpting the future in the air before him.

"Or perhaps," Jātadhāra, "you will have Candra killed while he sleeps."

"As I understand it, *you* are the ones who kill men in their sleep," Rāma snapped, barely containing his temper. "My purohita, my mahamāntrin, and the mahasenāpati of my army. My three most valued advisers and bosom friends, executed for no reason in the dead of night, while they slept."

Puzzled, Candra looked to Jātadhāra, but he, too, was baffled, as were their senāpatis.

"Don't pretend you know nothing about it," Rāma said disdainfully. "I speak of my three boyhood friends—Kubera, Karabhaka, and Nandana."

Now Candra understood. He had in fact visited their cells and questioned them soon after their capture. They had seemed so perverse and unsavory a trio that he could hardly imagine their providing a king with any useful advice, and so had dismissed their boasts of being Rāma's advisers as a ploy for better treatment and special favors.

"Their execution was certainly by no order of mine," Candra said. "I suspect one of their enemies is to blame. You would have a better sense of that than I."

"I will see your three closest advisers executed in compensation," Rāma said. "Only that will make amends for the pain I feel."

"Impossible," Candra said.

"Well, you must compensate me. They were my bosom friends, my comrades. I have no one else."

"We shall buy you some crocodiles," Jātadhāra said, "so you will not feel alone."

Candra's men laughed, and even Rāma's own senāpati were hard put not to smile.

"Old man, I will have your life for that!" Rāma said, reaching for his sword. But before he had it half drawn from its sheath, he found himself gazing cross-eyed at the point of Jātadhāra's sword pressed against the tender part of his throat. The old man had moved with such extraordinary speed that even Rāma's guards had been too slow to intervene, and now they were afraid to move lest some act of theirs inadvertently result in Rāma's injury or death.

"Provoke me, *please*," Jātadhāra said. "Make this day the most pleasant of my life."

Candra stepped between them. "As for your request that our

armies join forces," he said to his brother, "I will confer with my senāpati and send you an answer by courier at dusk. Now let this unpleasant meeting come to an end."

Princess Dhruvādevī traveled with her husband's army, according to custom. When they camped, the soldiers pitched a pavilion for her, a platform with poles and a billowing canopy overhead. She loved to lie on her sleeping mat, one hand on her stomach lest she miss her unborn child's slightest twist or kick, gaze at the canopy, and dream of the sails of the ships of her homeland coming into harbor.

Now she was too restless to enjoy such pastimes, knowing that Candra was meeting with King Rāma and that the outcome of that meeting would shape her life for years to come. Instead, she spent the morning berating the servants for the most minor offenses.

About noon she caught sight of Dattaka striding toward her, wearing the stern expression that reminded her so much of Samudra Gupta. But then he leapt up on the platform and smiled and embraced her.

"How did you fare?" she asked anxiously.

"Between husband and wife," he replied confidentially, "I have never been so terrified in my life. He reminds me of the creatures of the depths whose cold coarse skin one dreads to touch. But I pretended to be the stronger and fooled him."

"You did not fool him. You *are* the stronger."

Candra pulled away from her and danced around the platform as he spoke, elated over how well he had handled the confrontation. "I must tell you what he said. At the end, once all the talk of war was done—"

"War?"

"He plans to conquer the Śakas."

"By the eyes of Śiva! He is mad."

"Quite certainly. And I am madder, for I will fight by his side."

"You'll do no such thing!"

"If I war with him first, the Śakas will prey upon our wounded armies as jackals do upon sheep. You see, he is cleverer than you think. Not only has he stopped me from fighting him, but he has reversed the situation and made me his ally—for the moment, at least."

She stared at her husband as though she had never seen him before. Why was he too not filled with dread at the prospect of war? Why did he sound as if he were planning a festival day? Although she had never seen battle, she had heard tales of the devastation, the countless dead, the villages plundered and burned, the families turned to bands of beggars and refugees. Suddenly, she saw into him: despite his sensitivity, his love of Buddhist ideals, his kindness and generosity to all he met, the blood of a kṣatriya beat in his veins.

He wanted this war.

He longed to raise his sword and challenge the enemy like some character in the *Mahābharata*.

"But why do you stare at me so strangely?" Candra asked.

"Forgive me, my husband, but my thoughts wandered. Candra?" she went on, after a moment's hesitation. "If we war with the Śakas, will we win?"

"They are savage warriors and excellent horsemen. When years ago their armies battled those of"—he was about to say Samudra Gupta, but instead he said—"my father," just to feel the strangeness of the words upon his tongue, "our losses were nearly equal and a truce was struck. This time, if Rāma is to be believed, our army will be vast. Yet we lack my father's courageous leadership. Men cannot fight for that which they despise."

"I could not bear to lose you."

"Would the gods have given us a boy if they did not intend me to be king?" He was grinning again.

"Arrogant fellow!" She pushed him away. "You say it is a boy, but I who carry it *know* it is a girl."

"Whatever it is, boy or girl, I shall treasure it all the same. And now, if I am to keep the favor of my senāpatis, I must seek their advice about joining forces with Rāma. Though in truth the decision is already made."

For days the army gathered on the open plain to the west of Pāṭaliputra.

The elephants, kept separate in times of peace lest they denude entire valleys with their insatiable appetites, were consolidated by their patient mahouts into a vast herd a hundred times the size of any existing in the wild, that would keep a formation even in the face of arrows and battle cries, and present a wall of flesh and tusks that would strike terror into even the fiercest enemy.

One hundred corrals were built to hold the ten thousand horses expected to arrive from Khamboja, Sindhu, and Aratta in the north, and of course Arabia, or Vanayu as it was called.

Under the supervision of the mahāvaidya, vaidyas and veterinarians inventoried their wagons of linen bandages and iron surgical tools, of medicines, and unguents, and pain-killing drugs. In the evenings they sat about the fire comparing techniques for amputating limbs and extracting arrowheads from bone.

The commissariat brought a hundred wagons of food drawn by hump-backed oxen and set up cooking fires at regular intervals to feed the masses.

From the royal arsenal came wagons of weapons, armor and shields, and a million arrows, as well as spare wheels and axles and yokes for the chariots.

Smiths and carpenters arrived, coopers and masons and potters, and, most important, those engineers who specialized in digging trenches and improvising earthworks.

Proud kṣatriyas, including those culled from local guards and guilds in exchange for tax relief, poured in from every direction, cavalry on strutting horses, charioteers steering brightly painted vehicles, and foot soldiers one hundred thousand strong.

Last to arrive on their armored elephants were the commanders—King Rāma, Prince Candra, and King Jātadhāra—their gold and silver breastplates glittering in the sunlight. Behind them, in howdahs strapped to the backs of smaller elephants, rode their purohitas and astrologers, ministers and courtiers, numerous wives and concubines. Next on foot came the handmaidens to the queens, the royal porters, and the rest of the servants. And finally the camp followers—the prostitutes, jugglers, acrobats, fortunetellers, magicians, bards, and anyone else who stood to earn a kākinī by helping the soldiers amuse themselves of an evening.

Rāma was so enthralled by the vastness of his own army that he immediately decided to tour his troops, even before decamping in the pavilion that had been raised for his use. He ordered his royal chariot made ready and was furious to learn that a cracked rear axle would require hours to repair.

"There are a thousand chariots at least," Rāma said. "Get me another!"

The charioteer prostrated himself and rushed away.

Meanwhile, it had grown dark, and bonfires dotted the plain like rubies on a black cloak. Finally, a chariot—not his own, Rāma was irritated to note—arrived with four fine horses. He climbed into the back and, standing tall and proud with sword upraised, allowed himself to be driven among his forces. The ranks of elephants, horses, chariots, and soldiers seemed endless. At first he worried that he might be humiliated by their lack of enthusiasm. He had heard about the conquest of Nālandā, about his army defecting to Candra's side. Yet to his pleasure, his appearance was met everywhere with wild cheers and shouts of victory. Obviously the reports about Nālandā had been incorrect. His army revered and adored him. Their adulation was balm to his wounded spirit. For that brief moment, he was invincible, immortal. He was Rāma of the ancient epic, he was Ārjuna battling the Kauravas.

Dismounting at the end of his tour, he noted that the chariot he had been riding bore his brother's insignia and colors.

"What's the meaning of this?" he demanded of his charioteer.

"As I told you before, my lord," the charioteer replied, "your chariot was being repaired. Prince Candra offered his instead, so I took it."

"Knave!" Rāma shouted. "Fool!" And he hit him across the chest with the flat of his sword so that he sprawled in the dirt.

One of the porters ran up to him. "Prince Candra and King Jātadhāra have been waiting in the pavilion for some hours. They wish to begin a war council but will not start without you."

"Let them wait!" Rāma screamed. "I am king and I do as I please!" He took a few deep breaths and, when he had regained control of himself, told the porter to announce his intent to join them shortly.

And as he walked slowly to the pavilion, he reassured himself that the cheering had been for him, despite a night so dark that even the sharpest eyes might have mistaken him for his brother.

* * *

When Rāma arrived at the pavilion, he found his own military advisers, including Yājñavalkya, as well as Prince Candra and King Jātadhāra and their senāpatis, squatting around the perimeter of a large map, tentatively arranging figures of elephants, horses, and soldiers as though for some magnificently complex version of Caturaṅga. Rāma's forces were carved of ivory, Candra's of pink coral, and those of the Śakas of the blackest ebony.

Candra and Jātadhāra described their plan to Rāma. They proposed to move the army by barge down the river Narmada and then proceed north across the Vindhya Range and stage a surprise attack on Ujjayinī from the south, where the city, believing itself unapproachable because of the mountains, remained unfortified. It was a bold plan, involving as it did not only travel over supposedly impassable terrain, but also dispensing with chariots. Candra believed that their chariots would be nearly useless against the light, mobile forces of the Śakas.

Rāma would not even hear them through. All he had been taught of tactics and strategy involved the four forces of classical warfare—elephants, cavalry, infantry, and chariots—and the thought of going to war without one of them was, to his mind, like losing his sword before a duel. With so much at stake, he did not care for innovation.

Furthermore, it was his war, the war he had planned and dreamt of nearly all his life, and simply because he was allowing Candra and this dried-up king of some second-class state to share in his glory—for so he perceived it—he was not going to allow them to usurp the command. *He* was king of Magadha, King of Kings and Lord of the Land. Not they.

"Where there are many commanders," he said to them, "one must be superior. Otherwise, the army, like a chariot with many drivers, will try to go in every direction at once, and go nowhere as a result. So let us decide now, before we proceed any farther. Of we three"—he looked back and forth between Candra and King Jātadhāra—"who will command? The king of Magadha, the king of the Śālaṅkāyanas, or the prince of silk farming?" He was ever trying to humiliate Candra by referring to him thus.

"Prince Candra should be the superior commander," King Jātadhāra said. "He is wise, courageous, and compassionate."

"Thank you," Candra said, "but it cannot be. For the time that Rāma is king, Rāma must command."

"Then you swear to obey my rule," Rāma said, "like an obedient kṣatriya?"

"Until this war is done," Candra said, emphasizing the point carefully, "we shall acquiesce to you. As long as your orders are reasonable."

"Reasonable by whose standards?"

"By the standards of the *Dharmaśastras*," Candra said.

"Do you swear it on the Garuḍa seal, as our father did when he made his most solemn pledges?"

Candra and Jātadhāra both agreed, though the latter could barely bring himself to do it.

Then Rāma, with a great grin of triumph, squatted over the map and rearranged the little figures according to his own plans, which involved a frontal attack from the northeast.

Yes, it was the direction from which Ujjayinī was most vulnerable and therefore best fortified, but what of it? The very obviousness of it made it the last trick the Śakas would suspect. They would probably surrender at the sight of his vast aksauhini army, but if they foolishly insisted on fighting, then he would crush them with manpower and conquer their fortifications with elephants and the instruments of siege.

Even his own men listened with discomfort. Plans that placed manpower and military strength before tactics and strategy were troublesome despite one's allegiance. Men were men and not stones to be heaped in piles to stop an enemy advance. They all argued respectfully with Rāma, but in the end the king had his way, as was to be expected.

Afterward, Candra returned to his pavilion and made the most tender love to Dhruvādevī. Then he lay beside her, his hand on her warm, smooth belly, imagining the son she would bear him. All around him he could hear the sounds of the vast army falling off to sleep, the creak of tent poles, the whinny of horses, some soldiers laughing over a jest.

Would any of them survive Rāma's battle plan?

It seemed unlikely.

And perhaps that was the point of it: their destruction.

Perhaps Rāma, without knowing it, preferred the annihilation of the Gupta dynasty and the loss of Magadha to another man ruling in his place.

A most selfish and terrible form of suicide.

And Candra, though he was awake most of the night mulling it over in his thoughts, could see no way out.

Well before dawn the quiet was shattered by the savage pounding of drums, the blare of the trumpet, the cry of the conch.

The plans of the day, having been approved by Rāma and Candra and Jātadhāra, were passed along to the mahāsenāpatis, the senāpatis, and so on down the line to the nāyakas, who were in charge of the smallest fighting units, the pattis, each consisting of an elephant, a chariot, three cavalry and five foot soldiers. Like the army itself, the chain of command was ponderous but effective.

Meanwhile, the sky began to lighten, the bonfires were refueled and the sounds of the waking camp swelled from a rustle to a roar. Those who had brought their lovers gave them a last caress before rising from their bedding, while those who had taken prostitutes pushed them away without a thought.

The elephants, seeing their mahouts prying up the pegs by which they had been constrained during the night, bellowed in anticipation of freedom and rattled their chains. The great beasts knelt while howdahs were lifted onto their backs and girth belts tightened until they cut into the thick gray folds of their bellies.

Horses, driven from the corrals, snorted and tossed their manes, and rolled their eyes at the soldiers saddling them.

Pavilions were dismantled, their striped awnings rolled up, the tent pegs stored in bulging leather sacks, and all of this lashed to the backs of long-suffering camels. Soldiers, killing time till the march began, could be heard taunting a pet mongoose, cursing an unlucky toss of the dice, shouting insults at the prostitutes, and otherwise amusing themselves.

Dhruvādevī and the other queens and courtiers climbed ladders set against the sides of kneeling elephants and made themselves comfortable on tasseled cushions within the howdahs.

Finally, when Rāma and Candra and Jātadhāra had mounted their elephants, the instruments sounded again, and the great procession began to advance, ever so slowly, like a lumbering giant rising from a hundred years of sleep.

First the standard bearers, their silk banners displaying the Garuḍa seal, then the musicians, then the elite palace guard surrounding and protecting the elephants of the two kings and the prince. The rest of the army spread out behind them like the train of some unimaginably vast robe.

Some of the elephants, straying from the procession, trampled the hovels of a few poor Śūdras, whose village lay at the edge of the plain. The villagers screamed and shook their fists, threw clods of dirt, and called on friends to witness their misfortune. The soldiers laughed. Some of the braver Śūdras ran to the heaps of grain and leftover foodstuffs left behind by the commissariat, and making pouches of their vasanas, took with them as much as they could carry.

Dawn broke to find the entire world engulfed in dust.

The distance from Pāṭaliputra to the Śaka capital of Ujjayinī was some six hundred miles, but the trek took more than four months. While the roads around the capital were broad and smooth, allowing progress of as much as ten miles a day, they grew worse toward the interior. There were rivers to be forded, jungles to be cut down. The savage tribes who dwelt in the foothills of the Vindhyas—the Goṇḍas, and Kols, and the like—raided their camps by night, stole stores and horses and even killed two of their guards. At the end, three miles a day seemed an excellent accomplishment.

Some hundred and fifty miles east of their destination they reached the great valley where they had planned to rendezvous with the armies of the Parivrājakas, Ucchakalpas, Vākāṭakas, Mālavas, Ārjunāyanas, and the rest. Yet, though they were more or less on schedule, not a single soldier, chariot, elephant, or horse awaited them there. Rāma, puzzled and dismayed, sent a rider on a fast mount to visit the governors of the three closest states and discover what had delayed them.

The rider returned within a week. The regional governors, he told the king in a grave voice, had refused to see him, even after having been shown a letter with Rāma's seal designating him as an emissary. Inquiries regarding the status of their armies, however, had brought forth the information that no battle preparations had been made whatsoever.

"The whore's sons!" Rāma exclaimed, his face turning red, his words hissing through the cleft in his lip like gas through some fissure where the earth grows molten. "They promised to fight the Śakas at my side, and then, when I have traveled too far to turn back, they pretend to know nothing about it. Now I must face the enemy alone, with barely an anikinī army, or return home humiliated! Ah, what sly knaves they are, what honorless rogues! Behind my back they conspire and plot my defeat. They would see the mighty Guptas fall and the empire dissolve into a hundred little warring states! Well, I will not have it! I have not come this far to trudge home like some whipped dog. No, I will fight the Śakas, and I will conquer the Śakas. And then I will make a digvijaya, and for every state that promised me an army and did not send one, I will execute their ruler and a thousand of their kṣatriyas."

A further, graver setback came a month later, when they reached a tributary of the river Cambal that ran from north to south, some fifty miles east of their destination. Rāma had expected it to be little more than a stream and easily forded. Yet because of unseasonable rains both there and in Pancāla, the state to the north, its waters were broad and treacherous. They rushed white and foaming over outcroppings of glistening black rock. The river banks were crumbling, exposing the roots of the tall palms that leaned gracefully across the water. Occasionally, with a great painful groan, the weight of one of the trees would topple it into the river, the roots carrying a huge clod of earth along with it, and it would be swept downstream as though it were a twig, until it snagged on some stone.

The low-lying areas of the fields on either side were swamplike and mosquito-infested, their color vivid green from the moisture. Rice and barley were coming to ripeness, but no one was there to harvest them; the little village had been deserted by its inhabitants in fear of the carnage that was to come. An offering of fresh ghee dripping from the Śiva liṅgam in the village square indicated the haste with which they had departed.

To the west, one could see the range of mountains called Vindhyas, snow-peaked and mist-shrouded, so mighty they had once challenged the Himalayas for dominance of the earth; and in the foothills, like the jeweled pendant that nestles between the concubine's breasts, the ancient city of Ujjayinī, the prize that might make King Rāma the greatest of Gupta emperors.

But first there was one further obstacle to overcome: the dark pavilions of the Śaka army arrayed on the far bank, the soldiers as numerous as locusts, readying themselves for battle.

"I had not planned on this," Rāma said, standing on the near bank, shading his eyes with his right hand as he surveyed their forces.

Prince Candra suddenly started to laugh and found himself unable to stop.

Rāma scowled at him and said, "This hardly seems a time for levity."

"Forgive me," Prince Candra pleaded, "but there is something about your irritation with the enemy for doing the unexpected that strikes me as unbearably funny."

Now the others began to chuckle, too.

"Stop it this instant!" Rāma screamed. "We are in grave danger and we must devise a plan! If we do not act immediately, we will certainly be killed. Let us build barges and send our troops across the river. We will surprise them and catch them off their guard."

He was, all the others saw, hysterical with fear, and they lowered their eyes with shame.

"Brother," Candra said gently, feeling sympathy for Rāma despite all his terrible acts, "they have already surprised us. They observe our every move. We cannot surprise them. The best we can do now is play a waiting game, like the cobra and the mongoose when they circle each other, searching for a weak point, an advantage."

"He is right," Yājñavalkya agreed. "We must wait. The troops are weary from marching. Even the astrologers agree that the time for battle has not come."

"Is it the astrologers?" Rāma asked, glaring at them. "Or is it my brother's desire to make himself appear the hero by talking me out of attacking, and then leading his own army to victory?"

Candra sighed. "I have no desire to play the hero or steal your glory. I worry only for the safety of my men."

"You would have us believe," Rāma said, in his most sarcastic tones, "that the dharma oozes from you like sap rising in a palm."

"Brother," Candra said, "you test my goodwill."

"Would you prefer I test your courage?" asked Rāma, reaching for his sword.

"Fight him," Jātadhāra growled, "and put an end to this rivalry once and for all."

But Yājñavalkya stepped quickly in front of Rāma and, grabbing his sword hand, forced the half-drawn blade back into the scabbard.

"My lord," he said, "we are all tired from so much travel. Our nerves are frayed, our tempers on edge. Let us make camp and rest. Meanwhile, I propose the following: we send scouting parties up and down the river to find all likely crossing places, and post a patti at each. Another group seizes all rafts and barges that are regularly run upon the river and delivers them to some concealed yet convenient spot. Then, when and if a time comes to attack, we will be prepared."

Through the red haze of his fury, Rāma saw the sense of Yājñavalkya's advice. With a last glaring look at Candra, he returned to his pavilion.

Camp was laid out in a great quadrangle a mile or so back from the riverbank. The fields of rice and barley cultivated by the villagers in the hope of staving off famine for another year were ground to a muddy pulp within the course of a few hours. Ditches were dug to drain off the water, that the land could be made dry enough to hold tent pegs and foundations for watchtowers, and the excavated dirt was piled high and tamped into ramparts. Trees were felled in the nearby teak forests and dragged back by elephants so that construction of the towers might begin. Because of the excellent engineers and enormous manpower, work that might have taken months was accomplished in days.

When the ground was dry enough to sleep upon, each of the four army corps crowded into its own corner of the huge camp, while King Rāma, King Jātadhāra, and Prince Candra occupied pavilions in the center. Though Rāma's pavilion featured a splendid bed, he chose to sleep on the floor of his chariot instead, his sword and bow beside him. Each morning his backache, the result of not having sufficient space to stretch out on the chariot's uneven floorboards, grew worse, yet he had dreamt of the dramatic gesture so long that he could not bring himself to abandon it.

Soon after settling in, Rāma ordered a magnificent banquet for his senāpatis and royal guard, in order to slight Candra and Jātadhāra by not inviting them. Concubines wearing tinkling bells and zills upon their fingers danced to the lively music of the vīṇās. Many delicacies were served and many toasts drunk, to Rāma, to the war god, Kārttikeya, and his six foster mothers (who were those stars the Greek Yavanas called the Pleiades) and his wife, Kaumarī, the embodiment of the army itself.

Rāma made speeches to stir the blood of these, his best warriors, but the effect was not as intended. A poor and cynical orator, they thought him jesting when he spoke of courage and nobility.

When a servant announced, halfway through the evening, that Prince Candra desired to interrupt the festivities, Rāma feigned annoyance, though in fact he was delighted that his brother's desire to join them afforded him with another opportunity to reject him.

"Send him away," he said with indescribable satisfaction.

"But he has taken a Śaka prisoner," the guard replied.

Hearing this, the senāpatis sitting about him pressed Rāma to see his brother that they might question the prisoner. Rāma had no choice but to agree.

Candra entered the pavilion propelling in front of him, dagger blade to the throat, a man like himself, but somewhat paler and taller, with a vaguely Oriental cast to his features. The prisoner was stooped with fear, and clutched his shoulder, to stem the bleeding from a wound he had taken there. Someone had shown the mercy to wrap it with linen bandage.

"Brother dear," Rāma said sarcastically, gesturing with a pheasant bone he had been gnawing, "did we not speak of the cobra and the mongoose? Of a waiting game? Of observing the enemy until a weak point could be found? I see now that it was as I suspected, that you urged me not to fight so that you could fight in my stead and make me look the fool." He rose and shook the bone at them menacingly, and his voice grew grimmer still. "I warn you, I will not tolerate such trickery, even in a brother."

"He and a dozen others crossed the river on horseback,"

Candra replied. "They leaped the earthworks and rode through the streets of our camp, firing arrows into the barracks, knocking over torches, and creating what other destruction they could."

"Was anyone harmed?" Yājñavalkya asked.

"Five men were killed, and an elephant, made to rampage, trampled a tent, killing two more men and breaking the back of his mahout."

"And where are the rest of the invaders?" Rāma inquired.

"They escaped," Candra replied.

"You caught only this one?"

"I am only one man. Had our army been alert rather than sleeping with whores, playing dice, and drinking palm wine, then no doubt the rest would have been captured, too."

"Do you criticize my soldiers?" Rāma said, bending forward and fixing Candra with his gaze.

"Would I criticize cows if they wandered into the stream and drowned? Or would I fault the cowherd?"

One of the senāpatis laughed at the analogy. A glance from Rāma silenced him. For a time Rāma said nothing, simply stared at his brother with a cold eye. The prisoner was all but forgotten. Then, in a whisper: "And what of you, dear brother? Do you not sleep with the whore Dhruvādevī?"

Candra leaped across the banquet set out on the floor, overturning brass bowls and goblets of wine, grabbed Rāma by the neck, and drove him back against the pillows.

"Apologize," he hissed, "or I'll wring your throat like a rag!"

Rāma's eyes bulged. He tried to talk, but the pressure of his larynx reduced his voice to a wheezing, grunting rasp.

The guards rushed to separate them and held them apart.

"Kill him!" Rāma shouted. "He dared attack your king."

None of the soldiers made a move to carry out his orders. Candra, having regained control of himself, shook free of their hold and, looking around, demanded, "Where is the prisoner?"

Apparently he had taken advantage of the confusion and fled.

Having dispatched guards to find him, Rāma said, "The banquet is over. Go to your nāyakas and tell them that any man found whoring or gaming or drinking will suffer a hundred strokes of the cane. From this moment on half my army will be on the alert while the other half sleeps."

The prisoner was recaptured later that night. Hours of questioning brought little information they did not already know. The next morning, despite the objections of those who would still uphold the dharma, Rāma had him executed, his head embedded on a pike, the pike erected on the riverbank that the Śakas might see. An hour later, however, the bit of bank crumbled and the pike washed downstream, as though even the dumb earth did protest the sight of prisoners being so mistreated.

The next night, at the hour when men are in the profoundest depths of sleep, Śaka archers drifting on a barge near the bank launched a volley of incendiary arrows. Some fell within the earthwork walls and one tent canvas went up in flames. Every night thereafter the Śakas made an attempt on the camp, either by barge or on horseback, and always in the dead of night. Soon Rāma's soldiers were so troubled they could not sleep. Two nervous platoons, awakened by an animal prowling through the stores, mistook the other for the enemy and crossed swords. The resulting deaths were a terrible blow to morale.

Meanwhile, the daylight activities around the Śaka camp, the foraging from neighboring fields as well as the construction of elaborate earthworks, gave every impression that the enemy intended to hold its position until the river abated and could be crossed in force. In its way, this was as disturbing to Rāma's soldiers as the nightly attacks. Were it a waiting game, the Śakas, encamped only fifty miles from Ujjayinī and having a direct supply route for reinforcements as well as provisions, could easily outlast any army stranded half a continent away from home. Furthermore, malaria had begun to appear among Rāma's soldiers, and his elephants were consuming forage at a most alarming rate.

Again Rāma began to fear that if something were not done soon, the army would crumble from its own inner weakness, like a palace whose columns have been eaten by rot. It occurred to him that since they could see only those warriors who appeared on the bank above the river, it was conceivable that the Śaka army was a small force, made to look greater through clever display. Were this indeed the case, a powerful frontal attack along with a pincer movement to cut off supplies might be just the advantage that would bring about surrender, or at least negotiations that would permit an honorable withdrawal. At worst, they would get the measure of the enemy and give their own troops an opportunity to stretch their bowstrings. Many auspicious omens further encouraged him, as well as reports from the astrologer that the next few days would be excellent for such an undertaking.

Alas, these speculations on the size of the Śaka army reflected more Rāma's wishes than the facts gathered by Gupta spies. But for one who had spent his whole life enjoying the toadying atmosphere of the court, the distinction between how one would like the world to be and how the world really was became increasingly difficult to draw.

When Rāma called a meeting of the commanders to explain his plan, Candra, who was beginning to understand the nature of his brother's irrational suspicion of everyone and everything, held his objections in check. He knew that any criticism would simply encourage him in his folly. Jātadhāra, however, feeling no such constraints, openly expressed his opinion that the plan was reckless and stupid in the light of intelligence that suggested a Śaka force at least as big as their own.

"Of course you criticize my plan," Rāma replied, precisely as Candra had anticipated. "You try to talk me out of it, so that when my back is turned, you can implement it yourselves, pretending it was you who thought of it and steal my glory. Well, I am not so easily fooled. Neither you nor your army will have a part in the invasion. You will have to watch from the sidelines, and when victory is ours, you will be turned away from the celebrations and adoring crowds and forced to wear the mantles of cowards and traitors."

May the gods help us, Candra thought to himself, but said nothing.

The next morning, at dawn, the trumpets and drums set up a fearful racket. A camū force came charging across the embankments with a clatter of hooves and a thousand cries of "Victory to Rāma!" The elephants, more than two hundred of them bellowing with joy, plunged into the river and crossed completely submerged, only their trunks rising from the water like the necks of sea monsters. Each one carried a mahout and three archers, who, hanging to the girth strap for dear life, seemed propelled across the surface of the water as if by magic. Nearly eight hundred horses leaped in the water too, paddling frantically against the current, riders hugging their necks and shouting encouragement. Meanwhile, twelve hundred infantry were crossing in stout wooden barges and rafts and other crafts commandeered from the local ferrymen. At the same time, a few miles south, the pincer force was being deployed in a similar manner. Such swarming of man and beast was an awesome sight.

The currents were far worse than anyone had imagined. The inexperienced pilots, ignorant of the river's treacherous flow, lost control, and their boats were swept downstream, smashing into the paddling horses and breaking their necks, and finally being battered to splinters against the rocks. Some of the soldiers managed to escape the sinking crafts and swim back to shore; others foolishly tried to reach the far bank and drowned, or were filled with Śaka arrows as soon as they came within range. Volleys of arrows rained down upon the boats and horses that neared the far shore. The soldiers held up their shields, but the shafts penetrated the thick leather and pierced their bodies. The horses that climbed onto the opposite bank were so enfeebled they could scarcely stand. The Śaka cavalry swooped down upon them and dispatched their water-soaked riders with a few strokes of their swords. A number of elephants survived the crossing too, and those noble beasts, bellowing with rage, climbed the bank and actually got far enough to knock down the Śakas' earthwork walls. Śaka cavalry came at them with lances, stabbing again and again, screaming and riding back and forth until the beasts were so confused and angry that they turned and trampled their own soldiers and gored their own horses. They ran back down to the river, but this time, wounded and tired, they could not reach their own shore and drowned or were battered to death against the rocks.

Candra stood on the bank and wept.

The force deployed in the pincer movement was neither seen nor heard of again.

Thus was concluded the first skirmish between Rāma's army and the Śakas.

One night during a thunderstorm, in the blue-white illumination of a jagged trident of lightning, a sentry from the small outpost upriver was spotted galloping toward camp. A short time later, standing in the commander's pavilion, water dripping from his vasana and pooling around his feet, he told the just-awakened kings and Candra and the senāpatis the urgent news.

Having decided that no one could possibly ford the river in this terrible weather—so the sentry began his report, speaking loudly to be heard over the rain pounding on the canvas roof—he had crawled into his tent and fallen asleep. An explosion of thunder had awakened him to the sounds of men creeping through his small outpost. Seeing a shadow steal into his tent and plunge a dagger into the soldier sleeping across from him, he grabbed the sharpened metal throwing disk called the cakra that he kept by his bedding and hurled it at the intruder, slicing him across the face. In the ensuing confusion, he rushed from the tent, found his horse, and rode to camp with all haste to tell them of the Śaka invasion. Alas, the impenetrable darkness of the storm, with its whirling winds and rain, had made it impossible to estimate the number of those who had crossed.

A furious discussion ensued among the commanders. Was this "invasion" only another raiding party bent on further harassing them? Or was it the majority of the Śaka force being positioned for the final confrontation? And if this were so, why had no one noticed the army amassing on the far bank, as well as the barges or pontoons or whatever they had used to cross the rapid water?

The sentry, who knew the area well, pointed out that a number of wooded islands in that vicinity would supply cover for men and boats alike.

Once the sky had grown light and the rain turned to a drizzle, a few scouts on horseback were dispatched upriver to estimate the number of Śakas. Ten thousand foot soldiers, they reported on their return, as well as some five thousand cavalry. But as yet neither elephants nor chariots.

Much as they hated the enemy, the senāpatis could not help but admire their skill and audacity in successfully undertaking so daring a maneuver.

Rāma, skin crawling with fear at the thought of being trapped, lashed out at the sentry, berating him for laziness and cowardice, ordering his nose and ears cut off, and banishing him from his class. He would have proceeded to send his entire army north to battle, but the other commanders intervened.

They reminded him that the invasion might be only a

splinter group. After all, the bulk of the enemy's force still appeared to be encamped across the river. At their insistence, Rāma contented himself with sending a small army, a double pritapa, comprising twenty-five hundred infantry, fifteen hundred cavalry, and five hundred each of chariots and elephants.

Candra asked to lead the silk guild army in the offensive, but Rāma, again fearing that glory might be diverted from himself, insisted that the double pritapa be drawn from his own men. Yājñavalkya, who in everyone's opinion was unsurpassed as a senāpati, would lead it. At noon that excellent soldier, standing in his battle-chariot, gave the order for his troops to begin their march. Meanwhile, the forces that remained in camp were to marshal themselves in preparation for battle.

All day the commanders paced back and forth in the pavilion, chewing betel quid and waiting to learn the outcome of the first skirmish. Scouts were dispatched every few hours, but they were confused by the chaos and returned with conflicting reports. One said that the Śaka army had grown to fifty thousand in size, while another reported victory almost in Yājñavalkya's hands. A third scout did not return at all.

Around dusk of that day, Yājñavalkya's war chariot, easily recognized by its banners and brightly painted insignia, came rolling along the riverbank toward Rāma's camp. It moved slowly because only one of the four horses meant to pull it remained in harness. No driver sat on the yoke holding the reins. Only the horse's desire to return to his feed steered it right.

In time the heavy chariot rumbled through the gates. Rāma ran around to the back of it, hoping to find Yājñavalkya there, squatting with fatigue, perhaps, or lying on the floorboards wounded. All he found was a leather sack. He picked it up and opened it. Yājñavalkya's severed head fell to the dirt and rolled face up. The giant pearl that he wore as a false eye had been plucked from its socket, but the other eye appeared to focus on Rāma with an accusatory gaze.

Fear closed like a pair of rusty manacles round Rāma's heart. Yājñavalkya had been his teacher. Since boyhood he had guided Rāma in every decision that concerned the prince's military career. Now Rāma found himself without guidance at what was likely the critical juncture of his life. He had excellent senāpatis to confer with, it was true, but he wished to appear to them as an authority. He felt an extraordinary loneliness and desolation.

"What shall we do now?" his senāpatis asked him. But Rāma did not seem to hear. He squatted in the mud, holding Yājñavalkya's head in his lap, as though for security, and rocking back and forth.

Candra tried to bring Rāma to his senses. He knelt in front of him, and called to him, and shook him by the shoulder. He reached for Yājñavalkya's severed head, but Rāma clutched it in his arms and bared his teeth like an angry dog. Having assigned guards to watch over the king and alert him if there was improvement in his condition, Candra called for Jātadhāra and all the senāpatis to meet him in the command pavilion.

When they were assembled, he said, "As some of you have guessed, the encampment across the river was no more than a diversion. I climbed the watchtower at dusk this evening and saw the real army, sixty thousand strong, gathered on our side of the river, beyond the cane fields to the north. How they crossed in the midst of that terrible storm I cannot guess. But the fact is they are here, and they are ready for battle. That may come as a relief after so much waiting."

Some of the senāpatis laughed to hear him say this, for it was as though he had read their thoughts.

"When I was on the tower," Candra went on, "I saw for myself what many of you already know: that the Śakas have a great many cavalry, but no chariots or elephants to speak of. It seems to me there is a wisdom in this, for on ground so muddy, a chariot is dangerous and difficult to control."

The senāpatis murmured agreement among themselves. They had all lost chariots on muddy ground.

"Channa," he called to the senāpati in charge of chariots, "can the horses that pull the chariots also be ridden? Do they have experience as mounts?"

The senāpati replied that the chariot horses and cavalry horses were frequently exchanged for the sake of exercise.

"And Yaśodhara," he said, addressing the senāpati in charge of cavalry, "is it true that we have many more riders than horses?"

The senāpati in charge of cavalry agreed that this was in fact the case.

"Then it is as I hoped," Candra said. "Though my idea may at first sound strange, consider it carefully. Let us leave the chariots behind and give the horses to our cavalry. Then we will be more our enemy's equal in number and mobility."

He looked around at the senāpatis, and they all nodded agreement. They had been listening to him as though passing time until Rāma arrived, but by and by it became apparent that Rāma was not coming. It was no great surprise, for the king had been late for other meetings, had appeared disheveled upon arriving, and had behaved in a distracted and often irrational manner. They seemed as grateful for Candra's intercession as the passengers of a runaway cart might be to someone who sought to grab the reins and bring it back under control.

"As for elephants," Candra went on, sensing their approval and gaining confidence, "though I have seen only a few battles in my life, they too seem more hindrance than help. Since each elephant carries at least four riders, let us reemploy these men as cavalry and foot soldiers and leave the elephants behind, too."

The senāpatis found this idea far more difficult to accept. While certain armies regularly fought without chariots, no one except the Śakas dared dispense with elephants. They were so much a part of Āryan warfare, so comforting and auspicious in their wrinkled gray bulk, that it was difficult to conceive of a battle without them.

Yet such was their faith in Candra that they acquiesced. His innovations still were not at an end. For days he had been considering the special problems of war with the Śakas, and now that Rāma was gone, he had many, many ideas to discuss. He suggested that since their army, freed of chariots and elephants, was now more mobile, they might dispense with the rigid formations of classical warfare—the staff, the snake, the circle, the diamond, the alligator, and the like—and deploy themselves instead in mobile columns, holding a quarter of the army in reserve.

The senāpatis, fascinated by the boldness of his vision, were so busy flooding him with questions that they did not notice Rāma entering the pavilion, at last, holding Yājñavalkya's head to his breast as though it were a babe, until he was nearly by Candra's side.

Bit by bit, all conversation ceased and everyone gazed with horror at the muddy, blood-soaked king and his grisly burden.

"Is it treason you plan here tonight?" Rāma asked good-naturedly.

"I tried to include you," Candra said, "but you were in a daze from your grief."

"I believe it is treason," Rāma said, nodding to himself. And lowering his gaze to the severed head he held in his arms, he murmured, "Little brother tries to win away my senāpatis with wild schemes and bribes."

"I offer no bribes or schemes. Battle plans had to be made," Candra said. "Just north of the cane fields, the Śakas ready themselves for attack."

"He thinks I have made no plans of my own," Rāma whispered to Yājñavalkya's head. "He must suppose me a fool, to lead an army into battle without plans. Yes, I have many plans."

"I was simply offering a strategy in your absence," Candra said. "Now that you are here, we are all eager to hear your plan." Though he tried his best, he could hardly withhold his anger and impatience.

"But whose plan will the army follow?" Rāma asked, looking up at his senāpatis slyly. "The plans of the king of Magadha or the plans of a silk farmer?"

"Let us once and for all pledge our fidelity to Prince Candra," King Jātadhāra said impatiently. "This Rāma is mad! He anoints his skin with dirt and blood and talks with a severed head!"

The other senāpatis began to murmur assent.

"Ah, but he swore on the Garuḍa seal," Rāma reminded them. "He promised he would follow my orders as long as they were in accord with the *Dharmaśāstras*."

"I did," Candra agreed. "I swore it."

"Damned Demon King!" Jātadhāra exclaimed.

"Perhaps we can reach some kind of accord," Candra suggested to Rāma, hoping to save at least some element of his plans.

"We will reach no accord battling without chariots and elephants," Rāma said. Apparently he had been listening for some time from outside the pavilion before entering.

Candra sighed. "Then keep the chariots and elephants. Their fury inspires the troops, I suppose."

"And we will reach no accord marching in columns."

"March as you like," Candra said.

"But which of the formations will best serve us come tomorrow?" Rāma asked. He looked down at the severed head and murmured, "Ah, my friend, if only you were here to advise me. But wait!" He grinned at his brother as though it were a great jest. "I think he speaks!" Rāma raised the head so that the dead man's mouth was to his ear, and furrowed his brow and nodded as though listening with the greatest intensity.

"He says, 'Employ the Garuḍa Vyūha, that most auspicious formation that, viewed from the heavens, resembles the cosmic bird that is Viṣṇu's vehicle.' "

"This madman will lead us to our death!" Jātadhāra cried in vain. "Once and for all, let Candra command."

"I am king," Rāma said with a smile. "If Candra wishes to seize rule this night, then who is the real enemy of Magadha?"

"Let us make some kind of battle plan," Candra pleaded, "lest the Śakas arrive at our gate and find us bickering like a bunch of old women."

Yet though the moon rose high, no progress was made, for Yājñavalkya would speak only the words King Rāma put into his mouth, and Candra would not abandon his pledge, and old Jātadhāra, despite the temptation, refrained from burying his blade in Rāma's heart.

The next morning the mahouts arranged their elephants, each with its complement of archers and weapons, in a line the width of the battlefield, leaving fifty feet between them, so they resembled the pillars of some massive veranda.

The infantry arranged themselves behind the elephants in the shape of a great bird, with "wings" on either side and a "tail" in back. On command they would charge between the elephants, swinging swords and firing arrows, then retreat to the safety of the elephant's shelter.

The chariots, each carrying several archers and shield bearers, as well as a charioteer straddling the yoke, were clustered beyond the "wings," so that they might ride back and forth protecting the flanks; the cavalry performed a similar function around the tail.

While Rāma himself rode his chariot in the center of the formation, at Garuḍa's "heart," and allowed Jātadhāra, as king, a similar honor, Candra was assigned to a position at the very tail, where possibilities of heroism seemed least likely.

It was excellent warfare according to rules set down by pedantic brāhmaṇas in śāstras about warfare, but idealized as it was, it failed to take into consideration variations in terrain, climate, and the makeup of the enemy's army; it lacked the guidance of that greatest of gurus, experience.

The armies marched until they could see each other through the tall stalks of sugarcane. The horses, sensing the tension, danced nervously from side to side, and the elephants shook their trunks and snorted. The men, however, were silent. They could hear birds singing in the cane field and the soothing sound of water rushing over the rocks.

In time the air was pierced by Rāma's trumpets, the drums struck with such might that the earth trembled. Bellowing with fury, the elephants charged forward, the infantry running behind them, the chariots clattering along the flanks, the cavalry galloping at the rear.

When they were close enough to see the faces of their enemies—faces not much different from their own—a thousand Śaka horsemen split off from the body of the army. They galloped to the east of the elephants, avoiding them entirely, and, without breaking stride, raised small compound bows and fired a volley of arrows into the infantry. Hundreds of foot soldiers stumbled and fell and did not rise up again.

Rāma was at once astounded and dismayed. He had never seen a man on horseback fire a bow, never heard that it could be done. His own cavalry fought with lances and small shields, for the bows of Magadha were so long a man had to stand to fire them. One did not need to be a military genius to see the Śakas' advantage.

The king screamed for the cavalry on the western flank to cross behind the army and assist the cavalry on the east lest they too be so easily slaughtered by these mounted archers.

It seemed like a logical step, but then two more regiments of Śaka horsemen came charging forward, one part attacking the western flank as it crossed to the east, the other regiment vanishing into the hills, where it might cut a broad circle and return to attack the "tail." Their fleet stallions avoided the elephants as easily as a grown man outwits a child in a game of tag.

Rāma's chariots tried to protect the flanks, but slid about on the muddy ground, overturning and knocking into one another. As for his infantry, the mud foiled them too, for they had difficulty finding a firm foundation on which to plant the end of their bows, which were so unwieldly that they could not be fired otherwise.

The elephants were fierce aggressors. Prodded to a fury by the Śaka lances, they charged forward, breaking the enemy ranks. But before Rāma could close up the space behind them with infantry, the Sáka cavalry had ridden in, dodging between the elephants and assuming a position where they could begin to fight their way through the guard surrounding the king.

The battle raged on without break for a day and a night and a day, consuming men as a raging forest fire would timber. Any soul who doubted the importance of morale need only have compared the armies of the two brothers: Rāma's, which fell before the Sákas like wheat beneath the scythe, and Candra's army, which, though only a fraction of the size, continued to hold back the enemy despite the mud and confusion. The prince himself was always in sight, riding among his men on a stallion rather than in the chariot that was the traditional vehicle for a commander, cheering them on, conveying orders to his senāpatis and commending them for their valor. Now and then he would stop to lift a wounded soldier to his saddle and take him to the vaidyas before galloping back to the line of battle.

This army of healers, recruited from the ranks of ayurvedic students and monks and camp followers, all trained by Nanā and under her supervision, worked feverishly setting broken bones, amputating limbs, removing arrowheads and suturing flaps of skin.

Dhruvādevī, wishing to help her husband's efforts in any way she could, had volunteered to serve with them. Once she had conquered her revulsion at seeing a man's stomach laid open, an arm dangling by a ligament, a sword through the bowels, she became a useful servant to those who were adept with splints and bandages. She ran about helping wherever she was needed, without ever a thought for herself, until her fatigue was such that she thought she would drop if she took another step. And then she redoubled her efforts. One sight of Dattaka—still alive and well!—galloping back on his horse in order to deliver a wounded soldier, was enough to sustain her for many hours. Still, as the ranks of the dead and wounded grew to vast numbers, she became ever more dubious of the righteousness of the war her husband now led. Couldn't he, with all his cleverness, have devised another way to settle this without such terrible squandering of life? Or was it simply the way of the kṣatriya, as she had thought before, for the quiet times to be naught but an intermission between the violent acts for which he lived.

At one point during the fighting—she could not remember when precisely, for the whole experience quickly became a mire of fatigue and pain and bloodshed—while running to help a soldier whose shoulder bone lay exposed like the end of an ivory walking stick, she spied Nanā dragging a corpse to the pyres with all the strength of a man. The women's eyes met in a moment of extraordinary understanding.

They seemed to say to each other, "Is it for this that we give birth, and nurture, and learn to heal?"

Sometime in the evening of the second day of battle, Rāma realized that he was being defended by Candra and the silk guild army. They were everywhere around him, felling the enemy with their broad swords, or even with their hands.

Perhaps Rāma could have lived with the knowledge of his brother's troops defending him had he not recognized several of the soldiers taking orders from Candra as his own. Were it allowed to continue, the entire army might soon be under Candra's influence. The erosion of authority had to be stopped at all costs. As Rāma knew only too well, he who controlled the army controlled the throne.

He waved to Candra, and when the prince's horse was galloping alongside the chariot, he shouted, "Call off your men! I did not order them to guard me! Get back to the rear or I shall have you all executed for insubordination!"

To which Candra shouted back, "If you care not for your own life, think of Magadha!"

"Do as I say!" cried Rāma, his mouth foaming in anger.

Candra hesitated, contemplating seizing command there and then. But the sanctity of an oath made upon the Garuḍa seal restrained him, and he turned and led his puzzled soldiers to the rear, which was nearly as well, since a Śaka regiment was attacking there, too.

Vyāsa, the sage of ancient times who was said to have composed the great poem of war, the *Mahābharata,* used all the tricks of his craft to make hand-to-hand combat seem something great and glorious. Yet there was nothing glorious about the way in which fifteen thousand of Rāma's soldiers were brutally hacked to pieces with swords and axes that day or had their vital organs pierced by iron-pointed shafts. If anything, it resembled the butchering of meat, were the animal allowed to remain conscious throughout the process. Another nine thousand kṣatriyas were taken prisoner. Nearly all the elephants were killed or fatally wounded, and the horses fared not much better. These animals, having died in dumb loyalty to their masters and without the vaguest understanding of what had transpired, were particularly pitiful. One hoped they would be reborn as brāhmaṇas in homes of wealth and piety.

As for Rāma, no sooner had he sensed a final defeat and turned his chariot to flee, than an excellent Śaka horseman galloped up alongside him and leaped from his saddle to the chariot floor, where he wrestled but briefly with the Gupta king before taking him prisoner in the name of Rudradāman, king of the Śakas.

King Rudradāman was the greatest of the western satraps, as the Śaka kings of that time were known. Like the śūdra who, inheriting his master's money, conveniently forgets his past and begins to live like a vaiśya, the Śakas had done their best to forget their history as nomads. Famine and flight from other nomad tribes had driven them down from the steppes of Scythia to the Land of the Sons of Bharata some five centuries before. Since then, like everything that came in the path of the omnivorous faith of the brāhmaṇas' faiths, they had been nearly completely assimilated. While once they drank the blood of their human sacrifices in cups made from their skulls, and dragged their women and children about in carts covered with animal skins, they now lived in cities, patronized the arts, and practiced pūja to Viṣṇu and Śiva and Brahmā. Like all converts, they often outdid their instructors, becoming more Āryan than the Āryans themselves.

Thus, with the exception of decoration and color, the Śaka camp resembled the King Rāma's in its quadrangular layout and division into quarters, and the royal pavilion to which King Rāma was led reminded him very much of his own. As for the guard surrounding it, they could have been the royal guard of Magadha. They were not so very different.

By the flickering torchlight illuminating the pavilion's interior, Rāma could see a tiger's skin laid out on the floor and the king's bench standing upon it. The Sáka senāpatis were squatting around it in a semicircle, like a tribunal waiting to judge him.

King Rudradāman sat on the bench wearing a costume not unlike Rāma's, a necklace of linked golden plates, jewel-encrusted earrings, and bangles and rings, and the little tiaralike crown called the uṣṇīṣa.

He was a man in his sixties, bald, with high cheekbones, a face that narrowed like an inverted triangle to the chin, and a proud and piercing stare. He wore a silk bandage around his shoulder and another around his ribs, both dark with freshly clotted blood. A vaidya squatted before him, probing a wound in his outstretched leg with tweezers and scalpel and removing pieces of shattered sword blade. Although the vaidya continued his surgery throughout their audience, never once did Rudradāman flinch, or cry out, or allow his voice to express any discomfort whatever. Yet suffer he did, for, despite the cool night, sweat beaded on his brow and cheeks, and at times his left hand, resting upon his knee, clutched so tightly that the nails made red crescents in the skin.

All this made Rāma self-conscious regarding his own smooth skin, which bore only a scratch on the shoulder from the fall he had taken against the chariot floor during his capture. Fearful of being wounded, he had avoided ordering his chariot too near a place where swords clanked or arrows flew. He had stayed well back among his infantry as long as there was infantry, and when there was no more, he had tried to flee.

"I knew your father," Rudradāman began without preliminaries. He spoke a passable though oddly accented Sanskrit, in a voice that vibrated like the low strings of the vīṇā. "We met on this same battlefield twenty-five years ago. I defeated him almost as easily as I defeated you. Yet I honored him, for he respected the dharma. He did not go to war without issuing a declaration. He did not kill his prisoners without reason and stick their heads on pikes. He did not use poisoned arrows." Rudradāman picked up an arrow and showed it to Rāma, who recognized it as one of the millions he had ordered treated with a particularly virulent poison. "And he did not turn, when he realized defeat was inevitable, and try to flee the battlefield, leaving his troops to be slaughtered like so many dogs."

Rāma, seeing that Rudradāman was waiting for a reply, swallowed again and again, trying to gather enough saliva in his mouth to speak.

"I have only been king a short time," he finally managed, his great brown eyes growing moist. "I am still quite young, you see. My father's untimely death brought me to the throne unprepared. I wanted to please my people so I sought to give them the glorious kingdom of the Śakas, as my father had tried to do before me. I wanted to show them that I was as much of a man as he. Perhaps I did violate the dharma in my desire for success. But please try to understand me. I had to be victorious. I had to win the love of my people."

He paused, as if to gather the courage to go on. "They have always hated me because of this disfigurement with which I was born, the cursed cleft that divides my palate and lip and makes me hiss like a snake whenever I speak. You cannot imagine what it is like to be born deformed and suffer the mockery, the insults. As a child, they called me Little Camel."

"They called me Vulture Claw."

"Excuse me?" Rāma said.

"Give me your hand."

Puzzled but pleased by what seemed a display of friendship, Rāma came forward and did as the king asked. But then he drew back in disgust, for Rudradāman's right hand was twisted and clawlike, with only three fingers.

"We are disfigured at birth," Rudradāman said, "not to supply us with an excuse for our weaknesses, but so that, by overcoming these handicaps, we may achieve greatness."

"Yes, but you don't understand the problems I've had. A hand you see, is different from a lip. You can keep it hidden and it does not torment you whenever you try to speak."

"I will have half your kingdom," Rudradāman said. "All the land west of the river Yamunā and south of the Ganges will be mine. All cities that touch upon those rivers shall be mine, too. And Pāṭaliputra shall be the seat of my reign."

"It is impossible!" Rāma cried. "My people will never live

under Śaka rule. My wife's tribe, the Śālāṅkāyanas; my grandmother's tribe, the powerful Licchavis; my cousins who are married into the Vākāṭakas—they will not stand for it. There will be rebellion in every quarter. Your empire will be torn apart by war."

"Why do you suppose the armies of those states never rendezvoused with you?" Rudradāman asked. "They never intended to. Instead they sent battalions to strengthen my army. They were frightened by the Demon King of Magadha. They wished to see him defeated."

"*No*," Rāma said, though he knew instantly that it was the truth.

"Oh, yes. Indeed, yes. They wished to see him dead. They told me as much."

Rāma paled. "Certainly you do not intend to execute me. Such behavior is unheard of among civilized people. The karma of it would take a thousand lifetimes to undo. Make an alternative suggestion. Anything you want can be yours. Our treasury contains the most precious gems, the rarest metals. Why, I have a golden statue of Viṣṇu that weighs one thousand pounds."

Rudradāman was so amazed he could not help but laugh. "You are every bit as lacking in honor as I have heard. Naught would be gained by killing you, for a man so devoid of respect for the dharma is already dead. Guards, confine him and see that he does not escape."

Now one of the king's advisers, an elderly brāhmaṇa with a long jaw, spoke up. "My lord, with such a king as this—that is to say, a Demon King—might we be wiser to set him free and return him to his troops? For if we keep him here, he seems to be of some value, and thus perhaps worth battling for, but if we release him, does he not then appear worthless, even to the enemy?"

"This is an interesting idea," the king agreed thoughtfully. "We might return him under some particularly humiliating circumstances—strapped to the back of an ass or with his nose cut off."

"I pray of you," Rāma said, nearly weeping, "do not cut off my nose."

"This Demon King," the brāhmaṇa went on, "has been much criticized among his own people for taking men as his wives. Perhaps we might play upon this weakness of his to further degrade him in their eyes." He turned to Rāma. "Demon King, let me ask you this. Do you care so little for your women wives that you would exchange one for your own freedom?"

"I treat my wives well! I dress them in splendid style and see to it that—"

"Answer the question, please," the king insisted.

"Yes," Rāma whispered.

"Excuse me. I cannot hear you."

"I said, yes. Yes, yes, yes. I will give you a wife for my freedom."

"It must be the most beautiful of your wives," Rudradāman insisted. "There is one named Dhruvādevī, whose grace, the poets say, surpasses that of Parvatī."

"You may have her," Rama said quietly.

"What did you say?" Rudradāman inquired, cupping his hand to his ear, as though it would make him hear better.

The other senāpatis smiled to see him carry on thus, like a teacher with a shy student.

"You may have her!"

"I applaud your wisdom," Rudradāman said, "for I can think of no exchange more appropriate and humiliating." And turning to his advisers, he said, "The Gupta empire crumbles before our eyes like a house of unbaked brick during the rains."

Though King Rāma had been captured and the war won, still the armies battled on, as the hair and fingernails of a man continue to grow for some time beyond his death.

All night Candra galloped back and forth among his men, urging them to victory. When the dead bodies littering the field were so many that his horse began to trip over them, he abandoned his mount and fought side by side with them. Later he helped care for those who had been wounded, and still later, he organized the building of funeral pyres, one for the brāhmaṇas, another for the kṣatriyas, still others for the vaiśyas and caṇḍālas and those without a class, lest the classes be mixed, a situation intolerable even in death.

Come dawn, his work was done. He looked around the battlefield and found it resembled nothing so much as a nightmare quilt of limbs, heads, and torsos, stitched in blood. He thought he could see, by the sun's first ray refracted in his tears, a fleet of the rainbow chariots of legend, driven by apsarases, carrying the spirits of his valorous warriors upward, to paradise.

Surrounded by his men, he limped toward camp, favoring his right leg, where he had taken an arrow. The oozing scars of innumerable sword wounds crosshatched his chest and arms.

What he had mistaken for the glare of the sun rising over the ramparts was, he saw when he drew closer, flames from the burning pavilions. The Śakas had set a torch to them. Clouds of black smoke filled the sky. Terrified for the fate of Dhruvādevī, who had returned to camp with the vaidyas the night before, he forced himself to run the rest of the distance despite the harrowing pain in his leg.

In time he reached the fortification and saw to his relief that most of the inhabitants had fled. A parade of refugees, their clothes dirty and tattered, their belongings in bundles over their shoulders, their heads lowered in the despair of defeat, wound for miles along the trail in the direction of Magadha.

Prince Candra pushed his way through, asking if any had seen Queen Dhruvādevī. They shook their heads or stared at him vacantly, their eyes glazed with loss.

Hours later he thought he recognized her—by the tilt of her head or the sway of her hips he could not say for sure, for in all other ways she was simply another tattered refugee among the multitudes.

"Dhruvādevī!" he shouted with all his voice.

She stopped and turned, pressing to hold her place in the crowd.

Cupping his hands around his mouth, he shouted her name again, and this time she saw him, and began to push her way backward, like a swimmer struggling against the current.

He, in turn, shoved forward to the anger of those around him. Even when they saw his strange honey-colored hair and realized who he was, they made no amends, for they were all despairing of their future and cared naught for the fallen dynasty of the Guptas.

In time, despite what seemed like all the human race having been placed between them, they reached each other and embraced, and clung as though they were the only fast point in a universe of flux.

"I thought you were dead," she whispered. "I thought I would never see you again."

"And you," Candra whispered. "I worried you had died in the fire."

"Oh, never leave my side, my love," she gasped, "never again, not for a second! Let us go live as forest hermits and shun this terrible world that would let dark triumph over light and evil over good!"

Later, when the embracing was done, and the whispering of endearments, and the worrying over Candra's wounds, they took each other's hand and rejoined the train of refugees.

"What of Rāma?" she said, sometime later.

"He will bother us no more."

"Then he is dead?"

Candra shook his head. "A prisoner of the Śakas."

Dhruvādevī grew silent. Behind her, the smoke from the burning camp had filled the sky with ash and turned the sun the dull, dark red of a blood blister.

At dusk, the refugees made a simple camp. Whatever they had to make their lives more comfortable, they shared. Some of the men built a bonfire, while others went hunting for boar and deer. The gods smiled on them and supplied them with game, which they were permitted to kill since they were kṣatriyas.

While the meat was roasting, one of the men admitted he was a bard and, to the delight of the others, began reciting the *Rāmayāna,* a poem all Āryans knew and loved and would listen to again and again. When he came to those verses in which noble Rāma slays the evil Ravana, every man hung on his words. In the wavering red light of the fire their troubled, battle-scarred faces grew serene. Such was the bard's art that their own defeat was forgotten in the glorious deeds of the past.

Then Rāma, reminded
by the words of Matali
took his flaming arrow
like a hissing snake . . .

And speaking a mantra upon it
as the Vedas ordain,
Placed it in his bow
That great and mighty arrow . . .

Enraged, he fiercely bent
His bow against Ravana
And intent on his mark, he shot
The entrail tearing arrow . . .

Bearing the death of the body
The arrow flew with great speed,
And tore through the heart
Of the evil-working Ravana.

The spell was broken by the hoofbeats of a horse charging into camp. The Śaka soldier who dismounted announced that he had brought a proclamation from King Rudradāman. He stood before them and, opening a scroll, began to read:

"Thus does Rudradāman, the King of Kings, Greatest of the Western Satraps, and Conqueror of the Mighty Guptas, proclaim: that he has, by his own great bravery and the bravery of his soldiers, and by his strict and loving observance of the dharma, conquered the armies of Magadha and taken nine thousand prisoners and also taken prisoner King Rāma Gupta of Magadha, who is known as the Demon King.

"That King Rāma has agreed to trade his own freedom for that of his mahiṣī, Dhruvādevī, whose beauty is celebrated by poets and artists throughout the land.

"And so Queen Dhruvādevī must come to the Śaka camp by dusk tomorrow or else one thousand prisoners will be executed, and one thousand more for each following dusk, until all the prisoners have been executed. Then King Rāma will be executed."

He read it through again in its entirety, loudly, to be sure that no one had missed a word. Then he climbed on his horse and rode to the next refugee camp, to repeat his proclamation there.

After he had left, the refugees urged the bard to go on with his recitation, and the bard complied. They had no interest in the fates of kings and queens who had failed them. They longed only to lose themselves in a story of ancient times, when heroes protected the poor and the weak.

Only two of their number left the circle of listeners and went off by themselves to the edge of the camp. In the distance they could see the glow of other refugee camps marking the trail of defeat back to Magadha.

"What a villain he is!" Dhruvādevī exclaimed. "Even miles away and imprisoned, his evil reaches out for us. Oh, my beloved, what will I do?"

"Once again," Candra whispered, placing an arm gently around her, "it seems a question of one person being sacrificed for the good of many. If only that person were someone other than yourself, what a simple decision it would be!"

"I must give myself to the Śaka king. I have no choice."

"I will not permit it," Candra said. "I have spent too long a time finding you to lose you again so quickly."

"Then you will see a thousand more brave kṣatriyas executed for no cause but your own selfishness. And a thousand more the day after that."

"I know not what to say." Candra shook his head with frustration. "It is a dilemma that would confound the wisest sage. All I know is that I would die myself before I let you go."

"Are there not lovers who, faced with impossible odds, make a pact and drink poison?"

"Would that we were allowed such a simple solution," Candra said. "For while poison would spare us, those nine thousand kṣatriyas would die none the less."

"I had forgotten," Dhruvādevī admitted, "that the world would go on without us."

"I have an idea!" Candra began, but she put her fingers over his lips to silence him.

"Dattaka—excuse me for calling you that, but my heart knows only your old·name—Dattaka, my love, we both know what I must do. No more talk, please. Hold me in your arms and help me forget the past and the future, and make the few moments left to us last long enough to fill a lifetime."

13

King Rudradāman's bench had been set outside, in the middle of the Śaka camp, so that he might oversee a victory feast for his senāpatis and nāyakas. The air was filled with music and laughter. Whole deer and boars roasted in pits of glowing coals. The men milled about, bragging of their exploits in battle, drinking palm wine and indulging in tests of strength, such as lifting logs and wrestling with each other. Yet the king, like a child promised a long-wanted toy, could think of nothing but his new bride, the beautiful queen Dhruvādevī. From where he sat he could just make out the blue and yellow pavilion he had ordered erected for his coming tryst. Inside, all had been readied for her arrival, soft rugs spread underfoot, silks and cushions piled here and there, low rattan tables set with decanters of Yavana wine, and dates and nuts, and all other manner of delicacies.

"Go see if she has come yet," he said to the manservant attending him.

He was as nervous as an adolescent anticipating rati for the first time, rather than a king with eight queens and a dozen concubines. For some reason, he wanted desperately for her to like him, and had even gone so far as to prepare a present for her, a star sapphire in a golden bangle. He tapped the fingers of his good hand impatiently against his knee, while he hid the other, the disfigured hand, beneath his shawl.

"But, my lord, I went just a few moments ago, and a few moments before that. The more you send me, the more slowly the time will pass."

"If I enjoy the tension of waiting," Rudradāman said patiently, "then why not draw it out, as one would any pleasure?"

"Yes, my lord," the servant said, and ran to the new pavilion to do the king's bidding. When he returned a few moments later, he was beaming. "My lord," he said, "she has arrived."

"And is her beauty as they say?" Rudradāman inquired eagerly.

"I did not glimpse her, for she was already within the pavilion and awaiting you."

"Very good," Rudradāman said, rising from his bench. "Very good indeed."

At least twenty of the queen's handmaidens were gathered outside the pavilion, all dressed in their best veils and bangles and shawls. They prostrated themselves as Rudradāman approached and did not rise again until he had entered the tent. He was impressed at their discipline, that they did not giggle nor cast him flirtatious glances as did the handmaidens of Śaka queens. His estimation of the Śālaṅkāyana queen grew by the moment.

Now he entered the tent and saw her, in the delicate light of the ghee lamps, reclining upon a pile of cushions. Though her face was hidden by a veil, and her hair by a shawl, her form appeared pleasing.

"Welcome, my queen," he said softly. "You honor my harem by your presence. Come, turn your face to me, so I may see that beauty that is legend."

She shook her head and kept her face averted.

"You have nothing to fear," he whispered, noticing her shoulders heave as though she were weeping. He knelt beside her and placed his good hand upon her arm. "I am as kind as the king you have left is cruel."

He raised his finger to her chin and gently rotated her face toward him. How ugly she was! He struggled to make sense of it, but just as the truth began to dawn on him, she drew a dagger from her waist and plunged it into the soft space between his ribs. He rolled over backward, onto the soft rugs where he had hoped to have rati with her, gasping from the pain. Crouching beside the dying king of the Śakas, the woman whispered, "You celebrate your victory too soon, I fear."

Now the princess rose and walked calmly from the tent. The handmaidens fell in neat ranks behind her, and they moved together toward that space in the middle of the camp where the senāpatis and nāyakas were enjoying their feast.

The drunken officers caught sight of them as they approached the bonfire and, mistaking the queen for a concubine or a wealthy prostitute, wooed her and her servants with promises of food and jewels. As far as they were concerned, women were the one element missing from the evening's festivities. One could argue that the gods were favoring the procession by hiding the moon behind the clouds and shrouding them in shadow for the longest time. There came a moment, however, when the women stepped into the light and the senāpatis, though dead drunk and heavy with food, finally noted that their breasts and hips were crudely padded, their features coarse, their cheeks dark with stubble.

"They are men," one of the Śakas said stupidly.

"And so we are!" Prince Candra shouted, gratefully tearing away his veil and drawing his sword.

At this signal the handmaidens, who were really kṣatriya, did the same. Swinging their broad swords, they charged the Śakas gathered there.

In a few moments the entire command of the Śaka army, the mahāsenāpati and all the senāpatis and nāyakas, were lying dead on the ground, one sprawled on top of the other. Candra and the kṣatriyas whose aid he had enlisted grabbed flaming sticks from the bonfire and hurled them at the tents until the whole camp was ablaze. Śaka soldiers, awakened by the commotion, staggered from their tents, prepared for nothing worse than a drunken brawl.

A new Gupta army hastily fashioned from the remains of the old had rallied just beyond the earthwork walls of the Śaka camp. Though it was barely a thousand men in strength, its morale was magnificent, for the Demon King was gone and Prince Candra was in command. Their ranks swelled as the thousands of prisoners, overcoming their guards in the confusion, joined them. Those Śaka soldiers who fled the burning camp on foot were taken prisoner, and those who tried to break the ranks on horseback were felled with arrows.

Because so many of their own were mingled with the fleeing enemy, the Gupta soldiers were particularly cautious with their arrows; it was probably this caution that saved them from firing on the frightened and bedraggled figure that stumbled from the gate even before they realized that it was King Rāma.

* * *

During the triumphant march back to Pāṭaliputra, King Rāma found it ever more difficult to command the respect of his troops. Although Candra deferred to him in all matters, no one else paid him any mind. A joke about "the peacock who gives his hen to the tiger for safekeeping," was frequently heard. In order to avoid situations where his orders were ignored, or carried out grudgingly, or intentionally misinterpreted in order to cause him discomfort, he gave none. At the end, he kept to himself, walking at the end of the procession, a king without subjects, authority, or respect, a bizarre and pitiful figure.

One night, a week's march from Pāṭaliputra, Candra returned from foraging with his senāpati to find Dhruvādevī kneeling in front of their pavilion, crying.

"What is the matter?" he asked, squatting beside her.

"*He* is in there," she said. "I asked him to leave, but he would not. He called me names and"—she stopped to catch her breath—"and he said he had hired a sorceress to cast a spell that would"—she gasped again—"that would make our baby stillborn."

Candra's face turned red with rage and his hands closed into fists. He strode into the pavilon and found Rāma lying on the cushions, drunk from palm wine, his hair and clothing disheveled, his ornaments in disarray. The mockery of a king struggled to his knees that he might smile and bow when Candra entered.

"Darling brother," he said with reeking breath, "I am so pleased to see you. I hope I have not offended your wife. Or *our* wife, I should say. Since no one else dare tell you this, it becomes my duty. The rest are too afraid. They think you'll be king in the end and—well, you know what kings do when they're displeased."

"Tell me what?" Candra demanded.

"Our wife. She's a whore, you see. A slattern. She has a yoni this big"—he described a circle with both hands—"and she can't get it filled. She's slept with every kṣatriya in camp trying to find a liṅgam that would fill her up, and last night, after you fell asleep, I spied her trying to have rati with an elephant. But the elephant found her unsavory and, despite her kisses, refused to grow hard."

Candra walked over to him and placed the tip of his sword to the rolls of flesh at Rāma's stomach. "Retract each word you have said, or I will cut out your bowels."

"The silk farmer threatens me!" Rāma said rolling his eyes in mock terror.

Then suddenly Candra stepped back and hesitated. "I think I understand. You try to provoke me so I would kill you. You wish to go to the five, but have no nerve to do the act yourself."

"Bravo, little brother," Rāma said, applauding his observation.

"And you hope that if I kill you it will weigh on my conscience and spoil my sleep for years to come. It will be your last bit of evil, your legacy to me."

"You are so clever!" Rāma grew suddenly angry and commanding. "Now kill me and be done with it."

Candra breathed deeply, trying to calm himself and regain control. He shook his head and sheathed his sword.

"Then I will make you kill me," Rāma whispered.

"You will make me do nothing," Candra said, and turned to leave. He took a few steps toward the door of the pavilion and suddenly felt all of Rāma's weight slam into him from behind, knocking him to the platform. When he rolled onto his back, Rāma fell on him, a thing of jiggling, reeking flesh, and closed his fingers around Candra's throat.

"Kill me," Rāma whispered, squirming sensuously on top of Candra's body, as though enjoying kāma of the finest sort.

Candra, his vision beginning to swim from loss of air, saw his brother's face change like melting tallow into demonic visages, skulls, Durga faces, bhūtas, asuras, rakṣasas.

"I will not let you triumph," Candra whispered.

"But you will," Rāma replied, tightening his grasp. His voice was as calm and rational as that of a stranger asked the time. "For finally, evil is the path of life—else why would all of man's struggles be against it? Give in now and save yourself years of frustration. For you will come to it finally, one way or the other. We are all evil at the end."

The world began to flicker and darken. A fatigue, a longing for death overtook him. Yet at the same time something within him rebelled, authority was to that part of a man that acts without thought. An astonishing strength rose within him, and he threw off Rāma's weight. The king flew backward, hitting the tent pole with such force that it fell, and the canvas roof came down upon them.

The canvas impeded Candra's movement and blocked his vision. He was trapped beneath its folds like the silkworm in its cocoon. Though he could not see Rāma or determine which of the adjacent folds his brother was trapped in, the canvas, like the bond of blood made tangible, still transmitted his struggles. From nowhere, a sword slashed through the fold, missing him by inches. Candra cursed, and he heard Rāma laugh in response. Then the motion of the cloth became more intricate, and he heard another voice, the voice of Dhruvādevī, calling for him.

"Candra? Candra, where are you?"

"Stay back," Candra shouted. He guessed from the position of her voice that she was crawling along the top of the tortuous canvas, searching for him. What if Rāma's sword accidentally found her instead? He was a fool for not killing his brother when he had the opportunity! He cursed the part of him that had clung to the dharma even when it conflicted with common sense.

He drew his sword and watched the canvas around him. Suddenly it was completely still.

"Rāma?" he shouted.

Rāma's sword punched through the canvas, catching him in the thigh with a terrible stinging pain. Immediately Candra returned the blow, but his blade met only with cloth and air.

Again the sound of Rāma's cackling.

"Candra, are you all right?" Dhruvādevī's voice came from the same direction as Rāma's sword.

"Move!" Candra shouted. "He's right beside you!"

Dhruvādevī screamed. The canvas in front of Candra bulged, as though a body had fallen against it, and before he could stop himself, he had plunged his blade into it, delighting in the resistance of flesh after all this sparring with shadows. The canvas, pinned to the body, slumped forward, blood blossoming around the sword hilt.

He has tricked me into killing her, Candra thought with horror.

Quickly he drew his dagger and slashed through the cloth, like the emerging moth, into the blinding sunlight. For an instant he could see nothing. Then he saw Dhruvādevī, lying on her side on the canvas before him.

"May the gods forgive me," he whispered, kneeling beside her. Ever so gently he turned her over.

She raised her head, and frowned, and rubbed at a discolored bruise on her forehead.

"You live!" he said with delight.

"I would sooner be dead the way my head aches."

"What happened?"

"I was about to seize Rāma—at least I think it was him beneath the canvas—but the cloth was jerking so and twisting this way and that that I could not keep my balance and fell and hit my head. Oh, my darling husband, I hope I did not accidentally cause your injury in the meantime!" She had noticed the wound on his thigh.

"You cause me only delight," he whispered. "I would suffer a hundred wounds for one touch of your hand."

Candra turned to a bulge in the canvas and slit the fabric as though it were a shroud. Rāma's body lay there, slain by his brother's sword.

"Is he really dead?" Dhruvādevī whispered. "Are we finally rid of him forever?"

"So it seems."

Candra looked around, filled his lungs with the sweet air, and smiled at the woman who was to bear his child.

"What a fine day it is!" he said. "I have the most excellent feeling, as though we have weathered some dark and turbulent storm, that we may now enjoy all good things the world holds in store. Come, my princess, and give me a kiss."

But Dhruvādevī could not turn her back on Rāma's body. She laughed nervously. "Somehow, though I see the sword planted in his heart, I do not trust his death. I fear that I will hear his footsteps behind me every time I walk alone through some dark place and that his cursed split lip shall hiss at me in my dreams."

Joyful crowds greeted the new king and his victorious army as they crossed the drawbrige into Pāṭaliputra. Men and women leaning from the balconies threw garlands and rice and roasted grains as the procession passed along the Royal Way. Such rejoicing had not been seen since the coronation of Candra's grandfather, the beloved Candra Gupta I. Later, the Sanskrit poets said that the heavens themselves rained flower petals, but as everyone knows, poets live by such hyperbole.

Candra's first act upon reaching the palace was to free all those who had been imprisoned for their loyalty to Samudra Gupta. Alas, Vahara Mihira, the astrologer, had died of a chill in the dungeon, exactly as he had predicted from his own calculations. Vasubandhu, though barely a skeleton, survived, as did the old Purohita. It was the last of these men whom Candra most desired to see, for he had questions about the dharma that only the holiest of brāhmaṇas could answer. Yet he refused to come when Candra summoned him, explaining that his first duty was to restore the purity of the temple that had been so defiled by Rāma's reign. Candra, impatient for answers, proceeded to the temple, hoping he could steal a moment of the priest's time as he worked.

What he found there, in that dark and sacred hall of pūja, appalled him. The air stank of rancid ghee. The sacred fire, lacking fuel, had burned to an ash, and mice had gnawed at the sesame sweets left long ago as an offering, and left their own black pellets in exchange. The incense was a gray powder, the sacred water a dried film within the vase. The garlands adorning the golden altarpiece of a four-armed four-faced Viṣṇu were shriveled with age, like necklaces of dried hemp.

The Purohita was whispering purificatory mantras as he washed the rancid ghee off the altarpiece. Candra prostrated himself at the entrance and remained bowed there until the Purohita noticed him and, with some embarrassment, bade the young prince rise.

"Forgive me for not coming when you sent for me," the Purohita said, "but the purity of the temple must come before all other things. After these many generations the Guptas must not lose Viṣṇu's favor. Once my work here is done, I will leave for a hermitage, and you may choose your new Purohita."

"I had hoped I would enjoy your excellent counsel," Candra said humbly.

"But . . ." The Purohita was clearly taken aback, and pleased. "Well then, I should be honored to serve you as I served your father."

"There are many questions involving the dharma that have been weighing heavily upon my conscience. Were you to unravel them for me, I would be grateful."

"Let us discuss them while we clean the temple," the Purohita replied. "If we work with industry and piety, we may gain

Viṣṇu's favor, and he in turn may help clear our minds of delusion and lead us upon the path to wisdom."

He gave Candra a bunch of hen feathers bound to a stick and instructed him in dusting the alcove around the altar.

The prince worked silently for nearly an hour, building up his courage. He understood for the first time the trepidation other men felt confessing to their fathers, for the Purohita was father to all brāhmaṇas, keeper of the dharma, final arbiter of right and wrong, good and evil. While Candra had come to terms with his own recent, unorthodox deeds, he was certain that the dour judge would be less lenient. And this frightened him more than an army of Śakas on horseback, for he knew that he would abide by the Purohita's edict, even if it meant banishment or the loss of Dhruvādevī.

Finally, he said, in a voice so soft that it was all but swallowed up by the high-ceilinged chamber, "I have killed my brother and taken his wife as my own."

"Oh?" The Purohita paused in his work and gazed at the new king. "And how did this come about?"

Candra explained the circumstances leading to Rāma's death, dusting ever more industriously as he spoke in order that he might have an excuse to avoid the Purohita's hawklike eye. When he finally dared glance in his direction, he was surprised to see that the old man's expression was more bemused than stern.

"It is as Vahara Mihira predicted at your birth," the Purohita said. "What an extraordinary astrologer he was! Our land shall not see his equal for ages to come."

"What prediction was that?" Candra asked, intrigued.

The Purohita lowered his lids and exercising his extraordinary memory, quoted, " 'In his eighteenth year the prince shall commit an unspeakable crime—' "

"Yes, that is my concern. What shall be the karma of my dreadful crime?"

"Let me finish: '. . . the Prince shall commit an unspeakable crime, yet the gods shall favor him.' *The gods shall favor him.* Do you see?"

"I see only that I have killed my own brother," Candra replied.

"You have killed a Demon King. Every *Dharmaśāstra* warns that the people will not tolerate the rule of an evil king. You have served the dharma at a time when such a service was woefully needed. Be proud of yourself, my prince."

"You are certain of this?"

"Quite."

Candra looked unconvinced. After a few more minutes of cleaning, he said, "But what of the other crime I mentioned—taking his wife for my own?"

"You call crime what another man would label benevolence."

"I have practiced rati with her, not once but a hundred times at least." And he added, "She is with child."

The Purohita stopped his cleaning. For one of the few times anyone could recall, the dour old man smiled. "The gods grace us," he whispered, "with another Gupta prince."

"But what of the princess?" Candra pressed, wishing to leave no detail of the complex event unexplored. "She was my brother's wife. She neglected the path of the satī and fled from her husband's funeral pyre. Rather than mourn him, she celebrated his death."

"Did she ever practice rati with him?"

"No," Candra said.

The Purohita shrugged. "Then the marriage was never consummated. There is no law against a widow who is still a virgin taking another husband."

"But she was not a virgin *before* Rāma's death. You see, she had already practiced rati with me."

"Does not the *Mahābharata* tell of the five Paṇḍava brothers sharing one wife?"

"But we were never married by a brāhmaṇa. I have never even been initiated into my class."

"We must attend to that," the Purohita said, as though noting it on some slate in his mind. He sighed, and went on, "In my youth I lived by the letter of the Vedas. Now I see that the ancient sages, in all their wisdom, could not anticipate every situation that would ever arise. In that you will be king, your exploits must be judged in terms of how they have benefited your subjects. As far as I can see, you have done only well by them. Your father, were he alive, would be pleased."

Both men returned to their cleaning of the temple. Sometime later, Candra said, "Good Purohita, you knew my father better than anyone else, didn't you?"

The Purohita nodded. "He came to me when he was a child. For years I instructed him in that which the twice-born must know."

"Then someday when you have time—after the temple is purified, naturally—would you tell me about him?"

"I would enjoy that," the Purohita admitted, "for I miss him very much, and when we reminisce, it is as though we visit with those who are no longer among us."

"If only we had met," Candra said sadly. "It is something I will regret all my days."

"But you did meet—once. Against my advice, Samudra Gupta shaved his head and, dressed as a Buddhist monk, visited the home of Govinda the silk merchant, simply to set eyes on you. It was a daring and foolish plan, but his longing to see you was such that he could not resist."

"But I recall it well! A man with bow scars on his left wrist. He made an odd monk indeed, so tall and powerful. I gave him food. We had a good talk, he and I. Now that I know it was my father, I will cherish the memory forever."

Part IV

THE GOOD VAIDYA

14

As soon as the mourning period for King Rāma had passed, two festival days were proclaimed, one for Candra's coronation, and another for his wedding to Queen Dhruvādevī. Stalls and businesses were closed that everyone might celebrate. Their adoration of the new king and queen was obvious from the way they bedecked their homes with flowers and banners of colored cloth, as well as in the mountains of presents heaped upon the wedding pavilion. They were grateful that the war was over, that the onerous taxes had been reduced, and that they were no longer forced to give all their grain and ghee and cows to the army.

Now that the Śaka empire had become feudatory to the Guptas, the goods that passed through Barygaza, Lothal, Dvāraka, and the other ports on the western peninsula could be regulated to their advantage, promising unheard of prosperity. For once, however briefly, everyone felt as though he had enough to eat.

But most of all they were grateful that they were rid of the Demon King with his endless sacrileges and travesties of the dharma, and the capricious executions that filled every new day with terror.

The materials that had been gathered for the vast palace he had planned to build for himself were used instead to build shelters for the beggars.

Nanā, alas, was too troubled to take pleasure in the new prosperity. Following her splendid service during the war with the Śakas, Candra had requested she return to Pāṭaliputra with him to care for Dhruvādevī during her pregnancy. They were all concerned by the history of difficult births that had plagued the Gupta dynasty and wanted the princess to have every possible advantage.

Nanā paid daily visits to Dhruvādevī's chamber and, making her lie prone, probed her great, tight-skinned belly to determine which way the infant lay. It was a rare skill, more a result of experience in midwifery and an almost supernatural sensitivity than her training as a vaidya. Maddeningly, the infant would one day assume a perfect position, head down, arms folded across the chest, only to reverse himself another day so that suddenly the feet were first, the head last. Then he would turn again. She worried too about his shoulders, for they seemed exceptionally broad, and she had witnessed births where broad shoulders might halt the baby's progress through the yoni, forcing whoever was attending to break a collarbone or resort to extracting the baby surgically through the naval. At such times the fate of a golden-haired queen who had died some eighteen years before was much on her mind.

Observing Candra and his wife walking hand in hand through the garden each afternoon, feeding the peacocks, contemplating the lotuses that floated so tranquilly across the face of the pond, and gazing at each other as though they two alone existed in the world, Sutanukā vowed there would be no mishap. She prayed to the bodhisattvas, chanted secret mantras, had the queen drink herbal potions, did everything within her power to ensure a normal birth.

One night she dreamt that she was alone outside the moss-covered Śiva shrine at the outskirts of the city. Hearing Samudra Gupta's voice calling to her from within, she took a scalpel and cut the stone as though it were cheese. The shrine turned inside out, engulfing her in darkness. She would never find her way without the Vaidya's help. She tried to call for him, but she had lost her voice. She woke sweating and knew at once what she must do.

Arriving at Nālandā a week later, she was shown to the chambers reserved for special visitors. She sat upon a carved bench with columnar legs, waiting anxiously. The sounds of chanting and smell of incense reminded her of the wonderful years she had spent at the monastery attaining, through meditation and selfless work with the sick, a level of closeness to Buddha such that all things had come to be lovely and fascinating to her, and she could accept life and death with equanimity.

Yet her detachment was never complete. As long as desire remained, the Buddha said in a voice that echoed down the ages, suffering was inevitable. And try as she might, Nanā could never entirely shed her desire for the man who was her teacher.

She heard the clip of sandaled feet on paving stones, and her heart began to flutter frantically. The Vaidya appeared in his saffron robes, his head shaven smooth, his body bare of ornaments. For an instant he regarded her in her secular garb, her jeweled ornaments, her bare breasts, her lustrous black hair that had grown long enough to make a sleek chignon at her neck; then he looked away and refused to meet her eye.

"Why won't you leave me alone?" he asked, and his voice was truly plaintive.

"Grant me one last favor and I will never disturb your work again." She kept her voice level so he would not perceive how hurt she was by his reception.

"Speak."

"Queen Dhruvādevī has been carrying the child of king Candra eight months now. So far all is well. Yet I fear the child lies feet first in the sack and must be taken through the naval by surgery."

The Vaidya sighed and rubbed his hands across his face. "It seems to me we have played this scene before."

"Perhaps we have," Nanā agreed, now gazing down at the floor.

"With disastrous consequences," the Vaidya pointed out.

"King Candra is not his father."

"Well, you are an excellent surgeon. You have no need of me. Do the operation yourself."

"I would have both mother and child live."

"You know that is unlikely."

"So it was in the past," Nanā agreed. "But now you have the secret of stopping the fever. You can ensure that both survive."

The Vaidya smiled and shook his head. "If you refer to the use of lamb's wool soaked in alcohol, well, I have had some small success, but it far from a proven cure. Kings, I have learned, do not like to roll the dice for the lives of their loved ones."

"We are talking about King Candra," Nanā said, growing annoyed." The infant *you* delivered. The boy whom *you* instructed in Buddhism. You yourself have spoken on numerous occasions of his compassion."

"That was long ago. When men become kings their minds cloud with illusion, while their power over others makes them hopelessly corrupt."

"Candra is different!" She was nearly shouting, a most unusual exhibition from someone as controlled as herself.

The Vaidya raised an eyebrow. "May I remind you that this is a monastery."

"I am sorry," she said, and began again in softer tones. "I only mean to say that if you fail to save the queen's life, he will understand, I am certain of it. Who knows? The infant may decide to come head first after all, making an operation unnecessary."

"Making my long journey to Pāṭaliputra also unnecessary." He glanced at her again and looked away.

Suddenly a startling thought occurred to her. His nervousness, the quickness of his breath, his refusal to gaze at her body—was it possible that he desired her, even in her pockmarked ugliness, as he had for an instant years ago, when her beauty was flawless? No. She banished it as a fiction too dangerous to enjoy for even a moment.

"You could see your students," she went on. "You could teach them about the new techniques you have perfected here at the monastery."

Although he had often spoken about seeing his old students, he barely responded to her suggestion. His oddly self-conscious behavior certainly seemed to mask some strong emotion.

Now she threw herself at his feet and pleaded as a mother might plead for the life of her child: "Vaidya, please. Do this one thing for me and I will trouble you no more."

Prince Candra, in a rite as ancient as marriage and coronation, sat in his bedchamber, chewing betel quid and playing Caturaṅga with the dwarf (still alive and well despite his numerous soliloquies on the short-livedness of his kind), the dour Purohita, and Vasubandhu.

The last had nearly recovered from his time in the dungeon by eating even more gluttonously than before, in order to restore the fatness that had been such a comfort to him. He was delighted with the new Buddhist-trained king—far more than he had been with his Viṣṇuite father. The two of them were on the path to becoming bosom friends.

As could be expected, King Candra played an atrocious game, deploying his infantry to no purpose, neglecting to protect his king, and now and again forgetting even that he was involved in a game at all.

"And this is the great warrior who conquered the Śakas?" the dwarf would say, raising his eyebrows, each time Candra lost a man.

To which Candra would reply, "How much time has passed?" Or, "Is there no news yet?" and dispatch yet another messenger to join the score of them already running back and forth between his chamber and the harem.

Meanwhile, in a distant chamber of the harem, isolated so that her screams would not be heard, Dhruvādevī lay on a wooden couch suffering the pains of childbirth. Though at first the inner yoni had expanded to the width of three fingers, it had grown no more after that, just as Nanā had feared. Her delicate touch suggested that the infant's heels and buttocks were foremost at the opening.

Reluctantly, the Vaidya agreed with her diagnosis: the baby would have to be delivered through the naval. A horrid sense of the past recurring nearly overwhelmed him. He was not in the least relieved to learn that Nanā had already informed the king of this possibility and received his consent to perform the operation.

The Vaidya administered the soma preparation, and when Dhruvādevī was in a deep trance sleep, slit the dark skin of her stomach. Nanā and the Vaidya's old student Kaṅka, now a vaidya of some renown himself, held the sponges where they might stem the bleeding.

Then he cut through the sack-that-holds-the-bowels, and the slick purple muscle of the womb, and reached down, godlike, into the primordial mire to extract a squirming pink thing tied to its mother by a pulsing cord.

And once again the sound of an infant's screams filled the quiet corridors of the harem.

"A prince," Nanā said, weeping.

"Let us hope he resembles his father," the Vaidya said cautiously, "and not his uncle." He examined the baby with care.

"He seems to have fingers and toes in the right number . . . nothing wrong with his lip or palate . . . a perfect infant, as far as I can see."

"Oṃ namo bhagavate Vasudevāya," she whispered, in praise of Viṣṇu, who added generations to the Gupta dynasty as a jeweler would pearls to a priceless necklace.

Once the Purohita had performed the jātakarma ceremony, the cord was cut and the infant passed along to the wet nurse. Now the Vaidya set about closing Dhruvādevī's incisions, rinsing each layer of membrane and muscle with alcohol before going on to the next. He was glad none of the courtiers could observe him, for they would surely have thought him mad or part of a plot to kill the queen. Even though he was nearly convinced of the efficacy of the technique, he still felt foolish doing it. Finally, he sutured the outermost layer of skin with the mandibles of black ants and applied a dressing over that of lamb's wool soaked in more alcohol, and then poured more alcohol over that, and kept on until the rugs beneath his feet were soaked with it and the whole chamber stank from the smell.

"Make the demons drunk," he murmured to himself.

"What did you say?" Nanā asked.

He shook his head. "Nothing."

"And now?"

The Vaidya shrugged. "We wait."

"Might I bathe you in the meantime?" she asked. "You have worked very hard."

"Woman," the Vaidya said angrily, "for more years than I can recall, I have struggled to resist your charms. Now you tempt me like this when I am exhausted and lonely, and frightened that I have just killed the only queen of Magadha. Have you no pity?"

She looked at him, hurt. "Hate me if you must, but do not mock me. I have seen myself in mirrors and still ponds, and I know how ugly I am with my pockmarked face. I could not tempt a beggar."

"You are the most beautiful woman in the land," the Vaidya replied, and in that weak moment confessed the feelings he had harbored these many years. "You haunt my waking hours and invade my dreams. Am I never to be free of you?"

With that he turned angrily and hurried from the chamber.

* * *

The Vaidya kept a close watch on Queen Dhruvādevī over the following hours. Although he noticed neither flush nor perspiration nor excessive heat of the brow or chest, he applied cold compresses nonetheless, to ward off what might come. The hours became a day, and then a night, and still the queen's flesh remained cool to the touch, her breath slow and even, her pulse regular. The incision stayed a healthy pink color. The more hopeful the Vaidya felt, the more pessimistic and cautious he appeared.

Now the soma wore off and the queen awoke, weeping from the pain in her belly. Her attention was diverted, however, when King Candra came to visit, and the wet nurse gave them the baby to fawn over and admire, to compliment according to his length and weight and redness, as though these qualities were the results of profound thought or artistic inspiration on the part of the parents, and not simply Brahmā, the creator of all things, having his inevitable way.

Kumāra Gupta was the name they decided on. The conch sounded from the highest parapet of the palace, and the festivities continued for days. Surely, the people agreed, the dharma had been renewed, the cycle of ages had begun anew. Without question, this was the beginning of the glorious Kṛta-yuga, which would last 4,800 years, when men would be pious and moral, tall, and strong, and long-lived. A thousand miles to the north the ferocious Hūṇas had already begun the trek south in search of fertile pasture, the journey that would spell destruction and devastation for those of the Land of the Sons of Bharata the likes of which they had never dreamed. But for the time being, life had never seemed so sweet.

Weeks passed and Dhruvādevī grew steadily stronger. The Vaidya, his pessimism mellowing ever so slightly, kept her in bed until the incision was completely healed and then permitted her to take short walks in the garden with her husband. In time, when her health appeared faultless, he began to think about returning to Nālandā. Kaṅka, his old student, now guru to a second generation of students, pleaded for him to remain in Pāṭaliputra and teach his wonderful new techniques. King Candra and Dhruvādevī also begged him to stay, for they had come to regard him like a beloved uncle.

One day while strolling through the royal garden, admiring the sprays of brilliant blossoms, the swans gliding so effortlessly across the surface of a pool, he overheard a jingle of bells, a sound of laughter.

There, behind a screen of cypresses, Nanā—but now he had to think of her as Sutanukā, for little of the nun or Nanā remained in her—sat on a swing, swinging back and forth, one arm hooked around the rope, the other resting casually on her thigh. The little bells on her anklets made the jingling. The sound brought a spasm of memory. She saw him and became quiet and self-conscious.

"What were you laughing about?" the Vaidya asked.

"I was laughing because I am happy. Our land has a good king. Our people are prosperous." She smiled. "There is a fine new prince. And my mynah bird has remembered how to talk."

"Then all your needs are satisfied?" the Vaidya asked.

"Nearly." She became ever so slightly the coquette.

"I have been thinking about staying here in Pāṭaliputra," he said.

Sutanukā pretended to have only a polite interest. "But what of your inquiry into the fever?"

"I can continue my work here, with Kaṅka."

"I see. Well then, what about your quest for Nirvāṇa?"

The Vaidya sighed. "It is not, I fear, something the gods shall grant me in this lifetime. So I will console myself with life's other joys."

"And what are those?" she asked, hoping he could not hear her pounding heart.

"First and foremost," he replied, "a woman's love."

They said no more, for there was nothing more to say. The Vaidya moved behind her and gently pushed her swing so she could soar through the sky like a bird.

AFTERWORD

I had decided as early as 1979 to write a novel about "ancient" India, the India of the brāhmaṇas, before the Muslīms came and drove out the Buddhists, and certainly before the time of the English and their "superior" Christianity. This still left a rather long period to investigate, from the invasion of the Punjab by the Āryans, circa 1500 B.C. whose melding with the Proto-Indus Valley civilization eventually formed the culture of the brāhmaṇas, to the invasion of the Hūṇas in 485 A.D., which effectively brought an end to it.

I had no definite idea for a story in mind. The time of the Buddha interested me, as did the period of Aśoka, the great Buddhist king, and that of the Gupta dynasty, when the poet Kālidāsa lived.

One day I ran across a reference—I do not remember where—to a king named Rāma Gupta, who supposedly ruled between the two kings Samudra Gupta and Candra Gupta. Scholars debated his existence, for, aside from a reference to him in a fragmentary Sanskrit play *Devī Candra Gupta*, by the great Sanskrit dramatist Viśākhadatta, there was no evidence supporting his existence, no coinage or edicts, no monuments in his name (although recently certain Jain images have been found that appear to be dedicated to him).

The legend, as put forward in this particular play, was that Rāma Gupta, a cowardly king, surrendered his queen Dhruvādevī to the Śakas in return for his own life. His younger brother Candra Gupta, disguised as Dhruvādevī, went in her stead, killed the Śaka king, and won the throne and the princess for himself.

I found this a most captivating little story—or kernel of a story—as evidently Viśākhadatta had before me, and I began to wonder about the sort of relationship the two brothers might have had that would make one cowardly, the other ingenious. Five years later this incident appears about four-fifths of the way through my novel about the good Prince Candra, his evil brother Rāma, and the beautiful Dhruvādevī.

As in my earlier novels, the Faustian *Inner Circle*, and the erotic fairy tale *The Beast*, I had taken a simple story and embroidered it into a full-length novel. I find the challenge of such an approach stimulating.

Since the Indians disdained written history—and oral history for that matter, concerning themselves, to paraphrase Thoreau, "Not with the Times, but with the Eternities"—writing a book such as mine is rather like the rope trick, wherein a vast weight of conjecture is supported by the narrowest filament of fact. Still, I did my best to acquaint myself with everything that was known about the era and the ages preceding it. I read upward of sixty books, everything from Edgerton's meticulous translation of the *Mātañga-Līlā* of Nīlakaṇṭha (The Elephant Lore of the Hindus) to Lieutenant Colonel Gautam Sharma's dreadful *Indian Army through the Ages.* Of all these, by far the most helpful to me, and thus the work to which I owe the greatest debt, was A. L. Basham's *The Wonder That Was India.* Wherever I found conflicting views regarding the period when my story takes place, as to whether, for example, the women kept their breasts covered and veiled their faces before the Muslīm invasion (they didn't), or whether the Gupta army knew the secret of manufacturing and employing gunpowder (they didn't), Professor Basham was my final authority. For anyone with an interest in ancient India, I cannot recommend this book highly enough.

Among the many people who gave of their time and knowledge, I would like particularly to thank the virtuoso linguist Alexander Lehrman of Yale University, who set aside his Hittite and his translation of Nargarjuna, to read through the manuscript and galleys of *Golden Fire,* putting the Sanskrit in order. Thanks also to Wendy O'Flaherty of the University of Chicago for information about various social customs of ancient India, and Professor Stanley Wolpert of UCLA for helping me with some of the problems of Gupta warfare.

More thanks to Scott Waugh, also of the UCLA history department, and Joan Waugh, for their encouragement and good council.

And to Sterling Lord, my agent, who has stuck by me through the worst of times; Marc Jaffe, for his unflagging faith in me; Arnold Ehrlich, *Golden Fire*'s first editor; Ann Harris, its final editor, who is, to my good fortune, never quite satisfied with anything; and Natalie Robbins, who took time from her own book to read mine and offer excellent criticism.

And thanks to Barbara Grace Fast, for cheerfully enduring that most difficult ordeal of being a novelist's wife.